To: Sue and Laurie

Good friends.

[signature]

FINNINGHAM 9.4.13

The Forgotten Tsar

Terry Nathan

authorHOUSE®

AuthorHouse™ UK Ltd.
500 Avebury Boulevard
Central Milton Keynes, MK9 2BE
www.authorhouse.co.uk
Phone: 08001974150

Published by AuthorHouse 3/12/2013

ISBN: 978-1-4817-8539-6 (sc)
ISBN: 978-1-4817-8540-2 (hc)
ISBN: 978-1-4817-8538-9 (e)

I am proud to dedicate this novel to my friend Mike Dwyer from Surrey, England and La Manga Club, Spain, and to my wife Liliane. Mike gave me the confidence to believe The Forgotten Tsar was a story worth telling. He's with the angels now, gone but not forgotten. Liliane persevered through months of proof reading, endless cups of coffee, and the occasional tantrum. I love them both.

Introduction

The story you are about to read is one of great rank and privilege, of huge wealth and power, and of treachery, corruption, and lies. While it is a story of our times, its origin lies more than two hundred years earlier, back to 1798 when the Emperor Napoleon invaded the island of Malta and forced the Knights of the Order of Saint John of Jerusalem to seek refuge elsewhere. The Crusader Knights sought protection at the Russian Imperial Court, where Tsar Paul issued a Royal Proclamation placing those knights under his protection and patronage.

The dynasty, of which Tsar Paul was an early incumbent, was brought to a tragic end in the early hours of 17 July 1918, in the Siberian town of Yekaterinburg. This was where Tsar Paul's great grandson, Nicholas II, together with members of his family and immediate circle, were murdered by the Bolshevik hordes, and it is there that we take up the story.

My name is Alec Johnson, or so I have always believed, and as it would have stayed had the stranger not come and brought with him the notebook that was to make a lie of my entire life. Perhaps it would have been better had he not come, but it is too late for that now. There is no going back.

"What of that notebook," you might well ask, "and if Alec Johnson is not your true name, who then does that name belong to?"

To tell of the book will fill many pages, whereas the story of the true Alec Johnson but a few sad lines. He was born on 27 January 1937 in the Borough of Stepney in East London, within the sight and sound of Bow Bells; he was a true Cockney. Alec's life was cut short in

April 1941, a casualty of the indiscriminate bombing raids carried out on the orders of Adolf Hitler. The gravestone that recorded his name disappeared in the confusion of war, as did the record of his passing. I was given the name and the identity of this supposedly orphaned child, who had been evacuated from the dangers of wartime London to the safety of rural Scotland.

I ask only that you keep an open mind as you progress through the pages, being thoughtful as each new revelation unfolds before you, and that you take my words on trust where proof is hard to find or credibility stretched too far. Only when you reach the final pages will you be able to weigh everything in the balance and ask yourself whether the events I portray could really have happened or are they merely the dreams of an old gamekeeper who has spent too much of his life alone on the high moors

ROYAL PROCLAMATION

We pride ourselves that, placed by divine Providence and the right of succession on the Imperial throne of our ancestors, through the power and the force deriving from it, it is granted to us to protect, increase, and maintain an Order so ancient and so distinguished among the Orders of Chivalry, fully convinced through it we are rendering a most signal service to the entire Universe, We have graciously accepted to come to the aid of the Russian Grand Priory of the Chivalric Order of Saint John of Jerusalem. We have deigned to this effect to gather it, in its distress, to the bosom of Our Empire, as a safe haven, and We have established its new residence in Our Capital. Recalling to Our memory the merits of the Illustrious Chivalric Order of Saint John of Jerusalem, both toward the Religion and as toward all Christian Princes, We have resolved to turn Our attention and Our strength, not only to re-establish it, to the general advantage, in its property and in its ancient state of splendour, but also to give it again greater extent, radiance, and solidity. It is for this reason, and through a particular benevolence towards that Order, that We have showered it with new benefits. Particularly We bequeath to it all the natural wealth the earth has to offer in all that land which lies to the East of the Ural Mountains, on a line from My City of Serov east to My City of Surgut, and straight north as far as the Sea. Thus with their energies, their skills, and their devotion to serving all mankind, the Order can develop the resources of Siberia to the advantage of that illustrious Order.

In deference to the wishes of the Order, We have graciously accepted the supreme Majesty, with the firm intention to use all Our power and Imperial authority to its advantage and its needs, and such shall remain forever the same

Given at Our Imperial Residence of St Petersburg the 21st 'December, the 1798th of our Era, the 3rd of Our Reign and the 1st of Our Majesty.

Signed *Paul*

Chapter One

I'd spotted the headlights of the vehicle shortly after it turned from the Scottish Highland road onto the rocky track that winds its way over moorland to my home. The noise of its engine disturbed the chickens in their coop, and Randy, my faithful old border terrier whined, wanting to be let out to investigate. We waited together in the doorway, heedless of the midges that hovered all around us, and curious to see who was making the difficult journey. Visitors were rare, especially after dark when going off the track and getting stuck in the soft bog would be such an easy thing to do.

The car was a Range Rover, black and mysterious, with darkened windows and several aerials protruding from the roof. The chauffeur was first to step out. I could see him clearly in the light from the conservatory; his suit was black, as was his shirt and tie. He had a swarthy complexion, his head was shaven, and he was stocky of build, reminding me more of a prize fighter than a chauffeur. He had an ugly scar that ran from one side of his razor blade thin lips almost to his left ear. "Son of Satan" sprang to mind; I'd obviously read that somewhere, and in my subconscious mind it seemed an apt description. In fact, as I was to learn later, his name was Hawk, and his complexion an unfortunate gift from his Anglo-Saxon father and Mohawk Indian mother.

The two rear doors opened more or less simultaneously. An elderly gentleman appeared from the seat on the driver's side. He was tall and very slim, better than seventy years of age, but still with a nicely coiffured head of dark hair with silver streaks at the sides enhancing his already aristocratic look. He was wearing an elegant, well-tailored, grey suit and carried himself very upright, a habit left over perhaps from an earlier military career. My attention however was riveted to the other passenger. That was my twenty-year-old son Nicholas. He's a tall, good-looking lad with long, light-brown hair combed straight back, accentuating his high forehead and his fair complexion and amazing blue eyes, which were all qualities inherited from his mother. I like to think his other attributes – honesty, self-reliance, and raw intelligence – he'd inherited from me, but perhaps like all parents I tend towards prejudice. He was wearing his customary jeans and roll-neck jumper and a pair of extravagant Nike sports shoes on his feet. Nicholas was supposed to be in America where he lived with his mother and where he was studying Russian language and history at university. We spoke on the telephone every week and saw each other twice a year; we enjoyed a very close relationship, so it was a real surprise he should come unannounced in this way.

Randy bounded over to Nicholas, jumping up and trying to lick his face in welcome. The other two people stayed back, the elderly gentleman smoothing his hair with one hand and holding a document case in the other, while the chauffeur had lit a cigarette and was lounging against the side of the car, indifferent to what was going on around him.

Nicholas came to where I stood with Randy hard on his heels. A hug was a special feature of our relationship: manly, extremely physical, almost as though we were engaging in a mutual trial of strength. Today, however, it was somewhat reserved on my part. What was Nicholas doing here and in such unusual company?

He came straight to the point,

"Dad, I'd like to introduce you to Sir James Sinclair," Nicholas said. "Sir James, this is my father, Alec Johnson."

The elegant stranger came towards me, offering his hand in friendship and, curiously, bowing his head to me very slightly. I was becoming more anxious by the minute, wondering what all this was leading up to.

The chauffeur, meantime, was trying to beat off the midges that were attacking him; clearly he was more used to the ways of the city than to remote areas such as this.

"Forgive this intrusion, Mr Johnson. I've envisaged this meeting with you many times, wondering even if it was the right thing to do, but a serious and unwelcome disease meant I couldn't prevaricate any longer."

His voice carried just the softest trace of a Scottish accent. As he stood closer to me I could see the deep lines that ravaged his pockmarked face, and the way his eyes had sunk into their sockets gave the appearance of a death mask. The stranger would not be long in this world, but what on earth was he talking about? I suggested we should go inside partly to escape from the ever-present midges but also to shut out the unwelcome sight of the chauffeur – he frightened me!

I live in what used to be a bothy, a Scottish name for a moorland hut, which over the years had been home to a succession of keepers on the grouse moor; me included starting thirty years ago. At that time it had been a very primitive affair with no sanitation or drainage, and water had to be carried from the burn fed by the nearby mountains. It had just one room, dominated by a huge fireplace, which consumed massive amounts of peat.

My life had been very simple; eating was a monotonous diet of porridge for breakfast and a stew for supper, usually made from a rabbit or hare, which His Grace allowed us keepers to snare, with lashings of fresh vegetables and potatoes dug from my own patch of a garden. To this day I still use the old stewing pot which I'd inherited from a previous keeper almost fifty years ago, and it is constantly simmering on the open fire. It was a time of early to bed and early to rise partly because the only artificial light came from a smoky, old paraffin lamp which had definitely seen better days but also because ours was a grouse moor, and dawn and dusk is when most pilfering takes place, by two as well as four-legged thieves.

When my father died in 1981, I took his place as head gamekeeper and moved from the bothy into the gatehouse, which guards the driveway to Rannoch Castle, and lived there for twenty years. I retired in 2001, and the American owner of the castle, who we called the Grand Master, told me he needed the gatehouse for the new keeper. As a retirement present he proposed upgrading this old bothy to make it a modern cottage, and giving me a couple of acres of ground to grow vegetables and to rear chickens.

This suited me very well as the gatehouse held too many painful memories and was too near the goings on at the castle. I was accustomed to leading a solitary lifestyle, that goes with being a gamekeeper, and the moors had been my home and my living for so many years it would have been impossible to live anywhere else. Neither did the Grand Master stint on the upgrading; a spacious conservatory was added to the front of the house, and a dividing wall built across the lounge to provide a separate bedroom. Electric lighting and a boiler were installed, and water was piped in from a well, which provided crystal clear water, totally free of the kind of pollutants you find in the city. The drainage went into an enormous underground sceptic tank.

I'd never had a television set before – satellite television hadn't been invented the first time I'd lived in this bothy – and reception from the BBC and ITV channels was at best spasmodic, so it would have been a total waste. Reading had always been a particular pleasure for me, a way to pass the lonely hours and days when the winter weather made going outdoors impractical. The travelling library called at the village every week and always carried a good supply of biographies and the like, which I particularly enjoyed. By the time I retired, satellite television had become commonplace, so it was a welcome addition to my new lifestyle, as was the telephone, too. I'd insisted on keeping the open fireplace, and with a plentiful supply of cut logs, this kept the cottage warm without the need to install central heating. The kitchen continued to be a fairly rudimentary affair; old habits die hard and my eating routine had hardly varied from my youth, so a modern kitchen would have been a waste and out of keeping with the rest of my surroundings.

I made coffee for my guests, choosing to ignore the chauffeur outside, and placed the tray on the small table. Sir James meantime had opened the document case he was carrying and removed a small jewellery box, from which he took a locket on a chain.

"This belongs to you," he told me, "it came into my father's possession many years ago in circumstances which were highly controversial. He'd been instructed to take this locket, and a notebook which I'll bring another time, to the safe keeping of the authorities in London. He must have sensed they would be buried away in official archives and conveniently lost forever, so he disobeyed the instructions, something totally out of character for him to do. My father died some years ago, and I'd found them in his papers, together with his note explaining what it was all about. Frankly, I wasn't sure what I should do; he'd been a very senior official in the Foreign Office. The notebook contains information of a highly political nature, which perhaps should not be in the public domain. At one point I'd actually made an appointment to meet the man who'd replaced him when he retired from the Foreign Office. I'd intended handing them over, hoping that I wouldn't be doing something which would sully father's good reputation, but in the end I decided if he kept the notebook, and of course the locket, it was for a good reason, and I should respect his judgement."

To say I was mystified was an understatement. Who was this man, what was he talking about, what was so special about the locket? I took it from him; it was about the size of my thumbnail, heart shaped, made of gold with an enamel inlay. It opened easily; inside was a picture of a very young baby, and on the opposite face of the locket were engraved the initials "N" and "A", intertwined in gold letters, surrounded by diamond chips in the form of a crown. A tiny catch beside the picture opened a secret panel, revealing a lock of light brown hair. I became agitated. I knew I'd seen this before, but where and when, I couldn't remember.

The stranger noticed the perturbed look on my face.

"I can see the locket looks familiar to you," he said, "though you were a very small child when you saw it last. You have much to learn about your past, many things that continue to be secret even to this day. I thought it best that your son should be with you when you learn of these things, because they will concern him too, equally, if not more than you. That's why I made the arrangements through an old acquaintance at Harvard to fly Nicholas here for this meeting. With your permission I will leave the locket with you and return to my home, which isn't too far away.

"If you agree, I will pass by again in a couple of days to continue with this story, because there is much to tell. Meantime, from the discussions I had with Nicholas on the journey here, it is obvious he knows almost nothing of your life, at least your life as you know it.

It would help him to understand things much better if you would put that right, and you and he can then read the notebook with more understanding."

With that the stranger stood to leave. He again gave that old worldly bow of his head, let himself out, and in a minute we heard the engine of the Range Rover come to life and he was gone. Silence descended on my little home, and even old Randy sensed the atmosphere and nuzzled his head against my hand, seeking some kind of reassurance.

I passed the locket to Nicholas for him to examine and went to the drinks cabinet; whisky was a rare luxury for me, but my need was great and I was sure that Nicholas was feeling the same. I passed a tumbler to him, and still without a word being said, I drank mine in one swift gulp and returned to the cabinet for a refill. Hardly had I done so, when Nicholas, who, to the best of my knowledge, rarely drank, did the same. Then it was as if a curtain had been lifted. We both started talking, loudly, I think almost incoherently, neither listening to what the other was saying. This must have gone on for some moments before we looked at each other in realisation of what we were doing and lapsed again into silence.

It was true; as the stranger had intimated I'd told my son little of my life, though what that could have to do with any of this was beyond me to know.

"Let's first have some dinner, and then we can decide what we should do," I suggested.

Dinner was the usual rabbit stew, washed down with a jug of cider, which Ned, the old shepherd on the nearby *hirsel*, had given me in exchange for a dozen eggs the previous week. It was probably the effect of the whisky and polishing off the cider that finally loosened our tongues. We left the dishes in the sink unwashed, something I'd rarely done before. Nicholas brought in some logs from the lean-to by the back door and made them ready as if we were in for a long night. We settled into the well-worn armchairs, which I'd brought with me from the gatehouse, and then Nicholas seemed to find his voice again.

"Dad, I can't even begin to understand what this is all about, and it doesn't sound as though you do either, but I'm quite sure Sir James is being deadly serious. He didn't bring me all the way from Boston without good reason, so why don't you do as he suggested. Tell me about your life, the people you knew, where you went, what you did. Spare nothing, and then we should ask him to visit us again."

It was going to be a long night.

Nicholas returned the locket to me as I began to speak. I told him that my earliest recollections of life were confused and that I could remember nothing at all of the wartime devastation in London, which I'd been told had killed my entire family and forced my evacuation to Scotland when I was just four years old.

"I presume I would have travelled north by train and would have had many other young children as companions, all in the same predicament as I, but of that I have no recollection, which is perhaps surprising. I do seem to remember my first sight of Rannoch Castle, though that too is very confused. Even today, it looks grey and cold, almost threatening, so you can perhaps imagine how it would have appeared to me as a young child."

Nicholas knew the history of the castle quite well from his mother. It had been built five-hundred years earlier as a fortified tower house; it dominates the skyline for miles around. The four turrets glare out defiantly from each corner, challenging anyone to approach only at their peril. Those on the southwest and southeast corners overlook the glens and the strategically important track leading from the east coast across the Central Highlands and on to Fort William and the Western Isles, while those on the north side stare deeply into the distant mountains. Rannoch Castle is unique in that it has never been taken by force of arms.

I looked across at my son, briefly wondering if I should share with him a recurrent dream that has haunted me for as many years as I can remember, but he'd asked that I tell him everything, so I pressed on.

"I seem to remember another castle Nicholas, very different to Rannoch; this one had a wide staircase sweeping down from the main entrance to the marvellous lawns below. The grass was a shade of green I find impossible to describe, and so meticulously manicured you might be afraid to even step on it. In my dream I always see this couple sitting on a blanket, having a picnic. A toddler is playing at their feet, and a pair of beautiful horses is grazing nearby. Then the dream changes, and suddenly people are running around, shouting in alarm; I can see the horses as they crash through the nearby trees, clearly in panic, and then the vision fades and all I see is darkness."

I was feeling a little foolish, and wondered if Nicholas might think me crazy, but I needn't have worried. His facial expression hadn't changed, and he was absorbing every word and no doubt trying to fit each into the puzzle that was unfolding.

"Of course everyone has strange dreams at times, dreams that are totally meaningless in real life, and no doubt this is just one of them."

I was trying to play it down, even though deep inside I knew it was more than a dream.

To come back to reality, I told Nicholas of the duke and duchess of Dumfries, who owned Rannoch Castle back then. They were an elderly couple, childless themselves, and had taken me in for reasons I've never been able to understand. It seemed curious that in making such a charitable gesture they should have chosen to take only one poor refugee, while they could have accommodated many more in that huge castle. Even more curious, as I was to learn later, no sooner had I arrived than they promptly offloaded me to their childless housekeeper and her husband, who to all intents and purposes then became the only parents I was to know.

I learned that His Grace's many-times-removed great grandfather had chanced to give his loyalty and his army of Lowland Scots to William of Orange in the Glorious Revolution of 1689. His troops were routed at the Battle of Killiecrankie in that year, but ultimate victory eventually followed and William was pleased to reward the loyalty with the dukedom. The castle, which then became their home, had been appropriated from a less fortunate warrior who'd chosen the wrong side and had his bowels removed in retribution!

My mother, as I always called her, had been in service to the duke and duchess since the age of fourteen, and through a process of elimination had graduated to become the housekeeper. By the time I was thrust into this family in 1941, the necessary economies of wartime were being felt all over the country, and ours was no exception. All the other household staff had left to undertake war work, leaving mother to do everything that was required in the castle. Likewise on the estate, all the male workers had been enlisted to serve their country in foreign parts, leaving just my newfound father to take care of the vast estate.

He'd been gifted by the duke with exemption from military service, something he hadn't asked for and really hadn't wanted, but in those days you knew not to argue. He was given the title of chief gamekeeper, an anachronism for odd-job man, and worked twelve hours a day, seven days a week for the privilege. Our home was the gatehouse lodge, a two-bedroom cottage positioned to guard the long driveway to the castle. As was customary in those days the lodge was provided partly in lieu of wages, which anyway were a pittance and which their Graces' paid as infrequently as possible.

The smoke from the fire was beginning to burn my eyes, and I thought I'd seen Nicholas's head starting to drop, which was hardly surprising; the poor boy had only flown in to Glasgow from Boston earlier in the day, and was now showing signs of jet lag.

"Let's step outside for a while. I think we could both do with some fresh night air to clear our brains."

There was something very special about being in the Highlands, a long way from civilisation, on a night such as that one. The air was crisp, the stars shone more brightly, and the nearly full moon illuminated the ridges of the distant mountains, while around us it created long shadows from the nearby trees. The sounds of the night were special too; at this time of year the fox had moved up from the lowland, and he was on the prowl to feed his family, either a rabbit, which was his favourite food as well as mine, or even a young lamb that had strayed too far from its mother. Even though I was retired, I still enjoyed walking the moors, keeping a sharp eye out for predators, and using my Yeoman twelve-bore shotgun to good purpose when opportunity presented itself.

I continued with my story as we felt our way across the open moorland with Randy running on ahead, pausing from time to time to sniff the night air as he searched for any intruders.

"I was almost six years old when I started school, a bit older than my classmates. Mother had bought me a new pair of trousers and a very smart pair of shoes. I remember feeling very proud of them.

The night before I should start school, Mum and Dad had sat me down. They had something serious they needed to tell me. They told me they were not my real parents. They told me about the wartime bombing in London and how I'd miraculously survived when the rest of my family had been killed. My family name was Johnson, whereas theirs was McCabe.

"Mum did the talking – she always seemed to be the one who was in charge at difficult moments. I suppose I should have felt devastated, but I didn't. I wouldn't have known the word 'humble' at that age, let alone understood it, but in retrospect that was my feeling. I was so grateful they'd cared for me, had treated me as their own, and had loved me. This was 1943, and the war was at its fiercest. Germany seemed to be sweeping all before her. Morale everywhere in this country was at an all-time low, and young as I was, I knew from the wireless of the enormous problems people had to contend with: soldiers coming back from the war front with terrible injuries, food rationing, and people without money to live. I had good cause to feel lucky.

"You would think I would have a memory of the wartime bombing, Nicholas, but as I told you before, my memory of those days is very confused, almost as though I wasn't there, like I was somewhere else. I suppose it blanked out the terrible scenes I must have witnessed, as I understand memory can do at times of stress.

"I pass my old school every time I go into the village; it hasn't changed one bit, except its closed now of course. Had your mother not taken you to America you would have gone to that school too – perhaps it's lucky for you it didn't happen. It was a typically small village school: one classroom, a playground devoid of anything remotely resembling play, and a teacher who spent a disproportionate amount of time spanking young boys for misdemeanours they hadn't committed. I made some good friends at that school, and as is the way in small communities like ours, many of them are still my friends to this day. In the beginning, we had difficulty understanding each other. I found the Scottish accent to be almost incomprehensible, and likewise, my friends had difficulty understanding what I suppose was my Cockney accent. Over the years, that has changed, and now I sound every bit as Scottish as they."

Even as I said this to my son, I wondered how he'd have got on at that school had his mother come back from America and we'd had another try at making a success of our marriage, which is what I'd prayed for but hadn't happened.

I continued, "My parents encouraged me to bring young friends home after school; we invented many exciting games to play in the castle grounds. Best of all though was when the duke and duchess went away, which they did very regularly, either to see their friends in London of whom they seemed to have many or going sea fishing from the Island of Mull where they had another house.

"Unbeknown to my parents I'd found a secret entrance to the castle. To be honest it wasn't exactly a secret entrance. It was an iron grate at the back of the castle, which in former times would have been used by the wood cutter to drop logs into the storeroom ready to fuel the enormous fire in the main kitchen. The castle was supposed to be strictly out of bounds to us children, which made it all the more exciting; we'd remove the grating, gently lower ourselves into the storeroom, and by standing on a convenient table we could replace the grating so no one knew we were inside.

"From there we'd pass through the kitchen and up the stone stairs to the ground floor. I said it wasn't exactly a secret entrance, but we did find a secret room one day, a real one this time, indeed one that had some history attached to it. We were in the duke's study, a small turret room on the second floor of the castle. My friend Jimmy had tripped over the corner of a rug, fallen on his face, and hurt his nose, which was bleeding quite heavily. He was crying, but I was more concerned to clean up the blood in case someone should see it and realise we'd been there.

"That was when I saw the iron ring set into the stone floor. I suppose originally it would have been well hidden from view, but just then it was only covered up with the rug. Anyway, Jimmy stopped crying and helped me pull the ring, which easily lifted a stone block set in the floor. In the opening was a ladder that led down into the secret room. Can you imagine our excitement? I was a bit nervous and had decided to stay on guard, so it was Jimmy who went down, bloodied nose forgotten. I soon changed my mind when I heard Jimmy laughing at what he'd found. One wall was covered with pin-up pictures of pretty girls wearing bathing costumes, mostly of the kind that appeared in soldiers' magazines in wartime, and the floor was littered with more of them. Of course they were innocent by today's standards, but we could imagine the old duke hiding himself down there with his girlie pictures. There was also a notice on the wall, maybe written by the duke, I don't know, which said that Bonnie Prince Charlie had slept in that secret room for two nights while he was hiding from the English.

"Sadly, Jimmy was killed in a motorbike accident on the road to Blair when he was just sixteen."

Nicholas stopped in his tracks, and turned to face me.

"Surely someone must have found out what you were doing in the castle, and anyway I remember you once told me that the duke and duchess had died while they were on a fishing trip. Where does all that fit in?"

The impatience of youth!

"First of all, no one ever discovered our secret. Jimmy and I, with our other young friends, formed a secret society and swore terrible things would happen to anyone letting the cat out of the bag. As for the duke and duchess, their fishing boat capsized in rough seas off the Isle of Mull in 1946, and they were presumed drowned. Because they had no living relatives, the castle was put up for sale. That was a worrying time for my parents; the war had only just ended, and work was scarce. They were kept on at the castle while the solicitors were looking for a buyer, which fortunately didn't take very long. The new owner, a Mr Hutchinson, was a wealthy American who'd been grouse shooting on the estate before the war. As soon as he'd heard it was for sale he snapped it up, together with another three-thousand acres of moorland, which as it turned out was a lucky thing for me, but more of that later. We then had one of the largest moors in the Highlands on which to organise the castle's post-war future. Mr Hutchinson still had an active business in America and only visited the estate two or three times a year, always in time for the Glorious Twelfth of course, but usually at Hogmanay as well and other times as he could get away from his work."

For some minutes we'd been assailed by the smell of burning, and the reason became apparent as we breasted the hill: a gamekeeper had been burning the heather that day and a part was still smouldering. Heather is considered to be at its best nutritional value between six and ten years old, so the keeper carries out systematic burning on his moorland, replacing old heather with tender new roots, usually in small patches such as the one we'd encountered. It was unusually careless of him to leave the heather smouldering, even though the risk of fire was very small. Nicholas promptly removed the risk completely by emptying his bladder at the appropriate spot, much to Randy's apparent amusement.

I'd confessed to myself I was quite enjoying reminiscing, bringing back many pleasant memories. I'd told Nicholas how the school holidays were a time of real joy for me and my friends. With no television to distract us we had to find ways to amuse ourselves and keep out of the way of our hard-working parents and, even more, not to be a nuisance to the toffs who were there for game shooting.

Rannoch Moor, over to the west of the castle, is a high, empty, moorland area; once it would have been covered with vast, dark forests where bears and wolves would have roamed freely, but today it is the home of red deer, grouse – and the predatory golden eagle. My friends and I would hike for hours over the moor, imagining ourselves to be Royalist troops searching for rebel Jacobites or pretending we were with Bonnie Prince Charlie, marching north to Inverness and swearing revenge on the Duke of Cumberland's forces.

"Adolescence brought a move to a school in Pitlochry, which meant enduring a head teacher every bit as vindictive as his predecessor at the infants' school, so it was a blessing to leave school at age fourteen, even though I'd gained no qualifications at all. To become a gamekeeper today you must go to college for four years and have at least a higher national certificate, but in those days you learnt on the job, following in your father's footsteps, and I was no exception. Father showed me how to handle the traps and how to dig out the ferrets when they were laid up in the burrows. By the time I was twelve, he would send me out on my own, especially if it was a rainy day and the larder was empty. Dad taught me to paunch rabbits and disembowel them, and I became very good at it, even though to this day I hate the mess it always makes on the kitchen table."

We paused by the side of the burn, trying to spot the stepping stones in the moonlight so we could cross without getting our feet wet.

"Like me, your grandfather was a man whose entire life had been spent on these high moors. He was also a man of few words, so whenever he spoke you would pay particular attention. 'Respect,' he would often say to me, 'must come before everything else up here. You must respect the hill farmers and the shepherds and the very moor itself, because each can be your best friend or your worst nightmare.' My father was a wise man, largely unschooled but gifted in many earthy ways, a quality that is missing in today's better educated gamekeepers.

"Highland people can be wonderful neighbours, but they can be vindictive if they feel sinned against. Dad made it a point to get along with them all and taught me many of the finer points of being a shepherd's best friend, rounding up rough sheep and handing them to the clippers or helping pack newly shorn fleece into enormous sacks ready to be taken to market."

We returned to the cottage. The walk on the moors had been very welcome, Nicholas had hardly uttered a single word since we'd stepped out, listening attentively to everything I'd said, but it was getting cold and we'd not wrapped up properly. Even Randy was pleased to be back in the warmth and went to lie on his blanket at the foot of the bed without any bidding from me. Nicholas made coffee, strong the way we like it in the Highlands, and added what he called Dad's special spice – a generous tot of Highland whisky – while I put some more logs on the fire. He didn't seem to be in too much of a hurry to go to his bed. I had only one bedroom, so he was confined to using his sleeping bag on the settee, and Randy usually finished up sharing that with him on a cold night.

I continued my story.

"Nineteen fifty-five came, and with it my introduction to the outside world; it was a rude awakening. I'd been out with the ferrets, getting them ready to go hunting that night. When I returned, father gave me an envelope, buff coloured with 'On Her Majesty's Service' boldly printed on the top and franked with an official seal. It had come that afternoon, and was addressed to me. I think it was the first envelope I'd ever received, and I remember suddenly feeling very insecure and very frightened. Father had a worried look and mother was sitting by the fireside, hiding her face. She was crying. The letter was short and simple: I was to attend the army recruiting office in nearby Perth within the next fourteen days and failure to do so would render me liable to imprisonment. I'd been called up for National Service.

"This is neither the time nor the place to go into details of my life for the next two years. Suffice to say I attended the recruiting office as I'd been ordered to do. The sergeant, a very thick set and aggressive looking man, surprisingly scruffy in his heavy brown uniform, was short and to the point. He handed me a long paper, told me it was a legal document concerning my rights and my duties, and said I must sign it. I did so, and then he told me to stand up. A young officer came from the next room, told me to place my hand on the Bible, and repeat the words of the oath after him. His work done, he returned to his inner sanctum. The sergeant handed me a travel warrant made out for a single journey from Perth to Aldershot and said I'd better not be late or I'd really be in trouble. I was in the Army.

"I can't say that was a happy time for me, but looking back there were some good moments. Comradeship was something missing in my lonely life on the moors, and suddenly I was sharing a barrack room with twenty other men, none of us happy to be there, all of us totally out of our depth, and worrying whether we could possibly survive whatever the Army had in store for us. I had an advantage over most of my comrades. I was accustomed to getting out of bed before 6.0 a.m., whereas for many of them this was an altogether new and unwelcome experience.

"I'd only been there for six weeks when the sergeant major sent for me. This was a worrying development. *What had I done wrong?*

"I stood in front of him, heels together, back straight, head upright as I'd been newly taught, desperately trying to focus on a spot on the wall above his head and avoid the piercing look from his eyes. He was surprisingly gentle, a very different man from the one I knew on the parade ground. He told me my mother had been admitted to hospital. She was seriously ill, but he didn't know what with. I'd been granted fourteen days compassionate leave and was to go home immediately.

"I remember fighting back the tears from my eyes and was shocked at my reaction to the news. I didn't want to go home. I wanted to return to my friends in the barrack room. I suppose I didn't want to face the reality of what I might find when I got home, and the barrack room and my new-found friends offered me a place to hide from this crisis in my life.

"Mother died shortly before I arrived at the hospital in Perth. She had breast cancer. She must have had it for a long time, because by the time she went to the hospital it was too late to save her. I don't remember much of those fourteen days. The funeral took place on a cold, rainy day in the churchyard behind the castle. The priest gobbled through the service at the graveside, probably worried he'd catch a cold. My father hardly spoke to me at all. He stood as though in a trance, his eyes glazed and his actions slow and ponderous. I'd hugged him as the coffin was lowered into the ground, desperately anxious to share my sorrow with the only other person in my life I truly loved, but he was as a statue – cold and rigid. It was hard to avoid the smell of whisky on his breath, and this was to become a feature of his life without mother.

"I spent most of the next twenty months in Germany, living a life as different from anything I'd known previously as it is possible to imagine. My first experience of sex came within a few days of my arrival in Bielefeld."

I suddenly stopped speaking. *Should I really be telling this to my son?* I decided yes, and so I continued.

"A corporal in the Women's Royal Army Corps was teaching me the finer points of driving a three ton truck on the 'wrong' side of the road, using a disused airfield as the training ground. I quickly mastered the art of manoeuvring the truck, but the coffee break was another matter. She attacked me with a passion bordering on insanity. My knowledge of sex was almost non-existent. In the barrack room we would all talk knowingly of doing 'it', but probably few of us had any real idea what 'it' entailed and very definitely none of us knew how to do 'it' in broad daylight, in the cramped confines of the cab of an army truck. I can only say I was stunned by the gymnastic gyrations she performed on the floor-mounted gear lever, and when she screamed at me to flash her headlights, I lost the plot completely.

I bear the shame of my wet army underpants to this day. I don't even remember her name, and for sure she won't want to remember mine!"

I looked at the clock on the mantelpiece and wasn't surprised to see it was almost three in the morning. It had been a very long night, but now Nicholas was constantly rubbing his eyes, trying to stay awake. I could hear the wind getting up outside, as indeed it can on the high moors, and rain was beginning to fall too. Clearly it was time to sleep. After saying goodnight to Nicholas, I went to my bedroom. Randy had been sleeping on the bed, as he is want to do if I let him get away with it, so when I pushed him off, perhaps none too gently, he slunk away in a huff and no doubt spent the rest of the night curled up on the settee with my son.

Chapter Two

Mamdoubh Rifaat looked out at the gathering of journalists waiting in the car park of the Marriott Hotel in the Zamalck district of downtown Cairo. If he was disappointed at the lack of turnout, he wasn't showing it. Just minutes earlier he'd closed the extraordinary meeting of the League of Arab States of which he was the secretary general, and had hurriedly made the journey across town to the hotel in time to hold a twelve noon press conference. Protocol demanded that the minutes of the League meetings first be ratified by all the governments concerned. This usually involved several months of wrangling, and only then would the secretary general inform the outside world of their deliberations, but today was to be an exception and this had caught the media organisations by surprise.

The League meeting had been extremely difficult, even though he personally had done a lot of arm twisting before the session had convened. The delegates were unanimous in agreeing it was wrong for so many Coalition troops to be on Islamic soil. They all wanted to send a signal to the invading countries, as they called them. It was time for them to take their troops back home, but therein lay the problem. They knew that if the Coalition did indeed withdraw, the vacuum would quickly be filled by a very different kind of enemy, one much more difficult to control, the one from within. They also knew the Coalition countries, particularly America and Britain would be only too pleased to oblige; they desperately wanted to withdraw their troops, but as all sides realised, it was too late for that now. Too late the White House, strongly aided by Downing Street, had come to understand there had been options other than sending in a massive number of troops with an overwhelming technical superiority. Their objectives could have been achieved quietly and efficiently by a judicious use of special forces, such as the US Navy Seals or Britain's SAS, taking out the Iraqi political leaders, as in fact they had done with Saddam Hussein's own two sons, without causing the massive destruction to lives and property that hundreds of air strikes had done. Hindsight was a cruel master. The wars in Iraq and Afghanistan were hugely unpopular back home. Too many families had to see their loved ones buried, albeit with military honours, and the cost in financial terms was crippling, not to mention the cost in terms of political support. So, unusually, both the Coalition and the Islamists wanted the same thing, and neither could have their way.

The Arab League delegates would be satisfied with repeating the motion that had been approved at various meetings since 2003 – namely the demand for the withdrawal of all foreign troops from Islamic territory – and leave it at that. Mamdoubh Rifaat, however, needed more, much more. He needed penalties to be applied if the withdrawals didn't happen, and he'd done his best to justify that to the delegates.

"Did anyone take any notice of us in 2003?" he'd asked. "Did one single soldier leave Iraq or Afghanistan or Gaza or anywhere else for that matter, as a result of our demand?"

Around the table heads had shaken but without conviction. The delegates were afraid of where the secretary general was going with this. He'd done his best to smile reassuringly at them despite his inner feeling of frustration.

"No, they did not," he said, "not even one, and why? Because we didn't back up our demand with action, and the same will happen this time. Is that what you want? Is that what the leaders in your own countries want? To be ignored by the rest of the world, to be treated with such disrespect?"

Mamdoubh's voice had risen by nearly an octave as his apparent anger at the insults that were being heaped on their peace-loving countries was taking hold of him. He looked across the table at Mohammed Hajri, his Yemeni deputy, and gave a slight nod of his head. That was the signal for him to read the censure motion, which they'd prepared earlier that morning.

Hajri nervously tapped the table with the end of his pencil, causing the delegates to turn to look at him. He was a passionate advocate of Islamic fundamentalism and did his best to use his position on the Arab League Council to further that cause.

"Brothers," his voice quivered as he spoke, "the motion on the table says that we, the members of the League of Arab States, unanimously demand the immediate withdrawal of all foreign troops from Islamic soil."

Around the conference table heads were nodding in silent agreement, which encouraged Hajri to continue.

"I propose an amendment to that motion, to add the words 'If the invading countries fail to accede to this demand, we will expel them by force."

Hajri was well aware there would be serious dissent to such a controversial choice of words; he knew many of the delegates were much less militant than he, but even so he was taken aback by the ferocity of the reactions around the table. Pandemonium had broken out in the room, and everyone trying to speak at once. Voices were raised, and tempers were becoming frayed. Rifaat let it run for several minutes before calling the room back to order.

"Brothers, you've all heard the motion. Can I have a seconder, please?"

The Iraqi delegate didn't waste any time; he raised his hand straight away, as he'd agreed to do at a breakfast meeting earlier that morning.

The secretary general nodded his approval and said, "The motion is put before the meeting. Can I have a show of hands in support?"

The Kuwaiti delegate had started shouting again, asking where they thought they would get the necessary soldiers and equipment to take on the entire allied Coalition, and others round the table were nodding in agreement. Mamdoubh could see he was going to lose the vote. He'd been warned if he allowed that to happen the video tapes, which were of a very explicit sexual nature and which he'd foolishly kept in his office safe, would find their way to his family and to the media. He would be disgraced and held in ridicule everywhere. He could not afford to let that happen.

"My brothers, I can see we need more time to reflect on such a grave issue. With your approval I will simply record in the minutes that we discussed the use of force to expel the invaders and agreed to defer the item for the time being. Can I have a show of hands in support of that please?"

The secretary general noted that the Kuwaiti's hand still hadn't moved, and both the Saudi and Jordanian delegates were wavering, unsure of what they were being asked to agree to. Fortunately, the motion passed on a majority vote, and Mamdoubh moved the meeting on to the next agenda item, relieved to have that one out of the way even though he hadn't achieved all that had been demanded of him.

After taking leave of their colleagues at the League's headquarters, the secretary general and his deputy hurried down to their waiting taxi and half an hour later arrived at the Marriott Hotel. The traffic had been as chaotic as ever, even though this was Thursday afternoon and most businesses had shut for the Arab weekend. To make matters worse, it was an unusually hot day even by Cairo standards, and the air conditioning in the taxi was broken so they had to ride with the windows open, forcing them to inhale the highly polluted air of the Egyptian capital. It had been a most uncomfortable journey.

Rifaat had two reasons for going to the Marriott. He'd asked the hotel's manager, Ali Sharif, a man he knew well from his many visits to the Marriott, to summon as many media reporters as he could find to attend an emergency briefing from the League of Arab States. His other reason was that the Lebanese representative of a senior Saudi Arabian government minister was staying at the Marriott. In fact, he was using the minister's presidential suite, an indication of how much importance the minister attached to his representative, and they were due to meet immediately the press conference finished. The Lebanese man had the incriminating videos that belonged to Rifaat, and he wanted them back.

Mamdoubh Rifaat turned to his deputy and said "Let's not keep the pack waiting any longer, Mohammed. We promised a twelve-noon briefing, and that's what we're going to give them."

They pushed through the swing doors of the side entrance to the hotel in single file. Rifaat's bulk, somewhat disguised by the djhowtey he was wearing, forced a group of Italian tourists who were trying to enter the hotel to give way.

A dais had been placed on the pavement, slightly to one side of the entrance; it had a single microphone attached to the lip. Rifaat wasn't a man to take chances, and he certainly didn't want his deputy stealing any of his thunder. The dais had the hotel logo superimposed on its face. Rifaat would have preferred the green flag with its white wreath enclosing a crescent and the name of the organisation Jama'at ud-Dawlaat il-Arabiyya, but there hadn't been time to organise that. The waiting journalists went silent as he started to speak, only for him to stop again when he realised the microphone wasn't working. A hurried shout from the deputy secretary general quickly solicited the attention of a porter, who turned the microphone on at the transformer hidden under the dais.

Rifaat spoke first in Arabic, giving the reporters who understood that language the benefit of getting their copy on the wires before their international colleagues, and as he knew they would, they'd taken the hint and scuttled away to do just that. Immediately he'd switched to speaking in English.

"Gentlemen," he'd realised while he was doing the Arabic briefing there were no female reporters in the gathering. "The following is a very brief press statement, which I've been authorised to make on behalf of the League of Arab States."

Mamdoubh Rifaat had been a diplomat long enough to know full well what he was doing was wrong – that the members of the League would most certainly not have authorised him to make this statement – but he also knew that such were the sensibilities in the Arab world that they would not want to show dissent between brothers. They might object privately, but not in public. His fear of being disgraced and that his young son and daughter would learn of the video tapes and the kind of deviant they had for a father drove him on.

"We have watched as foreign armies have invaded many of our member states. In every case they have cited as their reason for interference in our domestic affairs the need to restore democracy, to give freedom to the people, and in every case they have done the opposite. They try to enslave us, and they do it for one reason and one reason only – they need our oil! The League has decided it is time for Islam to show its unity of purpose. We will be the guardians of our own peace. We demand the immediate withdrawal of all foreign troops from Islamic soil."

He paused at this point, and looked out at the journalists, trying to create a sense of climax.

He went on, "If the invaders fail to accede to this demand, we will expel them by force. That is all."

One lone English journalist was waving his arm in the air, trying to attract Dr Rifaat's attention in order to ask a question. Colin Jackson, the Cairo bureau representative for the BBC news channel, was himself new in town; he still had a lot to learn about the subtleties of Arab politics. He was at that delightfully naïve stage in his career where he believed that politicians and diplomats actually meant what they said. His Egyptian cameraman was busy recording the scene, though he'd been around long enough to understand there was nothing sensational to be had here.

A couple of other reporters had raised their eyebrows at the threat of force being used, but otherwise the reaction from the group was fairly muted. There were no gasps of surprise, and except for Colin there'd been no clamouring for more detail. They seemed to Colin not to have understood the significance of the threat the secretary general had just uttered. What Rifaat hadn't reckoned with, and what Colin didn't understand was most of them had been around long enough to remember the League making similar demands from 2003 onwards – demands that neither the United Nations nor the great Satan America had taken any notice of at all, and they doubted that today would be any different.

Certainly none of them had noticed the sudden jolt of surprise from the Yemeni diplomat at the last full sentence the secretary general had spoken. They couldn't know that very sentence had been rejected by almost every delegate in the meeting, and neither had it been included in the Arabic briefing just a couple of minutes earlier. As they were gathering together the tools of their trade, eager to return to their families and enjoy the weekend, none of them had realised the trick Rifaat had just perpetrated.

Mamdoubh Rifaat ignored the one lone reporter still trying to get his attention and started back to the air-conditioned comfort of the hotel, pausing long enough only to ensure Hajri was following him.

Once back inside, Hajri turned angrily to the secretary general.

"Mamdoubh, why did you use that sentence about using force? That was forbidden by the delegates. All our governments will turn on you when they understand what you've done."

The secretary general's sheer bulk was enough to intimidate his deputy.

"Mohammed, my friend, for how many years have we worked together? Please don't tell me now you don't trust me." Rifaat poked the Yemeni in the chest as he spoke. "You are a skilful diplomat. You know better than most that to make people pay attention you must first threaten them with a stick and then offer a carrot, and this is particularly true of the spineless politicians in the West. Anyway, the politicians in our own countries will read only the Arabic newspapers, and they cannot print the sentence that offends you, because the Arabic reporters weren't there to hear it. In a day or so, when they do find out, we will say it was a simple misunderstanding on our part and a plot by the West to justify sending even more soldiers to invade Islamic territory. We have nothing to fear Mohammed."

If only that were true, thought Rifaat, *if only that were true!*

"Forgive me for doubting you Mamdoubh, Hajri said, "Of course you are right. I know I worry unnecessarily."

Hajri looked at his watch, a gold Rolex he'd bought in the market in Alexandria for twenty Egyptian pounds. It wasn't very accurate as watches go, but it looked expensive, and appearances counted a lot in his line of work.

"I have to return to my Embassy to finish some papers. Perhaps you'll have lunch with me and my family on Sunday."

Rifaat readily agreed, not that he had any intention of keeping the appointment any more than Hajri had been sincere in making the offer, but they were colleagues and politeness dictated the offer had to be made and accepted. Come Monday Rifaat would apologise, pleading a sudden family emergency, and Hajri would understand. Honour would be satisfied.

"I must go to meet with his Excellency the Saudi minister. I've kept him waiting long enough," Rifaat said.

It wasn't for Hajri to know that he was only meeting with the minister's representative or that indeed he'd never actually met the minister. That wouldn't do at all. The Yemeni had only agreed to go along with Rifaat's actions because he'd been assured the Saudi Government was backing him but didn't want to be seen publicly to be doing so.

Mamdoubh Rifaat made his way to the Saudi's suite of executive rooms on the top floor of the Zamalek Tower. The security guard saluted him as he came out of the private lift. Clearly, he was expected, and the other guard stationed at the far end of the long corridor watched as he approached and then tapped three times on the door, which was immediately opened from the inside.

The first thing Rifaat noticed as he entered the lobby was the smell. Like something out of the *Arabian Nights* was how he thought of it. It was a sickly kind of smell, very sweet, a cheap aftershave lotion maybe, but Rifaat knew better than that. This was the scent of the perfume the hotel management used to cover up the smells of cigarette smoke or even the shisha pipe used by some of their guests.

The suite was in need of decoration; the sand-coloured paint on the walls looked drab, the heavy red curtains were badly frayed, and the dark wood furniture was tired, but still the impression was one of opulence. Two enormous chandeliers, which had their dimmers turned down so as not to reflect too much light on the drab walls, and the huge oriental carpet, which covered every inch of floor space, woven with intricate designs, and in all the brightest colours imaginable more than compensated for the rest of the drabness.

Of course the view from the windows would distract even the most ardent room critic. The majestic River Nile seemed but a stone's throw away, and the bridge that crossed it at this point, so elegant in white stone with two tall minarets in the background making a perfect frame. In the foreground the Hotel Marriott's own dinner cruise ship, the *Nile Maxim* moored by the river bank was being prepared to take the next group of foreign tourists on their journey through history, as the hotel brochure so eloquently described it.

As Rifaat entered the sitting room he saw the Lebanese man was speaking on his mobile phone so, unbidden, he'd made his way to the bathroom and closed the door, out of earshot of his host. He was kept in the bathroom for more than an hour, a display of arrogance he was accustomed to. It was the price you had to pay if you wanted to work with such powerful people, and especially if they had a hold over you, as the Lebanese man had over him.

His host was Majed Dajani, supposedly the representative of a senior Saudi Arabian Government minister. Rifaat wouldn't have known the name of the high ranking Saudi, which was fairly usual practice in the Middle East where black money was involved. In fact it was highly unusual that he should know the Lebanese man's name either, but Rifaat had been shrewd enough at their very first meeting some months earlier to catch a glimpse of the name on the credit card which Dajani had used to pay for Rifaat's paedophilic delights at a rather seedy night club in Heliopolis.

In common with many of his Lebanese countrymen Majed Dajani was a shrewd businessman, a natural linguist in Arabic, French and English, and accustomed to being a fix it man for oil rich Arabs from the Gulf states. He was also a Christian, and was a long-time member of the Lebanese Priory of the Chivalric Order of Saint John of Jerusalem, both things he tended to keep pretty much to himself. "The luck of birth," he often said to his closest friends, "meant that we were born without oil under our feet, so we were given a brain in our heads instead; in life," he would insist, "you could have one or the other, but you couldn't have both!" He was privately resentful of the way his country was forever being used as a pawn in other people's games; in times of peace the wealthy Arabs would come to Beirut to indulge their fantasies, and in times of war huge segments of the country would become battlegrounds at the whim of the Israelis, the Syrians or the Iranians, indeed at times by all of them, or so it seemed.

Majed pushed open the bathroom door; he hadn't intended to keep Rifaat waiting so long, but under the circumstances it was unavoidable. He could hardly have had the Egyptian listening in while he was speaking to the Grand Master of the Russian Priory of the Chivalric Order of St John of Jerusalem who, in common with most Americans, didn't speak any languages other than English! Majed had been telling the Grand Master about the press conference, which had been carried live on local radio. Neither of them was particularly impressed with Rifaat's performance; it was highly unlikely the press release would attract much international attention, evidenced by the lack of enthusiasm shown by the reporters, but it was only the opening step in the campaign, much more was to follow.

Mohammed Rifaat for his part was feeling humiliated, being obliged to wait so long in the bathroom, where the only seat to be had was on the toilet! It was closed of course, he wasn't doing anything, just sitting there, waiting. This most definitely was not in keeping with his status as Secretary General of the Arab League. To make matters worse, the Lebanese man's demeanour demonstrated very clearly what he was thinking of the Egyptian, and it wasn't very high. Rifaat felt severely disadvantaged, but he'd done what had been asked of him, or at least the best he could under the circumstances, and he wanted his reward.

"Mr Dajani," the Egyptian began, not waiting for words of explanation from his host, "the Kuwaiti delegate made the meeting this morning very difficult, but I did what I could, and I think you can report positive news to the Saudi minister. The majority of the League countries will now form an Islamic coalition against the foreigners, as he wanted. Even better news, I'm sure the Godless Americans and all the lackeys who have been seduced into siding with them will even now be making plans to pull their troops from our lands."

Majed stared long and hard at the Secretary General of the Arab League, making Rifaat feel even more uncomfortable than he had before. Was he really so naive to believe their objective was to remove the Coalition from Arab soil? If so, he could add 'stupid' to the Egyptian's other perceived qualities of greed and sexual perversion. And how had he known my name? On the few occasions they'd talked together he'd never introduced himself other than as 'the representative of a very senior Saudi Government minister'. If Rifaat's fate had been in doubt before, it certainly wasn't now!

"Mamdoubh, I'm grateful for all you have done for us, I really am;" being nice paid dividends sometimes, and he wanted to get Rifaat out of his suite! "I'm waiting for a call back from the Saudi minister, and rather than having to ask you to wait in the bathroom again, why don't you go to your room; I'll join you there as soon as I can."

Rifaat was pleased to escape, and to have time to bring himself back under control. He fairly ran from the presidential suite, and took the waiting lift to the ground floor. He was also feeling very hungry, not having had anything to eat since an early breakfast that morning, so he bought a rather generous sized pastry from the patisserie on the ground floor of the hotel which he ate on his way up to his own room on the eighth floor of the Gezirah Tower.

As soon as Rifaat had left the presidential suite, Majed dismissed the security guard from outside the door, giving him a handsome gratuity for his diligence. He'd hired him by phone from one of the agencies in town just for that afternoon, and it was extremely unlikely anyone would think to trace him. For the few seconds they'd met, Majed had worn glasses and a moustache to disguise his features somewhat, so identification was virtually impossible.

Dajani then set about removing all evidence of his having been in the suite at all. He hadn't visited any of the other rooms. Indeed, he hadn't even been to the bathroom, so there was little enough for him to do. He did not however try to remove the evidence that the secretary general of the League of Arab States had been there. Majani wanted that to be found in order to bolster the story of the Saudi Government minister, who did indeed rent that suite very frequently, though he had no idea who Majed was or what he was up to and didn't even know that he himself was paying the hotel bill. The reservation had been made by telephone, with the instruction to charge the account to the usual credit card. No one argued with a Saudi Government minister. Majed wondered what the hotel would do with the collection of videos he was about to leave on the coffee table, videos which he himself had burgled from Mamdoubh Rifaat's office safe and which would no doubt do justice to any inventory of sex videos in pornography shops around the world.

As he pulled closed the door of the presidential suite, he looked down the long corridor and noticed the security guard push the button to summon the lift for the hotel's important guest.

Good service, he thought to himself.

Still wearing the false moustache and glasses and lowering his head as he walked past the guard, as though deep in thought, which indeed he was, Majed climbed into the waiting lift to go to the ground floor. There he walked past the reception desk, which was as chaotic as usual, past the wonderful patisserie, which had so tempted Rifaat moments earlier but which he forced himself reluctantly to resist, and took the corner lift up to the eighth floor where Rifaat was waiting for him in his room.

The man had changed into a freshly laundered djhowtey, and by the look of such little hair he still had on his oversized head, he'd had a shower too. The room was much smaller than the suite of course, but it was very pleasant, recently redecorated in neutral pastel colours, and with a couple of prints of ancient Egypt on the walls. The room had a balcony that offered as wonderful a view of the Nile as Dajani had from his suite, and which had a couple of chairs and a small, glass-covered coffee table as furnishing. In fact the accommodation was as typical as a visiting businessman would expect to find in a five-star hotel anywhere in the world, or at least the civilised world! Dajani refused the offer of coffee, and suggested they sit on the balcony.

"Now that the work of the day is done, it's time to relax and get to know one another better," Dajani said. "Tell me what you are going to do when all this is over?"

Rifaat decided this was his opportunity to push a little for his own reward.

"The million dollars your Saudi friend is transferring to the account you kindly opened for me in Zurich will change my life for the better. It will allow me to do many of the things which until now I've been unable to afford."

Dajani gave a conspiratorial smile. He had a pretty good idea what things this obscenity of a man had in mind to do. He'd heard enough sly remarks to realise Rifaat had a great liking for young boys, and it hadn't been too difficult to get him talking about it. He'd boasted enough to Dajani about the collection of videos of himself and his young partners, which he kept in the safe in his office where his wife's prying eyes wouldn't see them. It had been a simple enough matter for Dajani to break into the safe, remove the videos, and then use them to blackmail the man into doing what he wanted with the Arab League.

Rifaat still had something on his mind. He wanted the videos back, and he was concerned to see that Dajani was not carrying them with him. He tried to make his voice sound as casual as he could to ask when he would get them back. Dajani smiled at him across the balcony.

"Relax old friend," he said, still playing at being conspiratorial. "I've left them in my hotel suite. I'll get them in a few minutes, and maybe you and I can get some beer up here and perhaps a couple of young guests. We can sit and watch the videos together."

Looking at Rifaat from the corner of his eye, Dajani could see that met with the fat Egyptian's approval – time to put the next step into motion.

Suddenly, Dajani jerked himself upright, gave a loud grunt, and fell to his knees, folding his arms tightly across his chest, clearly in great agony. He rolled his eyes back to the point where the pupils almost disappeared, a trick he'd learned during his younger days when he would feign illness to avoid going to school.

"Rifaat, quickly man – a glass of water. I'm having an attack."

Rifaat had no idea what kind of attack Dajani was on about, but he rushed to the bathroom to do his bidding. He ran back to the balcony, his left arm outstretched in front of him, holding the glass of water. Dajani was on his feet again by now, and it was an easy enough matter to grab the man's wrist so obligingly stretched forward , and using Rifaat's own momentum had pulled him to the front of the balcony, reached down to grab an ankle, and lifted him over!

It was that quick, and that simple.

The same Italian tourists Rifaat had inconvenienced immediately prior to the press conference were in the car park, waiting to board their mini bus to be taken to the airport. Their visit to Egypt was over; it was time to go home, but they had one more sight of Egypt to experience, one that most certainly was not included on their itinerary and one that would probably stay with them long after they'd consigned the romantic memories of Egypt's ancient civilisation to their photograph albums.

They heard Rifaat's terrified screams as he fell from the eighth floor. They saw the way his arms and legs thrashed about in mid-air as he made his involuntary journey thirty metres down and how his spotlessly white djhowtey billowed out like some kind of monstrous tent caught in a whirlwind. They heard the dreadful squelching sound as his body hit the tarmac. Mamdoubh Rifaat had served his purpose for the Grand Master, and he wouldn't be troubling any more young boys either.

Taking a tissue from the box on the bedside table and using it to mask his fingerprints, Dajani carefully withdrew the suicide note, which he'd skilfully forged in the handwriting of the secretary general of the League of Arab States. This he placed on the balcony coffee table, apparently the last act of a man with suicide on his mind.

Majed Dajani left the five-star Marriott Hotel in one of the regular black taxis, which cruise the streets of Cairo, without so much as a backward glance at the crowd of Italian tourists and curious onlookers who were hovering like vultures around the mess of what had once been a human being. Majed's destination was a rather less salubrious guesthouse, one which he always rented whenever business brought him to the Egyptian capital. This had the advantage of being owned by another Lebanese businessman, who asked no questions and made no record of his stay. Thus, Majed had the anonymity he craved, and his friend didn't have to pay tax on the rent he received.

Dajani's work for the day was done. He had another task to accomplish the following day, fortunately less strenuous than today's had been, and then he could leave Egypt for another capital city where he had more work to undertake on behalf of the Grand Master of the Russian Priory.

Both Sky News and the Fox News channels carried the wording of the Cairo press conference in their news bulletins, while the BBC played the video tape Colin had transmitted to them. It was a quiet day from a news point of view, but even so none of the channels had paid over much attention, none bothering to call on the talents of their so-called experts to give instant analysis, and the same was true of the news channels on mainland Europe. On the East Coast of the United States most middle-class Americans were just finishing their breakfast and were busy preparing to leave for work. In all probability, few would have barely registered the fact that Fox News was even reporting the news – that's how insignificant it was.

The stock markets in Europe, always ultrasensitive to issues in the Middle East, had barely registered any reaction either, and it was highly unlikely that Wall Street would be any different. If any of the governments in the West had any intention of doing anything about this latest news, they certainly didn't show it. It was nothing new. Unity in the Arab world was confined to their Islamic faith, and even there they were divided between Sunni and Shi'ite. They all had very individual political beliefs, often as different from each other as night and day and usually determined by whether they had black gold beneath their feet or relied for charity from those that had. It was this very disunity that in the past had kept the West safe.

The Grand Master of the Russian Priory of the Chivalric Order of St John of Jerusalem – or Oliver Emerson to give him his Christened name – was alone in his study on the second floor of Rannoch Castle, sitting behind his large, executive-style desk. The screen of a modern desktop computer was glowing on the side extension, the screen saver a picture of Rannoch Castle with the Knights of the Order of St John processing towards the chapel. On the facing wall, three plasma television sets were mounted next to each other, each tuned to a different channel, and these were now holding his attention. The news channels of the BBC, Sky, and Fox were all permanently pre-tuned; the Grand Master had little use for any other programmes, which he regarded as poor entertainment fit only for the masses.

He hadn't been best pleased by the telephone call he'd received a little earlier from Majed Dajani in Cairo. He'd hoped for rather more tension to be created by the threat of action by the Arab League, and that didn't seem to have happened.

Oliver Emerson could justifiably be accused of being intolerant of anyone possessing less than a single-minded dedication to the work in hand. His father had been a minister in the Presbyterian Church with a congregation in the mostly Catholic suburbs of wealthy Boston, a congregation he'd ruled with a hand of iron. He'd claimed to be able to trace his family lineage back to what became known as the Pilgrim Fathers, in fact to one of the thirty-five members of the English Separatist Church who had travelled to America in the ship *Mayflower* in 1620 to escape religious persecution in England. This hardy group of colonialists had established the first permanent settlement in New England, where they'd been able to practice their religion free from the bigotry they'd had to contend with back at home. His father had been a modern-day Puritan, filled with the same sense of moral certitude, a straight-laced, narrow-minded vision that the only way to Heaven was to live a life free from the sins of the flesh and he'd practiced what he preached.

Oliver Emerson was an only child. His mother had died in somewhat mysterious circumstances when he was barely eight years old. The way his father had explained it to him, the Good Lord had called her, and she'd taken her own life to be nearer to Him. Around the community and at school the opinion of the day had rather more to do with the simultaneous disappearance of the priest from the nearby Catholic church and the discovery of his body some weeks later, smashed almost beyond recognition on the rocks of the nearby lovers' beach.

Oliver's father had never remarried, and he'd brought his son up with a truly misogynistic attitude to women, so it was hardly surprising that young Oliver had never had so much as a platonic relationship with a member of the opposite sex, much less committed himself to marriage. In fact he hadn't moved on all that far from those forebears who'd waded ashore from the Mayflower four-hundred years earlier. His code of dress was as strict as his morals. From the time he left his dressing room at six every morning, until retiring for the evening nearing midnight, he was never without a shirt and tie, the latter bearing the Maltese Cross symbol of the Order of St John, as too did the badge on the pocket of his double-breasted, military-style blazer. His trousers had a crease so sharp as to cut the finger of anyone rash enough to get that close and black shoes, which his manservant spent at least an hour every day polishing to a mirror-like finish. He was as fastidious in his dress as he was with everything else in his life.

Apart from having been extremely austere, his early life hadn't been particularly noteworthy. His father had intended for his son to follow him into the church, indeed to inherit the congregation which he himself had spent the greater part of his life building up as a sort of family legacy. Oliver had attended Harvard University of course. His father had been determined that would happen. That prestigious seat of learning's very first class had been held in the summer of 1638, a mere eighteen years after his forebear and his likeminded friends, the Pilgrim Fathers, had landed at Plymouth. Even more appropriate, the school's very name had been inherited from a Puritan minister who'd donated his substantial library and an even more substantial sum of money to the college.

The sun had almost disappeared below the distant horizon, leaving just a gloomy shadow caused by the last of the sun's rays filtering through the leaf-laden trees beyond the new courtyard of Rannoch Castle. It was time for the main evening news, and for several minutes the BBC channel had been scrolling a flash message over their screen that important news was coming in from Cairo. The Grand Master was paying very close attention; maybe things were about to get better.

❋❋❋❋❋

Colin Jackson was back outside the Marriott Hotel in Cairo in the same car park where earlier that afternoon he and his cameraman had reported the League of Arab States' press conference. It was already 11 p.m. in Cairo, and more than five hours since Mamdoubh Rifaat had apparently jumped to his death from the eighth floor of the Marriott Hotel. Those Italian tourists whose last memorable sight of Egypt had nothing to do with that country's antiquity would probably be arriving back in Rome at any time now, and their place in the car park had been taken by a multitude of newspaper and television reporters.

They were crowding round a small area, which had been cordoned off with yellow tape, inside which policemen were jostling against each other, desperately trying not to step on the spread-eagled body of the secretary general, which still lay where it had fallen. Colin Jackson, the new boy on the block as far as reporters were concerned, already had something of a scoop to report to his bosses back in London. He was standing on the wall of the car park, which gave the cameraman filming his report a wonderful backdrop: the exotic River Nile, and the hotel's restaurant ship, the *Nile Maxim,* just pulling into shot as it returned with its load of tired but happy tourists, who'd now taken another step on their journey of discovery through Ancient Egypt. That certainly did not affect the seriousness of Colin's polished performance, admittedly short as it was on informed content and long on guesswork. He was only too well aware that hundreds of thousands, maybe millions of people would be watching him in distant parts of the globe, courtesy of the franchise arrangements the BBC had with overseas television companies. This was the most important moment in his broadcasting career.

The deceased had left a suicide note in his hotel room; this had been requisitioned by the police, but apparently not before a canny hotel porter had read its contents, which he was willing to share with any of the television reporters – for a small fee of course. Colin's share of the bribe had been 400 Egyptian pounds, which was all the money he had until his next pay cheque would be transferred from his Barclays Bank account in Watford to its Egyptian counterpart in the not yet fashionable Cairo suburb of Sadr City, and he desperately hoped it would prove to be a good investment. He didn't have access to the kind of slush fund money rumoured to be available to some of his competitors.

The cameraman gave him the thumbs up, the universally accepted sign that all was well, and then started what they call 'the five-finger countdown': holding up his right hand with five fingers upright, then reducing one by one until it was zero, which was Colin's signal to start talking.

"The body of Dr Mamdoubh Rifaat, until a few hours ago the secretary general of the Arab League, lies spread-eagled on the concrete of this hotel car park, less than fifteen metres from where I am standing. The police seem unsure what to do. An ambulance has been standing by for some hours now, but the police are not allowing the body to be moved."

The camera meantime had panned through 180 degrees, taking in first of all the elegant houses on the east bank of the River Nile, then a long view south down the river, showing the bridges and the multitude of boats plying back and forth, and finally back to the island of Gezirah, where the crowds of police were managing to conceal the object of everyone's attention.

Colin continued with his report while the camera had moved on to where the ambulance was patiently waiting.

"Meantime, it is understood Dr Rifaat had left a suicide note in his room on the eighth floor of this prestigious hotel. This has been taken by the police, but my informant in the hotel has seen the note and exclusively informed me of its contents."

Colin was bending the truth more than a little, but he knew he was the only reporter from the British media to have paid the bribe, so his national rivals wouldn't be able to catch his lie.

"It seems the secretary general was being blackmailed by an unnamed senior Saudi Arabian Government minister. This followed a visit they'd made together to a night club in Cairo earlier this year, which Dr Rifaat didn't want to do, but which the minister allegedly insisted upon. Being a strict Moslem, Dr Rifaat had declined the offer of champagne or other alcohol, and had asked for a Coca Cola. In the darkness of the night club the minister had slipped some powder into Dr Rifaat's drink which made him behave in a way that was totally out of character, and of which he is deeply ashamed. It allegedly involved the minister and himself going to a bedroom which the night club kept for that purpose, where two young boys were waiting for them and with whom, apparently in the precise words of Dr Rifaat, he had indulged in disgusting sexual acts."

The camera had swung back to Colin, catching him as he paused for breath, and just as a passing *River Nile* cruise boat sounded the ship's horn, while the triangular sails of a dhow protruded mysteriously above and behind the wall on which he was standing, all of which obligingly added local flavour to the report.

"The letter apparently goes on to say the price of freedom from blackmail for Dr Rifaat, which I am led to believe meant the return of some highly controversial videos, was to add words to the press conference he held earlier today, that Moslems all over the world rise in Jihad against the invaders of Islamic soil. In his poignant farewell letter, the secretary general explained his devotion to Islam was so strong he would rather sacrifice his own life than risk a Jihad, and he had therefore changed the wording, simply saying the invaders would be removed by force if they failed to comply. Dr Rifaat begged his family and friends not to judge him badly, and to recognise the great sacrifice he had made in giving his own life. He urged them not to view the videos, but rather to destroy them for the filth that they were. This is Colin Jackson in Cairo, reporting for the BBC in London."

Just as Colin had signed off, ready to adjourn to a café for a welcome cup of strong Egyptian coffee, the powers that be decided the body of the deceased secretary general of the League of Arab States had lain where it was long enough. It was quite unceremoniously bundled into the waiting ambulance and despatched to who knows where. The cameraman continued to record the scene as the ambulance disappeared into the haze of pollution, which hovered over the Gezirah Bridge. This would give the newsroom some extra footage to use or discard as they saw fit.

The cameraman was Egyptian. Mohammed Wahba had worked a camera for the BBC ever since the occasion when, quite by chance, he was visiting the Valley of the Queens on the opposite bank of the River Nile from Luxor when terrorists opened fire with machine guns, killing seventy-eight foreign tourists. It had always been his ambition to be a professional cameraman, and he carried a Handycam everywhere he went, hoping and praying for the day when he would be witness to some event of international significance. That day had arrived, and he'd recorded almost the entire event on his Sony Handycam, adding commentary as he filmed, and then telephoned the company in London to barter his film for a job. It had so impressed the managers in the studios in London, who were only too well aware of the value of such an important scoop, they offered him the job he craved and a salary which by Egyptian standards was something to be dreamed of.

As far as the Grand Master was concerned, things had very definitely gotten better. The end of the video clip showed the ambulance as it departed from the car park, its siren busily wailing its message of crisis, the blue lights flashing in the darkness, neither of which had a hope in hell of bringing Dr Mamdoubh Rifaat back from the dead, but which the Grand Master thought was a highly appropriate conclusion to an exceptional piece of television reporting and to a job well done by Majed Dajani.

Chapter Three

Several times during that fairly short night I heard Nicholas moving about, and at one point thought I heard the latch on the outside door click open. People always told me that as you get older you need less sleep, but I can only say in my case that is not true. Since retirement, my two greatest pleasures have been getting a full eight hours sleep every night, then walking the moors after a solid breakfast of thick porridge, shotgun to hand and Randy to heel. That day however was clearly going to be different. By the time I finally prised myself out of bed the wind and rain had both stopped and bright sun was pouring through the window. I had no curtains, there seemed little point. The nearest house was a couple of miles away, and to shut out the glorious view would have been a sin. On that June morning, the different shades of purple heather on the gently undulating heath had married like a patchwork quilt and stretched almost as far as the eye could see. The distant mountains were bathed in that soft sunlight, which townsfolk can only dream about; who needs curtains? Nicholas had gone out. Presumably that was when I heard the door latch open, though what time that had been I didn't know, and of course Randy had gone too. I decided that breakfast could wait, so after a quick shower, and without bothering to shave, I too went outside.

Nicholas had been bathing in the burn, but when he saw me he waded to the bank, probably pleased for an excuse to get out. The water tumbles down from the mountains and is always very cold. Randy was running up and down the bank, clearly alarmed at this strange behaviour, but at the same time prudent enough not to jump in. Emerging from the water, my son looked like an Adonis; he was totally naked, his long hair tied back; his broad shoulders sloped down to an almost feminine waistline and then cascaded out to manly hips and muscular legs any athlete would be proud to own. He looked magnificent.

"Hi, Dad," he greeted me, totally unconscious of any feeling of embarrassment at his nakedness. "I couldn't sleep. My brain was working overtime, so I decided to resort to shock treatment. I hope it works."

The silly boy could have got hypothermia, but this was not the time to tell him that. He jogged back to the cottage, remembering to stay on the pathway and not trample such few vegetables as I manage to grow. Randy and I followed at a more sedate pace, better suited to our advancing years.

My son has never developed a taste for porridge, at least not the real porridge we so love in the Highlands, and which had its origin in the Middle Ages as a soup thickened with barley. His American upbringing had lead him to adopt New World tastes, like eggs Benedict, with a generous helping of hash brown potatoes on the side, and innumerable cups of black coffee, so I shouldn't have been surprised that his offer of making breakfast came with the proviso that it be on his terms. Breakfast over and dishes washed and put away, including those from dinner last night, we decided to walk down to the local village. I had some shopping to do, and Nicholas was looking forward to having a pint of real ale in the local pub. Randy became very excited once he realised where we were heading, running on ahead and doing his best to make us speed up. He has a doggy lady friend in the village, and seems to have taken more than a passing fancy to her.

Once we'd started our walk I continued with my reminiscences.

"I returned to the estate in 1957, having completed my National Service. It was great to be back in the Highlands, away from the pressures and temptations of life in large communities. After mother had died, Mr Hutchinson had employed a married couple to take her place. Tom, a jolly looking man who was never without a pipe in his mouth became the gardener, and his wife Mary, who baked the best homemade bread I've ever tasted, the housekeeper. They were a nice enough couple, not that I had anything much to do with them, they had a small flat in one wing of the castle and largely kept to themselves.

Meantime, my father had changed. Mother's death had robbed him of his best friend; she'd always been there for him, an anchor when times were rough, and he wasn't coping well on his own. It was difficult sharing a house with him. He would criticise everything I did, or didn't do. Each night he just sat in his armchair, morosely staring into space. The bottle of whisky by his side, new that morning, would be empty before he stumbled to his bed. When Mr Hutchinson arrived for the grouse season I took the opportunity to have a private meeting with him, to discuss my future. Fortunately, he seemed to understand the situation, and gave me a job as an under-keeper, working for my father but with an independent salary. He also agreed to my request that I live in this very bothy, or cottage as it is now."

Nicholas asked if Mr Hutchinson had agreed to let me live in the bothy as an act of kindness, to avoid problems arising between father and myself, but then, he was a stranger to life on the high moorland; he didn't understand the subtleties of how a grouse moor works.

"Having a keeper living on the open moorland had advantages for the estate, as well as for me. As I've already told you, Mr Hutchinson had purchased an additional three-thousand acres of heather-covered moorland, and that became my main responsibility. With his permission I rented the land to a local farmer for sheep grazing, on condition I could determine how many sheep he could graze there, and of course I retained the grouse-shooting rights for the estate. This is a common practice in the Highlands. Not only is heather the staple food of the grouse, it also gives them cover to nest and shelter from their enemies, so the keeper has to keep control.

"Those were carefree days. I was perfectly content with my own company, as every keeper must be, but on Saturday evenings I would walk down the rocky track to the village, the very track that you drove up yesterday. I'd go to the pub where I would meet with my friends and play darts, drink beer, and swap exaggerated stories. The return walk to the bothy was often made with some difficulty, and more than once I finished up flat on my face having stumbled over a sleeping sheep!

"Once a week, I would take the Land Rover to the gatehouse

lodge and have dinner with my father. They were fairly silent affairs; frankly, we didn't have much to discuss, apart from the tasks he wanted me to do on the estate, and toward the end of his life my visits became less and less frequent, something I now regret very much. As you know, Father died in 1981, and is buried alongside Mother in the churchyard behind Rannoch Castle.

"After dad died, Mr Hutchinson asked me to move into the gatehouse lodge. He also appointed me head gamekeeper and told me to find a young apprentice who could look after the smaller moor. That was easier said than done. To live with loneliness one must be used to it, and so I had to find someone who'd been brought up in that environment, who was self-reliant, and who could be extremely tactful with other users of the moor, especially the toffs during the grouse season. That was to be a constant problem for me over the years; at one point, I'd harboured the hope you would want to follow in my footsteps, but unfortunately for me, your mother thought otherwise."

Our walk to the village took us over the moor which I'd worked for so many years as an under-keeper. June is a difficult month for the keeper; young grouse are just beginning to show themselves, and they can make a tasty meal for a hungry wandering fox to take home for the rest of his family. The carrion crow too, what we call the corbie, is a menace to the grouse and to the young lambs. It's no surprise that at this time of year the keeper is constantly on the lookout for a new earth, or the nest of a corbie and will destroy any he finds.

Nicholas had never shown any particular interest in gamekeeping; he'd been raised in the city of Boston, and had enjoyed a life as far removed from the Highlands as it is possible to get, so I was a bit surprised at his next question.

"Presumably the month of June is also a busy time for the shepherds, which is why there are so few sheep on the moors today," he asked.

That was very observant of him.

"You are quite right; this month the flockmaster will have rounded up the ram lambs for castration and the year- old females, what we call the hoggs, will be shorn and the flockmaster's initials and their year of birth horn-burned into their ear.

"I saw the young apprentice digging out some old heather a couple of weeks earlier, so he'll have re-seeded this part of the moor and now must keep sheep away from these areas, otherwise they'll pull the new heather up by its roots from the soft peat."

As we walked I continued to tell Nicholas the story, which took a strange turn in 1982 when the estate changed hands again. The solicitor who represented Mr Hutchinson instructed Tom, Mary, the new under-keeper, and me to attend a meeting in his office in Perth. He informed us that Mr Hutchinson had sold the castle and estate; he didn't know who to. He gave us one month's salary in lieu of notice, and said we had just forty-eight hours to vacate our accommodation and remove our possessions from the property. He did at least have the courtesy to apologise for the lack of notice and by way of explanation said that his contract to look after the property had also been terminated. I doubted, though, that this would have quite the same detrimental impact on his way of life as it would on ours!

I paused my talking as a helicopter flew low overhead, in the direction of Blair Castle. It was a sleek-looking machine with a long, distinctive nose cone, but it was the noise from the constant thrashing of the blades that concerned me. It frightens the sheep and can cause injury as they try to run away from the noise. Perhaps it's not too difficult to understand why I've not much time for city folks bringing their flash money and city noises to these remote highlands.

When I picked up the thread of the story, I told Nicholas of how we returned to the estate in a very sombre mood, but if we thought that was enough bad news for one day we were to be sorely disappointed. When I manoeuvred the estate Land Rover off the main road and onto the castle approach we were stopped by two men wearing security-guard uniforms. They identified themselves as employees of the new owner, and told us that contrary to what we'd been told only minutes earlier, they'd been instructed to see us off the property without delay. They each had very pronounced American accents, of the kind I would describe as vulgar, and they clearly meant business. We could see a large removal van was parked further up the driveway, which Tom and Mary were told was for their use. No discussion, no negotiation, just get out!

Tom was understandably angry and perhaps unwisely shook his fist at one of the guards, who reciprocated by giving him a very heavy punch to his face that knocked him to the floor, and the other guard then kicked him in the groin! I tried to intervene, knowing that against such thugs I would be helpless, but honour required I should at least try. I perfectly expected to find myself on the floor beside the gardener, but instead the guards walked away, their message very plainly delivered.

We picked Tom off the floor, and the three of us climbed back into the Land Rover, while the young under-keeper made his way across the moor to remove his belongings from his bothy.

On arrival at the castle a further shock greeted us: what I can only describe as the biggest, blackest, most fearsome-looking woman I've ever seen blocked the driveway – legs apart, hands on hips, and her strange, ankle-length, brown tunic flapping in the wind. Her appearance was fearsome, but her smile was as wide and as warm as the noonday sun. She introduced herself as Sister Martha. She was the new housekeeper, and she was sorry for what was going on. Her accent too was American but softer than the two thugs had been, and as I was to learn later, she came from the deep south, from the state of Alabama.

A man appeared, as black as Martha, but as small as she was large. He was wearing a brown tunic similar to hers and with the same emblem on the left side, a white cross with four arms that I thought looked familiar, though I couldn't place it just then. Sister Martha introduced him as Brother James; he was the butler – and also her husband. A more incongruous sight it would be hard to imagine. The two of them stood side by side: Martha six feet tall and weighing all of 220 pounds and James not even five and a half feet tall, and I doubt he weighed half of Martha. She offered to help Tom and Mary pack their belongings, an offer which was none too kindly refused. Brother James meantime asked me to accompany him into the castle and led the way to the kitchen. It hadn't taken him long to find his way around; we'd only been gone to Perth three hours. Martha joined us there, making coffee without being asked.

Brother James started the conversation, his voice as warm as his wife's smile.

"Try to forgive the men at the gate, sir," he said to me, "they will be returning to the United States in a few days, in fact as soon as the Grand Master arrives. Once they've gone, you can move back into the gatehouse, and in the meantime we've booked a room for you at the pub in the village for which the Grand Master will pay, and of course you can continue to use the Land Rover."

My brain was whirling inside my head. What was going on? Two hours before, I, together with the other staff from the castle, had been informed by the solicitor that our services were no longer required, and we had to go. Now I was confronted by these two strangely clad people, calling themselves brother and sister, but saying they were man and wife, telling me that while I still had to get out of the gatehouse, I'd be able to move back in once the Grand Master, whoever he was, had arrived.

My emotions were threatening to get the better of me. On one side I was angry, humiliated, and extremely bitter. After a lifetime of service to the estate, I'd been cast off as casually as a man might change his shoes, and yet on the other hand, where just minutes earlier I'd been a forty-five-year-old jobless and homeless man, suddenly it wasn't like that anymore, and I felt relieved. And what was this about a Grand Master?

"What about Tom and Mary?" I asked, "Are they able to stay too?"

The way Martha shook her head gave the answer to that question, without the need of words, so I asked if it meant I was still the gamekeeper for the estate. James shrugged his shoulders and told me he didn't know. All he knew was that the Grand Master had instructed them and the security guards to be respectful to me, to ensure the arrangements they made for me were to my entire satisfaction, and to beg me, and he actually used the word 'beg', to await the Grand Master's arrival, at which time everything would be made clear.

"What could I do Nicholas? Of course I huffed and puffed, and I said things to them about dignity and respect. I said I'd have to think about it, but I knew and they knew that I had little choice but to go along with what they were saying."

I declined their offer of more coffee, drove down to the gatehouse to pack such things as I'd need in the pub, and drove away. As I pulled onto the Highland road the two goons closed the gate very firmly behind me. It was only afterward that I realised I hadn't even said goodbye to Tom and Mary, not that I could have faced them knowing I was apparently still in and they were out.

The few days that James had said would pass before the Grand Master came turned out to be almost a month. In that time I stayed away from the estate, a little fearful of the security guards and angry and humiliated at the way I'd been treated. I slept late every morning, and spent too many hours in the bar every evening. I could barely bother to shave. My friends pressed me to tell them what was going on, but I couldn't have answered even if I'd wanted to. The village was abuzz with rumours about the new owner and the mysterious goings on at the castle. Large trucks arrived every day, dropping their load at the castle and then returning from whence they came. The drivers never stopped in the village for a friendly chat over a pint of beer and a pub lunch. Twice during that month I received a recorded-delivery envelope at the pub, postmarked London WC1, each one containing five-hundred pounds in cash and nothing else.

It was almost a month after the incident with the security guards that Brother James telephoned me in the pub. He asked if I could be available at seven that evening to meet the Grand Master. Promptly on time, a Rolls Royce arrived to pick me up. The chauffeur, who introduced himself as Brother William, was dressed exactly as the housekeeper and butler had been: a long, brown cloak with the white cross with its four arms adorning the left side. He wasn't wearing the peaked cap a chauffeur would traditionally wear; presumably, it wouldn't have belonged with the rest of his uniform. He ignored my attempt to climb into the front seat (if indeed you do 'climb' into a Rolls Royce) and instead pointedly opened the rear door on the passenger side.

Old Matt, who'd owned the pub for more years than anyone could remember, scratched his bald head in bewilderment. In all his years here he'd never seen anything like it, as indeed had none of my friends who just happened to be there when the Rolls arrived.

For me it was a strange sensation, being driven in such luxury, through the newly installed wrought iron gates, past the gatehouse which had been my home for so many years, and up the newly paved driveway. The distance from the gates to the castle itself is best part of half a mile, but even as we'd turned in from the main road I could see a different flag was flying from the mast on the castle roof; no longer was it the flag of St Andrew, patron saint of Scotland, but instead I recognised the same emblem as on the tunics worn by the three newcomers.

The entrance to the castle, too, was very different from when I'd last seen it. An entirely new doorway had been created in the south face, with an elegant portico reaching out into what had previously been the car park and had now been transformed into a stylish courtyard, semi-circular in shape, paved in a latticework of different-coloured stone and fenced in by immaculately cut hedges. A magnificent pair of statues of medieval knights, facing inward to each other, overlooked the entrance to the courtyard, seeming to advise caution to anyone entering to do so only in peace or suffer the consequences. It only needed a drawbridge and a moat to complete the transformation back into the fortress it had originally been.

As I recounted the story to Nicholas, my mind took me back to that day.

Brother James was waiting in the portico and politely came over to the car to open the door for me to get out. I stretched out my arm to shake hands, but he kept his hands clasped firmly behind his back and instead gave a dignified bow, the long cloak adding an extra degree of finesse to the uncalled for deference he showed.

He ushered me through the new doorway, but not before I noticed the coat of arms engraved into the masonry above the entrance – again the same motif as on the uniforms. The lobby, once so empty and cold, had been transformed into a museum of armour, with statues similar to those I'd just seen in the courtyard dressed in coats of chain mail, the visor on each of the helmets pulled down as though the knight inside was preparing to do battle. Lances and fearsome-looking pikes festooned the walls, and ancient banners hung from the ceiling. I don't know how long this had all been in the planning but clearly much more than just the month since I'd last been here.

James didn't give me time to stop and admire the changes, and I have to admit they well deserved admiration. He led me up the stone stairs to the drawing room. The Grand Master was waiting for me inside. He was tall and slim, bordering even on being skinny; his thinning jet black hair was combed in such a way as to change the shape of his head, making it more rounded instead of its true oblong shape. His nose was thin, as too were his lips – cruel lips, tightly wound over his teeth making a mockery of his efforts to smile – but it was his eyes which held me: the pupils were black as night, and the eyebrows were long and bushy, as black as his hair, reinforcing the hostile impression created by the rest of his appearance..

All of this I took in as I walked across the room to where he stood waiting for me. The cloak he was wearing was floor length, black, with the same motif on the left side as I'd just seen above the newly created entrance, and around his neck he wore a medallion, again the same motif, probably made of white enamel, superimposed by a crown of yellow gold with a red backing, and suspended on a red ribbon. Not for the first time I wondered what on earth was I into.

As we shook hands, I felt almost repulsed by the touch of his skin. It was cold as death.

"Alec, thank you very much for taking the time to see me. I am the Grand Master," he told me. As though I had any choice in the matter! . "Let's go straight through to the dining room, we can talk over dinner."

Saying that, he placed his arm around my shoulder in an extravagant gesture of bonhomie and led the way into the dining room. I'd been in that room many times in the previous forty odd years, but now it had been changed beyond recognition; it was magnificent. A huge, crystal chandelier hung over a circular dining table that could seat upwards of a dozen people, but was now laid with just two places. The walls were newly painted, white as they'd always been but now hung with tapestries, all depicting various scenes of jousting knights. Heavily embroidered curtains graced each of the leaded windows. The rich, fitted carpet was bright red, and the chairs around the dining table were upholstered in a similarly coloured material. The table was laid with extravagant looking silver, the centre dominated by a huge silver tureen. The lights from the overhead chandelier reflected like stars in the tureen's engravings.

I'd put on my best suit for the occasion, indeed it was my only suit other than the gamekeepers outfit, which employers traditionally bought for their head gamekeeper. To say I felt inadequate would be a massive understatement. Never before had I been invited to dine in that room. I was totally out of my depth and tried desperately hard not to show it. I concentrated on my host instead, which frankly wasn't too difficult – he was a very compelling character.

By this time in my narration, Nicholas and I were more than half way to the village, and I suppose I felt a little bit gratified that my fit son was beginning to pant a little, whereas I was as fresh as when we'd started out. Habit I suppose. We'd just climbed over a stile and would have taken a short cut directly across the middle of the field used by the shepherd to sort his flock, but Nicholas sat on the bottom step of the stile; he needed to rest. We were in no hurry, except for Randy, and he was clearly becoming more and more agitated at our lack of progress. I hoped I wasn't boring Nicholas with my story, but it was something I felt he needed to know now, so I continued to describe that strange dinner.

The Grand Master indicated the place at the table where I should sit and then explained what the changes I'd noticed were all about.

"The emblem, which you see on my cloak, and no doubt you've already observed on the castle flag," he told me, "denotes the Chivalric Order of Saint John of Jerusalem, Knights of Cyprus, Rhodes, and Malta, to give our organisation its full title which," he explained to me, "originated in Jerusalem in the eleventh century.

"The founder, a merchant from Amalfi, wanted to build a hospice to care for the sick and injured Christians making their pilgrimage to the Holy Land. The hospice came to be known as the Hospital of St John of Jerusalem and adopted the eight-pointed White Cross of Amalfi as its symbol.

"Over the years, the pilgrimage route from Europe became increasingly dangerous. Muslims attacked and robbed the pilgrims along the way, and that led to the magnificent Crusades. The Crusaders attacked Jerusalem, massacring many of the city's Jewish and Muslim inhabitants. Their occupation of the Holy City lasted for almost two hundred years, in fact until the Siege of Acre near the end of the thirteenth century, when the knights were defeated and found refuge briefly in Cyprus, then on the Greek island of Rhodes, and then to Malta, where they stayed until Napoleon forced them to leave in 1798."

Quite why the Grand Master found it so necessary at that time to tell me this history was beyond me, and to be honest this Order didn't sound like something to be particularly proud of. They had noble origins certainly, but they seemed to run from one disaster to another after that, and as the Grand Master continued with his explanation, so the disasters continued to come.

The Order, which at that time was almost entirely made up of Catholics, fragmented after they were forced out of their base in Malta. Some of the knights went to Yugoslavia and found protection under the patronage of King Peter. Others went to Rome and became known as the Sovereign and Military Order of St John of Jerusalem, while a third group found their way to St Petersburg, where Tsar Paul the First was the emperor. There they pledged 'obedience, submission and fidelity' to his Imperial Majesty, who in return agreed to become the Protector of the Order. The following year, at the request of his Imperial Court in St Petersburg, he created a Russian Grand Priory which would be 'for members of the Russian aristocracy and all Christians', and he issued a Royal Proclamation granting to the Order certain inalienable rights. It is from that Proclamation, signed by Tsar Paul on the 21 December 1798 that the Order derived what the Grand Master called "our inalienable succession."

James, the butler had entered the dining room at this point. He was panther like in his movements: soft, deliberate, truly cat-like. His relationship with the Grand Master seemed to be based on fear. He was ingratiatingly servile, almost as though he was waiting to be punished. His floor length, brown cloak was made of a much heavier and coarser material than the black cloak that the Grand Master wore. It seemed out of place in such gracious surroundings, even more than my poor suit, which was saying something. He placed bowls of cabbage soup in front of each of us, then reached for the jug on the sideboard and poured water into our heavy crystal glasses. The soup was thin and watery, and the bread rolls were definitely not to the standard the previous housekeeper could achieve. Not everything was an improvement.

Randy was starting to bark at us, and it was time to get moving again; we still had better than a mile to reach the village. As we walked on, I told Nicholas of how the Grand Master continued with what seemed more and more like a history lesson about failure.

He said, "At the time of the Russian Revolution in 1918 many of the aristocratic families feared for their lives, justifiably so as it turned out, and fled to other countries. Some went to France, where they could continue to indulge the gracious living they'd so enjoyed in St Petersburg, but the majority went to the United States, which at that time was providing a safe haven and new opportunities to immigrants from all over the world. Members of the Russian Priory were amongst both these groups. The rival priories were established in France and America which is a cause of confusion even to this day."

The Grand Master told me very forcibly he was determined to sort that out, so that succession would be firmly placed where it truly belonged. He didn't say "in my hands" but I almost felt as though that was what he intended, and he did say "woe betide anyone who stood in his way!"

As he said those last words his manner changed. His eyes assumed an almost demonic look, and his voice started to screech. I felt a cold shudder run down my spine. This man was a dangerous fanatic.

"You know him, Nicholas," I said, "and you can perhaps understand what I mean."

I returned to my story of that night. The butler had padded into the room to remove the soup bowls and replaced them with an equally frugal serving of ham, boiled potatoes, and overcooked vegetables. My host remained silent for some time, almost as though he regretted his outburst and was trying to compose himself again. Eventually, I saw him bend his tight lips into what he probably hoped was a reassuring smile, and he continued his dialogue.

"I am now the Grand Master of the exiled Russian Grand Priory; it was my decision to move the headquarters of the Order to this castle, which we see as neutral ground between France and America." He went on, "this is a serious gesture of reconciliation, not only to our brothers in France but also to the Order that was established in this country about a hundred and fifty years ago, which is called the Venerable Order of St John and which has the Queen at its head.

Only when that reconciliation has been achieved can the Order return to its former glory and retake its place as the sovereign nation it once was."

None of this was news to Nicholas, though I hoped the detailed explanation would help him fit pieces of the jigsaw into place, so I continued.

"Brother James came back into the room just as we were finishing the last of the main course. If I thought we were going to have a dessert, I was disappointed. He whispered something in the Grand Master's ear, who straight away excused himself and left the room. I wondered what was happening, but James came to my rescue by holding the door open for me; dinner was over, and I was leaving. He padded along just behind me as I went back down the staircase; I remember my shoes making a hollow sound on the stone steps, whereas he made no sound at all as he walked. The presence of the suits of armour in the hallway now made more sense to me and the knights' statues in the courtyard too, or at least they fitted in with the lecture I'd just received from the Grand Master, because that was what it felt like. It certainly wasn't a conversation; I'd barely said a word from start to finish.

The heavy wooden door, clearly new but made to look as old as the rest of the castle, swung silently to behind me. Brother William was standing by the Rolls, holding the door open, almost as though he hadn't moved all the time I was inside the castle, and once back at the pub I headed straight to the bar. Normally I would have gone to my room to change from the uncomfortable suit into something more casual, but I needed alcohol. My brain was spinning.

The bar was empty save for Matt the owner, and he was busy polishing glasses and making sure the bar was as neat and tidy as he liked it to be, which suited me very well. I didn't need to talk; I needed to think. I was a gamekeeper; I'd always led a relatively uncomplicated life. I hadn't been anywhere apart from my short time away in the Army. I hadn't done anything out of the ordinary, and I knew my station in life and was happy with it. Now all at once my employer, a grand master no less, whatever that was, was treating me more like a friend than his head gamekeeper, confiding in me his ambitions, explaining things to me in great detail as though it was important I shared his enthusiasm for what he was doing. He'd said he would restore the Order of St John back into the sovereign nation it had once been. I knew little of such matters, but even I understood that to have a sovereign nation meant you had to have a sovereign. Was he deluded? Were his words the ranting of a deranged madman, or was he simply a very wealthy but bored old man trying to inject some glamour into the last days of his life? Very definitely I hoped it would prove to be the latter, but I was to be disappointed.

Some days after that dinner I was allowed to move back into the gatehouse. It was exactly as when I'd left it, except that a very expensive-looking alarm system had been installed in the hallway. Brother William explained its workings to me. Once set, it would trigger an alarm both in the house and the castle if anyone or anything crossed the driveway.

Guests continued to arrive from the USA and increasingly from countries in Europe and beyond. Meetings were held in what had been the main ballroom, usually preceded by a service in the chapel. The guests would assemble in the basement armoury, all wearing cloaks emblazoned with the Maltese Cross, and from there would process in formation to and from the chapel, a flag-bearer leading the way, and the Grand Master next in line, holding aloft a ceremonial sword.

During our strange dinner, the Grand Master had explained to me that the cloaks they all wore were of a simple material, designed to emphasise the virtues of the Order, which I remember he saying were prudence, justice, temperance, and fortitude. If that dinner was anything to go by, the Grand Master certainly practiced temperance, but the same couldn't always be said of his guests. Many of their cloaks were exotic, especially those coming from Austria, though why that should be I didn't know. They were black like all the rest, but had a brilliant scarlet lining. Everyone wore the Maltese Cross medallion, but the Austrians also wore other decorations pinned to their cloaks, and had gold chains joining the two sides of the cloak together, and one old gentleman even had a blue sash draped over the top of his. It looked magnificent, but hardly in keeping with a vow of prudence and temperance. In private the Grand Master seemed almost scornful of those who had adorned their cloaks in this way, privately calling them stuffed peacocks, but on the few occasions I saw them together he was always most respectful towards them all.

One of the most frequent visitors was an American friend of the Grand Master who brought his daughter along on a few occasions. She and I got on famously from the very beginning, and for the first time in my life I fell hopelessly in love. For her part she told me she loved my way of life, she loved the Highlands, and despite the difference in our ages – I was forty-eight and she only thirty-one – she loved me.

Maria's grandparents had migrated from Russia to the United States in the early years of the twentieth century to avoid the brutalities of the Russian Revolution. She told me they were aristocrats, highly connected to the Russian royal family who'd been murdered in 1918. They'd continued to prosper in their new country, and were very wealthy. I longed to ask her father for her hand in marriage, but was certain he would not think me a suitable husband for his only daughter. I remember the way every part of my body ached when I went to see him, to ask if I could have his permission.

My fears were groundless, evidenced by the obvious delight which he displayed as he gave us his blessing. It was as welcome as it was surprising.

An enormous surprise awaited me on the morning of our wedding day. The Grand Master asked me to join him in the chapel, where the chaplain and my father-in-law to be were already present. They were wearing their Knights of Malta cloaks. I was led by the right hand to the altar, where the priest stood, holding in his hand the beautifully engraved sword I'd often admired in the Grand Master's study. He bade me kneel in front of the altar, and by touching first my right shoulder, then the left, and then the right again he created me a Knight of the Order. This was an unbelievable honour. I was but a lowly gamekeeper, born of parents from the poorest part of East London, and not only was I about to marry the girl of my dreams, I'd now been invested as a Knight of the Chivalric Order of St John of Jerusalem. How my life had changed!

More than a hundred guests, few of whom I'd ever seen before, crowded into the little chapel to witness our wedding ceremony. I was wearing my cloak, the eight pointed cross emblazoned on the left side proudly announcing to them all that I was now a part of the Order, as indeed were almost all the guests. Maria looked simply fabulous. She wore a white floor-length wedding dress with a train stretching back a good ten yards behind her and managed by six page boys and girls. On her head she was wearing a wonderfully intricate coronet, encrusted with so many precious stones it must have been heavy to wear. The reception took place in the castle, and the Grand Master had gone to enormous expense to ensure it matched the occasion.

Maria then joined me to live in the gatehouse, that lovely old two-bedroom house built of local stone, which had been such an important part of my life from my earliest days, and having her share it with me only made my happiness more complete. She had introduced new furniture and softer fabrics, and with all her femininity, a touch of love and cosiness.

I told Nicholas, "We'd been married for just one year when Maria told me she was pregnant, and your arrival Nicholas crowned my happiness in ways I could never have imagined."

She chose the name Nicholas, a name which her father told me conjured up nostalgic memories of the family's past in Mother Russia. She also insisted on teaching me the rudiments of the Russian language – it never seemed strange to me that Maria, who had never been to Russia, should have taken the trouble to learn the language, but it was a small price to pay for the happiness I now felt.

Maria's father settled a very generous endowment on us the day you were christened, and had made just one stipulation, that you too must learn the Russian language and in time should go to university to study Russian history and literature. It would have been churlish of me to suggest this was going too far in preserving the family history, though privately that was what I had thought.

"Your christening," I said, "took place in the chapel where your mother and I were married. Once again the chapel was crowded with guests, probably even more than on the wedding day, but this could perhaps have something to do with the following day being the Glorious Twelfth of August, and many of the guests were there for the start of the grouse shooting season.

"Your godparents were Count Gregory and Countess Sophia Bobrinsky, a lovely old couple whose own parents had left Russia at the time of the Revolution. I'd never met them before, and though they didn't speak a word of English they nonetheless made it plain to me they were sorry I didn't have anyone from my side of the family to share in the baptismal honour.

"How could I? Both my parents had been killed in the London Blitz in 1941, and my guardians were dead too. I had no other family, at least that I was aware of."

The actual christening ceremony was somewhat unusual, and no doubt unique. Those of us who'd been invested into the Order were obliged to wear our cloaks. We assembled in the armoury, and from there we processed up the stone staircase, through the hallway, and out to the pathway that leads to the chapel. My father-in-law led the procession, carrying the banner of the Knights of Malta, and behind him came the Grand Master, holding the ceremonial sword aloft. Next came your godparents, who others in the celebration referred to as 'kum' and 'kuma'. They were both wearing the cloak. Your godmother had the honour of carrying you. Your mother and I came next, your mother also wearing the cloak of the Order, which I'd never seen her do before. The chaplain was waiting by the Christening font. As he took you from your godmother, she began chanting some kind of proclamation prayer in a language I suppose was Russian. As your mother explained to me later, she was renouncing the Devil and all his works and asking God to protect you. Waves of incense billowed around the font; the chaplain held his hand over your face, and immersed you, head first, three times into the water. I've never heard you scream like that since, and neither do I ever want to again! Your little arms were thrashing the air, and your chest was heaving as you fought for breath.

"The chaplain then placed you in a sitting position in a special crib on top of the altar, safely held by restraining straps, and reached for the ceremonial sword, which had been resting on the altar, and touched you three times on your forehead with the tip of the blade.

"At that point I was prepared to leap to your rescue, thinking that perhaps this was some kind of sacrificial offering – that shows how far out of my depth I was feeling just then – but instead your mother approached the altar, undid the restraining straps in the crib, and picked you up. The chaplain draped a miniature cloak of the Order around your shoulders and bowed to you, then he took you from your mother and held you aloft for the congregation to see, at which point they all rose to their feet, and bowed three times, though whether that was to recognise God, or somehow was directed to you, I didn't know.

"A photographer had been waiting on the side, and he came forward and took a huge number of photographs. I used to have one of the photographs, but someone must have taken it. Anyway, we then all processed back from the chapel, the priest continuing to hold you aloft, still chanting as he did so, and only when we were all safely back inside the castle did he give you back to your mother. It was all so bizarre."

By this time, we had reached the village. Randy had disappeared in search of his lady-love, while Nicholas and I headed straight for The Speckled Grouse public house. The walk over the moor had given us an appetite, and the landlord was known for serving a wonderful cottage pie with mashed potatoes, which defied any kind of calorie count, and gravy heavily impregnated with a very crude metaxa brandy, which could easily fuel a rocket expedition to Mars!

The regulars were already at their customary places: Fred the postman, who always arrived on the dot of 12.30, was on his bar stool, leaning against the end wall as he'd done every weekday for as long as any of us could remember. His beer glass was almost empty, awaiting some kind newcomer to offer him a refill, which he always accepted, and never reciprocated. John, the only taxi driver within ten miles, was there too. He only drank double whiskies and had his own specially shaped glass, which he claimed prevented evaporation, though we all believed it was shaped to let the good brew soak into his luxuriant moustache, so he could draw on that for inspiration after the pub closed. Julie was at her usual place too. As you entered the pub the first thing you saw were her remarkable legs protruding from a short mini skirt; she got the free drinks instead of Fred. Last, but certainly not least, was Old Matt, the owner of the pub. He was a teetotaller and claimed he'd never drink alcohol in his life but was always happy to take money from those who did.

I took a table by the window while Nicholas went to the bar

to order our food and drink. Both Julie and Fred had immediately swung into action, Julie twitching her skirt just a little higher, which Nicholas certainly noticed, and Fred making loud shushing sounds as he drained the last dregs from his beer glass, which Nicholas appeared not to notice. He'd been here before.

While we waited for the cottage pie to arrive I continued with the history lesson.

"As I've already told you, the following day was the Glorious Twelfth, and many of the guests were there for the opening day of the grouse-shooting season. It is a day for townsfolk to stand amongst the heather, guns in hand, filling their lungs with pure moorland air, and their eyes with an unequalled scene of rolling purple carpet, and to feel envious of those of us who spend our entire lives here.

"As the head gamekeeper this was my day. For weeks I had patrolled the beat, noticing where the young grouse were nesting and adjusting the butts behind which my toffs would stand to best advantage. That these toffs were also my associates in the Order made it even more important that the day should go well. Somewhere out in front of the butts my beaters were already lined out, ready to bring in the first drive and waiting for the signal from the lookout man to tell them the guns were in position. I always used my old schoolmate Ned as my lookout. He's a shepherd who spent his life on the moors and has an uncanny knack of being just those few essential seconds ahead of the birds when they decide to take flight. One blast from his shrill whistle and the new grouse shooting season was underway. I was lucky on my moor to have fairly even ground, and with my line of beaters nicely deployed, the grouse will flush well in front of them and fly towards the butts, whereas with undulating ground the grouse would see this as being a gap through which they could escape the guns.

"Rather nearer to home, though, the storm clouds were gathering. Shortly after you were born, your mother told me that the pain of childbirth had damaged her inside, and not only could she never have another child, neither could she endure the pain of making love. Of course I understood; the temptation to continue the lovemaking which had been such a happy part of our relationship before you were born, would be unbearable for her, as to be honest it would have been for me too. It was for that reason I readily agreed to her request that we have separate bedrooms.

"The problems didn't end there though. From married friends I'd often heard their wives' personality had changed from the time of their first born, so I shouldn't have been surprised that your mother and I would now fall into arguing almost every night. She also started smoking, which was a total surprise to me, and drinking rather heavily too and would often go out in the early afternoon and not return until long after I'd gone to bed. Eventually, she struck the final blow. One afternoon she again went out, taking you with her this time, which was unusual. She didn't come back!

"She didn't take any of her own clothes nor yours. She left her jewellery; even her credit cards were left behind. The Grand Master actually came down to the gatehouse to tell me she'd been to see him, and he'd sadly agreed to arrange an immediate flight to America for the two of you. He'd been aware that all was not well between us and had not wanted to interfere, but when your mother went to ask for his help that afternoon he'd made the arrangements hoping that in doing so a period of separation would help bring us back together in a better way. I was desolate!"

My son didn't walk back to the cottage with me that afternoon, pleading a very justifiable tiredness and choosing instead to take a room at the pub in order to get some rest. It could have been he wanted to be alone to try and make sense of all that he'd heard or it could have been Julie's temptations, but the hug he gave me was as spontaneous as ever and to be honest I too was glad to have some time alone, except for old Randy of course. He was sitting on the pavement outside the door of the pub looking very sorry for himself. It's a pity dogs can't talk, Randy and I probably have a lot in common.

Back at the cottage I tried busying myself, but I could feel a depression coming on. I was seventy-two years of age; except for my son I was entirely alone in the world, and soon he would be going back to continue his university studies in America and to be with his mother again. I was feeling very sorry for myself. I folded his sleeping bag, which he'd abandoned on the settee, and put it away in the cupboard just inside the front door. I keep my Yeoman twelve-bore shotgun in that cupboard; seeing it reminded me it had been a while since it had been cleaned, so that kept me occupied for an hour or more, and then repacking some Eley cartridges in the gun belt passed a few more minutes. As darkness fell my depression only deepened. I picked at a stew and tried watching television to pass the time, but even that didn't work. I went to bed. Randy curled up on the bed next to me that night – I didn't push him back to his own blanket on the floor as I would usually have done.

Chapter Four

The London Stock Market opened at 8 a.m. this Friday morning, on time and normal, just as one hour earlier Frankfurt, Paris, and all the other European bourses had done. In Tokyo and Hong Kong, the markets had already closed for the weekend, their trading done, while New York was still sleeping. The Dow had closed very slightly down at the close of yesterday's session amid fears of renewed inflation. Business was quiet; no rumours of gigantic takeovers were insidiously being whispered out of the corners of nervous mouths, no profit forecasts were imminent, none of the Top 100 chief-executive officers were about to be given their marching orders, and none of the high-flying yuppies were going to earn big bonuses – anyway not today.

The night editors of all those daily newspapers, which even now were being pushed through letter boxes in towns and villages across Europe or displayed for sale on station concourses, had long since given up the struggle and gone home to bed. It was a tiring business trying to fill the front pages when nothing was happening. But tonight's shift would be very different.

The television networks and radio stations all over the world were having the same problem, desperately trying to find something to report. The newsreaders eked out every last morsel of unimportant verbiage in an effort to reach the next commercial break without having one of those embarrassing silences. They'd milked the news from Cairo about the suicide of the secretary general of the Arab League until that story appeared to have run dry, but there was nothing new to replace it – anyway not for the time being.

Today was going to be one of those days when everyone remembers where they were, like when President John F Kennedy was killed in downtown Dallas, or when Neil Armstrong took 'one small step for man, one giant step for mankind', as he became the first person to walk on the moon. It was going to be one of those days.

A mild case of the jitters had started getting to the day-shift people just after 12 noon GMT, which was when the Organisation of Petroleum Exporting Countries (OPEC) press conference in Vienna should have started, and didn't. Reporters were routinely deployed to cover the OPEC meetings. Today, in the absence of any other news, they had to provide fill-in to their news rooms, so the delayed start, which on a normal day would hardly have been noticed, assumed some significance, but still not that much. It had been duly noted that with the exception of the president, all the OPEC members had left town having first had a working breakfast together in their Vienna headquarters, so whatever the reason for the delayed start, it was hardly likely to be anything important.

In fact, all eleven OPEC members knew the press release, when it came, was going to be very important indeed, and they didn't want to be around when the flak started flying but even they didn't know everything. They knew the price of a barrel of oil was about to be dramatically increased to certain countries, what the president had referred to as the 'invader-countries', though that hadn't been a unanimous decision. The Nigerian and Venezuelan members had abstained in the voting because two of their main markets were about to be heavily penalised by these sanctions. This would cause a reduction in their demand for oil, and they couldn't support that.

Only two people knew the full content of the forthcoming press release, and they were total outsiders of the organisation. The Grand Master did, as indeed he should as he'd written it, though the OPEC president thought that had been done by the very senior Saudi Arabian government minister who was about to transfer two million dollars into the president's Zurich bank account. Sadly for him, the real minister didn't know anything about any of this, especially not the two million dollars.

Majed Dajani, sitting on his bed in the Cairo guesthouse, also knew the full content of the press release. It had been his duty to instruct the OPEC president on what he had to say. The fact that the

OPEC president thought Majed was the Saudi minister's personal representative, which he wasn't, didn't change anything. Did it?

The jitters became a bit more pronounced just after 1 p.m. GMT, which was when the reporters gathered in the OPEC press briefing room looked out the window and saw the president getting into his black, chauffeur-driven Mercedes 500SL. They calmed down again when the president's lovely secretary, Monika, came into the room to inform them there was nothing to be concerned about. The briefing had simply been transferred to the Hotel Sacher, where Dr Khalifa had some other business to attend to. In their hurry to get to the hotel, not one of the reporters thought to inform their editorial masters of the changed location, which was a pity because that would have given the news presenters a bit more gossip to fill the programme on such a quiet day.

By 3.30 p.m. the reporters were becoming restive. Some of the less conscientious amongst their number had already drifted away, and the others were demanding to know what was going on. The hotel manager had been called in to explain the delay, but he too was worried. He personally had taken the telephone call from Monika, who he knew was a frequent user of the hotel's well equipped gymnasium and sauna facilities. He'd readily agreed to let OPEC have the use of one of the conference rooms on the mezzanine floor for a press conference at 2 p.m., but it was long past that time now and it still hadn't even started. Eventually, the demands of the reporters were getting to him, he had to do something; he telephoned the OPEC president in his suite on the second floor.

Dr Ahmed Khalifa, the president of OPEC, was anxiously studying his watch as he paced the floor in his executive suite of the Hotel Sacher, in the middle of Vienna. From his extensive wardrobe he'd purposely selected the dark suit he was wearing, because he felt it enhanced the seriousness of the announcement he would shortly be making. His white shirt, delivered from the hotel laundry the previous evening, contrasted nicely with the suit, and with his complexion, which also was dark, reflecting his Bedouin origin. Strangely for the good doctor, whose choice of neckties usually varied between garish and flamboyant in a vain attempt to indicate a youthful passion, it was jet black, but only he, his secretary, and his doctor of course, would know that was in recognition of the devastating news he'd received by fax that morning.

It had been many generations since his predecessors had wandered the Arabian Empty Quarter, that vast stretch of inhospitable and infertile scrub land that reaches to the shores of the Red Sea. In common with the rest of his tribe, the discovery of oil had changed his life such that his predecessors would hardly recognise anything anymore, though whether they would feel the changes were for the better was another matter. In his more boastful moments Ahmed Khalifa was fond of informing his guests he'd been born on the very spot in Kuwait where the five-star Meridien Hotel now stood, though in those days it was his family tent that occupied that piece of land; it didn't have air conditioning, and it didn't have a bidet in the bathroom either, partly because they wouldn't have known what to do with a bidet had they had one, and anyway they didn't have a bathroom. This usually got a chuckle from his well-meaning guests.

Ahmed felt it was symbolic that in the last years of his working life he should be the representative for his fellow Arabs for the very substance that had transformed all their lives – oil.

It had been agreed that OPEC would hold their press conference at 12 noon GMT, exactly as the League of Arab States had done the previous day. The OPEC press conference was supposed to start with the words "The time is twelve noon", and continue exactly as the Arab League had done, so that political watchers across the globe would be aware they were acting in concert. Unfortunately, that was not possible now, the GMT time was almost 4 p.m. and the OPEC president was still waiting for the telephone call from the Saudi minister in Cairo authorising him to go ahead.

The telephone in the hotel suite rang just once before Khalifa grabbed it from its cradle, almost breathlessly giving his name, but he was to be disappointed. The voice on the other end was the hotel manager, who wanted to respectfully inform the OPEC president that the journalists waiting in the mezzanine conference room were becoming impatient. One or two had already drifted away, and another party had booked that room from 6 p.m. and he needed his staff to clean it first.

The manager had fairly gushed out his messages so they all seemed to roll into one. He was nervous not to upset his distinguished guest, but still the work of the hotel had to go on. Khalifa was undecided what to do, but he was the president of a very powerful organisation, and it didn't sit easily for him to do nothing. He'd lost count how many times he'd tried to contact the Saudi minister in Cairo, and each time he'd been told to sit tight, to wait just a little longer, and worse than that, the last couple of times no-one had answered at all! Khalifa unconsciously squared his shoulders and told the hotel manager he'd be down in exactly five minutes, and to inform the waiting reporters of that fact. He'd make one last attempt to contact the Saudi, and then he'd just have to work on his own initiative.

In fact it was the Grand Master who wanted the Vienna press conference to be delayed beyond the agreed hour of twelve noon. There was no Saudi Government minister of course, the Grand Master was concerned the Cairo report had generated so little interest anywhere in the world, he wanted the OPEC release to do much better so he'd instructed Majed to make sure Khalifa did nothing until he received further instructions. Several times Majed, who was in his very ordinary room in his friend's guesthouse in Cairo, had answered calls on his pay-as-you-go mobile phone. Each time he'd told the over anxious OPEC president to wait just a little longer, and he'd also neglected to answer a couple of times, thinking to himself he'd let the old fool stew a while longer.

Finally, the secure line on Dajani's satellite telephone in Cairo, the one the Grand Master always called on, rang with the instruction to let the Vienna conference get underway. The Stock Exchange in New York had opened for business, there'd been a slight fall on the Dow because of inflation fears, and it was the Grand Master's belief that it would be much easier to make the market go into free fall if it was already on a downward slope. Conversely, the European and Far East exchanges had all closed in fairly positive territory, so the shock when they reopened for business after the weekend would be that much greater.

No sooner had Majed hung up from the Grand Master than his other phone rang; it was the OPEC president, who'd sounded very relieved when the man he assumed to be the Saudi minister gave him the approval he'd been waiting for.

While I've been waiting here worrying, he's probably been gambling in the Marriott's Omar Khayyam Casino, Ahmed Khalifa thought, *but after tonight is over I won't have to put up with his arrogance ever again.*

There wasn't much love lost between Kuwaitis and Saudis.

Still muttering to himself, Khalifa left his room and took the two flights of stairs down to the conference room on the mezzanine floor. All the other OPEC delegates had left town immediately after initialling the communiqué they'd agreed to during a breakfast get together, leaving Khalifa to handle the press on his own. There were about forty reporters in the room, many of whom he recognised from previous press briefings. He took his place at the head table. The platform on which it rested was raised slightly, allowing the Kuwaiti to look down on his audience, the majority coming from western countries, which caused him a degree of inverse satisfaction. He smiled wryly as he took the prepared statement from his briefcase. This was not going to be the routine press briefing they were accustomed to; this one would make the whole world sit up and take notice.

His opening words had to be modified from the previously prepared script: "Ladies and gentlemen, please forgive me for making you wait so long. My name is Dr Ahmed Khalifa, as most of you may know I am the president of OPEC. The following is a very short press statement that I have been authorised to make on behalf of the majority of the OPEC members."

It was easy to tell which were the more alert reporters present in that conference room. They were the ones who had reacted at the president's use of the phrase "the majority of the OPEC members." They knew the press releases were always unanimous – this was different, and something wasn't right.

"In Cairo at 12 noon yesterday, our brothers in the League of Arab States issued a demand for the immediate withdrawal of all foreign troops from Islamic soil. We in OPEC support our brothers in their reasonable demand. By a majority vote OPEC has agreed to immediately increase to $120 a barrel the price of oil to any foreign country having soldiers on Islamic territory. This price will be increased by a further $5 a barrel every 90 days until the League of Arab States' demand has been met."

That was the end of the statement that had been agreed by the majority of the OPEC delegates at breakfast that morning, but Ahmed, believing he was acting under instructions from the Saudi minister, switched to reading from the falsified communiqué:

"Our brothers in the League of Arab States affirmed that if the invaders fail to accede to that demand, they will be expelled by force. We in OPEC will assist our brothers in the Arab League with all the means at our disposal. We will use the increased revenue derived from the oil price hike to fund the formation of an Islamic Self Defence Force. This will be the first time since our historic victory at the Battle of Acre in 1297, a glorious victory when we defeated the Crusading Knights as they called themselves, that we will once again be able to defend our own interests, without the need to rely on American or other imperialist invaders. That is all."

For some seconds after he finished speaking the room was totally silent, and then it exploded in uproar. The reporters gathered in front of the OPEC president were shouting over the top of each other, trying to be heard. The pictures being recorded by the television cameras in the room would be seen by millions of people across the world; every news channel would be showing them continuously for hours, if not days to come, and politicians in every Western country would be shocked by what they saw and heard. The dealers on the New York Stock Exchange would see these pictures, would hear Khalifa's words, and would watch as their exchange went into melt down, and the other exchanges around the world would follow suit soon enough.

Ahmed Khalifa then behaved exactly as the secretary general of the League of Arab States had done in Cairo the day previously; he turned away from the gathered reporters without giving them the opportunity to demand answers to their questions, leaving on the table copies of the falsified communiqué, bearing the initials of nine of the eleven member states' delegates. Those reporters who tried to follow him were quickly restrained by the hotel security staff, and Ahmed was totally unruffled as he walked back up the two flights of stairs to his room, and closed the door behind himself.

Tonight he would eat dinner alone in his room, perhaps with a very special bottle of French wine to celebrate, while he watched the news channels vying with each other to squeeze all they could from this latest crisis. Tomorrow he would tender his resignation from OPEC on health grounds, producing the medical report which his own doctor had faxed to him just that morning, telling the bad news that the scan he'd had in the clinic showed he had cancer of the oesophagus and that it was terminal. That had been a shock of course, as it would be to anybody, but at least it had made delivering the falsified press statement so much easier and made him that much more determined to enjoy every moment of life that was left to him. The two million dollars, which the Saudi minister would deposit in his account in Zurich and which he'd earned by adding those few extra words to the communiqué, meant he wouldn't even have to miss the little luxuries which OPEC had afforded him, like this exquisitely old fashioned executive suite on the second floor with its high ceilings and crystal chandeliers, original oil paintings, and genuine antique furniture, and of course the lovely Monika to keep him company. She'd joined the OPEC office staff earlier in the year as the public-relations representative, and while she had politely but very firmly rejected his sexual advances, she'd also made it clear she enjoyed his company and hoped they could be very good friends. He'd always known that some young people, men as well as women, worship being associated with people of money or power, and he had put Monika into that category and he hoped that in such little time as was left to him he could advance the relationship to his bed.

He counted himself lucky that she'd come along, much better to spend however many more days he had left on this earth with sweet Monika than with the fat woman he'd married years before, who'd failed to bear him the son he had so desperately wanted to carry on the family name. She was at the family home in Kuwait, and he would never have to see her again.

Khalifa had gone into his bedroom; he could afford to relax now. He turned to face the television in time to see the first flash announcement of his press conference being scrolled across the screen of CNN News. He hadn't realised he'd left the TV turned on, much less with the volume so high. Standing with his back to the wardrobe, he didn't see its door opening, and he didn't hear the footsteps, muffled as they were by the thick carpeting, as they came towards him. He was concentrating on the television so intently it is extremely doubtful he sensed the gun briefly being held next to his right ear, and whether or not he heard the heavily silenced whoosh from the pistol as the assassin calmly squeezed the trigger was totally irrelevant to the outcome. He couldn't possibly have seen the bullet that scattered bits of his brain all over the tapestry wallpaper of his executive suite. Ahmed Khalifa wouldn't ever hear anything again; his work really was done.

The assassin gently placed the pistol in the OPEC president's hand, taking care that one finger rested against the trigger, indicating its work had been done. The medical report, which she herself had typed on the cancer clinic's notepaper, she left on the dressing table where her unfortunate boss had placed it. From her very elegant handbag, she took the suicide note that would explain why poor Ahmed Khalifa had taken his own life, and placed it almost within reach of his left hand, except of course he was beyond reaching for anything now. She picked up the phone and pushed the redial button. The number she saw displayed was the pay-as-you-go mobile telephone that the Grand Master's man in Egypt had bought at the market in Cairo a couple of days previously and which would be at the bottom of the River Nile before the day was over.

The phone was answered on the second ring. Speaking barely loud enough to be heard over the noise of the television, she said, "It's done." She held the line open for a minute or so, as she'd been told to do, and then returned the phone to its stand. She turned the volume on the television down to its lowest setting before leaving the room – it wouldn't do for whoever was in the next room to be disturbed. Her work finished, she closed the door behind her and slipped the privacy sign on the handle; with any luck the lecherous old fool wouldn't be found until morning. She took off the surgical gloves she'd been wearing, and these went into the handbag to be disposed of later that night. She looked at her Cartier watch; if she hurried she'd be on time for her appointment in the hotel spa. It wasn't the first time she'd had to do the Grand Master's dirty work for him, and she found that a herbal sauna was a most effective way afterwards to rid herself of the unclean feeling.

Majed had listened on his pay-as-you-go mobile telephone to the words Monika had used, the ones he'd been waiting all day to hear. A sense of relief swept over him; he'd never worked with a woman in this way before, and though he trusted the Grand Master's judgement implicitly, the stakes were too high for mistakes. Majed wasn't to know this was by no means the first time sweet Monika had pulled the trigger on some unsuspecting enemy of the Order, and neither was it the first time she'd used her sex as a means of worming her way into their confidence, be they male or female.

Majed Dajani never wasted his precious time trying to decide whether he liked someone or not; he was a Lebanese businessman, and for him the act of liking was a hindrance. He remembered a proverb his old grandmother had taught him many years before: "Look upon your best friend as your worst enemy," she'd told him, "and you'll never be surprised or disappointed." Anyway, even though he'd never met Monika and the only words he'd ever heard her speak were those she'd just uttered, he'd decided he didn't like her so it didn't matter, did it?

For Majed Dajani, Chevalier in the Lebanese Priory of the Chivalric Order of St John of Jerusalem, all that was left for him to do was to consign a now unneeded mobile telephone to the depths of the River Nile, and then he could leave Egypt; he had a plane to catch, the Grand Master had another job for him to do.

For Dame Monika Wolff, the only female member of the Austrian Priory of the same chivalric order, she was already enjoying the soothing effects of the herbal sauna in the luxurious Hotel Sacher, heedless of the soon to be discovered suicide upstairs on the second floor. Tomorrow was another day, one to which she was already looking forward. She was flying to London, where she'd been booked as a date for a very senior Saudi Government minister at the Hilton Hotel on Park Lane.

*****

Each TV news channel was concentrating on the same subject: the increasing pandemonium around the world caused by the press conferences in Vienna and Cairo. The BBC's financial editor was in the studio explaining to a stunned population why the price of petrol and diesel had gone up by 20 per cent in the past few minutes. Both BP and Shell had implemented immediate price increases following the OPEC press conference, and it was beyond doubt that the other companies would be following suit before the night was out. On the same theme, Sky News cameras were recording outside a North London Esso petrol station, showing the cars waiting in line, engines running, moving another five yards forward every time someone at the front had taken his fill of the last cheap petrol. Even as the Grand Master watched on his flat screen television set and as the customers queued, the garage manager was adjusting the computer in his tiny office, and the price at each pump miraculously soared to equal that of BP and Shell. The fact that he was doing this on his own initiative didn't deter him; his profits would jump by the amount of the increase until such time as Esso officially instructed him to raise the price, at which time the profit would become theirs. He was a businessman after all, and if people were stupid enough to waste the petrol they already had in their tanks, just so they could replenish it at a higher price, who was he to complain.

In London, Frankfurt, Paris, and further afield in Mumbai, Singapore, Tokyo, Hong Kong, and Sydney, those dealers who spent their working lives manipulating stock markets to the hopeful advantage of their trusting clients were all sitting at home. Probably for the first time in their working lives, they were absolutely impotent. They could only watch as the Dow Jones Exchange in New York went into meltdown. Many of them were glued with their eyes on their Sony 42-inch plasma television screens, their ears filled with the latest mobile telephone gadgetry from Apple, their mouths working overtime, cursing everybody and everything, as they desperately tried to make contact with their colleagues in New York who could still buy and sell stock, but to no avail. Those dealers were busy on their own, dumping such stock as they could, even as they watched the market falling still further. The dealers who used the internet were having no better success; the overloaded system crashed, just as it had done eight years earlier when hundreds of dealers were caught in the middle of transactions. The shares traded but with no money in exchange.

By mid-afternoon the Dow had fallen from a high of 10,440, to 8,200, which was when the bell was sounded to signify the very premature end of trading for the day and therefore for the week. The previous year the directors of the NYSE had instituted a self-regulated strategy to cope with the impact of a market meltdown. They called it the trip-wire strategy, meaning that once the market fell by a certain pre-determined number of percentage points, the bell would sound and all transactions would have to cease immediately. The entire financial world fell silent, powerless to do anything until the first markets opened for business on Monday morning. Those more forward thinking brokers in America and Europe were already in the process of booking seats on the next available flight to Tokyo's Narita Airport; although they wouldn't be allowed on the floor of the Tokyo exchange, they could at least make sure their Japanese counterparts traded on their behalf, doing their best to minimise the losses every one of them was bound to suffer.

It would have been a rare treat for anyone able to see the Grand Master with such a satisfied smile on his face.

Back at the Hotel Sacher, the switchboard was jammed with incoming calls, mostly from Middle Eastern countries, all wanting to speak with His Excellency Dr Ahmed Khalifa. The harassed switchboard operator had lost count how many times she'd explained to angry and at times abusive callers that the good doctor was not answering his phone, and there was nothing she could do. Eventually, she was persuaded there was one thing she could do: what all good employees have to do when they are out of their depth, she passed the buck to the duty manager. He was a very nice young man, but even less able to cope than the older and more experienced switchboard operator, so he in turn called the hotel manager, who conveniently had a small apartment on the fourth floor.

He took immediate charge, but to do what? He tried phoning the room himself, but all that produced was a look of scorn on the face of the switchboard operator; she'd been doing that for more than an hour. He tried knocking at the door of the executive suite, but that proved equally negative. The only thing left was the master key, which the maid responsible for turning down the beds and placing a goodnight-chocolate on the pillow would have in her apron.

With the manager stood beside her she removed the privacy sign and inserted the master key in the lock. Both then hung back, willing the other to turn the round brass doorknob, either to face the wrath of their guest for having disturbed him, or to face whatever else was in the suite. There was nothing unusual in the sitting room. Everything was as the maid had left it that morning. They ventured into the bedroom, the manager nervously calling the guest's name, in the pious hope of avoiding any potential embarrassment should the distinguished gentleman be engaged in an activity too personal to mention.

Dr Ahmed Khalifa was beyond being embarrassed; he was well and truly dead, and it wasn't a pretty sight. With most of his head missing, and a gun clutched in his right hand, it didn't take a genius to understand the poor man had committed suicide. The hotel manager had rushed into the bathroom and was busy vomiting into the basin, an action that would later earn him the wrath of the police searching for incriminating fingerprints. The maid meanwhile, a very down-to-earth and mature lady, was wondering who would have to clean the man's brains from the tapestry wallpaper, determined it wouldn't be her.

The police force in Vienna is noted for being very arrogant in its dealings with the living and coldly efficient when dealing with the dead, but there are always exceptions, and so it proved in this case. Inspector Christian Wenger who had been given charge of the case swiftly looked for someone to blame for having disturbed his Friday evening at home, and he settled on the hotel manager. That stupid individual had dared to disturb what was possibly a crime scene; he'd pay for that. The maid meanwhile had proved to be a much more reliable witness; she'd given a statement that accorded with what the inspector had already decided had happened. She was allowed to go home, still determined it wouldn't be her who cleaned the wallpaper.

The envelope lying on the carpet, almost within reach of the dead man's left hand, was addressed to a government minister in

Saudi Arabia. It wasn't sealed, not that that would have made any difference; the policeman hadn't hesitated even for a second before removing the two sheets of paper from inside the envelope. The letter was written in English, which was convenient for the policeman as he understood that language very well. It had been written on hotel notepaper, very good quality notepaper as you would expect from such a hotel. He sank into one of the armchairs conveniently next to the large double bed, a bed that had held so many pleasant memories for the OPEC president, whose body with its terribly deformed head still lay on the floor almost by the policeman's feet. He began to read, not a jot concerned that he too had disturbed a crime scene because he already knew all there was to know about the suicide.

Dear Abdullah:

Today has been the cruellest day of my entire life. This very morning I received a medical report from my doctor here in Vienna. He told me the reason I've had the problems with my gullet recently, which I'd already mentioned to you, was a terrible cancer. The report told me that disease was very advanced, and in just a few weeks it would take my life in a very painful way. I've been blessed with a good life, Abdullah, and if it was the will of Allah for me to die in this way, I could accept it.

I'd decided after I'd done your bidding today, I would immediately retire from OPEC and live the rest of my life quietly in peace, perhaps in the south of France. The two million dollars you'd promised to deposit for me in a bank in Switzerland would make my last days on this earth more pleasant.

We've known each other since we were children, and our parents before us and their parents before them. How often did we hear their wonderful stories of the old times, when they would wander through the desert with their poor flocks of sheep and goats, searching for grazing, and the water which was even more precious than the oil which so changed all our lives?

Do you remember the time your family and mine were camped in a valley, with the huge sand dunes we dared each other to climb? Our fathers were sitting by the fire telling tales and smoking their shisha pipes; with our brothers and sisters we were supposed to be asleep in our tents, but we'd made the dare to climb those huge dunes. Do you remember how we looked up at the night sky? It was so dark, and the moon was nothing more than a thin sliver of gold, but it was the stars we loved that night. Do you remember how we tried to give them all names? We were both so innocent then; we hadn't been corrupted by the businessmen from the West, visiting our parents with their promise of riches if only they would sign their names to those pieces of paper. Do you remember how our fathers told us those Englishmen scorned them when they realised they didn't know how to sign their names, and how ashamed our parents told us they'd felt? Do you remember the promise we made to each other that night as we climbed those dunes? How we promised to take our revenge on those who had so shamed our parents.

And do you also remember how we got lost that night? How we were so sure all we had to do was climb the highest dune and the sea would be on the other side, only it wasn't, so we climbed another dune, and another, until we were lost. Do you remember how you cried when we couldn't find our way back to our parents, and how I promised I would find the way? We were as brothers then, Abdullah, maybe even closer than brothers, and I kept my promise to you. I got us back to our parents' camp, even carrying you when you hurt your legs falling down the side of the dune in the pitch dark and crashing into that thorn bush.

I know you will remember the night we met at the Hilton Hotel in London, a place you described to me as almost being your home from home. It was the ambassador's party to celebrate the Kuwait National Day. You were an important government minister in Riyadh, and you had come to England to see the new tanks the British were developing, which they were hoping you'd buy for the Saudi Defence Force. After the party you came back to the flat I keep in London, and we talked of the past. You reminded me of the promise we'd made to each other that night in the desert, to avenge our family's honour, and you asked me if I still wanted to keep my promise.

Because you and I are like brothers to each other, I did as you asked. I persuaded the members of OPEC to agree to increase the price of oil to the invader countries, as you had asked me to do. At the press conference I added the extra words you wanted about how we in OPEC would use the extra money from the increased price of oil to create a unified Islamic Defence Force, and that in future we'd be responsible for our own security without the need to rely on foreign infidel soldiers. I kept my promise to you, Abdullah, even though I didn't agree with what you were doing.

But you, Abdullah, you didn't keep your promise. When I telephoned you after the press conference, as you'd asked me to do, you scorned me. You laughed at me when I asked about the money; there was no money for me, and there never would be. You even insulted my family, saying we were still as Bedouin, and we should go back to our sheep and goats. I cried then, as you had cried all those years ago when we were lost in the dark desert.

Tonight I take my own life, Abdullah; I cannot live with the shame you've brought on me, that will be just as much a cancer as the one that is attacking my body even as I write this letter. I will wait for you on the other side, you who were once my brother, and I will have my revenge there. That is another promise I will keep.

Ahmed

It was only in the police canteen back at the station that one of the inexperienced, young police officers would confide to an equally inexperienced colleague how his boss had neglected to take even the most basic precautions at the crime scene. The boss's fingerprints were all over the suicide letter, and whatever evidence might have been left on the armchair had been removed by his boss's rather large backside. Had his arrogant boss been privy to the snide comments of his underling, which he most certainly wasn't, he would have answered it was so obviously a suicide such precautions were unnecessary. He would perhaps have added that such forensic evidence as might have been available had been destroyed by the stupid hotel manager before they'd even arrived.

For Inspector Wenger it was all such an open and shut case he didn't even bother to check with the doctor to confirm the authenticity of the damning medical report, so Majed Dajani's forgery skills and Monika Wolff's secretarial abilities had paid off yet again.

Chapter Five

It was mid-morning when I saw the car coming back up the Highland track, swerving from side to side as it navigated the many potholes and doing its best to miss the rocks which were littered everywhere. It was the same mysterious-looking Range Rover which had brought Nicholas and Sir James Sinclair a couple of days earlier. The same frightening looking chauffeur was at the wheel, but this time he didn't bother getting out – perhaps he remembered the midges that had attacked him on his last visit.

Nicholas was in the car and so too was Sir James Sinclair. Was this just a coincidence I wondered, or had it been pre-arranged? I shook hands with Sir James, and again he gave that curious little bow of his head. I found myself looking for it this time, and wondering what it meant; it was more than just an old-fashioned courtesy, I was sure of that now. I was a simple gamekeeper, and he came from a position in life far above mine. There was more to this than just courtesy, but what could it be? Perhaps today I might find out.

We went inside, choosing this time to stay in the conservatory. This was built almost entirely of glass from waist height up, making it a wonderfully light and airy place to sit. The sun was shining very strongly, warming the room, whereas outside it was quite cold, with a biting wind coming down from the north, gaining strength as it swept across the glens.

Sir James opened the discussion; clearly he was a man accustomed to taking the lead.

"My apologies for descending on you unannounced. It seems I am making a habit of doing that, which is most unusual for me. I understood from Nicholas you had almost concluded your life story, so it seemed appropriate for me to come along, and let you have the notebook I mentioned at our last meeting."

Whether or not it was a habit of his to descend on people like this, it was most definitely an unwelcome intrusion. I'd been looking forward to having more time alone with my son and finishing the story of my life's journey, as in fact this man had asked me to do, and his choice of words had been curious: how could he have known how far I had progressed with my story, unless he and Nicholas had been in contact? Had they met since I'd parted from my son at the Speckled Grouse, and was that by arrangement, or by chance? I was feeling more and more uneasy.

"As you so rightly say, my story is almost done," I said to them, and I picked up the narration where I had left off.

After Maria left me and took Nicholas to live in the United States, life became very quiet and very lonely. The happiness that I'd been privileged to share with them disappeared almost as quickly as it had come. I still had my work of course, and I continued to live in the gatehouse, though it no longer held the joy it once had. From time to time the Grand Master would send for me to discuss the estate or the prospects for the next grouse season, but even that had lost its magic for me. I came to hate the visiting toffs and to despise the self-indulgent look these people expressed, having pointed their hugely expensive side-lock Purdey shotguns at a flock of birds which had been expertly driven directly over their heads and which they couldn't miss if they tried! Of course it isn't that easy; even on the first day of the season, the Glorious Twelfth, when the young grouse have yet to gain the strength and the wisdom to fly higher and faster, a reasonable degree of marksmanship is called for, but those days I'd find fault with even the most expert gun.

How many times had I been there, congratulating them on their excellent shooting skills, and commiserating with the poor old man (there was always one) who'd been too slow getting his gun up to the shoulder and who'd discharged both barrels into empty air? Anyway, that is all in my past. Today another gamekeeper belongs up there with the toffs, pleasing them, praising them, sometimes commiserating with them, and always looking forward at the end of the day to a tip commensurate with their luck with the birds. I enjoy my retirement, and any bitterness I might have felt has long since gone.

In the month of June there would always be a large gathering of the Knights of the Order of St John to celebrate St John's Day. The numbers of knights seemed to grow year by year, to the point where the castle could no longer accommodate them all, and they had to take rooms at the Speckled Grouse pub in the village. This really got the village folks talking as you can imagine, but the Grand Master put a stop to that after one of our American brothers exchanged pillow talk with Julie, and her exaggerated version of the goings on at the castle were all over the village by next morning. Anyway, the pub couldn't cope with the international idiosyncrasies of our members, and we started taking an increasing number of rooms in the tourist hotels in Pitlochery, using large coaches to ferry them around.

With the increasing numbers of knights, coming from ever more countries to celebrate St John's Day, so the processions became more colourful. First in line came the serving brothers and sisters, supervised by the sergeant of the guard. These were the gardener and housekeeper, Brother James and his wife Sister Martha, the chauffeur Brother William, and four brothers who made up the security team. They were all dressed in the traditional brown robes, which, so I was told by the Grand Master, were unchanged in the Order's entire eight-hundred year existence. This group peeled off as we arrived at the chapel, to form a guard of honour for the rest of the procession, and then they returned to their own duties.

My father-in-law's responsibility was to be the principal flag-bearer of the main party, leading the procession as it wound its way from the basement armoury, up the cold stone staircase with its rough cast walls, past the armour-clad statues in the hallway, and out into the courtyard, from where we would solemnly march to the chapel. The Grand Master would follow him, holding aloft the ceremonial sword, followed by me, and then came the national contingents, each marching behind their national flag. As I'd said earlier, the robes became more colourful, creating a most impressive spectacle even if it was not what our forebears had in mind, but it would have been a sight to gladden the viewfinder of any visiting Japanese tourist's camera, except tourists were not allowed. This was a privately owned castle, and the Chivalric Order of St John of Jerusalem a privately registered institution; neither was open to the general public.

After the ecumenical service was over, we would march back to the Castle, with the chaplain leading the procession, to find coffee and biscuits waiting for us in the Great Hall. It was quite a spectacular sight, almost medieval, with the statues in their suits of armour seeming to mix with the visiting knights, while refreshments were taken around by the serving brothers and sisters.

The annual meeting of the Chivalric Order of St John of Jerusalem always took place on this occasion. This was held in what was called the Main Room on the third floor of Rannoch Castle. This room had been so neglected over the centuries as to be unusable, so when the Grand Master bought the Castle in 1982, like practically everything else, it had been totally refurbished and became a superb meeting room. The original wooden flooring had been removed to be treated for dry rot, then put back in place and varnished to a brilliant finish. It was almost a sacrilege to walk on it. The walls were covered with a heavy tapestry-like wallpaper, painted in a rich ochre colour, and the doors leading into the room were painted the same colour, but slightly lighter and with inset panels to provide some relief. Concealed lighting had been cleverly installed behind the coving, while all around the room were paintings of past Grand Masters. A stage had been created at one end, raised a foot or so above the level of the rest of the room, and this held the head conference table at which the members of the Supreme Council took their place, and behind which hung a magnificent painting of Tsar Paul I, the original Protector of the Russian Grand Priory. In common with all the other changes that the Grand Master had made to Rannoch Castle, this room lacked for nothing. It was wonderful.

There were five members of the Supreme Council: the Grand Master of course, the bailiff, who I'd never met but from the little I'd heard sounded a very sinister character indeed, the treasurer general, who was my American father-in-law, the secretary general, an ancient-looking man, stooped and scraggy and with a beak shaped nose, and the almoner, which was me. The audience at the general meetings consisted of the prior from each visiting delegation, together with a couple of each of their officers, usually totalling around thirty people.

The deliberations would often go on into the early evening, during which time all the other visiting knights would either break off into small working groups to discuss various activities the Order was pursuing, or just wander round the castle grounds. It frequently happened during the general meeting that disagreements would arise between visiting priors, usually on the level of oblations which had, or more usually had not, been raised from their members. It was part of my responsibility to take the arguing parties into the adjoining south-tower room, where they were obliged to settle their differences before being allowed to rejoin the meeting.

This room was as bare as a room could possibly be. The walls had all been replastered, and the ceiling replaced, but the original stone floor had been left exactly as it must have been over hundreds of years. The room lacked any kind of furniture or wall decoration. It was cold and uninviting; you didn't stay there any longer than was absolutely necessary.

With the exception of the Supreme Council members, all of the visiting knights would usually come by the Castle on the morning after St John's Day to take their leave of the Grand Master and then return to their own homes. The Grand Master, the treasurer general, and secretary general would then meet privately in the owner's apartment on the second floor. These meetings were always held behind closed doors. What struck me as odd was why I wasn't included, since I was supposedly a member of that body. Anyway, since all three of them were American and apparently had grown up in the same community in Boston, they probably wanted to reminisce on days gone by.

I bumped into various members of the castle staff from time to time as I went about my duties on the estate; I never saw them dressed differently than in their brown tunics. They were always very civil towards me, but never was there any display of friendship. A security guard was always on duty at the massive pair of gates guarding the entrance to the driveway; these had been specially built to replace the rusting and unsightly ones that had been there for as long as I could remember and now had the emblem of the Order engraved into them. They were always firmly closed to any curious passers-by. The security guards, or brothers as they were referred to of course, all came from Alabama, as did the housekeeper and gardener, Sister Martha and Brother James. They were all extremely attentive in the way they performed their duties, and even on the coldest or wettest of days would never accept even a cup of warming coffee from me.

I'd been watching Sir James Sinclair while I'd been talking. He'd not paid any attention at all to what I'd been saying. Instead, he had been looking at a notebook he'd taken from his fine leather briefcase. In appearance it was very similar to the kind of exercise book we used when I was at school, but its brown cover was rather faded and badly creased, and the back cover was missing. Whatever it was, it had seen a lot of use. Nicholas by contrast clearly had been paying attention, showing no evidence at all of the tiredness he'd displayed the previous day.

I turned to Nicholas and said, "I suppose it was three years after your mother had taken you away before I heard of you again. The Grand Master sent for me one day to suggest I should travel to America to see you in your new life. I didn't want to go. I'd been betrayed, my life had almost been destroyed, and I was fearful to reopen old wounds. But you were my son, my only flesh and blood, and I was desperate to see you again, so I went. As strange as it sounds, your mother and I never divorced; to this day she is still legally my wife. For me, to be divorced or not is totally irrelevant. There isn't another woman in my life, and I certainly don't expect one at this late stage. I would have thought Maria would have wanted to move on by now. Still, that is up to her.

"I'd never been to a city as big as Boston, and it was quite a frightening experience, I can tell you. I was met at the airport by a chauffeur and driven through Boston to the house where you and your mother still live today – when you're not away at university that is. Boston was cold. It was dark and raining too; the roads were so busy, and the driving so aggressive, it was intimidating. On the rare occasions I'd needed to go into Perth, even into Edinburgh, it was never anything like that. I was overawed by your house too. Remember, I was a man whose life had been spent in the remote Scottish Highlands where life tends to be rather rough and ready.

"Every room in your house was tastefully decorated and had fitted carpets. There was antique-looking furniture everywhere. I was taken into a room where your mother was waiting for me, and where you were sitting in a chair, barely four years old and already looking so confident with yourself. I remember your mother and I exchanged a few words, icily polite – though whether this was her doing or mine is difficult for me to say. Then she left us alone.

"During the course of that week the family encouraged me to spend as much time as I wanted with you. It took time for a relationship between us to develop. They'd told you who I was, but at that age it wouldn't have meant much to you. As for your mother, I didn't see her again until it was time for me to leave, and then surprisingly she was kind enough to invite me to come back to see you as often as I wished. As you know, I came back twice every year after that, and as you got older we would speak on the telephone every week too.

"As for the rest, you already know it, my son. I love you dearly and I count the days between visits, but if I am honest with you, as you asked me to be, I confess that I don't belong in your world and neither do you in mine. Our lives are so utterly different!"

Nicholas stayed slumped in his wickerwork chair for what seemed like a very long time after I finished speaking, but it was probably no more than a minute or two. Sinclair was watching both of us, waiting to see what would happen next, wondering perhaps if it was time for him to drop his bombshell. As it was, Nicholas broke the silence. He'd stood up and walked to open the conservatory door, looking out at the moorland and the distant mountains, a look on his face I would describe as wistful, though why he should do that I didn't know.

"Dad, how can you say we don't belong in each other's worlds? We belong to each other. Isn't that enough for you?"

I don't know whether he intended that as a rebuke or if it was some kind of a cry from his heart, but whatever it was, it hit home like a sledgehammer. He'd turned to face me as he spoke, and the wetness in his eyes had been very plain to see. This tall, strong, confident, young man was on the point of tears simply because I'd said something that was glaringly obvious. I wondered why?

Before either of us had the chance to continue that discussion, Sir

James Sinclair rose from his seat and put his arms around Nicholas's broad shoulders. He guided him, rather forcefully I thought, back to the wickerwork chair, and gently but purposefully persuaded him to sit. He himself continued standing, moving across the room so that his back was to the door Nicholas had left open. He was holding the notebook in his hand.

Sir James Sinclair was staring at me. His hand, the one holding the notebook, was trembling slightly.

"I can only guess at the thoughts going through your mind just now," he said to me, but he was looking at Nicholas and I wondered if that wasn't a conspiratorial look they'd exchanged.

"I do not propose to go into any further detail at this time," he said to me, "but as promised I will leave this book, which will help you begin to understand. It is written in Russian, a language I understand just a little, but fortunately your son is fluent, both reading and writing, which is another reason I arranged for him to be here. I have to tell you, there are quite a lot of pages missing towards the end of the book which must have been torn out at some point, and if you don't mind I will drop by tomorrow to let you have those."

Saying that, Sir James Sinclair placed the book on the wickerwork coffee table and turned to leave by the open door, but not before he very definitely bowed his head at me – not a slight nod as in the past, but a very clear bow.

I was dumbfounded; so much so I didn't even stand to see him out. I heard the engine of the Range Rover come to life, the tyres kick up several stones as the car was turned to face the opposite direction, and the noise of its powerful motor fade into the distance as it headed back towards the main Highland road.

By now I had become highly suspicious, wondering just how much my son already knew about what was going on. The look he and Sinclair exchanged moments earlier had not gone unnoticed, and the fact they'd met and come to see me together was perhaps not a coincidence. Add to those things the notebook, written in Russian, a language which 'by chance' my son happened to be studying at university, and this was adding up to something bizarre.

Even as I was trying to digest all this, still something else was trying to force itself to my attention, and with a shock I realised what it was. In the lapel of Sir James Sinclair's very elegant suit jacket I'd seen a small, round button with a scarlet base and a white, eight-pointed cross slightly raised in its centre. I knew what it was, as indeed I should. I have one too, though I rarely wear it. It was the badge worn by members of the Order of Saint John of Jerusalem. Sir James Sinclair was a Knight of Malta! Why had I never met him before at one of the meetings of the Order at the Castle?

Without saying a word, I left the conservatory and went to sit by the log fire in the sitting room. Here, in my own leather chair, my faithful dog by my feet, surrounded by such few possessions as I owned, here at least I was in control. The conservatory had suddenly become a hostile place where I felt insecure, out of my depth, suspicious even of my own son. I poked the ashes into showing a bit of life, and threw a newly cut log to feed the tiny yellow flame which had materialised. The only sounds to be heard were the noise of the sap from the newly cut log as it fell into the hot ashes, and the creak of the door hinges as Nicholas came into the room.

"I need to ask you some things about your relationship with Sir James Sinclair," was how I started the conversation. "I need to know whether it had been arranged in advance, or if it was a coincidence you came with him today."

Nicholas was in the process of drinking beer from a bottle he'd taken from the fridge. He stopped doing that and looked me straight in the face, a good sign!

"Sir James Sinclair," he told me, "comes from a family with a long history of service to the British Crown. As he's already told you, his father was a senior official at the Foreign Office and his father before him was for many years the British ambassador in Moscow. Sir James's career has been no less distinguished. For the last few years before retirement he was the head of MI5, the British Security Service. He actually resigned from the post in 1990, knowing that the following year the government intended removing the anonymity the head had always enjoyed, and he apparently felt his life would be in danger once that happened.

"In 1999 he was created a Knight Commander of the Royal Victorian Order by Her Majesty the Queen. This is an award held in Her Majesty's personal gift and is used to reward individuals who contributed something significant to the royal family. Sir James was rumoured to be the representative of the sovereign whenever the police were investigating incidents which might involve the Royals. That had its origins in the time of Queen Victoria, when the commissioner of police wanted to interview one of the senior members of the family about the Jack the Ripper murders."

OK, I thought to myself, *that goes some way to explaining the lapel badge, but the Queen's personal representative coming to see me, the notebook written in Russian which by chance my son happens to understand, and the locket which I have seen before – none of that is any clearer.*

Nicholas continued. "Sir James telephoned me in my room at the pub yesterday afternoon; I don't know how he knew I was there. He asked how your story was coming along, and when I told him it was almost up to date he said it was time to take the next step, which was to let you have the notebook. I asked him to pick me up on the way, and he agreed. It was as simple as that."

"Simple?" I almost screamed the word at my son. "You call this simple? I'm a retired gamekeeper. All my life I've tramped these moors. I earned less money in a year than the toffs I used to serve would spend on their shooting holiday. My colleagues in the Order of St John are all successful businessmen or politicians or I don't know what. Now I'm learning it is the Queen's personal representative who brought you here, who gave me the locket and now the notebook, part of which is missing, and who bows his head when he greets me – and you call this simple?

"It's enough Nicholas. Now I demand to know what's going on. I will not stand it that you, my own son, knows where all this is leading and you insist on taking me step-by-step, as though I am a child, a plaything for you and your influential friends. Either you stop this right now, or you can go back to your own life in America, and leave me to mine. If you are still here when I return, it's because you are going to tell me the whole story, or I will never see you again."

I left my chair and went to the door, calling Randy as I did so. He'd given up on his walk so it took him a second or two to realise what was going on; he was probably as confused in his own way as I was in mine.

I confess I stalked out of the cottage in high dudgeon, caring little where I was going, but I was back in seconds as the first blast of cold wind took my breath away. A short sleeved shirt and slacks are not appropriate walking gear in the Highlands in the middle of June! Nicholas was surprised at my quick return, and tried to hide the fact that he'd been making a call on his mobile telephone, and that did nothing to reassure me. In the bedroom I changed into more suitable clothes, including putting on my heavy walking boots, and retrieving my shotgun from the cupboard by the door. I didn't know what I was going to shoot, or even who, which perhaps gives an idea of the mood I was in. I left the cottage for the second time, taking care not to look at my son, though I knew he was sitting slumped in his chair.

Would he still be here when I get back?" I wondered to myself. I tried to convince myself I didn't care, but I knew that to be untrue.

I headed toward the Castle, which in the mid-afternoon sun I could see standing proud on the high ground overlooking the ancient track to the western isles. As a much younger man I'd made this journey very often, but scrambling up the shale-clad slopes was more taxing now, and I felt the need to rest much more often. Randy, too, had slowed down, though whether this was because of his advancing years or out of sympathy with me, I couldn't know. My chest heaved, my breath came in gasps, and my legs turned to water as they struggled to carry me up the next rise, but this was good therapy. I was physically pushing myself so hard my mental processes had switched off. I wasn't thinking about my son, or Sir James Sinclair, or even feeling sorry for myself. I was concentrating on the next rise, or keeping my balance as I slid down a steep, shale-encrusted slope.

As dusk was falling I reached the only peak high enough to overlook Rannoch Castle. The flag of the Order of St John of Jerusalem flew proudly from the highest turret, the red background fading into the night sky, leaving the white eight pointed cross majestically silhouetted against the darkness. A spotlight from the castle heightened this effect; it was eerily mystical, especially here in the otherwise empty Highlands. There were a few lights shining inside the castle, including from the Master's suite on the second floor. More intriguing though was the car parked in front of the entrance portico. It was Sir James Sinclair's Range Rover. Black, with multiple aerials – it had to be the same one. In an instant I was brought back to reality.

I don't know for how long I remained sitting there with different ideas swirling round in my mind, some crazy, some totally illogical, but what else could I do? I felt like a pawn in a game of chess in which either my son or Sir James Sinclair would move to the next square when they were ready.

I'd hardly left the cottage before Nicholas started using his mobile telephone, and the look of guilt on his face when I returned so unexpectedly told its own story. I had no doubt he was calling the man Sinclair but to say what? To tell him I was being difficult, even emotional? Or to ask about the remaining pages of the notebook? Unconsciously, I was fingering my shotgun, finding comfort running my hand over the stock, rubbed smooth by many years of use and many hours of oiling. What I would have given that evening to have had a bag full of cartridges, waiting for precisely that moment when hundreds of grouse would take to wing in front of me, firing first one barrel then the other, rounding my shoulder to take the recoil after each discharge, as I had taught so many city toffs over the years to do. A mad lust to kill was how I used to describe the antics of some of these types, and today that was precisely what I needed to do! Sadly, at any rate for me, there wasn't even a wandering fox to take my mind off my troubles, so I turned for home. Randy had been missing for quite some time; I had no doubt he was already lying sprawled on the carpet in front of the fire.

By the time I arrived back at the cottage I'd calmed down. I realised that continually blowing my top wasn't going to get me anywhere, any more than suspecting Nicholas of subterfuge was helping my state of mind. I had to let this thing run its course, see where it was going, and then decide what, if anything, I was going to do about it. I could do that.

To my great relief Nicholas was still there. He had put the coffee table in front of the fireplace and set it for a fireside dinner. The stew was, as always, simmering away in the old pot, the ladle already in place. I was more than a little surprised to see the dumplings floating on the top of the stew; cooking must be another of my son's store of special talents I wasn't aware of. Would we ever be able to have a normal father and son relationship after all this? I desperately hoped so; he was all I had in the world, except for old Randy of course, and I confess I rather took him for granted.

Nicholas had already taken another bottle of beer from the fridge for himself He had developed two unfortunate habits when drinking his beer: one to take it straight from the bottle, something I'd chastised him only alcoholics did, and second to drink it cold, which only the Americans did. My admonitions didn't do any good; my son very definitely had a mind of his own. Anyway, he reached into the kitchen cupboard to retrieve a bottle for me and poured it into my own special glass, managing to keep a decent head of froth on it. He was improving.

"I've spoken to Sir James," he said from the kitchen, cutting the bread into thick wedges, the only way when eating stew. "I was in the process of doing that when you came back to the cottage after stalking off. He wants to apologise for not bringing the other pages of the notebook. He phoned back about an hour ago and said he'd found them and will bring them to us tomorrow."

My paranoia was back. I'd seen Sinclair's Range Rover parked at the Castle not two hours ago. Was that where he'd gone to collect the missing pages? He'd originally told us his father had come into possession of the locket, and the notebook of course, in controversial circumstances during the war, so why would those missing notebook pages be in Rannoch Castle? I decided to let it pass, anyway for the time being, perhaps the end was in sight.

Nicholas plonked himself down in his armchair just as the BBC News was about to start, a programme he claimed to be streets ahead of any of the news programmes in the States. I was walking back to my seat, glass of beer in hand, as news was coming in to tell the world that the body of the president of OPEC had just been discovered in his hotel suite in Vienna, he apparently having committed suicide. I don't claim to be knowledgeable about or particularly interested in world affairs, but even my curiosity was piqued by this news, coming just a day after the secretary general of the Islamic League had also committed suicide, in his case by throwing himself off the balcony of a hotel in Cairo. I remembered seeing the pictures as they'd moved from an enchanting backdrop of boats on the River Nile, to the gruesome shot of the spread-eagled body of the Islamic League man, taken in between the legs of a scrum of policemen, all crowding round the body. Cairo and Vienna might as well be on another planet for all it had to do with me, or so I thought, but I did pause to wonder just what was going on in the outside world. Nicholas however had been paying very close attention, but then he was a real news hound; he'd also started to attack his bowl of stew. The poor lad must have been ravenous.

It is extremely difficult to hold a worthwhile conversation when trying to ladle spoonfuls of good stew into your mouth, and we didn't try. The dumplings were delicious, very unusually stuffed with cheese, something I'd never done but would from now on. He must have added some more vegetables and potatoes, all dug from my own patch of garden; since the weekend I'd been promising myself I'd top them up and hadn't got round to doing it. We each had two bowls of stew, and of course Randy had his too, he being as partial to stew or anything else that looks like food come to that, as any other dog. I cleared away the bowls from the table, preparing to stack them in the sink but Nicholas was having none of that.

"You wash, I'll dry," was all he said, and in minutes the job was done and we were once again sitting in front of the log fire. He opened the notebook.

Chapter Six

Weekends in Washington DC, are usually fairly quiet affairs. Most of the senators and congressmen have returned to their home constituencies all over the country, taking many of their staff with them. Even in the White House, incumbent presidents like to take off to the presidential retreat at Camp David for the weekend, but this was no ordinary weekend and no one had left town.

President George T. Riles had spent much of Friday afternoon watching television, as so many others in America had been doing. He'd watched as the crisis unfolded on the floor of the New York Stock Exchange; he'd watched as roving television cameras scoured the country to find those gas stations taking advantage of the situation to hike their prices as high as they felt they could get away with; and he'd watched and listened as captains of industries large and small had explained the devastating effect the oil price hike was going to have on consumer prices and on jobs.

American presidents don't have the luxury of simply taking it on the chin. They have to act, and President Riles was no slouch when it came to taking tough decisions, as he'd proved time and time again during his two terms in the White House. He'd spent the evening in consultation with most of his closest advisers, each giving their own opinion as to what was causing this latest crisis and, more importantly, what they should do about it. Deborah Adams, his charismatic and highly intelligent secretary of state was missing. Her entire evening was spent staring out the window of an Air Force Boeing as it winged its way through the night sky from Beijing. She'd been consulting with the Chinese leadership over the threat posed by the renewed North Korean nuclear testing and had been ordered home by her president. He desperately needed her input, but she was as lost on this issue as the rest of his team. She'd spoken on the telephone with the king of Saudi Arabia, and the emir of Kuwait, and neither had been much help. They hadn't said as much, but it was clear they'd been caught by surprise, just as much as everyone else.

※※※※※

On another part of the globe another young lady was looking out the window from her airplane seat too, but that was as much as she and Dr Adams had in common. Monika was flying in economy class on a British Airways Airbus A320. She'd left the apartment she shared with her mother near the State Opera House in Vienna before 9 a.m., and walked the short distance to her hairdresser's salon. Robert, a favourite with all the ladies, had looked up as she'd entered the salon. He was accustomed to Monika being dressed in a very elegant, even chic fashion, but today she was wearing a pink jogging suit with matching running shoes. He'd certainly never seen her like that before, but he'd been in the business of looking after his very special clients long enough to know never to show surprise; they might think he was criticising, and that would never do. He knew that Monika was always in a hurry, so he'd made sure to give her the very first appointment of the day.

By 10.30 a.m. Robert had worked his artistic magic. Monika's shoulder-length blond hair had been transformed from the frizzled look she'd had when she arrived, perhaps something to do with the sauna yesterday evening, to an extremely elegant and fashionable combed out style; he'd tried to capture the essence of free spirit, which was how he thought of his favourite customer.

A taxi driver appeared at the door of the salon, precisely on time as Viennese people always are, ready to whisk her to Schwechat Airport for her flight to London. Within an hour she was gazing out the window of her British Airways plane as it was climbing to altitude above Vienna, the River Danube glistening in the late morning sunshine, and the spire of St Stephen's Cathedral, a historic landmark, dominating the skyline for miles around.

Two hours later she was 10,000 feet above the Berkshire countryside, her plane on its approach to Heathrow. Monika was looking out of her window at the River Thames. This appeared to be trying to tie itself in knots as it twisted and turned its way toward London, just a part of its two hundred and seven mile journey from its source in the Cotswold Hills to the sandbanks where it merges with the English Channel. She much preferred this approach to Heathrow, coming in from the west of the capital city, especially on a beautiful June afternoon such as this, when the best of rural England was displayed in all its glory. The plane passed almost directly overhead Windsor Castle, favourite residence of the British royal family, where she had a view of the castle grounds not available to the tourists down below, and then on to Windsor Great Park, where the Magna Carta had been signed by King John almost eight-hundred years previously, and where more recently the memorial to President John F Kennedy had been inaugurated.

Monika was not a nervous passenger, but nonetheless it was always reassuring to hear that certain click as the landing wheels locked into place. In common with many of her fellow passengers, she took the last look out of the window, at the streams of traffic navigating the M25 motorway, then the perimeter road that runs all the way round one of the world's busiest airports, and finally, thanks to the skills of the pilot and no wind, the gentle bump as that mass of metal and humanity touched the runway. They were down, time for her to go to work.

※ ※ ※ ※ ※

By the time the American secretary of state's Boeing landed at Andrews Air Force Base she had decided on the course of action to recommend. She'd ordered, actually ordered, the Saudi and Kuwaiti ambassadors to report to the White House, and they were already there as her olive-green, US Marine Corps helicopter, which had almost seamlessly plucked her from the steps of the Air Force jet just minutes earlier, touched down on the White House lawn. They were immediately summoned to meet with the president, whose smile this Saturday morning was as stiff as his handshake, but if he was expecting some solutions, or even some reasonable explanations, he was to be disappointed.

The two diplomats had neither. The Kuwaiti Ambassador felt most disadvantaged. Because the OPEC president was also a Kuwaiti he thought the US president would assume they were acting towards a common goal, which certainly wasn't true. The ambassador's wheedling excuses did nothing to soothe the president's morning, but they were all taken by surprise when Dr Adams rounded on the Saudi ambassador. She thrust a folder into his lap, and demanded an explanation. The Saudi, a member of his country's royal family, wasn't accustomed to being spoken to like that, and never by a woman, but this was no time to stand on dignity. He opened the folder, wondering what was inside; he turned pale. His hands holding the letter were visibly shaking as he read Dr Ahmed Khalifa's suicide letter. The three onlookers were all staring at him. The president and the Kuwaiti ambassador wondered what on earth was going on and what was in the folder, while Dr Adams, knew precisely what was in there and was demanding an explanation.

President Riles was well accustomed to the antics his secretary of state could pull when she was in a bind, and this appeared to be a classic. He looked at her and raised his eyebrows, questioning. By way of reply she gave her president the barest hint of a smile, the corners of her mouth almost imperceptibly turning upwards and then returned to the grim expression that she was reserving exclusively for the Saudi. He was blustering, not knowing what to say, so Debbie, as the president (and only the president) called her, did it for him:

"Mr Ambassador, would you mind explaining to the president exactly why the president of OPEC would address a suicide letter like this to your brother-in-law, and when you've done that, answer the same thing from the secretary general of the Arab League?"

In saying this, she took the folder back from the Ambassador and handed it to President Riles, for him to read.

She continued, "Is he trying to do Osama bin Laden's work for him? Indeed, is he working with him, or could it possibly be that he is acting under instructions from your own government? Is your country doing its best to deliberately increase the already delicate relationship between Islam and the Christian world?"

The diplomat's brow was furrowed, his deeply hooded eyes still staring at the folder now in President Riles' hand. After some moments of hesitation, he stood from his chair and looked directly at the president:

"Mr President, I know nothing of these accusations being made by Dr Adams, and I am absolutely positive I speak for my government too. As you are probably more aware than any other leader in the Western world, it would be a devastating blow to my country if the coalition forces were to be withdrawn. There is no doubt whatsoever that the fundamentalists would seize the opportunity and try to overthrow the royal family. Were that to happen, they would then force a confrontation between East and West, and oil would be the weapon of choice. That would be very damaging to the economies of America and Europe, but it would also be seriously harmful to my country and all the oil producing nations in the Gulf region where we depend on the oil revenue to keep our people housed and fed. Surely you can see that?"

Mr Riles was nodding his head in apparent agreement as the diplomat continued, "As for the involvement of my brother-in-law Abdullah, this is not like him. His views are at times opposed to those of the Saudi government, and to be perfectly frank with you, that is one of the reasons the king appointed him as a minister. As one of your own illustrious predecessors reminded us, it is better to have your enemy inside your tent looking out, than outside your tent looking in."

The Saudi was being at his diplomatic best in quoting, or in fact deliberately misquoting Lyndon Johnson's maxim, perhaps out of respect to there being a woman in the room. LBJ had actually referred to your enemy 'pissing' in your tent, but no doubt everyone in the room knew that and let it pass.

The president of the United States of America had finished reading Ahmed Khalifa's suicide letter, his face expressionless, not betraying any emotion whatsoever.

"Debbie, how did you get hold of this letter? You've hardly been in the country for an hour, where did it come from? Is it genuine?"

The secretary of state's face was as expressionless as her boss's.

"Sir, this is a faxed copy. It came to me from one of our friends in Vienna. She'd found out from my office I was in the air, and she found the fax number from our embassy in Austria and sent it to me on the plane. I trust her implicitly. I have no doubt it is genuine. I will stand by that decision."

The president was far too wise to ask who the friend might be. Adams had said she stood by her decision, and she was not a woman to give her word lightly.

The Saudi ambassador was still standing, seemingly supporting himself on the back of the chair.

"I too have known Miss Adams long enough to take her word that this letter is as genuine as it seems. I have no explanation for it, nor will I try. I chance to know my brother-in-law is in London right now. I shall fly there tonight and confront him in the morning. What I do after that will depend on him. He is an honourable man and a very religious man; he is a wonderful husband to my sister and a very caring father to their five children. I cannot believe he has gone bad. In the meantime, I plead with you Mr President, keep this matter between us. It is better the world knows nothing of such matters, at least until we know whether they are true. Now please forgive me, but I have no intention of continuing this conversation until I have spoken with my brother-in-law and then with the king."

With that the Saudi Arabian ambassador made a very dignified exit from the room, closely followed by the Kuwait ambassador who hadn't said a word during the whole meeting and was extremely grateful he hadn't had to. Unbeknown to Dr Adams, the now deceased president of OPEC was his uncle.

*****

Monika had no checked baggage, and Terminal One was very quiet, fairly typical for Saturday lunchtime. Unlike the long-haul terminals Three and Four at Heathrow, where the queue at immigration even for European Community passport holders could be lengthy, there was no delay there either, and ten minutes after leaving the Airbus she was climbing into the back of a London taxi. Her destination was an apartment on the second floor of a modern block of flats in the Kensington area of London. This was owned by the Grand Master, and was available to his closest aides, always by arrangement with Brian the head porter, a man who accepted the unusual comings and goings in the flat as readily as he accepted the generous gift that came his way every Christmas. The block of flats boasted a full-sized swimming pool and a well-equipped gymnasium, both rarely used by the other occupants and both very welcome to Monika who liked to work out every single day whenever possible. In her line of work it was essential she stayed fit.

At 8 p.m. a very different-looking Monika took the lift down to the basement garage and walked through the automatic opening doors, unseen by the porter at the lodge. He could have spotted her on the closed-circuit television, which the owners of the freehold had installed just last year, but for some reason the camera in the garage area was forever being broken, and now no one bothered with it anymore. It was just as well. She was wearing a tight black skirt, which fitted like a glove. It was short but not ridiculously so; Monika had very shapely legs and the pencil slim skirt did them justice. The blouse she was wearing was open necked, showing just enough cleavage to be interesting, while a thin, gold chain with a delightfully small gold cross swung tantalisingly between her breasts. Her Ferragamo handbag and matching shoes, which would have seemed familiar to the now deceased president of OPEC as he'd bought them, were as elegant as the rest of her appearance.

Monika walked round the back of the flats and entered the rear door of another block a hundred yards away, to which she had a key. She left that block by the front door for all the world as though she lived there, which she certainly didn't, but the Pakistani chauffeur of the stretch limousine parked outside waiting for her didn't know that.

The limousine dropped Monika at the Ambassador Club, a very respectable gentleman's club in the heart of London's West End. This was a members-only gaming establishment, but she doubted she would be going to the gambling floor tonight. The Club boasted an excellent bar, where the tall, slim hostesses, with their floor length skirts, slit almost to the thigh, were on hand to serve drinks and delight the eyes of the gentlemen guests, and one of the best restaurants to be found anywhere in London. Her companion for the evening was waiting by the Club's inconspicuous front door. He stayed back as the liveried doorman opened the car door for Monika, positioning himself strategically to get the first glimpse of the legs, which he'd been assured were well worth visiting London for. He wasn't disappointed.

His Excellency Abdullah Qahtani, the thirty-nine year old Saudi Arabian deputy minister of defence, looked at his very best tonight. He was unusually tall for an Arab, and he made a fetish of always keeping in good shape. The extremely expensive Italian suit he wore had been tailored to perfection. Back home in Riyadh he always wore a traditional thawb, whereas when he was outside his own country he preferred to dress less conspicuously, but just as immaculately, in Western-style clothes. Monika offered her right hand in greeting, which he held for the briefest second in his own, then raised it ever so slightly as he simultaneously inclined his head downwards and very gently allowed his lips to brush her delicate skin, murmuring "*Enchante Madame*," as he did so. This was the first time Monika had met the minister, and while she was accustomed to always being treated very well by her dates, it was rare they were so perfectly gentlemanly. This was going to be an interesting evening.

The Saudi minister led the way through the swing doors to where the head concierge and the female cloakroom attendant were waiting to welcome their guests. As this was a gaming club, it was the law all guests had to be signed in, which presumably had already happened, albeit illegally, because Monika was ushered past the official and straight through to the bar. Dressed as she was, Monika certainly did not have any items of clothing to leave at the cloakroom. One of the Thai looking hostesses politely guided the couple to the seats, which had been reserved for them in the corner, discretely hidden behind the door so as not to be seen by new arrivals. The Saudi Minister was obviously well known here.

"What would you like for an aperitif, my dear?"

Those were the first words she'd heard him speak, other than the murmured greeting at the door, so she was surprised by the gentleness of his voice. Most of her other contacts from the Middle East, when speaking in English, spoke rather more gruffly, finding difficulty in losing the guttural sounds common in spoken Arabic, but not this man.

"A kir royal would be very nice, if that is not too much trouble, Your Excellency," Monika replied, doing her best to look sexy and sound demur at the same time, which was not easy. Her legs were crossed, the tight black skirt riding about eight inches above her knees, a pose which attracts looks but leaves a lot to the imagination.

The Arab snapped his fingers and a hostess glided across to their corner. It was no exaggeration to say she was a very beautiful girl.

"A kir royal for my guest and a large whisky and soda with just a little ice for me, please. Make it a Black Label."

With that formality done, Saudi Arabian Deputy Minister of Defence Abdullah Qahtani settled back in the armchair, opposite the settee on which Monika was sitting.

"My dear, can we drop the formality, please? It feels so unnatural sitting here, in such an intimate surrounding, to act as strangers. Please call me by my first name, Abdullah, or, if you prefer, by the nickname some of my European friends choose to use, Dandy.

Dandy is a nickname which suits him quite well, Monika thought. *He looks like a man about town, quite trendy, and with the olive-coloured skin he is certainly handsome. A good catch*, she thought.

"My name is Monika. I think you know that already; I don't have a nickname I'm afraid."

She even sounded apologetic.

"Then I shall think of one for you before the night is out," was his quick retort, "but to more serious matters. We have a guest coming for dinner with us tonight; his name is George Hamlyn, and he is the British minister of defence. It is a confidential meeting, and he will be very nervous to see you here. I will explain to him that you are German – I know he speaks a little of that language – and that you don't speak or understand even one word of English. I speak German myself, so we can all say a few words in that language in the beginning, then he and I will switch to English, and you must look as though you don't understand anything. You must look bored. At some point I will ask to be excused to go to the bathroom. If you chance to gently flirt with him while I was away, that would put him really at ease, which would be helpful to me. Now that is understood, how was your flight from Germany?"

"I like the name Dandy; it suits you very well," Monika told him. "As for my journey here today, my home is in Vienna, which is where my plane left from this morning. I don't have a problem to do as you asked, but if I get so bored that I go to sleep, can I rely on you to touch me under the table to wake me up?" Monika's look at her companion was more than mischievous.

"I think I'll remember to do that my dear, but maybe a rehearsal is called for."

As he spoke, he leaned forward in his arm chair and cuffed his right hand softly behind her neck, pulling her head slightly forward and giving her a delicate kiss on her left cheek, simultaneously moving his left hand up from her knee and under the hem of her skirt, her crossed legs stopping any further progress. He resumed his seat with a satisfied smirk on his slightly flushed face.

"Vienna is such a lovely city. Do you live alone?"

"Oh no, I share a flat with my mother. She's such a wonderful lady but very possessive of her only daughter, even though I'm twenty-eight years old. She hates it when I stay out all night, and if she knew I was in London, she'd really freak out."

Monika had used that line before. It wasn't true, but it always paid dividends.

"Then you must allow me to give you a little gift for her when we get back to my hotel," the Arab said. "It wouldn't do for her to think I don't appreciate her sacrifice in sharing you with me for just one night."

Monika nodded her head in agreement. It was difficult not to be impressed with this guy; he'd just killed three birds with one stone. There was now no question she would go with him to his hotel, and to his room, and to stay the night. The gift she knew would be a ladies' gold Rolex watch; his kind usually had half a dozen or more stashed away in the draw next to the bed where they kept their clean socks, though why there, she didn't know. She saw Dandy stiffen slightly as he looked towards the door. A man was being escorted to them – mid-fifties perhaps, balding, heavy rimmed glasses, florid complexion, grey-flannel suit, scuffed shoes – as different from her companion as it was possible to be! All this Monika took in as he was approaching them, led by the head concierge.

"George," the Saudi spoke to his British opposite number, "thank you for taking the time to see me. Thank you very much for coming. May I introduce my assistant, Monika Wolff from Germany. Unfortunately, she neither speaks nor understands a word of English, but perhaps under the circumstances of our meeting today, that is just as well. What she doesn't know, she can't repeat, hey?"

The British minister seemed at least a bit mollified by the words of his Saudi host. He addressed a few words to Monika in English, which got no reaction from her at all. Then he switched to speaking in German, and she immediately looked at him with a grateful smile, pleased at least one of them was paying attention to her. She replied back at some length in that language.

The steward from the dining room was hovering with the menus and the wine list, which broke the ice very well, particularly when Monika asked in her own language whether they had a menu printed in German. The steward seemed to understand and replied in the negative. This gave the British Minister the opportunity to offer his services, an offer she readily accepted. Perhaps it hadn't been necessary for him to have moved so close to her while he was doing the translation, but Dandy wasn't paying attention, or so George thought, and so he got away with it.

The Saudi took the lead, ordering the same food for each of his guests, having first ascertained what either of them didn't like, which perhaps gave them the first inkling of their host's arrogance. However, once in the dining room they certainly couldn't complain; the foie gras for starters was of the very best, followed by poached salmon for the main course, accompanied by a garnishing of salad and boiled potatoes, beautifully presented. It was at this point Dandy had made his excuses, allegedly to go to the bathroom, and was away for about five minutes. The waiters had seen his signal and gave the instruction to the kitchen to hold the dessert course until he returned.

George had used that opportunity to get to know Monika better, his spoken German more than acceptable. She gaily accepted his generous compliments and his card which had his private mobile telephone number. He said she could use his number any time she felt like talking with him, which he hoped would be tomorrow after the Saudi had gone home. By the time Dandy returned, clutching a briefcase his Pakistani driver had brought to him in the toilets, George and Monika were old friends.

The dessert, a thin slice of apple pie, correctly served cold on such a warm evening, and with the chef's special concoction sauce, which contained a liberal helping of calvados, was a wonderful conclusion to an excellent meal. Added to that the wine, and here the Saudi had at least given the British minister the choice of having red or white, was a very good Chablis, of which neither Dandy or Monika had any, and George finished the bottle, which no doubt had helped give him the courage to flirt with Monika the way that he had. It was fairly widely known in some circles that the British minister of defence had a great liking for expensive wines, and expensive girls.

"Dandy," the British minister of defence said to his Saudi colleague, "it's time we got down to business. I have to attend an urgent intelligence briefing at the Ministry of Defence later tonight; something to do with the suicide of the OPEC president. It seems there's been an unexpected development, and George Riles is hot on it."

Abdullah Qahtani didn't know the president of OPEC, and he didn't know he was dead, so it would have been extremely difficult for him to have explained how come a certain suicide letter, which even now was in the hands of the most powerful politician in the world, had been addressed to him. Monika had to fake a very delicate cough and cover her mouth with her hand as she did so, in order to hide the smile on her face. If only her two companions at the dinner table knew what she knew, in fact what she'd done, they wouldn't be looking so smug!

"The prime minister will be there, so I'll use the opportunity to break the news of the sales agreement we've reached. Give him some good news for a change. My briefcase is with the Special Branch policemen outside; it'll take me a moment to get it."

The three of them stood up from the dinner table. George Hamlyn waddled off to find his protection officers, while Monika led the way back to the bar, giving Dandy the opportunity to pat her bottom as a measure of his appreciation.

When they returned to the bar all the other guests had gone, which was very helpful – the discussion the two ministers was about to have needed to be discrete. They took the same seats as before, which placed George Hamlyn right next to his Saudi counterpart, and diagonally opposite Monika. She'd neglected to cross her very shapely legs this time, a sight which made the Saudi smile, and the Englishman stare. Abdullah Qahtani had opened his briefcase and removed a rather bulky document, which he placed on the coffee table. George Hamlyn did precisely the same thing; his document was a duplicate of the one which Qahtani had produced.

"George, in the end I decided to overrule my military colleagues back home. They much preferred the American tank, but I've decided we'll have the good old British one, even though the armour isn't quite so protective of the occupants and the range of the shells rather less. I don't like the idea of buying so much military equipment from just one source, it makes me feel uncomfortable. The Americans got the order for the new ground-to-air-missile system and the new AWACs, so they've done rather well. I'm worried they've been known to sell armaments to an overseas buyer and then refuse to sell the necessary spare parts I don't want us to be caught like that."

With that, the Saudi Arabian deputy minister of defence reached into the inside pocket of his Armani suit and withdrew the most exquisite gold fountain pen either of his companions had ever seen. As he unscrewed the top, he couldn't help seeing that Hamlyn's eyes had left Monika's shapely legs and were riveted on the Saudi's action. The Englishman had been negotiating this sales contract for many months and to have it signed was a real feather in the cap of his political career.

The British minister aped the actions of his counterpart, although neither his suit nor the ball-point pen quite matched the sophistication of the Saudi.

"Dandy, this is a very important day for both our countries."

As he spoke, the Englishman had opened his copy of the

document to the appropriate page and was signing his name. The Saudi meanwhile was desperately hoping he wasn't about to lapse into one of his long and boring political statements, which would be about as relevant and as sincere as the contents of the British minister's briefcase, which was resting under the coffee table.

"The 150 tanks covered by this agreement open a new chapter in the relationship between our two countries," said the Englishman.

By this time the Saudi regretted being so generous with the bottle of wine during dinner – this speech could go on all night! It was almost as though Monika had read his thoughts; she chose that precise moment to drop the napkin she was holding to the floor, and as she bent down to retrieve it, she allowed the British minister of defence a view of her breasts he would remember for a long time. Whatever he was about to say was forgotten.

George Hamlyn rose from his chair; he had to be going. He picked up the document that his Saudi counterpart had signed and put it in his government-issue briefcase, which he then closed. He held out his hand to Monika, to which she responded from the sitting position. He did his best to give her a meaningful look, a reminder of the offer he'd made while Dandy was at the bathroom. She gave him a wide smile in return; he could be hopeful! He turned to the Saudi, who'd remained seated, and offered his hand, but the Saudi instead patted the Englishman's chair, and reminded him their business wasn't quite finished.

"Oops, careless of me old chap. I almost forgot."

The British minister was rather hoping that in fact it had been his host who'd forgotten, which was about as likely as the moon being made of cheese! George Hamlyn reopened his briefcase and took out two large, oblong shaped packages, heavily sealed with scotch tape and stamped with the mark of the British Treasury. As he did this he was nervously looking around the room, but there was no one else there to see what he was doing, other than the Saudi, who already knew about it, and Monika, who hadn't known anything, but for sure she did now.

Monika Wolff, Dame of the Order of St John of Jerusalem, was now certain she would use that calling card the Englishman had given her, and was equally certain it would not be for his pleasure.

"All counted and correct, exactly as ordered, dear sir!"

He'd tried to sound amusingly casual, but it was very difficult to be casual when you were a government minister and you were paying a million pound bribe, in cash, in return for the signature from that exquisite fountain pen.

"The prime minister was very impressed that you will be using the money to set up a foundation for the underprivileged children in Africa," he said but didn't go on to add that the prime minister had wondered why it had to be given in cash.

Abdullah Qahtani took the two packages and placed them in his non-government issue briefcase. He held out his right hand to the Englishman and wished him a safe journey back to his office on Whitehall. He watched as the British official waddled towards the door where his two minders were standing waiting for him. As he passed the concierge's desk, the minister of defence heard Monika's sweet voice calling after him; he stopped in his tracks and turned. She was hastening towards him, her long strides causing the skirt to ride a little higher than it would normally. The two Special Branch officers looked at each other, eyebrows raised; they knew something of their Minister's reputation, and if this was an example of it, he was a very lucky man.

"Minister," Monika almost whispered, "my employer asked me to give you this, a memento of the excellent deal you made today."

With that she handed him the exquisite gold fountain pen, and as she did so she held his right arm and planted a slight kiss on his left cheek. The two Special Branch officers smirked at each other as they held the door open for their boss. Outside, the minister's chauffeur was waiting by the front passenger door of the Jaguar. The minister preferred to sit in front, reminding the people who'd voted for him that he still belonged to the working class, while the Special Branch officers climbed into the back seats; they were accustomed to the political idiosyncrasies of government ministers from whichever side of the House.

It was as the car was going round Leicester Square that George Hamlyn realised sweet Monika had said those last words in impeccable English.

While Monika was giving the fountain pen to George Hamlyn,

her host was busy settling the bill for dinner. The amount was Five hundred and seventy pounds, six hundred and fifty if you included the tip, plus another fifty for the beautiful bar hostess. He wasn't carrying that much cash – except in his briefcase. With the hostess looking on in total wonderment, Abdullah ripped open one of the packages, and peeled off fourteen fifty-pound notes.

"Keep one for yourself, and give the rest to the maître d'," he instructed, "and perhaps you'd be kind enough to write your home telephone number on the back of the receipt."

Monika was standing by the concierge desk when Qahtani came out from the bar, briefcase in one hand and putting a piece of paper, the receipt for his payment, into his trouser pocket. The name and telephone number written on the back of the receipt would be entered into his private diary, ready for the next time he was in London. One way and another, this had been a most successful evening, and it certainly wasn't over yet. He wasn't to know, but at that very moment an ocean away, his brother-in-law was climbing into his waiting ambassadorial car to be driven to Dulles International Airport for an overnight flight to London Heathrow just to see him.

Monika and the Saudi left the Ambassador Club together, the briefcase now held firmly in the hand of the Pakistani chauffeur who'd been waiting by the main entrance to the Club, talking with the doorman. Abdullah held the car door open for Monika to slide in – no way was he going to let his chauffeur have the privilege of seeing those lovely legs, and Monika didn't disappoint him. It was dark by now, and the traffic very busy, building up for another long Saturday night in London's playground. The journey to the Hilton Hotel would take only a few minutes, so Monika had to act fast, or the night was going to last a lot longer than she wanted it to.

As the car pulled away from the Club Monika turned to Abdullah, kissing him full on the lips. The Pakistani chauffeur, looking in his interior mirror, which he kept trained especially so he could see what his boss was doing in the back, could only stare as he saw his boss's right hand drop down below the level of Monika's face.

Lucky Arab, he thought to himself; he knew where that hand was going! Fortunately, Abdullah had two hands, and his other one was in use at that moment to press the button that closed the partition between the front and rear seats.

After what she judged to be a suitable interval and before her host got too involved in what he was attempting to do, Monika started giggling and pulled away from him.

"Dandy, I don't know what was in the packages the Englishman gave you, but it seemed to please you, and that's what matters to me. Why don't you pour us both a glass of champagne?"

On the journey from Kensington earlier she'd explored the drinks cabinet mounted in the back of the front passenger seat, so she knew it contained a bottle of champagne, Dom Perignon of course, and it was already on ice.

The Saudi reluctantly sat upright and did as Monika had asked. He opened the window to pop the cork; it hit a London black cab which was next to them at the traffic lights. No one took any notice; this was London at night! While he was opening the champagne, Monika had taken a small sachet from her bag and emptied the contents, a white powder, into one of the champagne flutes. Abdullah didn't see the powder; it was only a small amount, and the inside of the car was very dark and he had other things on his mind. He poured champagne for both of them, spilling some as he did so, and cursing his Pakistani driver loudly, though that was a bit unfair, it wasn't his fault the lights had turned to green, and anyway the driver couldn't have heard, not with the dividing partition closed.

Monika passed the doped champagne flute to the Saudi, holding her own glass steady as the car accelerated away from the traffic lights. He raised his glass to hers, to propose a toast.

"How does a million pounds sound to you, my lovely Monika? It would have been worthwhile coming to London just for that, but to have you as well, that is, as the English say, the icing on the cake. It's not difficult to understand why I feel so very satisfied with life."

With that, Dandy and Monika touched glasses, and each drank the full contents in one go.

The parking area in front of the Hilton Hotel on London's Park Lane is busy at any time, but never more so than on a Saturday night. Their limousine had difficulty edging into a parking place, and Qahtani was becoming agitated. He spoke into the microphone which connected the passengers in the rear seats with the driver.

"Stop the car. We'll get out here."

There were more stretch limousines in this parking area than in the rest of Europe; that was how bad it looked. Qahtani pushed his door open, and had one foot on the ground while the car was still moving. He was crazy. Then he was half way between the car and the hotel; this was something like being in no-man's land in World War I, on one side was the hassle and aggression of a busy city, on the other was the calm tranquillity of a five-star hotel. He almost dropped the briefcase he was carrying; it seemed to be getting heavier. That was when he remembered Monika; if he didn't go and get her she'd probably disappear, or spend all night sulking. He'd get nothing from her; he had to go back. In fact, Monika was already out of the car, running to catch up with the Saudi. She didn't want anything to happen to him out here. She was wondering about the briefcase.

She'd never seen a million pounds before; would she be strong enough to carry it?

The night air was cool, but Qahtani was sweating – unusual for him, but he was too angry to notice. He was a bit dizzy too, a touch out of focus, but he didn't notice that either. He wanted Monika, and he wanted her *now*. Monika recognised the signs; the powder was working, sooner than she expected. He'd drunk just one whisky before dinner and a glass of champagne in the car. She had to get him to his room quickly. She met him half way across the car park.

A black Rolls Royce, aerials protruding from its roof, flashed its lights, telling her to get out of the way, or was it telling her something else? Monika ignored it, Qahtani was her target, and she mustn't fail. She took him by the hand, pulling him towards the hotel's revolving door. His chauffeur had realised something was wrong; he'd abandoned the limo and come to help. She didn't need that.

"Fuck off," she told him, leaving absolutely no room for debate.

She got Qahtani to the revolving door, but he was staggering and a porter was coming across to help.

Good idea; he could be useful.

Between them they got the Saudi Arabian deputy minister of defence through the revolving doors, and into a lift.

"Which floor?" asked the porter?

Monika didn't know. She felt in the Saudi's trouser pocket for a key, found it, and gave it to the porter. He pushed a floor button, and they were on their way.

The Saudi was being sick all over his very expensive Italian suit. The floor of the lift was covered with his vomit, Monika's shoes were treading in it, and it was stinking. They reached the ninth floor, the door opened, and they were moving again. The Saudi's suite was at the end of the corridor, which seemed to stretch for miles, but finally they were there. The porter unlocked the door, and they were inside. Monika thanked him, she could manage on her own now – she'd just put him to bed; he'd be OK, perhaps a headache in the morning. The porter laughed; he'd been around a long time, and he knew the way these things worked.

Monika dropped the briefcase on the floor. At least she'd learned one thing: a million pounds wasn't too heavy for her to carry. She dragged the Saudi to the bedroom, letting him fall onto the king-size bed, a place where he'd eagerly anticipated such high hopes for that night's entertainment.

Forget it – no chance!

He was asleep by now or maybe unconscious. She took off his shoes, struggled with the jacket of his Armani suit, undid his tie, and would have left him like that but for the thin wire she saw running down the inside of his shirt. The vomit was all over her hands and the smell was overpowering, but she had to continue. She traced the wire to the belt of his trousers and found the small tape recorder.

The cunning bastard, she thought, *He'd recorded the meeting with the British Minister; the Grand Master would be pleased to have that!*

Monika went into the bathroom. She washed the vomit off her hands, and some had splashed onto her clothes, which she did her best to sponge off.

She was about to close the bedroom door behind her when she remembered something. Something she'd forgotten; something she'd been promised. She went back. Qahtani was lying on his back, snoring loudly with vomit trickling from the corner of his mouth and staining the beautifully white sheets. She opened a drawer by the side of his bed, the one which contained his socks, and also the gold Rolex watches. He'd promised one for her mother; it was important to keep your promises. She left the other five watches where they were; the cleaners would deserve a reward for the work they'd have to do before another guest could use that bedroom!

Once back in the lounge, the recorder went into her handbag, from which she withdrew and put on a pair of thin surgical gloves. She took an envelope from the bag, and removed the contents, four sheets of closely typed paper, which she unfolded and put into the Saudi's briefcase, next to the contract for the delivery of 150 British tanks. She removed the two oblong packages the British Minister had handed over, noticing as she did so that one of them had already been opened.

I wonder when that happened, she thought to herself.

Monika returned to the bedroom, still wearing the surgical gloves and did her best to remove all possible traces of her presence. She repeated the process in the bathroom and then in the sitting room. For the rest, it was impossible to hide the fact that someone had been there, but she was unknown in the hotel, she was one of many hundreds of people coming and going, the chances of her being traced were very remote, and anyway why would anyone try. An autopsy, required by law in the UK in the event of unexpected death, would reveal that Abdullah Qahtani had experienced a massive heart attack and died. His death would be due to natural causes.

Now her work was done; time to get out of there and let the powder finish the job, but she had a problem. The two packages were too bulky to fit into her handbag, and she could hardly take his briefcase. It would have been too obvious; a tart, for that is what the porter would have described her to his colleagues and eventually to the police, getting her Arab boyfriend too drunk to be able to stand and then running off with his briefcase. That wouldn't do, far too obvious. She put the two money packages and her mother's new watch into a Hilton Hotel plastic laundry bag. No one would question that, it happened all the time; young ladies coming to swish hotels with their rich boyfriends, providing the service that was demanded of them, and then being sent home, clutching their soiled underwear in a hotel laundry bag. One-million pounds was perhaps a bit excessive, especially since the poor man hadn't had his reward, but some you win, some you lose!

She left the suite, not bothering to display the privacy sign on the door, and took the lift back to the ground floor. She did her best to swagger slightly, as she thought a tart might do, clutching the laundry bag tightly in her right hand. She made for the revolving door; then she was through, unnoticed as far as she could tell.

A hand grabbed her shoulder as she took her first step on the pavement. Monika froze, undecided what she should do. People were thronging all around, all she had to do was scream and she would be safe, but that would attract attention, and she didn't want that. She turned round to see a tall man standing there, his hand now holding her arm, firmly; she couldn't run away. He had a finger to his lips, indicating she shouldn't make a noise.

He leaned towards her, whispering in her ear, "Majed Dajani – quickly, my car is over there."

He was pointing to a black Rolls Royce, which was double parked next to one of the stretch limousines, aerials protruding from its roof. A policeman was walking toward the car, notebook already in hand. Majed let go of Monika's arm and together they walked to the car, just in time to make the policeman's journey unnecessary. A chauffeur had jumped out of the car and held a rear door open for them. He was wearing a strange looking robe; anyway it looked strange to the policeman, but not to Monika, she had something similar, except hers wasn't brown, it was black with a very nice red lining, as were all the robes in the Austrian Priory of the Chivalric Order of St John of Jerusalem.

Dajani looked hard at Monika; he'd already decided he didn't like this girl, and now he was sure of it. She smelt awful.

Chapter Seven

The moment Nicholas opened the notebook it was as though an ominous presence had entered the room. My throat suddenly felt very dry. I curled my hands into a fist, and my body became tense. I was feeling aggressive; it was as though I was preparing to physically defend my son and me from whatever the book was about to reveal. Randy had been scratching at the door, wanting to be let out, but he too obviously felt something was wrong, and returned to sit by my side. A sheet of paper had fallen to the floor, and I bent to pick that up. It was a typed letter, on modern paper, and written in the English language. I read it slowly to myself. It was dated the first of January 1941 and was written at a place called Elbingerode in the Harz Mountains in Germany. As I was to learn later, what I had in my hand was a recent translation of the first page of the Russian language notebook that Nicholas was holding in his hand. This is the letter:

My dearest Son,

Germany is at war, conquering everything in its path. Every day the sky is darkened as squadrons of aeroplanes fly west, according to the wireless all taking their deadly load of bombs to England. If that country falls then the war in the west will be won, but what of the east? Will Mr Hitler take his war to our country? Will Mother Russia fall to him as easily as the rest of Europe? Mr Hitler has held talks with Cousin Wilhelm to discuss the possibility of restoring the German monarchy when the war is won, so maybe if he takes the war to Russia and wins, he will restore our Romanov family back to the Imperial Throne there too. We can hope so, but I have this terrible foreboding that disaster is not very far away. I fear for our safety.

Dearest Alexei, you are just four years old, and already you look so like your namesake, your uncle Alexei Nikolayevich. I cradled him in my arms as he lay dying in that dark forest in Siberia, bleeding to death after hitting his head on a tree as we fled from the house of death in Yekaterinburg. I buried him where he died. I, a Grand Duchess, daughter of the Tsar of all the Russia's, dug my brother's shallow grave using only my bare hands. I prayed that there he might have found the peace he never had while he was alive. You, my son, know nothing of the tragedies that have befallen our family. This book is for you that one day, if perhaps I am no longer with you, you can learn of the birthright that should have been yours. We must be patient and put our trust in God.

Your loving Mama,
Anastasia Nikolovna.

I truly do not know what I was expecting, but whatever it was, this wasn't it. I know where the Harz Mountains are, to the south west of Berlin. When I did my national service in Bielefeld we often had to arrange army convoys to Berlin to take supplies to our soldiers as well as to the French and American soldiers stationed there. At that time Berlin was still a divided city as a result of World War II, but it was in the Russian zone of occupation, and there were strict rules laid down governing allied access. We would drive to Hannover, and then turn east on the autobahn to a military checkpoint at Helmstedt, where the East German Grepo would inspect the convoy to see what we were carrying. The Grepo were like our military police, but capable of being brutal if the mood took them. There was always a Russian officer on duty with them, and we knew if we had problems with the Grepo he would sort it out; the Grepo always seemed afraid of the Russians. Anyway, once the convoy had been processed we were then allowed to continue down the east-west autobahn to Berlin, but under strict controls. We weren't allowed to leave the autobahn, and we were timed as far as Checkpoint Charlie in Berlin, which was where we came back into our own territory if you like. There weren't any signposts on the autobahn in those days, they'd all been removed during the war, and no-one had got round to putting them back, or perhaps they didn't want to. However, our maps were quite up to date, so we could see where the different autobahn exit roads led to. That's how I knew where Elbingerode was, but of course I'd never been there. It was in the Russian zone.

The writer of the letter was another matter. I remembered enough history to know that Anastasia was one of the children of the last Tsar of Russia, and I was quite sure I'd read the entire family had been wiped out one night during the Russian Revolution. Was my memory wrong, or was this some kind of trick? How could Grand Duchess Anastasia have written this letter in 1941, when she had been killed along with the rest of her family years before that?

Nicholas was staring at me, waiting for me to say something, but what could I say? What the hell did this have to do with me and with him too of course, and who was the child called Alexei she had addressed the letter to? A cold chill had run down my spine. Suddenly I knew where this was going; different things I'd learned in the past few days started to fit into place, like some kind of monstrous jigsaw puzzle. I was afraid, but I knew I mustn't let my fear get in the way of finding out the whole truth. It was surely time.

Nicholas was staring at me, the lines in his face accentuated by the lack of sleep.

How much does he know? I thought, and just as quickly changed that to *how much more does he know that I could still only guess at?*

"Dad, I was scanning through the book while you were reading the letter from Anastasia Nikolovna and saw the last entry covers the year 1918, the same year that the Russian imperial family were all murdered, or at any rate, that was what I'd always understood. I remember," he told me, "sitting with my mother watching a movie on television back home in the States. It was about a woman who claimed she was Anastasia. The movie was supposedly based on fact, but we all know what Hollywood is capable of. It was an entertaining film, but it meant nothing more, at least to me though Mother took it all very much more seriously, no doubt because of her own family history.

"I vaguely remember reading other things, about people claiming to be either the grand duchess or her brother Alexei; there was a woman who'd tried to commit suicide in Berlin by jumping off a bridge and who convinced many people she was Anastasia. She emigrated to America where she was feted by the Russian community, and there was a man in Vancouver who claimed to be Alexei, but their stories were eventually proved to be lies, and anyway to me it all seemed like some kind of romantic fiction, at least until now. In the letter you are holding, Anastasia, if it really is her, talked about how she and her brother had escaped from what she called 'the house of death'. Dad, maybe she didn't die that night!"

It took me some minutes to reflect on what he'd told me; my suspicious mind was in overdrive.

"So," I said, "what are we supposed to assume happened to her after she escaped from that house? Where was she in the years between 1918 and the year 1941 when she allegedly wrote the original of this letter I'm holding, and where did she gain this son called Alexei?"

It was this last part, the question about Alexei, which was frightening me.

"She surely carried on writing. It would have been totally illogical not to, and presumably it is in the pages missing from the notebook.?"

Nicholas clearly had no answer to that question; he looked almost embarrassed, as though somehow it was his fault, and for all I knew it could be.

"Dad, for the time being can I read this book to you, and the next time we see Sir James we can ask him about the rest?" .

"OK, Nicholas, let's put all that to one side, and as you said, concentrate on what we already have."

Nicholas started reading from the notebook, translating Anastasia's words as he went.

"When we were children our mother had always insisted that we each keep a diary; she made sure we wrote our daily happenings, so we would appreciate them more, and when we in our turn had children, the diaries would be important for them to understand what our lives had been like when we were their age. I doubt that even in our wildest nightmares we could have foreseen what would become of us, and nor would we have wanted to! Sadly, my diaries, and everything else I cared about were left behind that dreadful night in July 1918 when my brother Alexei and I fled from the house of death in Siberia. So this notebook is not my diary, but a recollection of my life until now.

"My patronymic name is Romanov. My father always referred to our family as a dynasty, something he assured us would continue forever, but sadly he was wrong about that, as he was about so many things, often through no fault of his own. Our dynasty had begun in 1613 when Mikhail Feodorovich was elected Sovereign of All Russia. My own father, Nikolai Alexandrovich Romanov, was born in 1868, of Tsar Alexander III and Tsarina Maria Fyodorovna. He was just twenty-eight years of age when he came to the throne when the untimely death of his father propelled him into something for which he'd been ill prepared. My mother, the Tsarina Alexandra Fedorovna, was German by birth. Her father was the Grand Duke Louis IV of Hesse, and her mother was Princess Alice, the third of the English Queen Victoria's nine children.

"Many unkind things were said about both my parents after they were murdered; they said that my father was weak and indecisive, that he lacked the experience to rule a country as vast as ours, and that he was dominated by my mother. Of her, it was said that she was the most hated person in all Russia. She spoke little of the Russian language. She seldom smiled, which I always found curious, as my grandmother's nickname for her was Sunny. She had a powerful influence over my father, but the main problem was her relationship with the Russian nobility. They disliked what they called her arrogance towards them. They were deeply suspicious of her relationship with the monk Rasputin, and she was German, which became an increasing problem when our two countries went to war with each other.

"Be all that as it may, they were wonderful parents – kind and loving and very generous, especially to all those obsequious courtiers who took every advantage in the good times and were nowhere to be found when things went bad!

"They were married in November 1894, and barely two years later my father was crowned Emperor and Autocrat of All Russia in the Uspensky Cathedral inside the walls of the Moscow Kremlin. My eldest sister Olga was already one year old by that time. My parents didn't even have time to get to know each other properly before the great burden of leadership was thrust on them, which I think contributed greatly to the problems which were to follow.

"The coronation itself turned into a tragedy. In Russia it is customary to celebrate a coronation by offering food and drink to the people, and this is what my parents did, to no less than seven-hundred-thousand ordinary Russian citizens. Tragically, a stampede happened – no one is sure why – and two-thousand people were crushed to death that afternoon in the Khodynskoe Field.

"To make matters worse, if that were possible, the following night was the Coronation Ball, which was to be attended by royal families and important dignitaries from all over Europe. My father always insisted he wanted to cancel the ball out of respect to those who had died, but those toady courtiers persuaded him rather than upset so many foreign dignitaries the ball should go ahead! To the ordinary Russian peasant this looked like my father didn't care about them, which wasn't true.

"I was born on 5 June 1901; that was by the Julian calendar, which was used in Russia until 1918, when the Bolshevik Government made the country change to the Gregorian calendar used by most of the rest of the world. I've since learned I was born into a life of privilege, but of course neither I, my brother Alexei, nor my three sisters appreciated that at the time. Nowadays, people like to compare the lifestyle of our hugely wealthy imperial family with that of the millions of poor peasants who lived in Russia at that time, but did it change when the Bolshevik's took power? Of course it didn't, except perhaps to worsen!"

Nicholas paused in his reading to take a drink of water from the glass by his side. It was maddening for me to know that my son already knew the contents of the notebook; as he'd told me; he'd stayed awake nearly all last night reading it, just to make sure he would do it justice when translating for my benefit today. I was floundering in the dark, wondering where this was leading and what the next page would reveal. Randy meantime had whined to be let out, no doubt bored by the unusual goings on in the cottage and wondering when we were going for our usual walk over the moors. That would have to wait.

Anastasia told us she was born at the Peterhof Palace on the shores of the Gulf of Finland, a favourite retreat for the Imperial family and one of several palaces which they called home. She particularly hated the Winter Palace on the banks of the Neva River in Saint Petersburg, telling us it was cold and draughty, and that it smelt musty. Their usual home was at the yellow and white Alexandra Palace in the Tsarskoe Selo, or Tsar's Village. The Tsar and Tsarina's rooms were on the ground floor, and the children's bedrooms, their classrooms, and rooms for the various ladies-in-waiting were upstairs. The village was about twenty kilometres from St Petersburg, to which they would travel on their private train.

Curiously, Anastasia went on to tell us that the four girls never had rooms of their own, they always shared just one bedroom between them wherever they happened to be, and the beds in which they slept, which she described as army cots, always travelled with them so they didn't have to get used to strange beds.

The Tsar was an enthusiastic hunter and loved to travel to the family estate in Spala, where he had a wooden hunting lodge. In the magnificent forests which surrounded the lodge was an enormous amount of game, like wild boar, deer, and even some brown bears. Anastasia described it as having small, dark rooms, and looked more like a country tavern than a royal residence; she complained that in the autumn, which was when they visited, it would often rain and be cold and damp. It clearly wasn't a favourite, particularly after Alexei had a near fatal accident there and the Tsarina refused to let any of the children go anymore. Spala is about a hundred kilometres south of Warsaw.

The family had a yacht called *Standart*, which they used for their summer cruises. Anastasia admitted that, even though she had a bit of a reputation as a tomboy, she had taken a huge fancy to one of the young crewmen called Mikhail and would flirt with him when no one was looking. She didn't say whether her fancies were returned. Interestingly, she mentioned one of the cruises in the summer of 1904 not in connection with flirting – she was barely three years old at that time. Her father had told her they'd anchored up for the evening at a place called Bjorko, and another yacht came alongside, which belonged to Kaiser Wilhelm II of Germany. It was ten years later that the reason for the apparently coincidental meeting came out. It had been privately requested by the German ruler, who wanted to discuss the possibility of Russia giving up some of its lands on the Baltic for the expansion of the German people. As Anastasia said in her own words, "this was to have a resonance with that of another German leader almost forty years later."

Nicholas carried on reading from Anastasia's book.

"Livadia was the clear favourite of all our palaces, although we referred to it as a villa. Father had this built himself, so he was particularly proud of it. It was beautifully white, sitting high on a cliff top overlooking the Black Sea in the Crimea. "Nearly every day we'd see a lovely blue sky, and the hot sun was a real blessing to us. We were much freer in Livadia; we didn't have so many of the irksome courtiers around us every hour of the day, and the ordinary people in the town seemed not to be curious about us, so we could wander around and even go shopping – unheard of in St Petersburg. Mother and father were much more relaxed here, and while they still had many official duties to attend to, they also had lots of time for us children.

"I remember particularly well the White Hall on the ground floor; this was where my oldest sister Olga had a ball to celebrate her sixteenth birthday. We younger children were only allowed to peep from the upstairs balcony; it was a wonderful sight which I will never forget. Olga really was the queen of the ball; she suddenly looked so mature and grown up, and the young men, most of whom were in military uniforms, were queuing up to dance with her. Was I jealous? Oh yes, we all were, even dear Alexei. I cried to Papa that night, and he promised me I would have an even grander ball on my sixteenth birthday. Sadly, that was a promise he wasn't allowed to keep.

"Outside the villa was an Italian courtyard – I can picture this as fresh in my mind as though it was only yesterday. It had tall white columns, enclosing a fountain ringed with palm trees and flowers. That was a wonderful playground for us young children. Later on that same night, Mama had come and tucked us into bed and told us to go to sleep, but that was impossible. I was so excited, picturing myself dressed in an exquisite ball gown, perhaps wearing a diamond-studded tiara – Olga didn't have one of those. Anyway, I looked out of the bedroom window, and I swear I saw Olga behind one of the columns, and one of the handsome Hussars was holding her hand. I bet Father didn't know about that!

"I have no memory of the times when the politics of Mother Russia started to turn badly. That was in 1905, when I was only four years old. Right at the start of the year the workers began to demonstrate against their living conditions. Papa talked a lot about this when we were old enough to understand, it had taken him completely by surprise. He honestly believed that the ordinary people in the towns and villages really loved him, and perhaps they did, but there were just a few militant people who were causing the trouble. Anyway, there was a day the Russian people call 'Bloody Sunday', which was when a huge crowd of workers had gathered outside the Winter Palace in St Petersburg. I have heard differing accounts of what happened that day, but mostly everyone seems to agree the demonstration was peaceful in the beginning.

"My father's special troops were on duty, mostly Cossacks who were intensely loyal to the imperial family. We girls really loved their ataman, or chief; when Mama wasn't around he would sit down with us in the nursery and tell us awful stories about what his soldiers did to their enemies. He had a huge moustache; he always boasted it was more luxurious than the German Kaiser's. I don't know if that was true, but he once told me he melted two candles every day to make the wax that he needed to make it gleam and turn up at the ends.

"Anyway, on that January day in 1905 one of the workers was standing on a box, talking to the crowd; he was a fanatic, and he was making the crowd become really angry. One of the officers, not a Cossack but a Hussar, ordered his men to arrest the speaker, otherwise he could see there would be trouble. The speaker didn't want to go with the soldiers, so they pulled him off the box, and stupidly one of the soldiers started kicking him. The crowd went crazy, attacking the soldiers, and the Hussar officer gave the order for his men to shoot over the heads of the people, to frighten them. That didn't work, so he told the soldiers to fire into the crowd. Hundreds of people were killed or injured that day, and that was the beginning of the end of the Romanov dynasty.

"That wasn't the end of the matter of course. By the start of that winter there was a general strike across the whole of Russia, and father knew he had to do something to calm things down. He was honestly trying to help the poor people to have better lives. You must remember he was the Autocrat of All Russia, that meant he was the absolute ruler, and he was always certain that God had given him that power so he could do his work. He promised the people a written constitution, something that would bring more power to the man in the street – democracy if you like.

"He created the Duma, or in fact recreated it, the original Duma having been discontinued by my illustrious forbear Peter the Great in 1711. The Duma still exists today, though not in the way Papa intended. Duma means 'to think', but perhaps there was too much thinking in those days! Anyway, in May 1906 and just before the first Duma was to take office, father made a paper called the Fundamental Laws, which elected people to positions of power in politics, but he retained to himself the right to appoint the government ministers and to fire them if they didn't do as he wanted, and to dissolve the Duma any time he wished.

"The political activists didn't agree with this at all. They felt it was not what they'd been promised, and they continued their protests. There were to be three more Dumas appointed while my father was the Tsar, each successively paving the way towards greater democracy. As I said, even to the end my father believed that God had given him the power to rule Russia, and personally, I don't think he was wrong. Of course most of the ministers he appointed were from the aristocracy and from the landowners and business people. These were people who had a much better idea how to do things than the ordinary peasant, but it didn't satisfy the militants, who were all from the working class; they wanted the power themselves. Anyway, in 1914 the Great War started, and while that put an end to the workers revolts, at least temporarily, it created many different problems."

I asked Nicholas to put the book down, to have a rest while I prepared lunch, which for me had always been a bit of a scratch meal taken as and when time permitted. Usually, I would be out on the moors during the daytime, so a packet of roughly cut sandwiches, which I would have prepared the night before, perhaps an apple or pear for dessert, and a bottle of beer would have sufficed, and that is what we had that day, though sitting in the conservatory. Randy for his part had given up on any thoughts of being taken for a walk so he was lying on the carpet in front of the fire in the sitting room; he was sulking!

Anastasia was speaking to us again.

"During the first year of the Great War things went well for our soldiers. They massed east of Warsaw and were pushing the Germans back, who were in full retreat. It was expected we would take Warsaw at any moment. I was working hard with my sisters, knitting scarves and socks to help keep the brave soldiers warm, and packing food parcels for them, always putting in little luxuries like bars of chocolate. We really felt as though we were doing our part to help Russia win the war.

"Then things started to go against us; once the winter ice and snow had melted away, the Germans were able to use their mechanised divisions to their full potential, and our soldiers were routed. It was said that one hundred thousand Russian soldiers died that spring in Poland, and we lost what we then called the Russian Kingdom. My father dismissed his cousin, who was in overall command of the Russian troops, and took control himself, travelling to the front to direct the war from there. I thought that was a very brave thing to do, and so in the beginning it seemed did the troops themselves, but by then it was probably too late. The morale of our soldiers was very low.

"Mother meanwhile had the impossible task of governing the country in his absence, and had to spend quite a lot of time in Moscow. We children were sometimes allowed to go with her; we stayed in the Kremlin where we had our own suite of rooms, which was very nice but we felt we didn't really belong there. St Petersburg was much better in every way, though in fact it had been renamed Petrograd when the war started, to try and lose some of the German influence. I think other countries fighting Germany were forced to do the same. The King of England, who was related to the German Kaiser, changed his family name from Saxe-Coburg-Gotha to Windsor to make the English people forget their royal family was more German than English, and poor Mama had that problem as well, but people wouldn't let her forget it. She wasn't welcome in Moscow at all. Everyone seemed to think she was still on Germany's side, and the decisions she made were in Germany's favour.

"Even more ridiculous were the rumours about her relationship with the monk Rasputin. The people were saying he was giving her advice about which ministers she should appoint and things like that, which was absolutely untrue. In fact, Mama believed Rasputin had mysterious powers that were able to bring healing to dear Alexei. He was born with a blood-clotting disease called haemophilia, and I know for a fact that Rasputin saved his life on more than one occasion and that was all that Rasputin did for us. Of course we all knew his reputation; he was supposed to have been a very heavy drinker and went around seducing many of the young girls who were sent to him for religious teaching. True or not, I don't know, and Mama seemed not to care, but others in the family became increasingly concerned about the damage he was doing to our reputation. One night in December 1916 my cousin Dimitri and a man called Felix Yussupov murdered him. If we believe the story, they first tried to poison him, then shoot him, and when all that failed they tied him up and threw him into the icy river! Anyway he died, but it was yet another black mark against the Romanovs, which wasn't at all fair.

"My sisters Olga and Tatiana even enrolled as nurses, and worked at the soldiers' hospital at Tsarskoe Selo, and Olga even had a nervous breakdown, that's how worried she was.

"The year 1917 was when things went really bad for us and for Russia. The Revolution was gaining strength, and the worse things were going in the war, the worse they went at home. By February the revolutionaries had taken control of Petrograd's government, and most of the troops had gone over to their side. They'd stormed the prisons and released all the prisoners – it was that bad. We were at

Alexandra Palace, and the Cossacks stayed to keep us safe. Then it seemed the army generals turned against Papa. The war was almost lost, and they needed to blame someone, so they blamed him. They wrote some strange letters to him, begging him to abdicate as tsar, and in March he did as they asked, he abdicated.

"In the beginning, he named my brother Alexei as tsar, but when a man called Prince Lvov, who was something to do with the provisional government at this time, told Papa that Alexei would have to live away from the rest of us, Mama refused. She knew that Alexei was too sick, and no one would look after him properly if she wasn't there. So then Papa named his own brother, the Grand Duke Mikael Alexandrovich, but he didn't want it. Then Prince Lvov formed the provisional government, but of course not calling himself the tsar. He couldn't do that; he was just a politician.

"After Papa abdicated he and Mama were placed under house arrest in the Alexandra Palace. When Mr Kerensky replaced Lvov at the head of the provisional government, he went to see my parents and told them it would just be for a few days in order to placate the crowds. He said as soon as we children were fit to travel – we all had measles just then – we would go to Murmansk, where a ship from the English Navy was already waiting to take us to England. I don't know if that was really true. Papa seemed to like Mr Kerensky, even though he had taken all our cars and horses and things, and he'd moved into the Winter Palace. As far as my sisters and I were concerned, he could have it!

"By the time my parents were placed under house arrest I was sixteen years old, the same age as when Olga had her ball in Livadia. What a difference this was! We were allowed to go for walks in the palace gardens, but always an officer was with us, and especially for Papa and Mama. In the beginning, my parents weren't even allowed to be together, except at meals times, and that was very hurtful. All the doors in the palace had to be kept permanently locked. Only the main door and the kitchen door could be used, and they always had a guard on them.

"I remember the Easter of 1917. This was the most important festival for the Russian Orthodox religion, what we called the 'celebration of all celebrations'. We weren't allowed to have the all-night vigil, which we'd always done in the past, but we did the Easter Kissings, an exchange of three kisses after which we'd say, 'Jesus Christ Resurrected', and you replied, 'Really Resurrected'. We then exchanged painted eggs, and each be given a piece of the Easter cake – kulich it was called – which had a cross on the top made from pastry. It was a very nice time, and Papa celebrated by giving all the staff little medals.

"We had lots of difficulties though. The soldiers became more and more rude every day, and the officers didn't dare do anything to stop them. Food and wine started to be rationed, and even wood for the fire became difficult to find. We weren't allowed to have any brought from outside, so we had to cut the trees ourselves in our own gardens. Papa became very good at cutting trees and also at breaking the ice on the river and shovelling the newly fallen snow off the pathways. Some of the soldiers stood and laughed at him while he was doing this, but Papa didn't get angry or anything, he said it wasn't their fault.

"For us children, some things continued as before. We still had our lessons every day; we could each speak German, French and English very well, and Russian of course. One of our tutors was from Switzerland, Pierre Gilliard. He was very formal, he wouldn't play jokes with us, but he was really loyal and stayed with us almost through to the end. Our doctor, Dr Botkin, was the same. He was always there when we needed him, and I'm sad to say he died with the rest of my family, but that was later on.

"We were kept in Alexandra Palace for five months. So much for Mr Kerensky's promise, but I think Papa didn't really want to go into exile in a foreign country anyway. He believed that if we ran away we'd never be allowed to come back, and he couldn't accept that. Anyway he was pushing Kerensky very hard to be allowed to live in our beautiful villa Livadia. We would all have been happy with that, but by this time the Bolsheviks were gaining more power and Kerensky was very careful not to do anything to annoy them. In July we were told to get ready to go, and even then they wouldn't say where they were sending us. Maybe they didn't know; maybe they couldn't all agree.

"I remember very clearly the thirty-first of July that year. After weeks of worrying about when and where they will send us, we were told to have our things ready that night. Dr Botkin overheard two of the officers from the Rifle Regiment saying we were going to Tobolsk. Apparently the soldiers from the Rifle Regiment were coming with us to act as guards during the journey, and then to stay with us in Tobolsk. The departure was shambolic to say the least. There weren't enough soldiers to carry all our luggage, and then when more came, they demanded extra money for their work. Our train was waiting about fifty meters away from the station, so we had to walk over the track to reach it and then unceremoniously push dear Mama up into the carriage, because there weren't any steps.

"Once on board though, things improved a lot. The carriages were from the French company Wagon Lits, easily recognizable from the outside by their distinctive blue paint with gold lettering and from the inside by their luxurious upholstery and curtains. In the restaurant car all the tables for our family and the senior people travelling with us were laid with exquisite crystal glassware and silver cutlery. Our sleeping car was equally comfortable, and for the first time we children had left our uncomfortable army cots behind and were able to use the lovely beds supplied by Wagon Lits.

"Our train finally left the station early the next morning. Some of the servants travelled on our train. People like father's valet, the chambermaids, the cook, and the wine steward had their own carriage at the back of the train. Then there was another one which had our paintings and rugs from the Alexandra Palace and the few bottles of wine remaining in our store there. A second train followed us, carrying the rest of the servants, and of course the soldiers who were our guards, more than three hundred of them.

"The journey was a bit like the old days. We didn't have to listen to the insults of the common soldiers. We were treated with respect by the staff on the train, but we had to promise to lower the window blinds when the train was standing at stations. At one point on the journey we left the train and boarded a river steamer; this was named the *Rus*, and it carried us up the Tura and Tobol Rivers to reach Tobolsk. All I can say is that we children enjoyed the whole journey, whereas our parents were fairly subdued, wondering what was in store for us when we arrived at our destination. I keep referring to my brother and sisters as children, but in reality by this time Olga was twenty-two years old, Tatiana was twenty-one (and for me she was the most beautiful of us girls), Maria was nineteen, and Alexei was fourteen. I was seventeen.

"I had never visited Tobolsk before, so I was interested to see what kind of city it was. In fact it was quite old. The very elaborate seventeenth-century stone fortress was particularly special because it contained some lovely churches and some very special buildings. The whole complex was in white and had been built high up on the bank of the river. Tobolsk was to be our home for the next eight months. We lived in a house which belonged to the former governor. No one told us what had happened to him, and we didn't want to ask, but I often wondered what he would have thought if he'd known that one day the Imperial Family would live there!

"Mostly we were confined to the house except for the few times we were allowed to go to a church, which was close to where we lived, and just once we prayed at the Cathedral of St Sophia, which was wonderful. The people of Tobolsk were genuinely nice to us; some of the older people would even bow if they saw us, but the soldiers didn't like that at all. Our lives were quite pleasant, even though it was a bit boring, at least until the end of that summer which was when a new commissioner was appointed to the city. He was a Bolshevik, and in no time at all he'd converted the soldiers to his way of thinking.

"Perhaps it wasn't too difficult to do; the whole country was in turmoil, the war was proving disastrous, food and drink were becoming scarce and very expensive, and everyone was suffering. Although it took some weeks before the news reached Tobolsk, things had come to a head in Petrograd that November. On the sixth of that month the cruiser *Aurora*, which was moored on the River Neva, and which I'd visited with Papa many times, fired just one shell, and that was the signal for the Bolsheviks to finally take the power they'd been threatening for so many months. The following day the Red Guards overthrew the Kerensky government, and the Bolsheviks had won!

"It sounds so simple when written in my notebook, but in reality there was so much suffering all over the country. Terrible atrocities were committed on all sides, and as always it was the simple peasants who suffered most, the very people the Revolution was supposed to help.

"That winter was very cold, even by the standards of Siberia, or so we were told. Fuel was difficult to find, more difficult for us because we weren't allowed to go outside foraging as the townspeople could, so we had to rely on our guards to help us, which they did very rarely. There was one soldier though who was to become very special to the whole family, and to me especially; his name was Mikhail, or Mika as I called him when no-one could hear me. He originally came from Irkutsk, which is in Russia's Far East. He'd been one of the sailors working on the Royal Yacht *Standart* when we had our annual summer cruises; his passion for being on the water came from living close to Lake Baikal when he was growing up. I mentioned him earlier; I used to flirt with him, which was very unfair because he wasn't allowed to even speak to me unless I gave him permission. Anyway, when no one was looking he'd bring in some firewood for us and do some errands when we asked.

"That winter passed in some sort of haze, and everything seemed unreal somehow. We knew we couldn't stay in Tobolsk forever, the soldiers guarding us all wanted to go back to Petrograd where their families lived. The Bolshevik government was making new laws, but by the time they reached far-away towns like Tobolsk in Siberia they'd probably been changed again. No one felt they belonged there.

"Toward the end of April the Bolshevik government sent yet another new commissioner to Tobolsk, with the responsibility to move us somewhere else. He told us the new government had been forced to sign a peace treaty with the Germans at a place called Brest-Litov, because almost the entire army had deserted! That finished Russia's involvement in the Great War. It seemed that Mr Lenin wanted Russia out of the war at any price so he could concentrate on building the Bolshevik political movement, and he got his way. He was having problems in the Crimea where the White Army was in control and also in the Far East where the Czech Legion was on the rampage.

"It seems the deal he made with the Germans was to give them the land in the Baltic States they wanted for the German people, and in return the Germans stopped fighting in Russia. I remember particularly well father's reaction to this news: he was shocked. I've already mentioned that father had met with Kaiser Wilhelm – that was in Bjorko in 1904 when we were on our summer cruise – and in that meeting they'd actually agreed to this exchange of territory but pledged to keep it secret for the time being. Father told us he had no intention of ever giving them that land but was worried that if he had refused the Kaiser there would be a war between us, so he agreed but it was never implemented. This was a tragedy for Russia.

"The new commissioner was called Vassili Yakovlev. He told father we would be going to Moscow. We would much rather have gone to Livadia on the Crimea at a place called Yalta, but that was obviously out of the question while troops who were largely sympathetic to my father were still in control there, so Moscow was probably the next best. Whether we would be allowed to live in our old apartments in the Kremlin or not was another question, which Comrade Yakovlev couldn't answer. Anyway, he insisted his orders were that we had to leave straight away, but we had a problem. Alexei was very ill, far too ill to make a long journey. Mama wanted to stay behind with him while Papa went to Moscow, but Yakovlev said he couldn't agree to that, his orders were that the tsar and the tsarina must both leave Tobolsk, as there was too much sympathy for the imperial family in this region. Eventually, it was agreed that Mama and Papa would go and Maria as well, which they did on the twenty-sixth of April; the rest of us would stay until Alexei was better, and then we'd follow them.

"It was heart wrenching for all of us on that day. None of us knew when we would be reunited as a family, and Mama was particularly worried about leaving Alexei, even though the lovely Dr Botkin was staying to look after him. We heard later that the train taking them to Moscow was stopped by a local Bolshevik committee at a town called Yekaterinburg. A part of the Trans-Siberian railway line between there and Moscow was under the control of the Czech Brigade soldiers, and the Bolshevik were worried they would try and free my parents, which in truth they probably would.

"The Czech Brigade was a force of about thirty thousand men, mostly deserters or ex-prisoners of war from the Austro-Hungarian Army. They'd been fighting alongside the Russian Army in the

Great War, but now that Russia was no longer at war with Germany, they wanted to return to their own homes. We learned there had been an agreement with the Bolshevik government to let them pass through Vladivostok, but the Czech Brigade refused to surrender their weapons, so the agreement fell apart. The Brigade disarmed the soldiers in a town called Cheliabinsk, and very quickly took control of the Trans-Siberian Railway all the way from Lake Baikal to the Ural Mountains, presumably to try to use the railroad to get home. So my parents and Maria stayed in Yekaterinburg, and the rest of us arrived there on May twenty-third.

"Yekaterinburg was founded by my many times removed great grandfather, Peter the Great, and he named it after his wife Ekaterina. That was in 1723; he was planning the colonisation of the desolate wastelands of Siberia, and realised he needed a town, which could be the gateway and as a base for stores – somewhere for the explorers to gather.

"It is a cold, forbidding city, closed to the outside world. Peter the Great knew there was an abundance of coal and iron ore in Siberia, and of course the diamond and gold mines are now legendary. The house we stayed in was owned by a rich Jewish merchant called Nicholas Ipatiev. When the local Bolshevik committee had decided to keep the imperial family in their town they had simply ordered him and his family to leave, which must have been very difficult for them, but it was worse for us.

"We were not allowed to go out under any circumstances. A high, wooden fence had been built all around the house, right up to bedroom window level, so we couldn't see out and local people couldn't see in. The food they gave us wasn't fit even for the animals, but father made us eat and not complain. The soldiers guarding us were awful; they followed us everywhere, even to the bathroom. We had no privacy at all, but I have to say no one ever tried to touch us, which was something at least!

"The guard commander at the house was a rough man called Avdief, and he encouraged the soldiers to treat us badly. The soldiers were from the Rifle Regiment who'd been with us from Petrograd, and that included my friend Mika, but even he was being more careful not to be seen to be helpful to us. There was one terrible day when Alexei was being sick and Mama wanted some boiling water from the kitchen, so she asked Mika to get it for her. He went crazy, shouting and swearing at Mama, and then he even slapped her face, something even the worst of the soldiers had never done. Later that day, I asked him why he had changed, and he laughed at me and spat in my face! I really felt that my last friend had deserted me. It was so degrading.

"That happened just after a new commander came to replace Avdief. This man, Yakov Yurovsky, was the worst of them all, and he had brought ten other soldiers with him, all as bad as him. They hated us. We'd done nothing to them, and surely we were suffering enough. But they made our conditions even worse, and they enjoyed doing it. One of them came in to the room where I was sleeping one night and urinated on the floor, right in front of me. Mikhail seemed to get on with them very well; all of the other Rifle Regiment soldiers had left when the new team came, except for Mikhail, who was usually on guard at the door in the night.

"We stayed in that house for almost two months, until the seventeenth of July. About nine o'clock that night Mikhail put his head round the door of the sitting room, looked at Papa and beckoned him with his finger. He'd been behaving so badly to us, we thought he wanted to do something bad to Papa. Anyway Papa had no choice; he followed him into the tiny kitchen, and after a few minutes came back and sat down with us, whispering very quietly.

"Mikhail had overheard Yurovsky telling his men to be ready and that they had received authorisation from Moscow to do 'it' that night. Mikhail didn't know what they were talking about, but it sounded very bad. He told father he would help two of us to get away, but we had to be ready very quickly. Papa had already decided it would be Alexei who would go, and I would go with him because Mikhail obviously liked me very much, and that would make things easier.

"Mama didn't agree; even though Alexei wasn't ill just then, he could change in just a minute, and she wanted to go with him. I can honestly say that was the only time I ever saw my father be so strict with Mama. He told her he'd made up his mind; her place was by him, and if anything happened to the rest of the family, at least Alexei would be safe. Alexei was the Tsarevich!

"All of us had sewn jewels and gold nuggets into bits of our clothes when we were leaving Petrograd, just so we would always have something if we needed it. Papa now collected as much of this as he thought Alexei and I could hide, and he also gave me a small bag full of gold nuggets, which I had to give to Mikhail when we were safely away. Then we waited!

"It was eleven o'clock that night when Mikhail came to the room and told us we must leave immediately. The rest of the soldiers were in a meeting in one of the basement rooms, leaving him in his usual position on guard at the front door. We were all crying, even Papa though he was trying very hard not to show it, and hugging each other, not wanting to let go, but Mikhail grabbed hold of Alexei and me by the hand and pulled us to the door. We crept down the stairs. Mikhail stopped at the bottom of the stairs and turned his head to listen. Satisfied, he went straight to the door, opened it, and we ran as fast as we could, through the gate in the fence and out into the street.

"I was holding Alexei by the hand; we were running towards the trees, which were away at the back of the house. The path we were on was very muddy, and I nearly slipped several times. It took us only a few minutes to reach the trees, even though it seemed to last forever. As soon as we were safely in the trees, Mikhail stopped, to let us catch our breath, but then we heard a dog bark and he must have worried it was chasing us, so we started running again until we were a long way inside the taiga, the Siberian name for the large dark forests that cover this region.

"Soon both Alexei and I had to stop, whatever happened. We couldn't run any more, our legs were so tired, and we were gasping for breath. Mikhail was very nervous and kept looking around, as though he was worried someone would jump out from the trees and catch us. He whispered to me that he'd met a girl who lived not far away; she was the housekeeper in a dacha owned by a rich businessman who was staying in Moscow with his family, so the house was empty except for her. He was sure she would shelter us for a few days while we decided what to do, but he had to warn her first. He was going to see her, and would come back to fetch us. With that he was gone; we were alone in that dark forest, very frightened, and I felt betrayed!

"Why should it matter to me that Mikhail had a girlfriend, but somehow it did. We didn't know why he was helping us now, when he'd been so bad in the last few days. We didn't know if he would come back. Alexei started crying again, and said he was going back to the house where Mama would look after him, and he started to run back where we'd come from. I chased after him, softly calling his name, telling him to stop running, but the closer to him I got, the faster he seemed to run.

"It was so dark in that forest, and the trees so thick, with branches jutting out everywhere. Even over the top of my heavy breathing I heard the thud as Alexei's head hit the branch of a tree hanging over the path we were on. I saw him fall to the ground. I was with him in a second, but it was probably already too late. The blood was running from his forehead, all down his face. I think he was unconscious, but even so his hands seemed to be clawing at the wound, perhaps in an effort to stop the flow of blood; he seemed to be having a fit. I saw blood beginning to come from his mouth, then from his nose and ears, and then he lay still. I was cradling him in my arms. He was dying.

"In Petrograd I'd been taught some things about first aid in the military hospital where Olga and Tatiana had helped nurse the wounded soldiers, but that was no help to me now. The bleeding was so fierce I couldn't have stopped it with all the first-aid equipment in the world, and of course I had none. That night my brother Alexei died in my arms, I was all alone in a frightening world.

"We had only left that horrible house less than half an hour ago, and my Mama's words were still in my ears, 'Look after your brother, Anastasia, he is your responsibility now.' I had failed my mother; my brother was dead. I was seventeen years old, alone in this dark, frightening forest. My dead brother was in my arms, and I was covered in his blood, waiting and wondering if Mikhail would be coming back to me.

"After what seemed like hours, but maybe wasn't even ten minutes, I laid my brother's body down in the grass and started to dig in the ground, which had been made soft by the recent rain.

I, a grand duchess, daughter of the tsar of all the Russias, dug my brother's shallow grave using only my bare hands. As I dug I prayed that there he might find the peace he never had while he was alive. In all my life I'd never had to work as hard as I did that night, but finally it was done.

"I had to drag poor Alexei's still body to the grave. The rain had started to fall again as I kissed his forehead, at the place where the wound that had taken his life was open, and then I started to cover his body with the soil. As I did this I was frightened by a noise; Mika was standing next to me, staring at me, trying to understand what I was doing. I stood up and threw my arms around his neck and held him tightly; he had returned, he hadn't let me down, not as I had let my own brother down. I cried and cried, and I was still crying when I lay down with Mika, and I went to sleep.

"When I awoke it was to a different world. Above me, through the top of the tall trees, the summer sun was shining, the sky was a wonderful blue, and all around birds were singing, a chorus in harmony with the rest of nature. It took a few seconds for me to remember where I was, to remember how I'd failed my brother and betrayed the trust my parents had placed in me, but I was alive and I had to go on.

"I looked around to find Mika, and was shocked to see him kneeling by the side of Alexei's grave. He'd reopened it and was doing something to Alexei; his hands were feeling around inside his trousers. The feeling of horror swelled inside me, and bile was churning in my throat. I wanted to vomit. Oh my God, what was this man doing to my brother?

"I screamed at him, his first inkling that I was awake; I pulled his hands away, out of my poor dead brother's trousers. He was clutching some precious stones and a locket which I instantly recognized as one my Mother always wore. It was in the shape of a heart and made of gold with an enamel inlay. When it was opened it would reveal a picture of a very young baby, and on the opposite face were the initials 'N' and 'A' intertwined in gold letters, surrounded by diamond chips in the shape of a crown. My father had presented it to mother after Alexei was born, to thank her for giving him a male heir to the Russian throne. I'd never seen her without it, and didn't even know she'd given it to Alexei; of course it was his picture on the inside of the locket.

"'What are you doing?' I was hysterical. 'How can you do this?'

"Mikhail looked at me. He was angry, I could see that. He was still holding the precious stones and the locket.

"'These things have a value, Highness,' he said to me; 'Last night when I was with your father in the kitchen, he told me he would give you and Alexei all the jewels the family had, and I was to use them as I thought best. Your father understood we were going to need money if we were to survive the difficulties which lay in front of us. When you buried your brother last night, you were too distressed to think about practicalities. The jewels were secreted in his clothes. I promised your father I would take care of you both, and I would do my best to deliver you to a place of safety. I have failed your brother; I do not intend to fail you. Now help me make sure we have taken everything, and then let us cover him again, and leave him in peace.'"

Nicholas put down the notebook. The log fire was still burning brightly, warming us and Randy too; he was stretched full length, hogging it as he always tries to do. I went to the drinks cabinet, then looked across at my son, questioning. He nodded. At this rate I'd soon have to buy another bottle of whisky. I took the tumblers back to the fireside, where each of us quietly sipped the golden liquid, enjoying the temporary silence, each wrapped up in our own thoughts.

I was thinking about Anastasia, trying to imagine what it must have been like, seventeen years of age, all alone in that dark forest, on the run from the soldiers. Just hours earlier she, together with her young brother Alexei and Mikhail had fled from what she'd called "the house of death", leaving behind her parents, her sisters, dear old Dr Botkin, and the servants, all to an uncertain future, but was hers any better I wondered. She'd mentioned a dog; his name was Jim, and she'd described him as being her best friend. Anastasia told us he'd tried to leave the room with her and Alexei, but her father had held him back.

I remember how lonely and frightened I felt when I got on the train to London to do my national service. I was a bit older when that happened to me than Anastasia had been, and of course I wasn't in any danger, and once I'd arrived in the barracks I had lots of other young men for company, all in the same position as me, and even so I was scared. How much worse it must have been for her, brought up to a life of privilege, with servants to do her every bidding, to suddenly find herself alone with a man who just days earlier had abused her and her mother, a man who'd then gone off to see his girlfriend leaving her all alone. She was totally vulnerable, but of one thing I was now convinced – this had really happened. Terrible.

Nicholas had already told me Sir James Sinclair had promised to bring the missing pages the following day, and of course earlier I'd seen his Range Rover parked outside Rannoch Castle, so it was logical to assume that was where he was collecting it from, but why from there? What was that all about? Just another of the mysteries which have invaded my life these past few days!

I poked Randy in his belly with my foot.

"Come on, dog. Let's go for a walk. How about you, son?"

I was still wearing the heavy walking boots from earlier in the evening, so all I had to do was pull on an old anorak and deer stalking hat I keep in the cupboard by the front door, and I was ready. I turned on the conservatory outside light, giving us something to aim for on our return, and headed out across the rocky track. Nicholas soon caught me up, handing me my old walking stick as he did so. I suppose we walked for about two hours, each deep in thought, hardly talking at all.

We returned to the cottage, both of us very subdued, no doubt each wondering what shocking news the missing pages had in store for us, and of course, when would we get them. We didn't have long to wait.

Chapter Eight

The Saudi Arabian ambassador to the United States of America gave an involuntary nod of his head when he heard the landing wheels of the British Airways Boeing 747 click into place, almost as if he were signifying to the captain his approval of the flight. The cabin service director came over to check his seat in preparation for landing.

"I trust you've had a good night's sleep, Mr Ambassador."

Gordon Mountford was one of the most senior cabin crew in the airline; he knew exactly how to behave with the many types of people he had to serve, but few were as easy as this gentleman had been.

"Windsor Castle is underneath us right now," he continued. "King John rode from there in June 1215 on his way to Runnymede, where he'd been given little option by the barons but to sign the Magna Carta, the nearest thing we in the UK have to a Constitution. Have you visited there, Sir?"

Saeed Al Turki glanced out of the window and was rewarded with the magnificent view of Windsor Castle from the air, just as Monika had less than twenty-four hours earlier. Twice he'd been a guest of the royal family at Windsor, once at a formal dinner hosted by Her Majesty the Queen on the occasion of the state visit of the king of Saudi Arabia and the second time when he was coming to the end of his tour of duty as the Saudi ambassador to the UK. Prince Charles had given a private dinner in his honour. Saeed Al Turki had good reason to have pleasant memories of his time accredited as an ambassador to the Court of St James.

"No, it's something I keep meaning to do, but you know how it is; like you I'm continually travelling to exotic places on business but never find time to see them through the tourists eyes."

It had been easier to pass the question off that way than go into detailed explanations.

"Your stewardesses gave excellent service; you have a very good team."

In fact, they'd had little to do. The ambassador had taken his dinner in the British Airways lounge at Dulles before taking off, so once on board he'd only asked for a pot of tea, "served with milk please, exactly as you do in England, and perhaps you'd be good enough to do the same thing about half an hour before we land in the morning." Then, he'd changed into the pyjamas the airline offered in the first-class cabin, meaning his suit would still be in its usual pristine condition for arrival into London. He'd reclined his own bed and gone to sleep.

Unusually for the ambassador, he wasn't being met at Heathrow. He'd purposely not told anyone he was coming, because that would have alerted his brother-in-law, which he didn't want to happen. He wanted to surprise him and see his reaction when he demanded an explanation why he'd been linked to the suicide of the OPEC president, and what the Islamic Defence Force, which had been mentioned in the suicide letters, was all about. The ambassador had never heard of it before, and neither had His Majesty the King of Saudi Arabia when Al Turki had phoned him from Washington.

He took a black cab from Terminal Four direct to the Hilton Hotel on Park Lane. It wasn't his usual choice of hotel in London – he much preferred the Grosvenor – but he was only staying the one night, so he might as well be in the same hotel as his sister's husband. He'd personally telephoned the hotel from his car on the way back from his meeting with President Riles in the White House, so even his own staff wouldn't know he'd gone to London, except for his chauffeur of course, who'd been sworn to secrecy.

The journey from Heathrow took just half an hour; there was much to be said for arriving in London early on a Sunday morning, and the hotel check-in desk was empty of guests, so in less than an hour from leaving the comfort of seat 1A on the British Airways Boeing 747 he was standing in the shower of the suite in his hotel.

At the check-in desk he'd casually asked for the suite number of Abdullah Qahtani, and was a bit surprised when the receptionist had looked at him so strangely, as though it was an unusual request, but she'd given it to him and even given him a suite on the same floor.

Ambassador Al-Turki was just towelling himself off when he heard a knocking on his door, loud and insistent. Certainly, this would be room service, wanting to put a courtesy bowl of fruit or some flowers in his room; why couldn't they phone first? Grumbling to himself he put on the bathrobe hanging in the wardrobe, hastily pushed his hair into place as best he could, and opened the door. It wasn't room service. The man who stood there, unusually tall, balding, and running slightly to fat, didn't waste time apologising for disturbing the hotel guest.

"Ambassador Al-Turki, may I come in and have a word please?"

It didn't sound like a request, more like an order.

"Since you appear to know who I am, you might do me the courtesy of waiting until I've had a chance to dress and had some breakfast, and then by all means we can meet – say in one hour from now."

It was characteristic of Saeed Al-Turki always to be gentlemanly, the polite but stern look on his face masking his true inner feelings.

His visitor pushed his way through the door, speaking as he did so.

"My apologies for not introducing myself. I am Detective Chief Inspector Morgan of the Metropolitan Police. I would like to know what is your interest in the deceased gentleman."

Saeed was utterly thrown by the question. He stood aside to let the policeman come all the way into his suite, and pointed to the settee, silently inviting him to sit.

"What deceased gentleman are you referring to, Chief Inspector? I am here to visit His Excellency Abdullah Qahtani, the deputy minister of defence in my country; he also happens to be my brother-in-law, and he's staying in a suite further along this corridor."

Mr Morgan looked carefully at the ambassador, trying to decide if he was telling the truth, wondering if he might be about to claim diplomatic immunity and order him to leave the suite. He'd better tread very carefully with this one.

"Then you will not be aware, Sir, that your brother-in-law, as you refer to Mr Qahtani, is dead?"

Saeed Al-Turki had been shocked a few times in his life, but never like this.

"Dead! Abdullah is dead? Where? Show me. Quickly, man!"

The two men left the suite and walked to the very end of the corridor, to the suite rented by the late Abdullah Qahtani. The ambassador had declined the suggestion he should perhaps pull on a pair of trousers and a shirt; he was still wearing the bathrobe. A uniformed policeman was standing by the door of the suite; he looked quizzically at the chief inspector, wondering who his guest was, wearing a bathrobe of all things; he wasn't about to be enlightened, anyway not by his chief.

As they entered the sitting room Mr Morgan paused, looking at the ambassador.

"The person who rented this suite is in the bedroom, Sir. He's lying on the bed, partly clothed. So far as I am aware, he hasn't been touched. If you feel up to it, I would like to ask you to identify him for me, and then perhaps we can talk some more."

Al-Turki nodded his agreement, too numbed to speak. They entered the bedroom. The late Abdullah Qahtani was indeed lying on the bed, dressed as the policeman had described. Saeed however hadn't been prepared for the stench of vomit that greeted him, nor the awful sight of his now deceased brother-in-law, normally so elegantly dressed, and so personal in his hygiene. His suit jacket was lying on the floor, carelessly discarded when he'd fallen on the bed; his shirt was unbuttoned to the waist, the zip on his trousers undone; he was wearing just one shoe; the other was lying on the floor in the sitting room.

Vomit covered the lower half of his face, had spread onto his chest, and covered much of the otherwise pristine, white, bed sheets. It had congealed in unsightly lumps. Saeed Al-Turki looked away. It was a disgusting sight.

"Perhaps if you don't mind we could adjourn to your suite to continue our discussion. The SOCO people haven't arrived yet," the Chief Inspector suggested, and Al-Turki was only too pleased to agree – anything to escape from that awful scene.

SOCO, or scene of crime investigating officer to explain it in full, hadn't meant anything to him, and he wasn't even curious to know what it stood for. He had far weightier things on his mind, even weightier than the fact that his brother-in-law was dead.

How much did the policeman know, and how much should he tell him? Did Abdullah's death have anything to do with the suicide of the OPEC president or the Islamic Defence Force?

These questions and more rattled through the ambassador's brain, but he was calm now and he could think logically. Once back in his own suite he telephoned room service and ordered coffee for them both without even asking the chief inspector for his preference. While they were waiting, he disappeared into the bedroom and pulled on the trousers and shirt as the policeman had suggested a lifetime ago, taking the opportunity to work out how much, if anything, he would tell.

Chief Inspector Morgan had asked the ambassador if he'd identified the deceased person, and could he confirm it was his brother-in-law Abdullah Qahtani; of course, the ambassador had confirmed it. The chief inspector was of the opinion Abdullah had died from natural causes, but that would have to be confirmed by a doctor, who was already on his way, and in due course by the coroner. The police had arrived on the scene at, coincidentally, about the same time the ambassador's plane had landed at Heathrow; they'd been alerted by the deceased's chauffer who had a key to the suite. He'd tried telephoning the deputy minister, and when that hadn't worked he'd gone to the suite to remind his boss he had to leave for the airport to catch the 10.40 a.m. Saudia flight back to Riyadh.

The policeman seemed satisfied with Saeed's explanation that he'd come to London for a business meeting, unconnected with the deceased, and had merely looked in on him to suggest they had lunch together. He'd offered no objection when Saeed told him he had to return to Washington that same afternoon, accustomed as he was to dealing with diplomats and politicians flying all over the world at short notice, of course at taxpayers' expense; whether those taxpayers be Saudis, or British, or any other nationality, it was always the same! They drank their coffee, and the policeman offered his condolences,

Saeed said of course he'd inform the deceased's family and the Saudi Embassy here in London, and the policeman left.

The ambassador went into the bathroom to do his ablutions, and was luxuriating in a hot bath, which was where he always did his best thinking, when he heard a loud and urgent knocking at his door. In his haste to leave the bath and pull on the bathrobe yet again, he almost slipped on the black, marble tiled floor, recovering by grabbing the towel rail. A Pakistani man was standing at the door; he was dressed as a chauffeur might in dark suit, white shirt, and a smart peaked hat, which he removed when he saw the ambassador.

"Good morning, Sir. Do you remember me?" he asked.

The ambassador did indeed recognise Rafi Akhbar; he'd been his chauffeur on numerous occasions, both during his time at the London embassy and on his frequent visits to the English capital subsequently, but what on earth did he want on this morning of all mornings, and how did he know he was here?

"Yes, Mr Akhbar, I recognise you, and I'm very sorry but this is a dreadful morning, I've no time for you today."

This would be too much if all he wanted was to know whether he could be of service to him, and anyway what was the hotel doing, allowing these people to visit the floors?

Rafi was trying to push his way into the room, just as Chief Inspector Morgan had done minutes earlier. The ambassador recognised the man was agitated, acting quite unlike a chauffeur normally would.

"You'd better come in, but I hope it's important, man."

It was important. No sooner had Rafi entered the room than he presented to the ambassador the briefcase he'd been carrying. It was an exceptionally good quality briefcase, that much was obvious even before the ambassador took it from the chauffeur's outstretched hand.

"I was downstairs when you checked into the hotel this morning, Sir. That's how I knew you were here. I was Mr Qahtani's chauffeur; it was me who discovered his body this morning. I panicked, not sure what to do. I started shouting, and a cleaning lady came; I showed her the dead body, and she used the phone to call the manager. He called the police, and then told me to wait downstairs. As I was leaving the suite I saw this briefcase lying on the floor. I grabbed it when no one was looking and took it with me. I remember Mr Qahtani had it with him last night, and it seemed important. I didn't tell the police I'd taken it, and now I don't know what to do."

Saeed Al-Turki silently opened the briefcase. Inside he saw a sheaf of official-looking papers. He fingered them cautiously inside the briefcase, not wanting to remove them in full view of the chauffeur, but then had second thoughts; no doubt the man had already looked inside, it wasn't going to be a surprise for him. Ambassador Al Turki scanned the documents. One was an agreement for the supply of tanks for Saudi Arabia's Defence Force, an agreement that his brother-in-law had boasted to him about. The other papers referred to a meeting that had been held to discuss the formation of an Islamic Defence Force.

"I think you did the right thing, removing the briefcase, Mr Akhbar. This has nothing to do with the British police. Please don't say anything about it to anyone, and if you've nothing better to do, perhaps you'd wait downstairs for me. I'll need to return to Heathrow sometime this afternoon; would you be kind enough to drive me?"

Rafi Akhbar, chauffeur to many of the wealthy Arabs from the Gulf States, knew a good thing when he saw one. He'd be only too pleased to drive the ambassador to Heathrow, where no doubt he'd be well remunerated for all his services.

Saeed Al-Turki gave up on the bath; the water was probably too cold by now anyway. He sat down to examine the documents that had been inside his brother-in-law's briefcase. They confirmed his worst fears. Each page of the thinner document was stamped with the word "Secret" in large red letters. It was typed in English, which struck the Saudi as a bit odd; he wasn't to know that Monika's word processor back in Vienna didn't have an Arabic keyboard. It was headed "Islamic Defence Force", and in the opening paragraph referred to a secret meeting that had taken place in Sana'a, the capital of Yemen, on the fifteenth of May, just one month earlier.

The opening statement concerned the aim of the Islamic Defence Force: 'The first time since our historic victory against the crusaders at the Battle of Acre in 1297 that Islam will be able to defend itself without the help of soldiers from infidel countries.'

It went on to quote a saying from Imam Khomeini: 'We shall be ferocious and implacable against the infidel invaders, the heretics. Muslims will be united and merciful between themselves.'

Ambassador Saeed Al-Turki shuddered. What was his brother-in-law thinking of? Where did all this come from?

Why have I never seen any evidence of this in his behaviour in the past? he wondered.

One paragraph in the secret document referred to the imminent signing of a contract with the British government for the urgent delivery of one hundred and fifty tanks; they were ostensibly destined for the Saudi Army, but fifty would be immediately deployed to the border Saudi Arabia shared with Yemen, where they could conveniently disappear across that border and be used to protect the entrance to the Red Sea.

Protect the entrance to the Red Sea – from whom? Saeed Al-Turki said to himself. *This is more than madness.*

Another paragraph referred to the order for a new ground-to-air missile system, which the Saudi Arabian deputy minister of defence had ordered from the United States on behalf of his government, a major part of which, by convenient coincidence, would be installed along that part of the Red Sea coastline close to the Yemeni border.

And where is the money going to come from to pay for this madness? the ambassador asked himself and realised the answer even as he thought of the question.

Of course, the extra income OPEC would generate by increasing the price of oil to what they'd called the invader-countries.

The second document in the briefcase was the contract that Qahtani and his British opposite number had signed at the Ambassador Club the previous evening. The ambassador recognised his brother-in-law's signature on the document, and underneath a scribbled note that simply said 'one million pounds, cash!'

Saeed Al-Turki used his mobile phone to speed dial his sister's home, a palatial and very modern mansion on the outskirts of Riyadh. He had some bad news to give her! During that call, she confirmed that her husband had indeed been in Sana'a on 15 May. The ambassador then telephoned his own national airline to learn that the nonstop Saudia Boeing 777 to Riyadh had left at 10.40

that morning. They have a saying in Saudi Arabia: 'If we can't do it, Dubai will always oblige!' He called Emirates Airline and with no problem at all booked himself on the afternoon departure to Dubai, with an onward connection to Riyadh. He had a king to see; the American president would have to wait.

Rafi Akhbar was waiting in his limousine, parked immediately in front of the Hilton Hotel entrance; he was doing everything in his limited powers to provide a service second to none to his client, including greasing the palm of the hotel doorkeeper to allow him to stay parked where he was. Saeed Al-Turki settled the account for his suite, including the overnight stay, which he hadn't had, reassuring the concerned cashier there was nothing wrong with the service. He was leaving early because he had to return home urgently. The cashier had smiled sympathetically, conveniently forgetting to apply the 20 per cent discount, which the Saudi Embassy had negotiated with the hotel for all Saudi nationals staying there. She reasoned he'd be too preoccupied with his domestic problems at home to think about that, and she was right.

His departure from the hotel was delayed by more than half an hour; this had nothing to do with Rafi Akhbar or the hotel management. It had everything to do with the protest march that was snaking its way down Park Lane, where it turned toward Buckingham Palace, and from there continued on to The Mall, turned into Whitehall, and finally into Downing Street where the barricades might or might not stop any further progress. Whether or not they made it to the famous front door, the marchers would be noisy enough so Prime Minister Gerald Smith would be only too well aware they were there – as if he wasn't already.

The rally had started in Hyde Park, where speaker after speaker had demanded the government must do something to ease the rocketing price of petrol and diesel. It had passed the two pounds a litre mark and was still rising as oil companies, distributors, garage owners, and forecourt attendants alike all did their bit to make something extra out of the crisis OPEC had started. All over the country similar demonstrations were taking place, all demanding the government take action, but the government was powerless; there was nothing they could do.

Cross-channel ferry traffic between Dover and Calais was at an all-time high, as was traffic through the tunnel, as anxious motorists found it cheaper to go to France to fill their petrol or diesel tanks, and however many other containers they could illegally fill, and transport back home. Trucks and coaches were doing the same thing, many having long-range tanks fitted, but all that came to a sudden end when the French government, which had no front-line troops in Iraq, imposed a 100 per cent fuel levy on all British registered vehicles.

Prime Minister Gerald Smith had telephoned his French opposite number, imploring him not to take that action, but there was a realistic concern in France that OPEC would penalise their country too if they helped the British evade the sanctions OPEC had imposed.

The French Prime Minister had summed it up very eloquently to his British opposite number: "Gerald, I've been assured by my contacts in OPEC, you have only to give notice to withdraw your troops from Iraq and Afghanistan, and they will immediately drop the sanctions on your country. OPEC don't want this any more than you do, but now fundamentalists have taken up the call for withdrawals, they daren't back down."

✻✻✻✻✻

The United Nations building in New York is normally like a small ghost town on a Sunday morning, with only the minimum number of staff present needed to maintain its vital functions, but today was very different. Without exception every single office was fully staffed as each delegation prepared to brief their respective ambassadors for a meeting under the chairmanship of the secretary general. Telephone lines from New York to practically every capital on the planet were red hot, while at the other end of those lines, regardless of the hour of day or night it happened to be locally, harassed civil servants were doing their best to instruct their delegation as to how they should proceed.

The UN ambassadors of the eleven member states of OPEC had met privately all night, desperately trying to find the wriggle room their respective governments were demanding of them. They'd entertained hopes the offending countries would agree to announce a gradual troop withdrawal, which would allow them to cancel the edict made by their counterparts in Vienna, but those hopes had been dashed early on. Taking their lead from the American president, the ambassadors of those countries affected by the oil price hike had refused to even countenance trying to find some compromising words, insisting it was tantamount to being blackmailed. They demanded the United Nations unanimously agree a resolution requiring both the ending of the oil price hike, and the threat of military intervention by the Islamic Defence Force.

No one knew what to do; the crisis had gone to full steam ahead without the usual preliminary skirmishing associated with such demands from fringe groups of whatever political or religious persuasion. Not one intelligence organisation had picked up any unusual activity either in the ether or on the ground – not even gossip. The world was stymied

Chapter Nine

At about the same time as Saeed Al-Turki was boarding the Emirates Airbus at Heathrow, Dr Debbie Adams was hurrying into the White House. When she'd left the Oval Office with the Saudi and Kuwaiti ambassadors the previous afternoon, the president had asked her to report back by 9 a.m. Sunday on the latest developments.

"And find Tom Lane!" he'd yelled at her back. Tom Lane was the former prime minister of the United Kingdom and currently undertaking a highly profitable lecture tour of the United States.

Other than more panic there was nothing new for the secretary of state to report. The concern being felt all over the world about what was going to happen when the stock markets opened for business in the Far East on Monday morning was increasing as the hours ticked by, yet she and everyone else knew, by the next time Europe and America opened their eyes from sleep the damage would be done; it would be irreversible. But at least she'd found Tom Lane.

The former prime minister of the United Kingdom was in New York as a guest of the Irish American Foundation at whose dinner he was the guest speaker. After leaving British politics he'd joined the lucrative American lecture circuit, as indeed had the only other former British prime minister to have held that office for so long, Margaret Thatcher. Mr Lane was seen in some circles as having been a prime mover in the settlement of the Northern Ireland problem; there were persistent rumours of a Nobel Peace Prize to be shared with his Irish opposite number. The chairman of the Foundation, a senator with strong Irish links, had given him a lavish introduction, regardless of the fact he didn't actually like him and had tried to block his nomination as a speaker. He'd also given him a piece of paper, which Mr Lane had held in his hand while giving the speech, but could only read after he'd sat down again to a tumultuous round of applause and stamping of feet.

The paper bore a telephone number and a name – Dr Deborah Adams. That was all, but it didn't need anything more. At the first opportunity, Mr Lane made an excuse to go to the bathroom, and while there had used his mobile phone to call Debbie; not that he called her by that name; it was the exclusive preserve of President Riles.

"I'll book you on the 6.10 a.m. United Express JFK to Dulles flight in the morning," she said when he told her where he was. "The boss wants to see you. I'll pick you up at Dulles."

She'd done what she'd said; he was seated right next to the door, and was the first off the plane. As the passengers from Flight 7315 walked into arrivals at Dulles Airport she was standing waiting for him, totally oblivious to the number of people staring at her, all recognising her and eventually Mr Lane too. There were those who thought him a more popular figure in the United States than in his own country.

The official limousine was waiting by the exit, just one of the privileges of the ruling class, as was the siren and the two police motorcycle outriders which hastened their arrival at the White House.

⁘⁘⁘⁘

The president of the United States of America was sitting behind his desk in the Oval Office. Two things were unusual for him this Sunday morning: he was in his shirt sleeves and he wouldn't be going to church, the former speaking volumes of his relaxed relationship with Tom Lane, the latter an indication of the seriousness of the situation that was gripping the entire world.

"Hi, Tom, thanks for making the journey. Have some coffee."

The president didn't know whether his friend had made the

journey all the way from London for this meeting or from a motel round the corner.

"Debbie here's bringing in a guy she swears knows all about the international oil problem and Russian reserves in particular, and he's gonna teach us what he knows, so listen in; then we can talk."

Everything in the Riles White House was synchronised; nothing was left to chance. Right on cue, almost as though he was listening in, which he most certainly was not, there was a discreet tap on the door and it opened to reveal one very smart United States Marine Corps corporal in his dress-blues uniform. Just behind him stood a distinguished-looking man, ultra-thin framed spectacles perched precariously on the end of his nose and with thick, grey hair falling over the collar of his plaid shirt. He wore a ridiculously pink bow tie. He had academic written all over him, and so it proved. The secretary of state introduced him as Dr Charles Weinberger, her special adviser on Russian affairs and an acknowledged expert on oil affairs internationally.

The most powerful man in the world stood from his desk and went round to shake hands with him, closely followed by Tom Lane.

The president wasn't in the mood for standing on formality as he said, "Thanks for coming Charles – it's OK for me to call you Charles, I hope. Make yourself comfortable and listen up. You know about the oil price hike from those guys in OPEC; as a good American you'll understand why we can't give in to their demands to bring our boys home, anyway not on their terms. All I need to know from you is how important is Middle East oil to us, can we do without it, is there anywhere else in the world we can tap for supplies?"

The president of America had briefings on this subject at least twice a week, so he knew as well as anyone what the answers were; today he wanted Tom Lane to hear an American's solution to the problem. George Riles was a master at this game.

"Mr President, when Deborah called me yesterday, she told me you wanted to learn about oil production to help you prepare a response to the OPEC demands. In my opinion the crucially important aspect is not so much oil production as the actual reserves, proven oil reserves, and note please I used the word 'proven.'

"OPEC, the Organisation of Petroleum Exporting Countries,

has its headquarters in Vienna. According to current estimates, it has 78 per cent of total proven, world crude-oil reserves, say around 900 billion barrels, but I need to explain what proven means.

"The amount of oil that OPEC members are allowed to produce on a daily and annual basis, which they all solemnly promise not to exceed, is based on a percentage of their proven reserve figures. If they produce too much oil, there will be a glut on the oil market, and prices will fall, which they don't want of course. So they have no interest exploring new wells because that would increase their proven reserves, and therefore they'd have to increase their daily output.

"Contrast that to the non-OPEC oil producers; they are mostly private companies and their figures are manipulated for economic, not political reasons. Their main motive is profit in the short term, so they need to produce to their maximum capability, not restrained as OPEC is. Furthermore, these same companies want to show their reserve figures as high as they can, to satisfy their shareholders and the world's stock markets, so they have an interest in new drilling and even exaggerating the likely yield from these wells.

"Here in the United States," he continued. "We consume almost twenty million barrels a day, of which we import twelve million barrels a day. We have a crude oil refining capability of seventeen million barrels a day, by far the highest capability of anywhere in the world. I'm sorry if this is boring, but it is necessary background."

He hadn't said anything new to either of the Americans, and Tom Lane's time in office back home in England had benefited greatly from North Sea oil revenues, so he too was on top of the subject.

"Continue please, Charles; we're all ears – I promise."

That was the president of course.

"For many years the main focus of American and, Mr Lane, UK foreign policy has been targeted towards the Middle East – in the 1980's supporting Saddam against the Ayatollah Khomeini in Iran, then against Saddam when he went bad, forcing him to take his troops out of Kuwait. Stability in the Middle East is paramount to our long-term interest, hence our policies on Libya, Lebanon, and Palestine."

Professor Weinberger had looked at each member of his audience in turn, looking for some kind of spoken support, but none was forthcoming!

"Each of our successive governments has tried to reduce our reliance on Middle East oil, but in reality the opposite has happened; as our economies have improved year on year, so the amount of oil we consume has increased. We import more from OPEC today than we did in 1990; like it or not, we are more dependent on OPEC now than we were ten years ago. Now OPEC has made these new demands on us, demands that will cripple our economy. But what if a significant part of the solution to America's problems lies in our own back yard?"

The president did his best to look sternly at the professor.

"If by this, Prof, you mean the Arctic National Wildlife Refuge, you can forget it. If, as Congress wants, I was to sanction exploration of only the minutest area of the ANWR, I will be crucified by all the eco do-gooders from Alaska to New Mexico, and there will be more demands from the rest of the world for us to sign up to the Kyoto Accord. I would be the bad guy; my place in world history will be as the evil monster who allowed the oil rich companies to become even richer, at the expense of the native Inupiat Indians living in the Reserve, and the extinction of all the Arctic wildlife, from the whale to the tadpole. Then I would leave office at the end of my second term, and what would happen? My successor, no doubt a Democrat, will continue to castigate me for authorising the exploration but sadly inform the good American voters it's too late now to stop it – it's been signed into law! They win the eco argument, and they get the votes for all the tax dollars it's gonna produce. No, Sir. We ain't going down that road."

Tom Lane had been paying very close attention to this latest exchange. He'd heard mention of the Alaskan Reserve, but knew little detail.

"George, if only for my own information, and so I can sound knowledgeable when the ANWR is discussed, can I hear what Charles has to say?"

The president stared at the former British prime minister.

"C'mon Lane, don't try to smarty pants me. How old are you, fifty-eight? And you're still on a crusade to save the world, just as your forebears did eight hundred years ago? Which dragon are you going to slay this time?"

Mr Riles was playing hardball.

Tom Lane had gone red in the face. Few people could speak to him like that and get away with it.

"George, I think it's important I'm aware of all the possible solutions to this problem, if only so I can shoot them down, as surely as you just did to Charles Weinberger here."

The president appeared to reluctantly give way.

"OK, Charles, tell Tom what's so attractive about the ANWR, but make it quick because it's not going to happen."

"Mr President, Mr Lane, the ANWR lies in the Arctic Circle and covers an area of nineteen million acres, ninety-four thousand acres of which is owned by the Inupiat Indians. Experts confidently predict there are billions, and gentlemen I do not speak lightly, there are billions of barrels of economically recoverable oil and trillions of cubic feet of gas waiting to be extracted.

"Some facts you need to be aware of, Mr Lane," he continued. "Of the nineteen-million acreage of ANWR, only 0.01 per cent would need to be developed to bring that oil and gas to the American people; that if I may say so, Sir, is the equivalent of Hyde Park to the whole of your country. Twenty years ago, the caribou herd in that part of the Arctic near Prudhoe Bay was counted at two-thousand-four hundred strong, today it is over thirty thousand. Those caribou are stripping the land of such food resources as are available, threatening extinction of the bear and wolf population. Despite the protestations of the ecological lobby in this country, exploration would be no threat to the native wildlife. Just think, Mr President, one word from you and we would lose our reliance on the Middle East for all time. They can fester in their own sand for all we'd care."

The president looked angrily across the room.

"Weinberger, I'd be obliged if you'd confine your briefing to matters of oil reserves, which at least you seem to know something about!" Turning to face his secretary of state, the president told Debbie, "Have a talk with the people at the UN; tell them if they want my support in the meeting with the ambassadors this afternoon, I'll want Tom here to be given responsibility by the UN to find a way out of this mess, and while Debbie's doing that," added the president, "Charles here can now tell us the global oil picture and leave American politics to me.

"It's no secret there's oil aplenty in Siberia, so Professor Weinberger, let's hear all about that, and then Tom, you can put your Russian friend President Schumakof under pressure to let us have some of it!"

It was time for Professor Weinberger to turn the discussion the way he secretly wanted.

"Thank you, Mr President, and let me start at the top end. Much of the information I'm giving you about Russia today is highly classified, most of it is derived from our friends over there."

Charles didn't have a single piece of paper in front of him; he was doing this off the top of his head.

"In November 2003, the Russian president signed a decree making the status of Russian mineral reserves a state secret. He then signed another decree, which you gentlemen know all about, which kept ownership of Russia's natural resources exclusively in their own domain. It is an undisputed fact that in Eastern Siberia, there are oil and gas deposits there that will dwarf the entire OPEC and non-OPEC sources added together, and that's not counting the gold and diamond mining possibilities. Successful mining in Eastern Siberia would result in Russia becoming *the* global energy powerhouse for the next one-hundred years and more."

The secretary of state re-entered the room just as the president was about to intervene.

"Mr President, I've just had a call back from our people at the UN; all the ambassadors have unanimously agreed to recommend Tom's appointment as deputy secretary general as you asked; he's been given the specific responsibility to resolve the current Middle East crisis."

The former prime minister of Great Britain did his best not to smirk at the welcome news of his new appointment, now a foregone conclusion once the ambassadors had unanimously made their recommendation. For many months, he'd been hoping to get the top job at the UN, even though he knew full well the appointment was rotational, and it was Asia's turn. That was one of the reasons he'd delayed his departure from Downing Street, waiting to see if the arm pulling by his many friends, including the president of the United States, could overturn that rotation, but without success. Anyway he was now the number two, and he could always hope!

President Riles wanted to get back to the briefing. An important ball game was about to start on TV, and he'd promised his wife Yvonne they would watch that together.

"Every time we meet with the Russian president," he told his guests, "we get around to talking about energy supplies, and every time he tantalises us by throwing in the temptations of Eastern Siberia. He then takes it back out again, by reminding us of the hostile terrain. Our own people have even been allowed to go there and make assessments of the reserves. I remember the paper they produced which told us it will never be commercially viable to mine there." The president looked scornfully to Weinberger. "And you're recommending we change our dependence for oil from the Arab Sheikhs to the Russian Bear? Do you think that's wise, Professor?

The good Professor was being bullied by the American president, and he didn't like it!

"No, Sir, we do not have to become dependent on the Russians, but if we learn to cooperate with them to our mutual advantage, we all become winners. Please let me explain: he felt in his pocket for the notebook that was never far away from him. Many times Dr Adams had seen him go for his notebook when he wanted to surprise her with some less well-known facts, and it had become a bit of a game between them.

"So, Charles," she asked, "what rabbit are you going to pull out of your hat, or should I say notebook, this time?"

Turning to the other occupants of the room she added, "That blessed notebook of his should be classified top secret; he's got enough information in there to win us a world war if he sets his mind to it."

The academic had rehearsed this next part so many times he didn't actually need the 'blessed notebook', as Dr Adams had referred to it, but it looked better if he did it that way.

"Mr President, might I be allowed to tell you what I believe is absolutely the best option for us, an option that will keep Europe and the United States awash with oil and gas for at least the next forty or fifty years? It's something we can bring on line very quickly, and much more cheaply than any other option

The other two looked at Charles expectantly, and the secretary of state had merely nodded her head. She knew what he was about to drop on them would be something he'd been secretly researching for weeks, and he'd never let her down yet.

"If you can envisage a line running south to north along the eastern edge of the foothills of the Ural Mountains, linking two towns, Serov, north of Yekaterinburg, and Salekhard, a mining town on the River Ob, a distance of almost 500 miles. Then imagine another line further east, linking Surgut to Yartsangi, an inlet on the Kara Sea, which is 350 miles. Envisage then, if you will, the corridor between those two lines; at its widest point in the south, this corridor would be 450 miles wide, and at its narrowest in the north, less than 100 miles."

Charles Weinberger knew he had their undivided attention and wished he'd had the foresight to bring a map with him. While he'd been talking, he'd roughly sketched the area he was referring to on the back of a sheet of paper he'd taken from his jacket pocket.

"In the mid-1980s, a geological survey was carried out by a joint Russian/Kazakhstan team, checking the feasibility of extending the existing Kazakhstan oilfields northwards. This survey proved huge oil and gas reserves in the corridor I'm referring to. However, nothing came of it; with the break-up of the Soviet Union a decade later I guess each side didn't trust the other enough to proceed with the project. So it was shelved.

"If we could get approval to drill in that corridor, we would then need to construct a pipeline just 250-miles long to the port of Amdema where we'd build a giant oil terminal. There's a narrow inlet just north of Amdema that links through the northeast passage into the Barents Sea; we can ship by shallow draft barges through that inlet to Murmansk, and by super-tanker from there to Europe and the American east coast."

Tom Lane was so excited he almost spluttered the most obvious question.

"How much, Charles," he asked, "would a barrel of oil cost taking your pocketbook solution?"

This was the moment Charles Weinberger had been briefed to expect.

"Including the cost of shipping to New York, less than fifty-five dollars a barrel. Add to that the cost of the licences, which the owner of the territory would be entitled to levy on the oil companies, say another ten per cent, for a total of sixty-five dollars a barrel tops!"

In his excitement, Tom Lane forgot that the shortened derivative of Dr Adams's Christian name was the sole preserve of the president of the United States and said:

"Debbie, this is incredible. A solution to the world's energy problems has been staring us in the face since the mid-1980s, and we've all let it slip past unnoticed. Can I have a copy of the survey report Charles mentioned? I'll need that to get Vladimir Schumakof on side."

Dr Adams was prepared to forgive Lane's use of her nickname.

Let it go this time, she said to herself. *"Let the Brit do his thing. As for giving him a copy of the report, he could just as easily get it himself from the internet.*

The president of the United States had been watching this exchange with some amusement. Debbie Adams had been one of the better appointments to his cabinet.

"Vladimir Schumakof," Tom Lane told them, " will look upon this as manna from heaven; by my reckoning we need to produce a minimum of ten-million barrels a day from this field, that's $55 million dollars every day for the next forty or fifty years for the licences, and that's not counting the revenue from the natural gas Charles says is there in abundance. Can you see anyone in this day and age walking away from that income?"

The three politicians were so busy looking at each other, they failed to notice the smirk on the face of Dr Weinberger.

No, he thought to himself, *I can't see anyone walking away from that income, but the Russian president's not even in the ball game. Tom is assuming the Russian government owns that territory – and they don't!"*

Wisely, he hadn't said that out loud; he didn't want to spoil their day.

President Riles stood up from the desk chair he'd been occupying throughout the meeting and faced his audience.

"Friends, let's wrap this up for today. I need to spend some quality time with Yvonne, or the world's oil problems will seem as nothing if she gets mad at me. Thank you, Professor, for your input. It's been truly invaluable; and as for you Tom, congratulations on your new appointment. You know what you've got to do but do keep me in touch through Debbie."

With that he opened the door. The ever-patient Marine Corps corporal on guard outside took charge of his boss's guests, while the boss himself went to join his long-suffering wife Yvonne.

The secretary of state and her very knowledgeable but somewhat devious special adviser escorted Mr Lane back to the bullet-proof limousine that had brought him and Deborah Adams from the airport earlier that morning. As she watched the car disappear into the afternoon traffic, accompanied by two police motorcycle outriders with their sirens wailing a message of urgency, the secretary of state turned to congratulate Professor Weinberger on his presentation.

"Charlie, you'll be the link man between our government and Tom and of course the Russians. Make sure you keep me in the loop at all times."

They too shook hands, and just as Dr Weinberger turned to climb into the car which had quietly pulled in behind Mr Lane's, she asked him:

"Hey, by the way, what's that neat pin in your lapel?"

It was round, with a white, eight-pointed cross slightly elevated on a red background.

Charles hadn't been at all embarrassed as he told her, "Oh, it's just a small, charitable organisation I belong to; you know, we help little old ladies cross the street – things like that."

That was about as massive an understatement as it was possible to make. Bailiff Grand Cross Charles Weinberger was a member of the American Priory of the Chivalric Order of St John of Jerusalem. In his youth he'd been a student at Harvard University, where he'd had a brief, intimate, and in those days illegal moment with Englishman James Sinclair. Unfortunately, this had been captured on film by an unscrupulous American who even now was sitting in his castle in the Scottish Highlands orchestrating the present crisis.

Tom Lane was driven to Dulles Airport, and due to the

considerable influence of the police motorcycle outriders, he actually caught the 4.55 p.m. United Express Bombardier shuttle back to New York's John F Kennedy Airport. However, he missed the flash announcement coming over the CNN news channel. Dr Adams for her part had gone jogging in the grounds of the White House, so she too had missed it. That only left president Riles; he'd been watching the ball game on television and had been irritated when they interrupted the game to make an urgent news announcement from Port Said in Egypt.

"The Suez Canal Authority this afternoon announced its solidarity with their Islamic brothers in the League of Arab States and OPEC. With immediate effect, the Canal is closed to all tankers delivering oil to invader-countries."

The announcer looked up, having read from the text he'd been handed just seconds before.

"I guess that means they'll have to take the long way round the Cape of Good Hope, which won't be very pleasant for those guys; the seas I understand can be mighty rough round there."

He hadn't yet realised in the heat of the moment that it wasn't only the seas which would be rough. The price of gas in the United States was about to hit four dollars a gallon, and that would only be the start.

Meantime, Dr Charles Weinberger, special adviser to the American secretary of state, was screaming at the driver to turn the car round. He had to go back to the White House. He'd left a sheet of paper on the president's desk, and he had to have it back. On one side was a map of Eastern Russia he'd drawn for President Riles' benefit, and that should be classified top secret, while on the reverse side was his mother's laundry list. If he didn't pick that up from the launderette this afternoon, he'd be in real trouble!

Chapter Ten

Early the following morning, I heard the sound of an approaching car; it was the Range Rover. This was becoming a most unwelcome routine. Even Randy didn't bark anymore, but those missing pages couldn't walk here on their own, so Sir James Sinclair's presence would have to be tolerated again.

In fact it didn't turn out like that. As I walked through the conservatory to answer the knock at the door I could see it was the chauffeur standing there. He was even more unwelcome than Sinclair; he gave the impression of being a man capable of causing great harm without letting it trouble him at all, a man without conscience. It was with some trepidation I opened the door, but my fears were groundless. He didn't say one single word, simply thrust an envelope into my hand, turned back to the car, and he was gone. Nicholas came behind me as the Range Rover was leaving. He'd been sound asleep on the settee when I'd passed through the lounge on the way to open the conservatory door, yet here he was looking slightly ruffled, and dressed only in his shorts and vest, but wide awake. How did he do it? Just one of the advantages of youth.

"What was that all about, Dad?" he wanted to know.

I held up the envelope for him to see. It was quite thick and sealed with Sellotape. My fingers were trembling as I nervously opened the envelope and withdrew what was clearly the missing pages of the notebook, substantially more than were in the part we'd already seen. Nicholas was going to have his work cut out translating this lot, though on flicking through I realised some of the pages towards the end were blank – an indication that this probably represented Anastasia's final chapter.

I sat in one of the wickerwork armchairs in the conservatory, carefully turning over the first few pages, noting the neat handwriting and the elegant way in which each paragraph was presented. It was a strange sensation, knowing that in the next few hours we, or at any rate I, because I still wasn't sure how much my son already knew, would learn more about this mysterious lady Anastasia Nikolaevna Romanov and my connection to her. I handed the document across to Nicholas, suggesting I get some coffee for both of us while he made himself comfortable.

Nicholas translated the first few lines word for word.

"My son," was how they started, "the events of those last weeks and months of 1918 were as terrible and as degrading as anything you could possibly imagine."

It was fascinating to watch Nicholas as he scanned each line; his eyes constantly darting from one side of the page to the other. The lines on his forehead wrinkled as his brain tried to translate not only the words, but the meaning behind them.

Anastasia told us how Mikhail had taken her to a dacha set in a clearing in the woods all on its own on the outskirts of Yekaterinburg. They had to be very careful not to be seen; Anastasia's clothing was covered in her brother's blood, and her hands and face were dirty after digging the soil for his grave. Mikhail too had to be careful; he was a soldier, and last night he'd deserted his post and helped two of the prisoners escape. If they were discovered they would both be shot!

Anastasia described the dacha as a rustic, timbered hunting lodge, with small dark rooms and hard, wooden furniture, not unlike the hunting lodge at Spala, but at least it had electricity. Mikhail introduced his girlfriend to Anastasia. Her name was Olga; she was around thirty years of age, rather older than Mikhail, and she originated from Irkutsk, as Anastasia knew Mikhail did too. That was the common bond that had brought them together. Olga had been in front of Mikhail in a queue at a butcher's shop in Yekaterinburg. When she gave her order in the thick, twangy accent common to Irkutsk, Mikhail recognised it, and that set them talking.

Irkutsk is the capital of Siberia, far to the east of the Ural

Mountains and an important stop on the Trans-Siberian Railway. In Yekaterinburg, Mikhail was living in a rough billet with the other soldiers, just around the corner from the house owned by the Jewish merchant Ipatiev, which was where the Romanov family was being held prisoner. Even in the summertime his accommodation was cold and was very crowded. They had little food, though no doubt more than their prisoners. He was only too glad to accept Olga's offer to visit her at the dacha!

Her employer, a *meshchanin* or petit bourgeois, had gone to Moscow, wanting to be at the centre of the Revolution. He'd told her it was necessary to see which way the wind was going to blow so he could make his own plans, and by the time any news reached their small town in the Urals it would be too late to do anything. He'd taken his wife and two children with him, leaving Olga with instructions to take care of the dacha but with little money to buy food. She was glad of Mikhail's company and his pay packet.

It was clear from Anastasia's writing that Olga resented her and did her best to treat Anastasia as a servant. Anastasia wasn't even allowed to sleep in the dacha. Mikhail explained it would be dangerous for her to sleep there; if the dacha was raided during the night she would be found, and her life would be forfeit; better to be outside, where you could escape, she was told.

"And what about you?" Anastasia had written, "You are a deserter from the army, and you helped me escape. Your life would be forfeit, too. Why is it OK for you to sleep in the house, but not me?"

That seemed to have fallen on conveniently deaf ears. Ridiculous as it seemed to Nicholas and me, it was apparent that Anastasia, until twenty-four hours ago a grand duchess, was jealous of a relationship between this common, private soldier and a housemaid.

Anastasia slept in the woodshed, which apparently was where Olga had to sleep when the owner was home, but for now she was in his bed – not for the first time it seemed. The woodshed was cold and draughty; it had no lighting, and it had no furniture other than a very uncomfortable bed. At least it was clean, which was a lot more than could be said for the building next door. If the woodshed was yet another cruel indictment of her previous life, the toilet was even more so. It was in a battered, old hut adjoining the woodshed. It was a very primitive affair, being little more than a hole in the ground with a bucket of water nearby. The smell she described as worse than anything she'd ever known in her life. I think both Nicholas and I grimaced just at the thought of it!

On that first night, Mikhail had come to see her in the wood shed. In the book she told how they'd discussed their plans, how he was going to keep the promise he'd made to Anastasia's father. He seemed to have been very rough with her, giving orders as he was accustomed to in the army, rather than having an even discussion.

"From now on," he told her, "your name is Anna, and you are my wife. I will always call you by that name, and you must always think of yourself by that name, otherwise we are both dead. You must respect me as your husband, like it says in the Domostrol you must behave in a chaste and obedient way to me! When it's necessary, we will be together as man and wife, but don't worry, I will always respect the promise I made to your father. You have nothing to fear from me. While we are here, Olga is my girlfriend, not by choice, but by necessity. I have what she wants, I'm a young man, and I'm a soldier. I can keep her happy. You have the jewels, so you have the money to keep us fed. She has the dacha, where we are safe. It's not our choice, but that's the way it is."

Olga went into town every day, listening at the market to the rumours sweeping this small community on the edge of Siberia, almost two-thousand kilometres east of Moscow. One day, she brought home a copy of the local newspaper. A reporter had heard rumours about soldiers being seen burying bodies late at night near a village called Koptyaki, about seventeen versts north of Yekaterinburg. Like everyone else in town, he knew the imperial family were being held prisoner, and their fate was in the balance. He presumably put two and two together, and went to the house of Ipatiev to see if he could learn anything there. His report was clearly very distressing to Anastasia.

Anastasia told us when the reporter arrived at the house it was deserted. A dog was lying by the front door; it had been stabbed many times, and had bled to death. Anastasia was sure that would have been Jimmy. A notice was pinned to the door, roughly written on a scrap of paper, saying the imperial family had been shot without bourgeois formalities but in accordance with the Bolshevik democratic principles.

Nicholas looked up from his reading.

"I translated word for word, exactly as Anastasia wrote that last sentence," he told me, "and I suspect she memorised it from the newspaper account. It makes awful reading even today, how much worse it must be when it's your own family they are referring to? Do you think people really thought in terms like that back then?"

How can one person be so well educated, as my son most certainly is, and yet so naive?

"Not only in those days," I told him, "think about the atrocities that were committed in the Nazi concentration camps, then in the Vietnam war, and more recently in the Balkans, and even today in parts of Africa. Ordinary rational people become worse than animals, the mass hysteria whipped up by corrupt politicians out to get votes, and newspapers whose only objective is to sell copies. The world hasn't changed Nicholas, it's always been wicked."

The reporter said the front door of the house was standing open; he'd gone inside. On the ground floor was evidence of soldiers having been billeted there for some time; scraps of food still clung to the unwashed dishes in the sink, cigarette stubs and empty bottles smelling of vodka were everywhere. All the upstairs rooms were clean, but the cupboards and drawers were open, the contents thrown on the floor. Items of clothing had been torn apart, as too had the thin mattresses and pillows, as though people in a frantic hurry were searching for something which might be hidden there; he saw several bibles, but nothing of value to indicate that just two days earlier, people of wealth had occupied those rooms.

He went down into the basement. As he pushed open the door of one room a wild dog leapt out, and ran up the stairs, blood round its mouth where it'd been gorging itself. In the room itself he counted more than a dozen rats, feasting on the bits of human remains that still remained. This was the room where the massacre had taken place. Every wall and even the ceiling were pockmarked with bullet holes. Attempts had been made to remove as many of the blood stains and pieces of human flesh as they could, but the entire floor was stained red, no attempt had been made to clean that—it was where the dog and the rats had been taking their fill. It was obvious the execution squad wouldn't have wanted to hang around once their foul deed had been done; the reporter ventured to suggest they'd probably deserted, and gone to their own homes, as so many of their compatriots all over Russia had done.

As we'd already learned from Anastasia, Mikhail had been left behind in the house when the rest of his army colleagues were replaced by what became the execution squad. We wondered whether it was his doing to persuade the team leader, Yakov Yurovsky, to keep him there, and if he already had an idea of the fate that was to befall the family? If so, we had to assume he'd already decided he was going to do what he could to help the imperial family escape.

Somehow Anastasia had obtained a copy of the report into the massacre written by Yurovsky. With some difficulty Nicholas translated this part of her notebook word for word:

"I had never visited that room in the basement where Yurovsky said his men murdered my family, so I can't comment on that. He said the shooting took place at about three in the morning. By that time of course I was deep in the forest, digging the grave for my brother Alexei; I didn't hear anything, which wasn't surprising. He said each of his men had instructions to shoot one person, he himself was to shoot my Father, and his bullet was the first to be fired. That apparently killed my father outright, a blessing I suppose. What came next was unbelievable carnage, which wasn't surprising; these people were peasants! Their orders had been that each member of the firing squad should take it in turns to shoot their designated target, but instead they all began firing at the same time, and bullets were ricocheting all round that room, as much a danger to themselves as to my family. After the soldiers had finished shooting, or Yurovsky had managed to stop them, I don't know which, my mother and sisters were apparently still alive. That sounds unbelievable, with so many bullets flying around, but that's what his report said; it went on to say one of the soldiers, a brute of a man called Yermakov who I remember only too well, then tried bayoneting them, and when that didn't work either, they started shooting again. Even then Yurovsky said, the job still wasn't done, that Alexei was still alive! He shot him in the head. That gives the lie to his entire report, as I know only too well. Poor Alexei was already dead by that time, but not by the satanic actions of these men."

"Yurovsky's report hints at the way his men then started stripping the clothing off the bodies, to retrieve the valuables each of the victims had attempted to conceal. These people were behaving as animals; if that part of his report is to be believed, it was a real frenzy of lust for gold and jewels, really repugnant. I doubt very much all the valuables were handed over, as he claims, but they're welcome to whatever they kept; I hope it brought them all bad luck. If Mikhail hadn't rescued Alexei and me, they'd have had a lot more!"

"His report talks a lot about the disposal of the bodies, and I find much of that unbelievable. According to him, he buried them twice. The first time, they threw the bodies into a waterlogged mine near a village called Koptyaki, about seventeen versts north from the city, in full view of some local people. Apparently the water barely covered the bodies, can you imagine the incompetence of the man! Anyway, they took the bodies out of the mine again, and moved them to another pit just off the Koptyaki road. They made fires to burn all the clothing, to remove all traces of the site, and according to Yurovsky they burned dear Alexei, and the servant Demidova's bodies on that fire, another of his lies. The man Yermakov then poured sulphuric acid over the faces of the dead bodies, and the pit was filled in, and levelled."

My mind was working overtime, trying to imagine the ghastly scene being enacted by Yurovsky and his men. "Why, Nicholas, do you suppose they went to the trouble of pouring acid over the faces, what were they trying to hide?"

"That's an interesting thought Dad. Sulphuric acid is not the kind of thing you would expect them to routinely carry, so they had to go and get it from somewhere, therefore there had to be a specific reason. Maybe he wanted to make identification of the faces impossible, and I would guess that had something to do with Yurovsky claiming to have burned two of the people, whereas we know they escaped."

Anastasia again. "Of course there were lies in the report which Yurovsky had allegedly made, but as Mikhail had told me, the man would have been shot if he'd confessed that two of us had escaped, so he had to distort the truth in parts. We'd known the Czech Brigade was getting closer to Yekaterinburg, and Papa was absolutely certain they would have orders to free us, in fact that had been our main hope of being saved. As incompetent as Yurovsky and his men were, I cannot believe they would so calmly take almost thirty six hours to bury, exhume, burn, then rebury my family, when the enemy they so feared was almost knocking on the door of the town. There is something very wrong with his account."

My mind was in turmoil. The Bolsheviks had murdered the Romanov family on 17 July 1918, and just nine days later they were thrown out of Yekaterinburg, and the Czech Brigade took the town. If Anastasia's father was right in his thinking, the Imperial Family would have been freed by the Czechs! Russian history, perhaps to the present day, could have been so different if only …

Nicholas went on with his history lesson. "To come into much more modern times, in 1991 the then President of Russia, Boris Yeltsin, who coincidentally was born in Yekaterinburg just thirteen years after the Imperial Family were massacred there, authorised the exhumation of the pit where the bodies had been buried. The remains were all carefully gathered together by scientists from the USA, UK and Russia and samples taken to those countries where the DNA was independently tested for authenticity. They were compared to the DNA of Count Nikolai Trubetskoy, who was a cousin of Tsar Nicholas II, and also to Georgij Romanov, Tsar Nicholas's brother who'd died of tuberculosis in 1899, as well as to the Duke of Edinburgh (and here my eyebrows raised as you can imagine), who was a grand nephew of Tsarina Alexandra. The scientists independently concluded they were more than ninety nine percent certain they had the remains of Tsar Nicholas, his wife and three daughters! They agreed the remains of the son Alexei, and one other daughter, either Maria or Anastasia, which later tests confirmed as Anastasia, were missing. They also confirmed the other sets of remains belonged to the unfortunate Dr Botkin, and three servants. What was quite unique in international relations terms, all three countries were unanimous in their results. There was no doubt."

Something was bothering me; something Nicholas had just told me did not fit with the Yurovsky account of the burial. We knew of course he'd lied, saying that his team had killed all the Imperial family, but something else was wrong.

"Nicholas, think about it; there were witnesses to the burial, ordinary people had seen what they were doing, and they would have been able to count nine bodies being buried instead of eleven. But look further; if Yurovsky had said they'd burned Alexei and Anastasia's bodies, that would fit with the DNA results which stated unequivocally the remains of those two were missing. But why would he tell a lie on a lie, why would he say it was Alexei and the maid Demidova they burned?" I think we both realised no-one would ever be able to resolve that mystery.

Nicholas started reading again. Anastasia and Mikhail stayed in that dacha until the end of August 1918. By that time the Czech Brigade was running the town, but for the people living there they'd simply swapped one unwanted occupier for another. The brutalities continued, as did the shortages of food, but no one had come near the dacha; they'd been left alone. Both Anastasia and Mikhail were becoming restless, but where could they go and what to do about Olga? She knew too much. Would she talk after they'd gone, thinking she'd get a reward for the information? They'd decided to confront her, and then decide what to do. Anastasia had written:

"The three of us sat down in the kitchen with our supper. Outside it was already dark; the strong wind was making the branches of the trees which surrounded the dacha move against each other. It was a grinding noise, quite unpleasant to the ears, and of course the rustling of the leaves was noisy, too. I knew that when I went back to my bed in the woodshed it would be cold and draughty; I would be lucky to get any sleep at all, and I was frightened to be on my own.

"Supper that night was like we had most nights. It was called a borscht, a kind of soup made with potato, onion, a cooked beetroot, salt and pepper, all things which were fairly easily available in the market, but we also needed some tomato paste, butter, sour cream and sugar, and these things were more expensive, and hard to find.

"Fortunately, money wasn't a problem; the Jewish man Ipatiev who owned the house where my family were murdered, had a stall on the market, and he would buy the jewellery in exchange for money. He never asked Olga where she got the jewels, but I was shocked when she told us how little money he gave her. It was like he was robbing us, but what could we do? I was very suspicious of her though, and one morning when she went into town and Mikhail was cutting wood in the forest, I went through her clothes but found nothing. Next, I went through the cupboard where the owner's clothes were stored. I found what I was looking for in a pair of boots, the kind the Cossack soldiers would wear, almost knee length. In the foot of one of the boots was a wad of money, tightly rolled into a ball. I wondered what to do? If I told Mikhail he'd probably do something stupid, either to her for stealing or to me for going through her belongings.

"I decided to keep the money myself and say nothing, but where to hide it? I had noticed high up in the toilet shed there was a piece of wood running from one side of the roof to the other; a rafter to keep the two sides in place. To be honest, whenever I was using the toilet I always looked up at the roof; it was clean, whereas the floor was disgusting! I wrapped the notes in paper and put them on that rafter, tying them with a piece of string. Olga never said anything about the money, anyway not to me and I think not to Mikhail either, and the rate of exchange she got for the jewellery suddenly got better. I was learning!

"After we'd eaten, Mikhail told Olga we were thinking about leaving and asked if she had any plans to do that as well? Olga told us she would like to go home to Irkutsk and seemed to be hinting to Mikhail he should go with her since they both originally came from there, but she didn't have the money to buy the tickets. I thought it would be a good idea if I went that way as well. The Trans-Siberian train from Yekaterinburg went to Irkutsk, and on to Vladivostok. From there I could get a ship to anywhere in the world, and I would be safe. I said that to Mikhail and Olga. I had the money to buy tickets for all of us, they could stay in Irkutsk and I could go on my own the rest of the way.

"Mikhail went mad! He told me I would be raped, and all my money stolen even before the train left Yekaterinburg. I thought the Czech Brigade soldiers would be better behaved than the Bolsheviks, but he reminded me what they were, deserters from their own army or prisoners of war. Many were convicts; none of them had anything to lose. It was out of the question. He'd already decided we were going to take the train to Moscow. It was only half the distance as Irkutsk, and winter was coming but it wouldn't be so cold there. He was sure we'd be safe. I started to ask what the difference was; according to what he said, a woman was in danger whichever way she went on the train, but he yelled at me to shut up. He'd also given me a look, as if to tell me to leave it to him. He didn't interrupt Olga when she said she didn't care what happened to her. If she had the money to buy a train ticket, she was going home.

"The next day, Mikhail himself went into town, the first time since we'd escaped from the house of death. He'd changed his appearance, and of course got rid of his uniform, and anyway Olga had told us there were so many young men in the town, probably all of them deserters from the army, what was one more? After a lot of difficulty arguing about the price, he bought two tickets on the Trans-Siberian to Moscow, and another one to Irkutsk, using one of the gold nuggets Papa had told me to give to him. Neither of us knew the value of gold, but while we realised he had probably being cheated , we knew he'd had no choice; in fact as we learned later, he could have bought the whole train for that nugget!

"Both trains would leave the next day, Olga's to Irkutsk about eight in the morning, ours to Moscow in the afternoon. I was relieved; pleased to be getting out of that horrible town which held only bad memories for me, pleased to get away from Olga, and happy to be on the way to find some of my relatives, somewhere I would be safe. Olga had found a bottle of wine belonging to the owner, so we opened that to celebrate our coming journeys.

"After dinner, I went into the bedroom she shared with Mikhail; I needed a change of clothes. One of the owner's daughters was the same age as me and, according to Olga, about the same size. All the clothes were old – presumably if she had any better ones she'd taken them with her to Moscow, but I did all right. The next morning, we said goodbye to Olga. She walked into town, carrying a small bag which had all her belongings. She looked so pathetic, and even though I hated her, I felt sorry for her too. When Mikhail wasn't looking I gave her a little of the money I'd stolen from her, which of course she'd stolen from me in the first place!

"We made a fire behind the dacha and burned all the clothes I'd been wearing when I left the house of death. I cried to lose the pretty underthings and the long frock; even though they weren't in a very good condition anymore, they were still better than the ones I would be wearing in future. After a last meal of borscht, which I hoped I'd never have to eat again, we left the dacha and walked to the station. On that day I was so happy, but if I thought things were going to get better for me, I was very wrong.

Chapter Eleven

Outside, the morning sun was making its presence felt, reminding me I hadn't even made breakfast yet. I'm not well organised when it comes to domestic chores. Nicholas went to have a shower while I fried bacon and eggs and made toast with the bread I'd bought in the village three days earlier. I'm not a very good cook either, but we both wolfed it all down, regardless of any cholesterol which might be lurking around. Randy had to be content with some of the stew left over from last night.

After brunch, which is what I suppose we'd call that makeshift meal, I showered while Nicholas did the dishes, and then we went outside to take some much needed fresh air. I looked around me at the familiar glens; the ground gently sloped upwards until the middle distance, where it became much steeper as it reached the mountains. The different shades of heather formed a multicoloured quilt, and the track ran unevenly past the cottage and down to Loch Rannoch. I tried to compare this wonder of nature with the place far away in the Ural Mountains Anastasia had described, and of course I couldn't. Here was absolute peace and tranquillity, while there had been misery and death.

Nicholas and I returned to the seats we'd occupied all morning. We'd been quiet with each other during brunch, each lost in our own thoughts, wondering what was coming next. Nicholas had done his best to translate that part of the notebook word for word, and it had been difficult going. Several times he'd had to turn to his Russian/ English dictionary to find the exact meaning of a particular word or to read the same sentence several times to put it into context with what had gone before, so progress had been slow.

"I don't know about you," I said to my son, "but I'm impatient to learn what happens to Anastasia, and where I fit into this intriguing story. Can I suggest you tell the story as she has written it, giving us the gist of it without being so perfect in the translation?"

Nicholas's eyes were already glued to the next page, scanning the lines quite quickly, no doubt getting the sense of what was coming next.

"I'm happy to do whatever you want, and I agree it's frustrating, going as slowly as we have. So, if you're absolutely sure, I'll speed it up."

I'd never asked Nicholas much about his time at university; we always had so many other things to talk about in the short times we were together, that had been a very low priority. I didn't know how he fared in competition with his fellow students, but if his ability to translate from Russian, and old Russian at that, into English was anything to go by, he was an exceptional pupil; much better than his Dad, but that wasn't saying a lot.

Anastasia told us how she and Mika, as she'd started calling him, walked to the train station in Yekaterinburg. She described the clothes she was wearing, stolen from the dacha where she'd spent the past six weeks. We found it amusing to think of her wearing the white-cotton pantaloons, into the waistband and each leg of which she'd sewn the last of the gold nuggets. She'd found a matching bodice lying on the floor of a wardrobe, the kind that had to be laced down the front; she'd had to wash it several times to remove the grease marks, clear evidence of use or was that misuse? Into one of the bra cups, which she described as being larger than she'd needed, she'd hidden the locket that Mika had taken from Alexei's trousers that night in the forest.

I gave an involuntary shiver as Nicholas read that out to me, as indeed I should have. That same locket was now sitting on the mantelpiece above the fire in my sitting room! Next was a petticoat, which covered her from the neck to below the knee and which had belonged to Olga; Anastasia had found this in the laundry basket; apparently it was just what she was looking for, so she could sew her collection of rubies into the hem! Presumably Olga didn't have any say in that matter! The outer layer of clothing consisted of a grey blouse, which unlike the bodice, was quite tight, indicating that the previous owner liked to flaunt whatever she had, and a woollen button-up cardigan which had more likely belonged to the mother than to the daughter! The black skirt came down to ankle length, and was of a coarse material, heavy, but with a red frill tacked onto the bottom, to add a bit of much needed colour. Finally she'd taken a pair of well-worn boots, too large for Anastasia normally, but with the rest of the money she'd stolen back from Olga pushed firmly into the toecaps of each, and which Mika still didn't know about, they fitted nicely.

Whether by accident or design she didn't know, but they'd turned onto Liebknecht ulitsa, and walked right past the house Ipatiev where she'd been imprisoned, and where her family had been murdered. In the notebook she mentioned looking in the garden to see if she could see her dog Jimmy, even though the newspaper had said he'd been killed by the thrust from a wicked bayonet. She hadn't said a thing about her family, but it wasn't too difficult to understand the thoughts which must have been going through her mind! At the station, the eastbound train for Irkutsk and Vladivostok was just pulling in as they arrived. It was some hours late, but better late than never! They'd scanned the crowds trying to find Olga, expecting to see her pushing through the hordes of people wanting to board the express, but she was nowhere to be seen. They'd watched as the train eventually pulled away from the platform, still with more than three thousand kilometres to go to Irkutsk, and about the same again to the end of the line at Vladivostok. Anastasia was positive Olga hadn't boarded that train. They never heard of her again!

According to the signs on the westbound platform, the Moscow train was supposed to arrive on time in the afternoon, but it still hadn't arrived by the time it got dark, and both Mika and Anastasia were hungry. She told us they'd saved some food for the train, not knowing whether they'd be able to get anything once they were travelling, and they didn't want to use that, so Mika left the station to find one of the peasant women in the station yard who sometimes had food for sale. These were mostly Buryat women whose men folks had been forced to join with the Cossacks in the war, and who'd disappeared. Tsar Nicholas had told his daughter they'd been used as front line troops against the advancing Germans in Poland. They hadn't stood a chance once the Germans had reorganised following the winter of 1915, and he thought many thousands had died. The women in the yard had fled from the famine in Mongolia, only to end up far from home, unable to go on, and unwilling to go back. They were a pitiful sight, but so too were many ordinary Russians, there wasn't much sympathy for these people. They lived in what they called yurts, a sort of tent, round shaped, and made from skins which they'd brought with them from Mongolia. From time to time they would barter some of the skins for food, which they'd then sell to passengers from the trains for a profit, but then the women from that tent had to crowd into one of the others, until eventually they'd have no tents left, nothing to barter, and nowhere to sleep! They lit fires all the time, to cook by and to keep warm on the cold nights, but also to keep the mosquitoes away; they used dung from the horses which passed by the station to fuel the fires; mosquitoes didn't like the smelly smoke!

It was while Mika had gone to see these Buryat women that one of the Czech soldiers came up to Anastasia on the station platform. She said he was a big brute, like a bear, and his breath was stinking of alcohol. It was very crowded, but that didn't make any difference; everyone was too afraid to interfere. The soldier pulled her by the arm, telling her she had to go with him for checking; she had a pretty good idea what checking he had in mind, and though she struggled, she couldn't do anything against him, and no-one else would help. He'd dragged her behind the shed that was used as a ticket office; the real one had been destroyed in the fighting between the Czech and Bolshevik soldiers. He was trying to tear her cardigan off, and had one hand inside her blouse, trying to pull that off at the same time. We could only imagine how terrifying that must have been, but according to what she wrote, she was more afraid he'd find the locket hidden inside her bodice than anything he might do to her! Thank God Mika heard her cries; he'd pulled the soldier off, and told him she was his wife. Surprisingly the soldier just walked away. Afterwards Mika told her if the soldier had wanted to fight he would have had to kill him, otherwise he would have reported them to his commander, and then anything could happen to them, they'd probably be made to disappear as so many others had.

It was early the following morning, 2nd September 1918 before they finally spotted the train, the wood burning engine pushing showers of sparks and thick black smoke into the dawn sky. The wheels of each carriage shrieked as they slowly passed over the sets of points. The driver leaned out of the window of his cab, his heavily sooted face peering down the platform looking at the mass of humanity waiting for him to arrive with his train.

Nicholas looked across at me.

"That driver probably had the best seat on the whole train, certainly less crowded than anywhere else and probably a lot warmer too."

Possession of tickets didn't necessarily mean you would travel on that train; you had to force your way on, pushing aside anyone smaller, weaker, or less determined than you. There was swearing and crying, but no one cared. It didn't help that the train was already full before it had even arrived at Yekaterinburg – full of refugees from the east who had the money to buy a ticket, trying to escape the starvation.

One old man left his window seat to go to the toilet; to his shame, Mika took his seat and refused to give it back when the man returned, despite his crying and begging. Mika then started blowing his nose in a disgusting way and making burping sounds, things Anastasia had never heard him do before. It was awful, and she felt really sorry for the woman sitting next to him, who eventually couldn't stand it any longer, she stood up and pushed her way further down the corridor. Quick as a flash Mika pulled Anna as he called her into the vacant seat. He'd got what he wanted!

Anastasia wrote how she couldn't help comparing the condition of the train to the Wagon Lits, which had carried the imperial family into exile. Now the carriages were filthy and were overcrowded. The body odours of her fellow passengers, many of whom had travelled for days without the possibility of washing themselves, were sickening. The heating had broken, so it was bitterly cold, particularly during the long nights, and the wind was howling through an open window in spite of efforts to block the opening. She wrote how she'd cuddled up close to Mika to keep warm. How she must have missed those army cots, which she used to complain about so bitterly, but to her credit, she quickly adapted to her new way of life. That was something Nicholas and I found remarkable.

There was no food to be had on the train, and they soon used up that they'd brought with them, so then they bought what they could from the peasant women standing on the platforms at each station – usually a loaf of old bread, perhaps some hard boiled eggs, once even some ham for which they paid an exorbitant price, even though it had seen better days. Anastasia would queue to take hot water from the samovar at the end of their carriage so they could make tea, and while she did this Mika would spread himself over both seats, defying anyone to take her place. As they travelled through the vast openness they saw the peasant huts, often huddled together for protection against the bitter winds blowing from the frozen tundra in the north. In one such settlement Mika had pointed out the black banners tied to posts outside some of the huts, indicating that someone inside had diphtheria. Stay well away!

In every station they passed, large and small, posters were on display, some showing foreigners who'd come to live in Russia and who now controlled the industries – and describing how the Bolsheviks were going to force them out, to get coal to make the factories work again, to keep the trains moving, and to bring food to the people. Other posters showed young men in uniform strung up from telegraph poles by the side of the road; they were deserters from the new Workers' and Peasants' Red Army, as the discredited Russian army was now called, but it was still in a mess. Strict discipline had been reintroduced following the failed experiment of Soviet Order No. 1, which had abolished ranks and made all the soldiers equal, but it would take time to get back to a position in which soldiers would automatically respect their officers once again.

From time to time they would pass a refugee train, eastbound like them, waiting in a siding for their train to pass; how long had they been parked there, waiting for the so-called express to pass, Anastasia had wondered. Many people were trying to flee Russia to avoid the famine that gripped the entire country. The summer of

1918 had witnessed a severe drought, the worst for many years; the harvest had been a disaster. Farm animals like sheep, cows and goats that weren't dying of hunger, were being eaten to save their owners from the same fate, but it was only a postponement of the inevitable. They didn't have the resources to replace the animals, so the horses and even dogs were next to be sacrificed, but the end was always going to be the same.

The people on these refugee trains were the really unfortunates ones; they didn't have the money to buy proper tickets. They were packed into cattle trucks. Entire families, carrying with them such personal belongings as they'd managed to save, somehow squeezed into a restricted space. Anastasia mentioned one particular train they'd passed. Like others, the sliding door was open while they waited in the sidings. People walked around off the train, beating their arms in a vain attempt to keep warm. A little girl lay on the grass, her thin, summer frock totally inadequate against the bitterly cold wind; her emaciated face and thin sticks of legs plain to see. She was clutching a rag doll, perhaps her only toy.

Nicholas translated Anastasia's plaintiff comment: "Is this what the Revolution was for? Is this the rosy future the Bolsheviks had promised the people? Is this their reward for ridding the country of a tsar who loved and cared for them?"

Nicholas looked up at me; his eyes were red, partly from emotion, but also from the sheer effort of translating such a moving testimonial to a country in ruin.

"If you don't mind, Dad, I'll just finish the next couple of pages and then take a break. I could do with a good drink!"

Anastasia was speaking to us again.

"As we travelled westwards we passed buildings whose windows had been smashed and whose walls were riddled with bullet holes. Large manor houses had all been destroyed; some were still burning. It was perfectly logical that the peasants didn't support the Whites, who were the forces opposed to the Revolution and who at this time were largely in control of areas to the east and south of the country. The peasants had been brainwashed that a White victory would restore the aristocrats to their previous positions of power and that the land reforms enabled by the Bolsheviks would be overturned.

They would have to give back the land they'd so recently acquired. It was understandable therefore they didn't support the White Army, but did they really want these Bolsheviks? As we pulled into Moscow station I saw one of Lenin's propaganda trains waiting to pull out on its journey across Russia, telling the peasants in the outlying areas what the Revolution was all about and why it had to succeed, about the abuses that had been heaped on the poor working classes. "Surely people couldn't be so blind; the truth was all around them!

"As our train came to a squealing halt and the doors were opened, a throng of unwashed humanity spilled out onto the station platform – journey's end, anyway for the vast majority of the passengers, but not for us. We'd been on that train for sixty-two hours, far longer than it would have taken in my father's day. It was a pleasure to be able to walk again and to have some fresh air instead of the highly polluted atmosphere on the train, but a shock was in store for us. In front of the station was a large square, which I'd seen many times when I'd visited Moscow with my parents. It looked as though nothing had changed. It was as busy as ever; buses, taxis, bicycles, people hurried around, and everyone seemed to have a purpose.

"This was not the way it had been back in Yekaterinburg. Here it seemed as though the Revolution had never happened. The place was alive, but slowly a sense of reality overtook us. I watched one nicely dressed woman step right over a young child curled up in a tiny ball on the pavement, as though he wasn't there. Later, when we had reached the comparative safety of Mika's grandmother's apartment in a suburb of Moscow, we learned what was happening.

"Of course we'd heard about the Cheka, Lenin's secret police. Their brutality was legendary. They were men who had rushed to answer Lenin's call for ordinary citizens to safeguard the new democracy. They were given a suit of clothes, black of course, and a gun, and told to do whatever they thought was necessary. They had no training, there hadn't been time for that; Mr Lenin wanted his spies out on the streets. The citizens of Moscow and Petrograd too, as we later found out, were terrified of these thugs, because invariably that is what they were. The lady I'd seen stepping over that poor child, and everyone else I'd seen rushing about, looking down but not seeing, were frightened, distrusting, and suspicious of everything, minding their own business as they went about their day in search of something to eat. There was food to be had if you had money - the markets were continuing to flourish, patronised by the aristocrat and communist, bourgeois and peasant alike, but if you had no money, you starved!

"Mika and I stayed in his grandmother's flat all that winter. He hadn't told her who I really was, or should I say who I'd been. By that time I'd lost all trace of ever having been a grand duchess; that had been in another life! He told her I was his girlfriend, that we were saving to get married, and had come to Moscow to look for work. Babushka was a lovely lady, and very kind to me.

She never once asked questions about my background, never about my family. Maybe this was a Cheka hang-up, or maybe she simply accepted things at face value. She had only one bedroom, and she insisted on sharing that with me, saying Mika could wait for his share until we were married. She had a mischievous glint in her eye as she said that, but to be perfectly honest, I would have been happy to share a bed with Mika. By that time I looked upon myself as his wife, even though he'd been meticulous in keeping our physical relationship at bay; he was taking care of me as he'd promised my father he would."

Nicholas put the notebook on the small folding table I'd placed between the two chairs and stood up.

"I need a drink, some food and a walk, in that order," was all he said.

Randy had followed him each step of the way, knowing he was going to get something out of this sudden movement, either food or a walk, hopefully both.

It wasn't quite 5.00 p.m. The sun hadn't slipped behind the mountains to the west of Loch Rannoch yet – too early for a tipple on a normal day – but Nicholas wasn't waiting for any of that. He poured a whisky for each of us, and took mine outside to where I'd moved to enjoy the last of the sun's rays, and went back into the kitchen to prepare supper. He'd raided the deep-freeze while I'd been making brunch and taken out a frozen pizza which he'd allowed to thaw. He'd also picked some fresh lettuce and spring onions from the garden, and with the rest of the tomatoes he'd found in the fridge he made quite a reasonable salad. Microwaved pizza isn't the best, but it was all I had in the cottage, and beggars can't be choosers.

Anyway, we wolfed it down and followed it with ice cream he'd also resurrected from the freezer. We were ready for walking, except Randy wasn't; he hadn't been fed. I filled his bowl with two good ladles of stew, and in no time he was a happy dog.

Meantime, Nicholas had picked up the notebook again; the walk was postponed. I'd laid the fire earlier in the afternoon, so it was a simple matter to light the kindling, wait a few minutes for the flame to catch, then gently place a couple of logs astride the fireplace and let the flames lick at the bark. In no time we had a good fire going.

"Are you happy for me to keep reading quickly as we did before dinner," Nicholas asked, "or would you prefer we took it more slowly?"

"Let's keep it the way it was, Son. We can always go back to anything which hasn't been clear to us."

Anastasia was in the small apartment, which belonged to Mika's grandmother or Babushka, and clearly she was enthralled with the woman.

"She treated me as though I were her own child, which for me was a new experience – to be loved by someone for my own sake, not by scheming courtiers who wanted to ingratiate themselves to us children in order to take advantage with our parents," was how she described her.

She told us they'd sit for hours in the tiny kitchen, drinking tea made from caked black bricks imported from China especially for poor people, while she told stories about her life. Her husband, his name was Kolya, was what she called a Katorga. She'd said this with so much pride in her voice Anastasia thought it must be something really important, though she'd never heard of it before. She was shocked to learn it meant someone who had been exiled to one of the very special high-security camps her own father's government had maintained in a huge uninhabited area along the Kara River in Transbaikalia. He'd been sentenced to ten years there for political agitation, but everyone knew that ten years in Transbaikalia was a life sentence: no one ever came back, except for the guards of course, and they only did one year out there, but it was a punishment posting for them too.

Babushka thought that Kolya must have died there, though she wasn't sure about that; she hadn't heard anything from him for more than five years, so she feared the worst. Kolya had been a political activist; he'd won a seat to the Duma at the beginning of 1906. The elections had produced an anti-government majority, so it was promptly dissolved by Tsar Nicholas, and some of the ringleaders were sent into exile, Kolya amongst them. Anastasia hoped that this wonderful woman wouldn't hold it against her if she ever found out she was the tsar's daughter.

Mika managed to find work from time to time, usually with a gang of labourers whose job it was to fill the holes in the roads. This was a job for life; the condition of the roads was so bad they would never be able to finish. Mika could only work when one of the other members of the gang was off sick, but it suited him that way; it left him time to explore ideas for their future plans.

Anastasia had asked him if they could get to the Crimea where she knew she would be welcomed by her grandmother, the Dowager Empress Maria Alexandrovna. A large group of the Romanov family, including the dowager empress, had left Petrograd when the troubles started in 1917 and had gathered at the Villa Ai Todor in the Crimea, a place Anastasia remembered well. Once there, Anastasia felt her troubles would be over. She wasn't to know they'd had their share of troubles too, resolved only when the Bolshevik Government signed the peace treaty with the Germans to end their involvement in the Great War, as a result of which the Germans had occupied the area and freed the group from house arrest.

While she was in Moscow, Anastasia wrote a coded letter to one of the housekeepers who'd worked for the imperial family at Livadia. The woman had a daughter Anastasia's age, called Sophia. She and Anastasia had become friendly, going shopping together and playing every day. Sophia had stayed with Anastasia the night of Olga's ball, and they'd sniggered together when they saw Olga and the young Hussar sneaking behind one of the pillars in the Italian courtyard. It seemed Sophia spent more time at Livadia than she did at her home, which anyway was very close by.

In her letter Anastasia reminisced about the times she and Sophia had spent together, without of course mentioning Livadia or any of her family's names; that would have been a dead giveaway if the letter had fallen into wrong hands. She hoped it would get through OK, and if it did, she knew the housekeeper would be able to see the dowager empress without difficulty. Anastasia had asked her grandmother to send someone to Moscow to collect her, and in the letter said that at twelve noon on the first and fifteenth days of every month she would be at a certain place near the Kremlin, where she could be contacted. That was as much as she could do. The letter was sent at the end of September, and Anastasia waited, not knowing whether the letter would get through.

The weeks seemed to pass pleasantly enough, even though both she and Mika were becoming very restless. On one day, before the snows set in, they'd gone with Babushka to a forest on the edge of Moscow, where they foraged for mushrooms, and on another day had visited her allotment and dug up the rest of the potatoes and vegetables, tilling the soil to make it fresh before the ground froze.

Once a week Anastasia went with Babushka to the bathhouse, which was on the ground floor of the apartment block. The first time was a shock for her; she'd never shared a bath with strangers before. It was women only of course, and she seemed to have coped with it very well and came to look forward to it. It was almost some kind of social event, which in some ways is what it was meant to be.

She also mentioned the first time she saw a dead body in the street. She'd gone out with Mika to the Kremlin Square on the first of November. She wanted to see if there was a message for her from the Crimea, even though she knew it would be too soon. They hung around the rendezvous point for an hour in the freezing cold, and Anastasia had been telling Mika about her life in the Kremlin, which she'd often visited when her parents had business there. She described the meeting rooms, where the main feature she seemed to remember were the wonderfully polished floors and the magnificent chandeliers. She also told him about the imperial family's quarters in the Kremlin, describing them as adequate for the few days they would be there, but quite basic.

At this point Nicholas looked up from his reading.

"A friend of mine was in Moscow on business just a few years ago. His host, a senior Russian politician, had arranged for him to have a private tour of the Kremlin. They were accompanied by the Mayor of Kiev and his wife, and of course my friend had an interpreter with him as he didn't speak the Russian language. The official conducting the tour at first refused to allow my friend's interpreter to go on the tour, but when my friend pointed out there was no point him going either, because without his interpreter he wouldn't understand what they were seeing and talking about, they relented. Apparently, my friend and the Mayor of Kiev, had to wait almost an hour while the official got permission for the interpreter to go along. Would you believe they didn't want any of the ordinary Russian population to know that, to this day, the tsar's quarters had been preserved almost as though he and his family had slept there last night! The sheets and towels are changed every week, and the rooms are cleaned every day. Isn't that incredible? Do you suppose they're waiting for him to reappear?"

Back to the book! On the way home from the Kremlin, Anastasia had been very quiet. Even though she knew it was extremely unlikely anyone would have been there waiting for her, she had maintained some hope and was disappointed. She'd also learned from a newsboard that Kaiser Wilhelm II of Germany, a cousin through her mother Alexandra, had been forced to abdicate and had gone into exile in Holland. It seemed the German generals had blamed him for losing their war, just as the Russians had her father, but at least the Kaiser was still alive! The fact that the Great War had ended was almost unnoticed in Russia, wrapped up as they were with their own revolution.

It was very foggy. She'd fallen over something on the pavement, and as Mika was helping her up she saw it was the body of an old man. He'd died where he'd fallen, and tragically it was becoming a fairly common sight in the big cities. She screamed and started to run, but Mika had pulled her back to the body; the old man was wearing a greatcoat, and Anastasia needed one! She'd described her feeling of revulsion as Mika forced her to put the coat on, and would have pulled it straight back off again, except Mika wouldn't let her. When they arrived back at the apartment, Babushka had taken the coat and cleaned it. As the winter progressed, Anastasia came to be very grateful for that greatcoat.

She continued going to the rendezvous point twice a month, but increasingly her visits were turning to despair. As the winter wore on, and her spirits fell, she and Mika would argue and Babushka would have to calm them both down. Anastasia told us that her letter had in fact been given to the dowager empress, though it had taken over six months to reach her. There was no explanation for that delay, crucial though it was.

On the morning of 11 April 1919 the Dowager Empress had embarked on the British ship *HMS Marlborough* at Yalta, with around forty other members of the royal family and their entourage. The ship had been sent at the express request of Queen Alexandra of England, the dowager empress's sister, who begged her to leave Russia before the Bolsheviks should murder her, as they had her son Nicholas and his family. Sophia, Anastasia's friend, had received the letter just the day before the ship was due to sail; she knew Marie Feodorovna was leaving on the ship and had hurried to the port to deliver it, but had difficulty persuading the port authorities to let her in. She finally managed to evade the security people and arrived at the quay side just as the last rope was about to be taken off. The Dowager Empress had seen her and had told her officials to allow the girl to come on board, thinking she wanted to escape, as they were doing. Sophia gave her the letter, and explained how it had come into her possession.

Amongst the royal family on board, in fact an aide to the dowager empress, was one Prince Dimitri Suvorin, a twenty-five-year-old bachelor. He knew Anastasia very well, and had often visited the family at their homes in Tsarskoe Selo, and Livadia. It was assumed he would one day marry either Tatiana or Maria; the oldest sister Olga having made quite clear she didn't want anything to do with him: he had a reputation as a womaniser.

The dowager empress asked him if he would leave the ship and keep the rendezvous with Anastasia and thereafter do what he could to take her to safety, to which he agreed. *HMS Marlborough* had already sailed from Yalta by this time, so the following morning it anchored off Halki Island, a dozen or so miles from Constantinople, where both Prince Suvorin and Sophia disembarked under a cloak of secrecy. The ship then carried on to Malta, where it arrived on the evening of 20 April, 1919. The dowager empress of Russia, mother of Tsar Nicholas II and Anastasia's grandmother, stayed in Malta just a few days, and on 29 April 1919 she embarked on *HMS Lord Nelson* for England, and subsequently to her parental home in Denmark.

Chapter Twelve

It was plain that both Anastasia and Mikhail became increasingly bored with their stay in Moscow, and neither was it an easy time for Babushka. Sharing her bed with an eighteen-year-old girl had been a noble gesture on her part when the pair had arrived back in September, but after three months she was becoming increasingly irritated with the arrangement. It wasn't helping that Anna, as Anastasia had been introduced to her, wasn't looking to find work.

The pair still had some gold and precious stones left, but those seemed to be disappearing at an alarming rate, and at one point Anastasia had actually accused Mikhail of stealing some of it. That seemed to us to have been a very unjust accusation; he could have walked away that very first night in the forest, taking with him all the gold and jewels that Tsar Nicholas had instructed Anastasia to give to him once they were away, and no-one would have been any wiser, but he hadn't. It could have been that he'd been hiding some of the valuables, perhaps to stop Anastasia exchanging them for money to buy the new clothes she wanted.

In the book she referred to seeing a *kapot*, a long gown traditionally worn by the wives of prosperous merchants, in a shop just off the Kremlin Square, and how she'd fantasised about wearing that at Christmas. We could only guess at how she must have felt. Her life as a grand duchess must have seemed as remote as the moon, but still she had a longing to be dressed nicely and knowing she had the wherewithal to buy the clothes must have made for a big temptation. Mikhail, on the other hand, clearly came from a poor family and would have had no idea of the worth of the jewels they were carrying.

No doubt every time he had to barter yet another jewel for cash, he was cheated by the clever businessmen, who presumably would have assumed he'd stolen it in the first place, so they were merely taking their share. However, it was also clear he had his feet very firmly placed on the ground. He realised if he allowed Anna, as he called her, to dress as she wanted, it would quickly draw unwanted attention to them.

Nicholas went back to translating what he said was word-for-word from the notebook, which even I could appreciate was not an easy thing to do.

"Babushka was determined we would celebrate Christmas, never mind that outside in the streets of Moscow everything was dreary; poverty and starvation was everywhere, what was there to celebrate? I felt like that too, but in ways I couldn't explain to her. The nearer we came to Christmas, the more I missed my family. Back then, we would practice the Christmas rite of Koliada, celebrating the birth of Christ by singing wonderful Christmas carols. As a family, always with Papa in the lead, we would go out into the streets in Tsarskoe Selo, and we'd sing carols as we walked, encouraging ordinary people to join with us; by the end of the evening, we would have a huge crowd of people in joyous spirits, and we girls would walk amongst the crowd, giving away little pieces of money. Alexei was the most popular however; Mama would give him little medallions, made in silver and showing Christ as an infant being cradled by the Virgin Mary, which the court jeweller made for her every year. Alexei would give one of these to anyone he particularly liked, and I remember Papa remarking on our last Christmas at the village how Alexei was only giving them to pretty girls!

"Now that's all gone; my parents and sisters are dead, murdered by the Bolsheviks, but at least in death they're still together. Only poor Alexei is alone, lying in that shallow grave in the woods; the ground will be frozen – it's too much to even think about. What is there to celebrate?"

Straight after Christmas Mikhail had announced they would be leaving Moscow. They were going to Petrograd where he'd heard there was a lot of work to be had and good money to earn. It was clearly a lie, told for Babushka's benefit. Twice each month, he and

Anastasia had returned to the Kremlin Square to see if there was a messenger coming from her grandmother in the Crimea, but always to no avail.

"We said goodbye to Babushka in the middle of January. It was a day of mixed feelings, sad because I'd come to look upon her almost as my grandmother, but I was happy to be moving again, though to what was uncertain. Babushka had cried when we hugged each other for the last time, imploring Mika to take care of me. Once we were gone she'd be back to leading the solitary life she'd had before we'd descended on her back in September, every day wondering if her husband Kolya would walk through the door of her little flat, free from his exile in Transbaikalia, but always knowing that as each day passed, the chance of it happening was becoming less and less."

Mikhail had gone to see the old Jewish man who had a tiny stall on the very edge of the market place. He sold what Anastasia called pierogi; these were dumplings which his wife had made with a flour substitute, mixed with water and some fat of dubious origin, salt to taste, then hollowed out and filled with cheese, if she could find any, or more likely old potatoes she'd have bought from one of the other traders. These she would then bake in an oven heated by a brazier, which the old man and his wife would sit round in their pathetically thin clothes, trying to keep warm.

His real business though was as a money lender, but he had to be careful; the Cheka were continually hounding the Jewish population, trying to force them out of business, and they would have taken his money if they'd known about it. He would also buy and sell jewels, not asking any questions where they came from. Mikhail liked dealing with him; he felt he was more honest than the businessmen he'd used when they'd first arrived in Moscow. They needed money to buy two train tickets to take them to Petrograd, and some extra so they could buy food on the journey; for that he'd given the old Jewish man a pearl necklace which the tsarina had worn on her wedding day.

Nicholas and I wondered where that necklace might be today.

Anastasia described the train journey as a nightmare. Their first mistake was in returning to the same station they'd arrived at four months previously from Siberia, only to find that trains going west left from a station across the other side of the city. It was freezing cold; the roads and pavements were covered in a thin layer of snow under which lay a much thicker layer of ice. They held hands to stop from falling. That was the first intimate contact there'd been between them since the night in the forest when he'd held Anastasia as she slept, and it seemed to have cheered her up.

"It was as though he really cared for me, and would protect me, as Babushka had told him to do. I remember looking up at his face as we walked, trying to understand what he was thinking, wondering if it was about me, but as always, he gave no signs. His face was red with the cold, especially his nose, which I found funny, and I even laughed out loud, but he just kept his eyes fixed on the pavement in front of us, carefully picking his steps. It was disappointing. I desperately needed affection, and he was the only one who could give it to me but he seemed oblivious to that."

Both Mikhail and Anastasia were wearing boots; she'd stolen hers from the dacha where they'd stayed in Yekaterinburg, and his had come from the body of the old man Anastasia's greatcoat had also come from, but both had been in need of repair. In the market Mikhail had seen a *sapozhnik*, an old Cossack man who made and repaired boots, and he'd lined theirs with the skin of a wild cat, many of which still roamed the forests on the outskirts of Moscow and would often be seen in town, scavenging for food, along with the poorer part of the population.

When Anastasia had mentioned repairs to her boots, she'd also mentioned the money she'd stolen back from Olga; she still had some left, which she continued to keep stuffed into the toecaps of her boots and which, according to her, Mikhail still knew nothing about. From her writing it was clear she saw this as her pocket money to spend on little luxuries like the occasional bar of chocolate.

The train they hoped would take them to Petrograd was pulling into the station platform as they arrived, the old engine puffing clouds of dense, black smoke from its chimney, while masses of hot steam billowed from the pistons, and the brake shoes locked onto the rims of wheels that squealed in protest at the harsh treatment. Anastasia and Mikhail pushed their way through the throng of people waiting to board the train; Mikhail had spotted an open window in one of the carriages, and quick as a flash he'd hoisted the slim Anastasia onto his shoulders and pushed her through the opening which, she recounted, she was shrewd enough to pull shut behind her.

Nicholas grinned at me and said, "She was a quick learner Dad, we should be proud of her."

Certainly I did feel very proud, not only because of the incident with the window but with the whole way she'd acclimatised herself to her new station in life, albeit she clearly hoped it would be only temporary. What I hadn't yet come to terms with, and I knew full well I couldn't put this off much longer, was what was her connection to my son and me?

Nicholas and I passed almost that entire day sitting in the conservatory, he remorselessly plugging on page after page with the book, determined to have it finished before the day was done, me topping up the pair of us, and Randy too of course, with food and drinks as seemed appropriate. It suited me fine; if I were to be honest with myself, which was something I wasn't being much of, I have to say I was enjoying all I was learning. I had a pretty good idea where it was leading, though if these were the last few pages, it was going to leave a huge gap somewhere, and hopefully we'd arrive at that point before bedtime tonight.

Anastasia described the train journey to Petrograd as being just as bad as the one from Siberia, though mercifully lasting only fourteen hours, which even so was almost four hours longer than it should have been. As before, they saw several refugee trains, cattle trucks as Anastasia described them, packed with people fleeing the famine in Siberia, but journeying to what – more of the same! The entire country seemed to be racked with ruin and despair. All during that journey they saw factories, which should have been busily belching thick smoke into the winter sky, standing idle; farms, which would have provided food for the population, were empty of people and animals. Villages they passed were almost deserted except for just a few old men and women, looking little more than bags of bones, their faces ash grey, hunch backed, weary of being alive, not quite ready for death. Only when they approached train stations did they see life, but for what? The platforms on both sides of the railway lines, westbound and eastbound, were packed full of people, a heaving mass of humanity, all seeking relief from the dreadful conditions where they were, all reassuring each other that whichever direction they'd elected to travel in, that was where there salvation lay; but it didn't!

Anastasia had convinced herself, as had all those passengers on the west-bound platforms, that in Petrograd things would somehow be different.

"Petrograd was such a civilised city," she'd written, "the people were not peasants, like those we'd seen along the way; they had proper homes and good families, they went to work, the children went to school; it was only eighteen months ago my family and I left from there in those wonderful Wagon Lit train carriages, surely little can have changed in that time. But I was wrong!

"Mika and I left the train and went into the square in front of the station. It was covered in a pristine layer of snow, blanketing the roads as well as the pavements, so it was impossible to tell which was which, but it didn't matter. Where were all the buses, the cars? Unlike Moscow, here nothing was moving. Two army lorries were parked in front of the station; they must have been there a long time because there were no tracks in the snow showing where they'd come from. Some soldiers were standing around, warmly dressed, well fed, smoking, laughing and joking with each other. Nearby were about a dozen women, mostly quite young, two with small children clinging to their mother's thin skirts, another was breastfeeding her baby, the sad little mite's lips clamped desperately to his mother's teat, draining what little strength the poor woman had left. They were huddled round a brazier trying to keep warm, even in that intense cold doing their best to appear attractive to the soldiers, so they would be chosen as the one taken into the back of one of the trucks where the man would get a few minutes relief, and her some near worthless roubles or a loaf of bread to feed her starving family. Their bodies were all they had left to give!

"I'd wanted to take a taxi from the station to a house near the Winter Palace where I remember my old nanny had gone to live after she'd retired. I knew she would look after us. But Mika had said no, we couldn't afford a taxi, and as it turned out there were no taxis anyway, the only things moving were people; thin, emaciated, all of them like scarecrows, their eyes staring down at the ground, skinny arms poking in the heaps of rubbish scattered everywhere, searching for a stick of wood to make a fire or a crust of bread to eat. So we walked.

"Once fine houses along the banks of the River Neva were in ruins: the wooden front doors and the exotic staircases long gone, as was the antique furniture and valuable paintings which had graced many of these homes, all to fill empty fireplaces to give just a little warmth so a family could exist for one more day in this hellhole.

"Is this what the people sacrificed my family for?" she asked.

"The house where my old nanny lived was in ruins, just like all the others. With Mika, I walked up the steps to where once would have been a very stout front door, but it had gone. We walked through room after room; not one window was in place, not one room habitable, not one stick of furniture, even the wallpaper which I remembered on the wall in the sitting room, and which Nanny had been so proud of – all gone. We found her in the basement where she'd been hiding, lying on the cold concrete floor, wrapped in a beautiful sable fur coat, the dark brown hair once so soft and glossy, now stiff and frostbitten. This had been a retirement present from my mother; somehow the pathetic, shivering creatures who'd robbed Nanny of almost everything she owned had missed the coat she'd used to keep warm, but even that had failed her. Nanny was dead; she'd frozen to death, the sable coat acting as a makeshift shroud."

It was as Anastasia stared at the sad bundle laying on the cold stone floor, a woman she'd loved, and who'd loved her, who'd never asked much of life, who in a last act of desperation had returned to the foetal position as though desperately trying to return to the warmth of the womb from which we all derive, that Anastasia realised the Russia she had known was gone forever. It was time to go away!

I think both Nicholas and I were damp around the eyes as we struggled to absorb what we'd learned. It was horrible; we couldn't imagine how Anastasia must have felt, after all she'd been through, then to find this.

Mikhail had taken Anastasia's hand and led her out of that awful place. All thoughts of trying to find a sympathetic face in Tsarskoe Selo were gone, they had to leave Russia. Mika knew the way to the docks in Petrograd from his time working on the royal yacht. He'd told Anastasia he hoped he'd be able to find friends there who would help them. He must have been successful, because the only mention in the notebook was of them boarding the German ship *Oberburgermeister Stettin* under cover of darkness as it prepared to cast off for its regular three-day run to Stettin in Germany. How Mikhail had organised that wasn't made clear, nor how many of their precious gold nuggets he'd used to seal the bargain. Totally without documents of any kind, the daughter of the former tsar of Russia had escaped from the country of her birth.

"Can you imagine how sad she must have felt Dad, standing as she probably did at the ship's rails, watching the lights on the shore disappearing into the night sky, her heritage, and her family, all gone forever! She was only eighteen years old, and remember, too, she was going into the totally unknown. At this point we don't know her plans or where were they heading. We need to read some more."

Nicholas had picked the notebook up, ready to start translating again, and then put it back down again.

"That ship they'd sailed on," he asked, "does the name mean anything to you?"

That was a silly question to ask of a Highland gamekeeper. What would I know of a ship sailing almost a century ago between St Petersburg, or Petrograd depending on your point of view, and somewhere called Stettin in Germany? Presumably, though, it meant something to my clever son.

"Yes, yes I remember now."

So he did know!

"There were two ships, the other one was the *Preussen*; they became known as the Philosopher's Ships because in the early 1920s, Lenin ordered the deportation of almost two-hundred intellectuals. It was claimed, or feared, these people would not be able to reconcile themselves to life in a supposed society where peasants held sway. In fact they turned out to be the lucky ones; just a few years later they would have faced almost certain death in the gulags in Siberia. In those days Stettin was in Germany, but today it is known as Szczecin and is in Poland."

Where did he get it all from? So much for a university education, but it hadn't held me back any!

Nicholas reopened the notebook.

"Leaving the ship in Stettin was sheer chaos, but that was lucky for us. The ship was overloaded, mostly with Russians, but also with some German soldiers and some others who must have been from the Czech Brigade, all trying to make their way home from a war already forgotten. Everyone was a refugee, many in the same situation as Mika and I with no documents and no visa to enter Germany. But Germany was in chaos too; even four months after the war had officially ended, whole families who'd been displaced were trying to put their lives and their families back together again.

"My first thought had been to go to the hunting lodge Papa had owned in Spala, but on the ship a German soldier, who'd been there with his unit when they were advancing in Poland, doubted it would be safe. Of course we hadn't told him who I was! The same soldier had shared a cigarette with Mika, and while they sat and smoked, he told him how Kaiser Wilhelm had been forced to abdicate, and was living in Holland. He'd joked with Mika, that in Germany they didn't kill their kings when they didn't need them anymore, not like we did in Russia. If only he'd known!"

Anastasia told us of their arrival in Germany.

"Once we realised we were safely away from the ship we looked for somewhere to sit and make our plans. On the ship that hadn't been possible; it was so crowded, people could easily have listened to what we were talking about, and secrecy had become second nature to us by then. It was very early in the morning; I remember how cold it was, and very foggy too. The cold felt different somehow to what we were used to in Russia. There it is a dry cold, whereas in Germany it was damp, so it seemed to penetrate to our very bones.

"We sat on a wall looking out over the sea. Our homeland was a long way away, there was no going back, and anyway what was there to go back to? We could only go on. Because of what the German soldier had told Mika on the ship, Spala was out of the question, though Mika was still of the opinion we should try; I think he fancied the idea of shooting wild pigs and things. Of course he was dreaming, and Spala was such a dark place and so damp. It would have been depressing after a while, and it seemed we might not be safe. We'd have to find my Cousin Wilhelm.

"Kaiser Wilhelm was the son of my mother's auntie, Victoria, princess royal of England, and he was the godfather of my brother Alexei. I'd only seen him a couple of times, and even then I was too young to remember. Anyway, I thought he was our best hope, but how to find him? We'd known for a while he'd been forced to abdicate, and the soldier Mika had met on the ship said he was living in Holland, but where?

"We saw a café, a welcome beacon of light on this foggy morning. Inside, a few old workmen were having their breakfast, which seemed to consist of thick black bread and some cold meat; one man had a boiled egg – I would have given a gold nugget just to eat that.

"There was a really bad-tempered looking woman serving behind the counter. She had a really hard face, and her hair was untidy and looked as though it hadn't been washed for ages. Maybe we didn't look too good either. We hadn't been able to wash ourselves on the ship, but that hadn't occurred to me at the time. She barked at poor Mika, like a dog would bark, and of course he didn't understand a word she'd said. She'd looked at her other customers and told them we were another pair of thieving Russians; we'd ruined our own country, now we were coming to Germany to steal from them. She told them to throw us out on the street. Until that time I'd always stayed in the background, letting Mika do the talking, but now I had to be in charge; like my brother and sisters I'd been taught German, French and English. I became angry; how dare this woman speak to us in this way, we hadn't done her any harm.

"We are not thieving Russians,' I yelled at her, 'we're from a good family, but your German soldiers killed them; they killed our mother and father, they raped my two sisters, and they would have done the same to me but for my brother Mika here, he saved me. He beat two of them off me, all on his own. As our mother lay dying, they tore her wedding ring off her finger. And you dare to accuse us of being thieves! Now we have no home, so we came to your country, hoping maybe we'd find some compassion for what your men had done, but obviously you don't care. It's not necessary to throw us out, we'll leave by ourselves. Your soldiers took nearly everything we owned, but we still have our pride."

Nicholas was trying hard not to laugh.

"Where on earth did she get all that from?" he wondered. "That doesn't sound like the young grand duchess we've known until now. She's become hardened, and it's not difficult to understand why."

Anastasia told us the woman was shocked to hear her speak German, and High German at that. She didn't go so far as to apologise, but did tell them to sit at one of the tables, and she'd get them some breakfast. When it came, both Anastasia and Mika were surprised. They each had two boiled eggs and some cold meat that looked like ham, though it didn't taste like anything they'd eaten before, and generous lumps of the black bread like the workmen were eating. They were given mugs of steaming hot coffee, a real delicacy, and laced with sugar too!

After the workmen had gone, the woman came and sat with them.

"I'm very sorry for what I said, I didn't mean any harm, but we've had a difficult time too. But you're so young, I'm sorry for what our soldiers did to your family."

Of course Mika couldn't have understood a word of what was going on, but that hadn't stopped him wolfing his breakfast down, no doubt wondering what Anastasia had said to deserve it. Anastasia had offered to pay, though she had no idea how – they had no German money at that point – but fortunately the woman wouldn't let her, telling her it was her way of apologising for being so cruel. Anastasia had brought the discussion round to the abdication, offhandedly asking if the woman knew where the kaiser had gone to live.

"Oh, I know where he's gone," she'd answered, "Though that wasn't good enough. He should have been strung up for what he's done to our country, and to yours too, and how many young men have died because of him. He's at a place called Doorn in Holland, and he'd better stay there. He's not welcome back here."

Anastasia didn't know where Doorn was; come to that she didn't know where Holland was in relation to where they were, but it seemed they still had a long way to go. But the café lady wasn't finished yet.

"He took off as soon as he realised we'd lost the war, and remember young lady, here in Germany we called it 'the Kaiser's War', and he'd lost it, so he was going to be in trouble, and believe me, he knew it.

He took his eldest son with him too, another Wilhelm, probably no better than his father, good riddance to both of them I say."

Anastasia had picked up her ears at mention of the Crown Prince Wilhelm. He'd visited them in Tsarskoe Selo, and her mother had been particularly impressed with him, remarking to the girls it was important the two families got on well together.

"I wanted to know about his wife more than him; she was the Crown Princess Cecilie, and was the daughter of Grand Duchess Anastasia Mikhailovna, a great friend of my mother. In fact, I think I was named after her. If I could only find her!

"I suppose the young Wilhelm took his wife with him to Holland,' I asked the woman, "and their children?'

"No, and there's a thing,' she'd answered. "That's one lady with her head in the right place. The rumour is, she told her husband he could run away if he wanted, but Germany was her home, and her children's home, and no one was going to drive them away. She's still living in the palace in Potsdam that's named after her.'" The café owner had referred to Schloss Cecilienhof, a castle which the Kaiser had arranged to be built in Potsdam for his eldest son, the heir to the Hohenzollern throne.

Once the woman had returned to her duties behind the counter Anastasia had explained to Mikhail what she had learned.

"We're not going to Holland, Mika; we're going to Potsdam. That's much closer to where we are now. It's next to Berlin, and I'm sure we're going to be safe there."

She'd gone on to explain the relationship between her and Cecilie's mothers. Anastasia hadn't said what Mikhail felt about the arrangement; it would surely have been mixed. They'd been together for more than six months, living what he, and most certainly Anastasia too, would have described as a common life, but once Anastasia was back amongst her own kind, what future would there be for him? We wondered whether Anastasia had even thought of that?

They left the café well fed, and from her writing it was clear their morale was the highest it had been for a long time. The journey to Berlin, a distance of around two hundred kilometres, was accomplished that same day. At the train station in Stettin they'd seen a money-changer's booth, and Mika had wanted to see if the man would accept a gold nugget in exchange for German money. Anastasia told him it wasn't necessary; she described the look on his face as he saw her sit on a bench on the station platform and take off one of her boots. Poor man, he must have thought she'd gone mad, and when he saw her take out a handful of money, his look had apparently changed to one of astonishment. Anastasia had confessed it didn't smell too good; she hadn't washed her feet or her thick winter stockings for more than a week, but the money changer didn't say anything about that, and he gave them what they thought seemed like a good rate.

"The 4th of February 1919," Anastasia had written, "was a date I will always remember. We'd arrived in Berlin the previous evening, tired after the long journey from Stettin. Straight opposite the train station was a hotel, not very good class, but better than we'd had since leaving Babushka's apartment three weeks earlier, and the rent was cheap. We checked in as man and wife, which caused me a bit of a problem a few days later, but it was all we could afford, and Mika had never once tried to take advantage of me. He paid for two nights; the landlady wanted money in advance, I suppose she didn't trust us. We wouldn't have looked too good to her!

"Our room was on the first floor landing. It was very small, little more than a cupboard, and had one tiny window which looked across the square to the station. It had a bed, what I suppose you'd call three quarter size – certainly it wasn't big enough to be a proper double – an old chest of drawers, and a wobbly chair. The linoleum on the floor was torn in places, and the net curtains at the window were dusty and grimy with age. The window hadn't been cleaned for many years; I tried to open it, but the hinges were rusty and wouldn't move. The window sill outside was full of bird droppings. No doubt it all sounds horrible, but to us it was bliss. For the first time in ages we had something we could call our own; no one would try to throw us out, we had a proper bed, and blankets so we wouldn't be cold, as we had been for so many nights since leaving the house of death. There was a bathroom on the same floor, and Mika allowed me to go first. It was heaven, just to lay and soak in hot water, and in private, whereas in Moscow, which was the last time I'd had a proper bath, the women all bathed together. I stayed in that bath until the water was stone cold, and then Mika went to have his. He was back in our room in less than ten minutes; poor man, I'd used all the hot water, so he had a quick scrub and that was all!

"That was the first time Mika and I had actually shared the same bed, but still nothing happened between us. In fact, we'd had a big argument. He accused me of not being truthful with him about the money in my boots, and when I told him I'd stolen it back from his girlfriend Olga in Yekaterinburg, he called me some bad names, and didn't talk to me any more that night. I think it hadn't helped that I'd used all the hot water!

Anastasia had worried how she would make contact with Cecilie, as she was referring to her.

"I can hardly walk up to her front door and say who I am. She's never met me, why would she believe my story? I decided to do the same thing I'd done with my grandmother. I'd write her a letter, and this time I'd ask Mika to deliver it for me. Then I'd have to wait and see what happens, and just hope for a better result.

"I wrote that letter in our hotel room; it was a bit difficult because Mika was still angry with me about the money, and he kept shouting, calling me a thief, while I was trying to concentrate. Anyway, early the next morning he left the hotel, still in a bad mood from the night before, and said he'd see me when he got back from Potsdam, but if they threw him in gaol I'd better start running again. Poor man, whenever he was mad, he wouldn't talk to me for days.

"All that day I stayed in my room, waiting to see what would happen, wondering where Mika was, if he was all right, and I slept a lot too. The bed wasn't very big, and the mattress was lumpy; Mika didn't snore, not like Babushka, but he'd been very restless, turning over and over and several times nearly pushing me onto the floor, so I hadn't slept a lot during the night. I didn't have anything to eat the whole day, and drank only water from the tap in the bathroom.

"It was the middle of the afternoon when I heard a commotion on the stairs. It would have been impossible to climb those stairs without making a noise; they were so old and creaky. I think we must have been the only people staying in the hotel, otherwise we'd have heard every time anyone climbed them. I heard Mika's voice, speaking in

Russian, telling someone I was in a room on the first floor; I confess I was feeling frightened, wondering what was about to happen. There was a discreet tap on the door, and then Mika opened it, mouthing at me not to worry, nodding his head as if to reassure me everything was all right.

"A lady stood behind Mika, and I mean a lady. She looked wonderful. She was as tall as him, about forty years old I should say. She was wearing a coat made of a beautiful fur, dark brown, very similar to the one nanny had been wearing when she died, and with a matching hat, designed I should say to keep her head warm more than being fashionable. Remember we were still in February. Her dress was full length, made of silk it seemed, pale blue with mauve spots. She was wearing a string of pearls round her neck and carried a leather handbag of the kind designed to be practical. A bit like her hat I suppose. I couldn't see her shoes; her dress seemed to sweep over her feet. I used to see ladies like her every day of my life in St Petersburg, but that was a lifetime ago.

"Behind her stood a man in a dark suit, wearing jack boots, and in his hand holding a peaked hat. He was older than the lady. As it turned out he was the chauffeur.

"The next few minutes passed in a haze of confusion.

"Anastasia, is it really you?' she asked, speaking in Russian.

"I could only nod, I was speechless. The lady was looking me up and down, desperately trying to reconcile the scruffy, poorly dressed and ill-kempt woman standing in front of her with the grand duchess she'd last seen on the night of Olga's ball in Livadia on the Crimea. I remember I started to cry, the pent-up emotion of so many months on the run, stealing food as we went, nights sleeping in the cold and wet, taking clothes from dead bodies so we could stay alive, and suddenly I was confronted with a vision of grace and elegance from my past; it was all too much. I sat on the bed and the lady sat with me, her arm around my shoulder, holding me as I sobbed. She'd shooed Mika and the chauffeur out of the room, not wanting them to see me in my distress. She was talking to me, urging me to cry more, using the kind of words Mika didn't know to comfort me, words I hadn't heard in such a long time. She was from my past, but I wasn't the sweet Anastasia she seemed to remember. I'd changed.

"I must pull myself together. Where was Mika? What must he be feeling? I pushed her away, perhaps none too gently, and stood up, drying my tears on the sleeve of my frock.

"'Yes, I really am Anastasia. Who are you?'

"Her name was Countess Maria Petrovna Bobrinsky; she'd been a lady-in-waiting to the dowager empress whenever she visited the Crimea. She'd chosen to escape to Germany, whereas the rest of the royal party and other nobles were waiting to be evacuated to England, including of course the dowager empress herself. She'd come to Potsdam to see the Crown Princess Cecilie, and now stayed at the Russian colony on Nedlitzer Strasse, just behind the Castle Cecilienhof. The crown princess had telephoned her that morning; a Russian man had just delivered a letter to her, from a lady calling herself Anastasia, daughter of Tsar Nicholas II. She was in a hotel in Berlin, and she wanted to meet with the Crown Princess. She asked me to see this lady, and if she really was who she claimed, bring her to the Castle."

The way Anastasia had written the next piece gave us an idea as to the kind of dilemma she was going to have to face, reconciling how she'd lived for the past six months, to her previous lifestyle of wealth and glamour.

"The Countess suggested I might like to take a few minutes to compose myself, while she would go outside to talk to my servant; she'd give him some money and send him on his way.

"'My servant!' I'd shouted at her. He's not my servant he's my...' What? All the old Imperial arrogance had returned in the flash of that moment, but then I went quiet. What is Mika to me, I wondered? If I asked the landlady downstairs who he was, she'd say he was my husband; if I asked the café owner in Stettin she'd say he was my brother, and if I asked Babushka she'd say he was my boyfriend. These were all lies we'd told to suit the particular circumstance we were in at the time, and now the countess assumes he's my servant, probably because anything else is unthinkable.

What do I feel for him? Last night, as we lay in bed together I'd spent long minutes watching him by the light coming in from the small window, while he was tossing and turning in his sleep. I can honestly say I thought of him as my man; I don't mean that as a servant, I mean he belonged to me and me to him, equally. I'd wondered last night if I loved him, and did he love me? I told myself yes to the first, and no to the second. Never had he shown me any sign of affection. He'd done what he'd promised my father he would do: he'd taken me to a place of safety. Now he'd kept his promise, maybe he wanted to go away, even back to his home town of Irkutsk, to see if Olga had made the journey safely"

Anastasia had apologised to the Countess for shouting at her. She'd told her for the time being it would be better for Mikhail to stay near her; they still had things to sort out. She hadn't explained to the countess what she meant by that, no doubt preferring to face that issue only when she had to. As they were leaving the hotel Anastasia had turned to the landlady and asked for the return of one night's lodging money, saying they wouldn't be needing the room any longer. The landlady was so overwhelmed by what was going on she'd returned the money without so much as a murmur, whereas the countess had looked askance, the look on her face being one of disbelief that Anastasia, if she really was who she claimed to be, could be so common as to demand the return of some money!

The problem of what to do with Mika surfaced again immediately they left the hotel to get in the car. The chauffeur had opened one of the rear doors for the two ladies, whereas Anastasia had made a beeline for the front door. It was a habit. You got the seat nearest to the driver; that was always the warmest place. In the past few months they'd travelled in all kinds of vehicles: trains, buses, even a *tarantass*, like a horse and cart on which you piled your possessions and then lay on top of them so they didn't fall off again, but never had they travelled in a chauffeur-driven car. The countess had exchanged a haughty look with the chauffeur and shrugged her shoulders, but Anastasia meanwhile had realised her error and joined the countess in the back seat.

Anastasia told us how the car drove through the entrance portal of the Chateau Cecilienhof, turned round the beautiful flower bed, and come to a halt in front of a covered archway, inside of which was a heavy double door. The crown princess was standing in the doorway, waiting to greet her visitors. She was wearing a pink ensemble, pink being her favourite colour, and a large matching hat. The contrast between the pink of her hat and her dark-coloured hair was really exotic, and her big eyes, so sad looking, yet her face glowed with sincerity and warmth; she was truly beautiful, perhaps the most beautiful woman Anastasia had ever seen. She immediately fell in love with Cecilie, who she went on to describe as being down to earth, not one to stand on ceremony. She embraced Anastasia immediately they met, without reservation, notwithstanding the clothes she was wearing, nor the poor condition of her complexion; she shook hands with Mikhail too, which was something the countess certainly hadn't done.

Once inside, she'd heard Mikhail gasp in surprise; they were in the main hall, which had a high-vaulted, wood-beam ceiling, reminding him of the upturned hull of a ship, which had sunk in shallow water not far from his home on Lake Baikal. Even more impressive was the staircase which faced them; constructed in richly engraved oak, fully two metres wide and richly carpeted, this led up to the private apartments on the first floor. Crown Princess Cecilie had led the way to her own private sitting room, another surprise not only for Mikhail, but for Anastasia too. This room was designed like a cabin on a ship, and served to remind Cecilie of her passion for sailing. Cecilie was very proud of her desk and its matching chair. They were made of birch from her mother's Russian homeland, and the desk had so many drawers she could never remember where she'd put anything.

Anastasia mentioned the bathroom; she'd never seen a sunken bath before, and the dusky pink tiles she thought very sophisticated. They were invited to sit, and instinctively did so side by side on the settee, an action not unnoticed by their hostess. A uniformed maid served afternoon tea, English style, a tradition the crown princess had adopted following a visit to England just before the war. She'd explained that her husband had been forced to go into abdication with his father, which of course Anastasia already knew, but she'd been allowed to stay in the palace with her children. Saying that, she'd invited Anastasia to look through the porthole shaped window, where they had a view of the Prince's Garden, and where two of the children were playing. Cecilie had six children, and was clearly a very proud mother.

Cecilie had immediately put them at ease. She hadn't asked a single question of either of them, but just chatted away while they were having their tea. She'd explained she'd had the idea to make the room they were sitting in like a ship's cabin when she'd travelled to Stettin to christen a steamship in the dockyard there, a ship to which she'd been privileged to give her own name.

No doubt the mention of Stettin would have caused Anastasia and Mikhail to look at each other. They'd disembarked there just two days earlier!

"This lady took me to her heart straight away," Anastasia had written. "She told me it was ridiculous to keep calling her Crown Princess; the Kaiser had abdicated, the future of royalty in Germany was in doubt.

"'My name is Cecilie, and if I may, I will continue to call you by your given names, too.'

"She'd included Mika in that! She confessed she had so many questions she was dying to ask, but first she should play the part of a good hostess, and look after her guests who'd been on the road for such a long time.

"There will be plenty of time to talk of your adventures later," she'd said.

"Unfortunately all the rooms in the palace are taken just now, so I have arranged for you to sleep in the Marble Palace," she told them. "This is just a short way from here, and has wonderful views over Holy Lake; no one else is staying there, so you won't be disturbed. Please look upon that as your home for as long as you wish. You and I are of a similar size Anastasia, and Mikhail, you aren't much different from my husband, and I'm sure he won't mind you borrowing some of his clothes. I'll have them sent down to the Marble Palace straight away."

With that, she escorted them back to the main hall, where the chauffeur and a butler were waiting to take them to their new home.

Nicholas looked across at me.

"That was one very trusting lady or one very clever one, probably both," he said, "to give them a chance to settle down, sort themselves out, and doubtless watch very carefully for any mistakes they make.

And can you imagine how Mika would have been feeling. He must have been so far out of his depth!"

I couldn't help but agree, and I would have added the word "kind" to his description of the crown princess. She would have watched the body language between Anastasia and Mikhail, she wouldn't have been able to make up her mind whether they were lovers or whatever; it would have been perfectly obvious to her that Mikhail was not of the same class as Anastasia, but who knows what they'd gone through together, and how they'd dealt with all their trials and tribulations? No doubt the maids in the Marble Palace would have been instructed to watch very carefully, and report back to Cecilie. Equally interesting to me, Nicholas had started to call Anastasia's friend Mika, instead of the more formal Mikhail we'd both been using until now.

"The relationship between Mika and me began to change within hours of our moving into the Marble Palace. The butler had been very discrete; he'd left it to us to choose our own sleeping arrangements, and it was my decision to have separate bedrooms, but right next to each other. I knew of course that protocol demanded we each revert to our respective stations in life, but I wasn't sure I could face up to that and I agonised over what to do for several days. Eventually, it was dear Mika who resolved it for me.

"It was on our fifth day at the Marble Palace when he suggested we go for a walk by the side of Holy Lake. I was pleased to agree; we were starting to get under each other's feet and bickering with one another, which was ridiculous considering all we'd been through together. There was a lovely pathway along the side of the lake, going to the Green House, then on to Cecilienhof. I remember it was a beautifully clear day, with a lovely blue sky, quite unusual for the middle of February. "Benches had been placed at intervals along the pathway for walkers to sit on, each with wonderful views over the lake, and Mika led me to one of these. I'll try to remember his actual words.

"'Anna,' he'd said, and how poignant it had sounded to hear him call me that. 'I've done as your father asked; you are now in a safe place. We've done many strange things together; we've faced great dangers, we've lied, we've cheated, and we've stolen things which didn't belong to us, and we did those things because we didn't want to die. That is behind us now. Over these weeks I've watched you change from a spoilt young girl, into a mature woman, and I'm proud to have been part of that change. You forced yourself to stop being a grand duchess, to become a peasant woman, and now you have to force yourself to change back again, to regain your true station in life. I have loved you from that very first time you talked to me on your father's yacht. I told myself my love for you was as a brother, but if I'm to be honest, with myself as well as with you, the temptations to believe otherwise were at times very strong but that too now has to change.

"'My station in life is not to live in a grand palace, to dress in fine clothes, and to have servants   none of those things. Our adventure, my dearest Anna, and at times it was a wonderful adventure, is over. When we leave this bench, you will no longer be my Anna nor I your Mika. I will go away, because I couldn't stand to be near you, but no longer a part of you. Last night while you were sleeping I took such few possessions as I own and left them further down this pathway. My dearest Anna, you now have your life back again, now I must try to find mine.'

And with that he stood up and held out his hand. The man whose bed I'd shared in that hotel room, who saved my life, who for so many months had been my guide, my saviour, was about to shake my hand and walk out of my life forever! I'd clung to my Mika in desperation, my arms clasped tightly together round his shoulders, my cheek next to his while the tears rolled down my face like a torrent, my whole body shaking in uncontrollable grief, how could he be so uncaring as to leave me in this way?

"I watched as he walked away, and I cried; oh how I cried. From the way Mika walked I could see he was trying to be brave; his head was upright, his shoulders back, his strides long and purposeful, but I know my Mika, he was crying just as much as I."

Chapter Thirteen

Grand Duchess Anastasia Nikolaevna Romanov, watched as the man who'd been her friend, her saviour, a man she felt she truly loved, walked out of her life forever. She stayed sat on that bench, trying to control her grief, desperately wanting to believe that Mika had been right to walk away, and knowing that in losing him, she'd also lost her heart.

Crown Princess Cecilie was at the Green House; she'd watched the sad scene take place. She couldn't hear the words Mikhail had spoken, but she could see what he'd done, and understood he'd had no choice. He was a very brave young man. As he walked out of sight of Anastasia, so Cecilie had stepped out in front of him on the pathway. She offered him her handkerchief to dry his tears. Such a delicate lace handkerchief had no place in his life. He waved it away, not ungratefully, and tried to dry his tears on the back of his hand. She kissed him on both cheeks and pressed into his hand a sum of money, enough to take him home to Irkutsk, if that was where he was going, and with more to spare.

I looked across at my son.

"Nicholas, I couldn't have done what Mika did. It was clear he loved Anastasia, but he'd forced himself to always remember his own place in life and not take advantage of her, as he could so easily have done. Wherever the rest of that book you are holding is going to take us, it has just lost something of huge importance in her life."

Nicholas nodded his head in agreement.

"Mika was clearly a very unusual man; he could so easily have lost his head in the clouds, but instead kept both feet planted very firmly on the ground. I would dearly love to have known him."

Nicholas continued with the notebook, trying to control the sadness he now felt for Anastasia and for Mika.

Cecilie had walked to the gate with Mika. Her car and chauffeur were waiting there. She told the driver to take Mikhail to wherever he wanted to go, which happened to be the train station in Berlin. After he'd gone, she waited a while and then walked down the pathway, to the bench where Anastasia was still sitting. She'd stopped weeping, and was looking across the lake, but not seeing anything, totally lost in her own sad thoughts. Cecilie had taken a small picnic, and together they moved to sit on the grass. Later that afternoon Anastasia moved into the Chateau Cecilienhof; the crown princess hadn't spoken the truth when she'd said all the rooms were occupied, she'd wanted to give Anastasia the time to sort herself out and to decide her own future. She put Anastasia in the guest suite on the ground floor. That was fully self-contained, and from the living room Anastasia could walk through the French windows into the Princes Garden, where she would spend hours on her own.

Late that night the crown princess had sat by the side of Anastasia's bed, holding her hand, as they talked of the past. Cecilie had noticed the beautiful locket Anastasia was wearing round her neck; for many weeks this had been safely hidden inside her petticoat. The locket was heart shaped, made of gold with an enamel inlay; inside was a picture of a very young baby, and on the opposite face of the locket were engraved the initials 'N' and 'A', intertwined in gold letters, surrounded by diamond chips in the form of a crown. A tiny catch beside the picture caused a secret panel to open, revealing a lock of light brown hair. Any doubts Cecilie might have had about her guest's true identity were gone; she knew beyond a shadow of doubt this girl really was the Grand Duchess Anastasia.

Anastasia had already warned us there were still difficult times ahead, and so it proved. The Prussian state had confiscated the entire fortune of the House of Hohenzollern when the Kaiser had abdicated in November 1918. As a result, Cecilie didn't have the financial resources to keep the chateau, so in the winter of 1920 she moved with four of her children to a renaissance castle in a small town called

Oels, in Upper Silesia, leaving her two oldest sons Wilhelm and Louis Ferdinand behind in the Prince's Wing of the chateau in order not to jeopardise any rights of succession they might one day have.

Anastasia, who by this time everyone understood to be a close friend of Cecilie's own family, moved with them. Other than remarking that both she and Cecilie much preferred being in Oels, away from the make-believe social life of Potsdam and Berlin, she said very little of that time in her life.

"The year after we moved to Oels, rumours began circulating in Berlin that Anastasia had survived the massacre in Yekaterinburg. This worried us a great deal; only a very small handful of people knew who I really was, and Cecilie was confident none of them would betray my secret. If that wasn't bad enough, worse was to follow. They published an interview in a Berlin newspaper with a woman claiming to be me. According to the newspaper, she'd jumped off a bridge in Berlin in an attempted suicide bid, to escape from the trauma of the murder of her entire family, and when that failed, she'd decided to openly declare her identity.

I read the newspaper interview with amazement; she knew so many details of my life and about my family – things which only someone really close to us could have known. Even Cecilie started looking at me strangely, wondering if in fact it was me who was the hoaxer, not this other woman. This was an extremely tense time; my biggest worry was if one of the few people who knew of my real existence became so enraged at this imposter they started dropping hints, to disgrace her, but in so doing, put me at risk."

It was curious how many things Nicholas knew of the Romanov family, notwithstanding he was studying Russian history at university. He knew about this imposter. She found her way to America. Her real name was Franziska Schanzkowska, but she also called herself Anna Anderson. She originally came from Poland. She succeeded in fooling quite a lot of people, including curiously Princess Irene, a close friend of Anastasia's mother, and her son Prince Sigismund, who'd known Anastasia quite well. Some years after the impostor's death, DNA testing was done which proved conclusively she was not a Romanov, but where did she get so much information about the Romanov family? The consensus of opinion seems to put the blame on Gleb Botkin, the son of the Romanov family physician who was killed in the house of death with the family, though why he would do that is not known.

Anastasia again:

"In 1923 Crown Prince Wilhelm was allowed to come back to Germany, having given a solemn undertaking to Chancellor Stresemann not to enter into political life. He had visited my family in Tsarskoe Selo, but that was in 1903, I was only two years old then, so of course I had no memory of him. Years later I remember my mother talking about him, saying how important it was for our two families to get on well together, and she seemed to have been most impressed by the young Crown Prince. Anyway he arrived at Oels on 9 November 1923, having spent five years to the day separated from his wife.

He was a very nice man, not arrogant, quite ordinary in many ways, but he was very quiet; he would withdraw into himself for days on end. Cecilie told me privately he'd changed; I suppose five years in exile can do that to you. I don't think he and Cecilie were getting on that well – maybe because they'd been apart so long; I don't know. Cecilie had secretly passed a message to him in Holland that I was alive, and staying with her, so he wasn't surprised to meet me, and in fact he helped a lot to prove I was who I claimed, and not an imposter. He told me there was a photo of my brother Alexei on his mother's writing desk in Doorn, though why she should have had it he didn't know.

"Was he just testing me I wondered? Anyway, I knew why it was there.

"'The Kaiser was Alexei's godfather,' I answered.

"It was as though my answer to that question had resolved any doubt in his mind that I really was Anastasia.

"Two things happened in the next year; Petrograd, what I continued to call St Petersburg, had its name changed yet again. It became Leningrad, in honour of the revolutionary who'd died some months earlier. It will always be St Petersburg to me! The other thing that year, much more important, was that Grand Duke Kirill Vladimirovitch Romanov, first cousin on my father's side, who was living in exile in France, proclaimed himself Titular Emperor of all the Russias. I remember him as being a rather arrogant and pompous man, a bit like the Kaiser, but of course I didn't say that to Cecilie, and giving himself the title of Emperor without the authority to do so, was in keeping with my memory of him. I wasn't surprised. Curiously, he did one thing, which is probably no more valid than his claim to the title, but which pleased me immensely; he cancelled the edict laid down by Tsar Paul I which decreed only males can inherit the title of Emperor. Why he would have done that, I don't know, but it meant I was the Empress and Autocrat of all the Russias, albeit in exile! Much good may it do me. If he'd known I was alive he'd have told the whole world – he was a bit like that – so he didn't do it to help me; he had three children, two girls and a boy, so perhaps he thought if something happened to his son Vladimir, then either one of his daughters, Mariya or Kira, could succeed him. Anyway, that's my guess."

We'd taken a break; I needed some fresh air. Randy was desperately clawing at the door, which probably meant that nature was calling him, and Nicholas's eyes were red from reading Anastasia's handwriting, which wasn't always of the best. He'd turned on the early evening news; he was worried about the effect of the oil price increase imposed by OPEC, and whether there was any connection between the apparent suicides of the OPEC president and the secretary general of the League of Arab States, both of which had been reported in the past couple of days.

"You know what I don't understand Dad," he said, causing me to stop in my tracks as I was about to leave by the conservatory door, "how can they threaten to use force to expel our troops from Iraq and everywhere; they don't have the number of troops, they certainly don't have the equipment, and the Islamic countries are never united enough to make a stand like that? What are they driving at, and who is this Saudi minister mentioned in the Egyptian's suicide letter?"

How was I supposed to know answers to questions like that, and really, what the heck had it got to do with us, although I suppose the oil price hike will bite hard? I hadn't bothered to answer, noticing that he'd gone back to watching the screen.

"Wow, look at that," he declared, "lines of trucks blockading the

M1 motorway, and all the other motorways, too, by the look of it. Sheer chaos!"

He wasn't exaggerating. The television coverage had moved on to show farm tractors blockading Whitehall, even the entrance to Downing Street; Prime Minister Gerald Smith was shown abandoning his official Jaguar car and walking back to No. 10, flanked by nervous looking security men. The port of Dover was blockaded too, by British motorists angry at the French imposition of the fuel tax on British registered vehicles. A scuffle had broken out between some French truck drivers, trying to get home for the weekend, and a crowd of what looked like English yobs taking advantage of the dispute to settle some supposed differences of their own. In major cities up and down the country demonstrations were taking place, demanding the government find ways to absorb the increased cost of petrol and diesel. All the airlines were imposing fuel surcharges, even those that had block purchased their fuel months before, taking advantage of the crisis to boost their own balance sheets.

"Nicholas, it's very reassuring sitting here in the Highlands, far away from strife like that. I don't know what it will do to the price of your plane ticket back to America though; I suppose since you've already got it, they can't do anything. When are you going back home anyway?

Nicholas's retort was unnecessarily sharp. "The airlines will do whatever they choose, as they always do, and as for when I'm meant to be going back to the States, we'll probably learn more when we have dinner at the Castle ."

"Dinner," I asked, more than a little surprised, "what's this about dinner at the Castle? I presume you mean Rannoch Castle?"

"Dad, you know all about the invitation," Nicholas said? "We've been invited by the Grand Master to have dinner with him, just us and Sinclair, as a sort of pre-St John's Day celebration. Remember my birthday also falls on St John's Day, and as I'm twenty-one this year, I can officially be knighted into the Order, so that's going to happen on Tuesday in the chapel. You remember, of course, I was baptised into the Order, but this is their official recognition of me as a fellow Knight."

As he was speaking he'd gone to the mantelpiece above the

fireplace, and pulled a large white envelope from where it was half hidden by the old-fashioned clock, which has sat there for more years than I care to remember. I examined the envelope carefully, deeply suspicious. It was addressed to me; the stamp had been franked in Perth last Monday, the same day Nicholas had arrived at the bothy.

"I put this here," he told me, "it was laying on the floor just inside the conservatory door when I arrived. I'm sorry; I thought you'd seen me pick it up. Anyway it's not a big deal is it? It's kind of the Grand Master to take the trouble."

Randy had been outside and done what he needed, and Nicholas had resumed his seat as he finished telling me about the envelope, all of which suggested we might as well finish the notebook.

Anastasia told us Cecilie and her family moved back to the Potsdam chateau in 1926, questions about inheritance and ownership of the chateau, and the financial affairs relating to the House of Hohenzollern having been amicably settled by the Prussian state authorities, but Anastasia was becoming restless again. She was twenty-five years of age, and she was complaining of having nothing to look forward to. She talked of wanting to be married and to have a child to continue the imperial succession, but marriage had to be to someone of royal blood, and there was no one like that around her.

"It was the same year the family had returned to Potsdam they had a private visit from Adolf Hitler. At the time he was an up-and-coming politician and presumably felt that the support of the Hohenzollerns would enhance his electoral chances. In his meeting with the crown prince he suggested a return of the monarchy was a possibility.

"Four years later a rather more senior politician had come calling. This time it was a representative of German Chancellor, Heinrich Bruning. Constitutional issues were being discussed in the Reichstag; there was growing support for the return of the monarchy, but of a constitutional variant, rather than the absolute monarchy, which Wilhelm II, and of course my father too, had enjoyed. He told us it was unthinkable that Kaiser Wilhelm himself be reinstated; he was held personally responsible by the German people for their defeat in the war, but there was support for the crown prince, and even more for his oldest son, Wilhelm. Unfortunately there was a problem, the president of Germany, Marshal Hindenburg, was an old man; he was steadfastly loyal to the Kaiser and would not support any other candidate for the monarchy, which meant there was nothing to stop the rise to power of the ultra-right wing National Socialist Party. The chancellor was asking Wilhelm to intercede with President Hindenburg.

"You can imagine how excited the crown prince and Cecilie were. There were endless discussions long into the night and many telephone conversations with the kaiser in his exiled residence in Holland. For me too, this was an exciting time; if the German monarchy could be restored, why not that in Russia too? But sadly it wasn't to be. The kaiser was convinced Marshal Hindenburg was right to hold out for the restoration of the monarchy exactly as it was pre-war. When Chancellor Bruning's representative returned to hear the family's news, he was clearly disappointed. He was sure that nothing now would stop Mr Hitler's rise to power, and of course that's exactly what happened.

"It was my birthday, the fifth of June 1931 when my whole world turned upside down, and in the nicest way possible. It was a glorious day, the sun was warm, there wasn't a cloud anywhere in the sky, and the water on Holy Lake was as calm as could be. I was sitting with Cecilie and her daughter Alexandrine on the lawns; we were chatting about nothing in particular. We heard a car drive up to the chateau, and Alexandrine walked over to see who had arrived. Cecilie and I heard her scream of delight, and she came racing back to where we were sitting.

"Anastasia," she was yelling, 'Anastasia, come quickly."

"Words almost fail me from here on.

"Coming across the lawn were two men and one woman; one of the men was striding authoritatively in front, beautifully dressed in riding boots, breeches, and an extremely elegant coat. When he saw me he broke into a run, his arms outstretched, and the look on his face one of delight."

"Anastasia Nikolaevna, is it really you!' he was crying."

"I recognised him instantly: Prince Dimitri Ivanovich Suvorin, the only son of one of my father's best friends and a distantly related cousin. I'd known him all my life; our families were together at every opportunity, especially in the Crimea where his family had a villa very close to Livadia. I stood up and he literally swept me into his arms, both of us laughing, crying, and shouting with emotion. He was whirling me round, which was when I saw the two people who'd accompanied him. One was Mika, looking much older than when he'd walked out of my life twelve years before, and the other was Sophia, the daughter of our housekeeper in Livadia, though to be honest I hadn't recognised her.

My world was turned upside down at that moment. How many times had I thought about Mika in those years, dearest Son? I thought about him every single day. With the passage of time I'd come to idolise him; he was a real man, he'd saved my life, and he'd taken nothing from me when he could so easily have taken everything. Suddenly to see him in front of me like that, he became instantly human again, no longer the hero figure of my dreams. He'd put on a little weight, and he was dressed quite well but not of the same class as Dimitri. I remembered the last words he had spoken to me: 'When we leave this bench you will no longer be my Anna, nor I your Mika.'

"He was right!

"The following day, I suddenly realised I was alone with Mika. I think the others had deliberately engineered that to happen. This was when he told me his story.

"After I left Potsdam," he said, "I made my way back to Moscow and back to Babushka. Every two weeks, I would go to Kremlin Square, always hoping for news from your grandmother in the Crimea. In July, six months after you and I had fought our way onto the train leaving Moscow to go to Petrograd, the contact was finally made. A young woman was at the appointed place, casually taking twelve steps one way, then twelve the other. That was the signal. It was Sophia, though of course I didn't know that at the time. She took me to a block of flats, to an apartment larger than Babushka's, but not particularly grand, where His Royal Highness Prince Dimitri Suvorin was staying. We sounded each other out, trying to make sure we really were who we claimed to be, that it wasn't some kind of trick. We arranged to meet again the following day, to plan our journey together to Berlin.

"I left the apartment, and Sophia came with me. She was staying with an uncle, near to where Babushka lived. Early the following morning I was awakened by a banging on the door of the apartment; it was Sophia, very distressed. She'd gone to the apartment where the Prince was staying, as she did each morning. Black cars were everywhere, surrounding the block; men were guarding the entrances, ominous looking men, all of them carrying guns. It was the feared Cheka. As she stood in the shadows she saw the prince being led out and pushed forcibly into one of the waiting cars; he hadn't seen her. He was taken straight to court, and was sentenced to ten years hard labour in Siberia. His crime; he was the bourgeois. I later learned he had been denounced by Sophia's uncle.

"Sophia came to stay with me in Babushka's apartment. In the beginning she shared a bed with Babushka, as you had done. Babushka spoke of her 'Anna' often, comparing Sophia to you very unfavourably! Eventually, Babushka moved to sleep on the settee, Sophia and I shared the bed. We were married the same year, and are very happy together. We wanted to start a family, but agreed we first had to wait for Prince Dimitri to be freed, so we could take him to find you. That was so important to both of us; Sophia wanted to keep the promise she'd made to your grandmother, and I believed I still had a responsibility for you, as I'd promised your father.

"'Every fifteen days for the next ten years either Sophia or I would return to the rendezvous point in Kremlin Square, waiting and praying for Prince Dimitri to suddenly appear. How many times we almost gave up, but always one of us would urge the other on, never to give up hope. We hoped he might find the way to escape, as we'd heard some had done from Siberia, or that he would be released early, but on both those counts we were to be disappointed. I was a bit worried he wouldn't remember the meeting place; it had been so long, and Siberia does strange things to a man's mind, but my fears proved groundless. It was exactly ten years after the raid by the Cheka that I saw him standing there, looking like a frail old man, but at least he'd survived. He'd had to make his own way back from Siberia, staying on the Trakt, the old Imperial post road, and taking rides from whoever was kind enough to stop for him. It must have been a very hard journey, but he'll tell you more about that himself.

"'He didn't have anywhere to stay in Moscow. I think he was worried the Cheka would come for him again; those people never give up, and they can do what they like. They don't have to have a reason. He didn't want to stay with any of his friends in case he got them into trouble. Like I said, he looked like a frail old man; he wasn't well enough to go on another long journey. I took him back to Babushka's apartment, and she looked after him for almost a month, feeding him to get his strength back. She did a good job too. I still had some of the money the crown princess gave me when I went away from you; I'd saved that in case of an emergency. So we used it to buy food at the market for him. We couldn't all stay in Babushka's apartment – you remember how small it is – so Sophia and I moved into a flat nearby, which we shared with some students.

"'The prince kept trying to persuade Babushka to let him leave, but you know what she's like. "You'll go when I say so, and not before," she told him. She didn't know who he was of course, but she's not stupid. She understood he was someone special; he could have walked out at any time, but I think he was a bit frightened of her!

"'Anyway, eventually she gave in. He'd sent me to see a friend of his, to borrow some money for the train and boat tickets, urging me to be careful and not to let anyone else know – as though I needed to be told, after all we'd been through. From then on it was all simple. The trains are back to normal, more or less. We all had documentation of a sort, so getting out of Russia wasn't a problem, and he browbeat the German immigration people to let us through. In just over a week we were here, and the rest you know.'

"Mikhail suddenly leaned across and took my hand, and looked me straight in the eyes, just as I remember him doing before, when he wanted to say something he found embarrassing. That was his way of dealing with it.

"'Many times I've thought of you, and what might have been between us. I meant everything I said when we parted on this very footpath all those years ago; I did love you, I still do, as a brother in those days, now as a loyal servant, and as circumstances permit, as a friend.'"

Anastasia didn't say how she felt at that moment, but later we learned that Mikhail and Sophia had stayed with her and Prince Suvorin as gardener and housekeeper almost to the end.

"Mr Hitler came calling again; that was in 1932. Chancellor Bruening had resigned, and new elections were to be fought. Hitler wanted the Crown Prince to support his campaign; it's not difficult to understand what Wilhelm wanted in return. Wilhelm also told Mr Hitler about me, and he insisted on meeting me straight away. I was very nervous. I'd heard so many bad things about him; I think it was Cecilie who'd told me in her opinion 'Fascism was the ugly child of Communism, and Nazism grew from Fascism.' I can only say in our meeting he was extremely polite, very solicitous as to my welfare, and gave me encouragement to believe, if he won the election, he would do all he could to support the restoration of the Russian Imperial family.

"Mr Hitler won the election of course, and he became chancellor of Germany. I was pleased with the result, and I think Wilhelm was too, but not so Cecilie; she'd decided she didn't like him. For me it wasn't a question of liking or not, it was a question of my possible future in Russia. There was a huge march on the day he opened the first Reichstag of what he called the Thousand Year Reich; maybe he'll have better luck than my father's dreams about our family dynasty. Wilhelm took part in the parade, as Mr Hitler had asked, showing solidarity between the former royal family and the new government. He was dressed in his uniform of the Danzig Hussars; he looked superb! He invited Mr Hitler back to Cecilienhof after the parade, and again there was talk of restoring both the monarchies. We had reasons to be hopeful. Wilhelm had done as Mr Hitler had asked, but there was to be no payback – politicians are universally the same: they get what they want and then forget you. It had been like that in Russia towards the end.

"Over the next few months there were several meetings at Cecilienhof with high government officials, and after one of them Wilhelm gave me a German diplomatic passport, made out in my full Romanov name, and he had one for Dimitri too, gifts from the German government. This was another good sign, and it resolved one of my problems; until then, I'd had no identification documents. Dimitri and I had fallen deeply in love and wanted to be married, but of course it had to be done secretly, and this too was arranged by one of the visiting officials. We were married in a civil ceremony in accordance with German law on the twelfth of January 1936 in the Main Hall of Schloss Cecilienhof, with Wilhelm and Cecilie, and Mikhail and Sophie as our witnesses, and this was immediately followed by a very short religious ceremony conducted by a priest from the Russian Colony in Potsdam. He was well known to Cecilie, and of course was sworn to secrecy. The marriage certificate showed our full names, Anastasia Nicolaievna Romanov, a Grand Duchess of Russia by profession, and Captain Dimitri Suvorin, a Prince of Russia and Captain in the Imperial Russian Guard. This was a risk on our part, but I insisted on it being shown this way in order that, if and when the Romanov's were restored to the throne of Russia, there would be no doubt as to the authenticity of the marriage."

Looking at the book in Nicholas's hand I could see there were only a couple of pages left to read. Either Anastasia had stopped keeping a record of her life, or a tragedy was in the offing. I desperately hoped it was the former, but was afraid it was more likely to be the latter. I said as much to my son.

"Remember this was a difficult time in Germany. After his election as chancellor in January 1933, Hitler's next objective was to remove any likely threats to his leadership from his own side. The Night of the Long Knives in June of that year, in which Ernst Rohm, the Head of the Stormtroopers, was assassinated along with several of his fellow collaborators, not only rid Hitler of opposition from that quarter, it also persuaded the Army chiefs to support him, since they'd distrusted Rohm too. That made Hitler's next task easier; when President Hindenburg died of old age just six weeks later, the Army supported Hitler to merge the offices of president and chancellor, with himself of course as the supreme authority, including being in command of the armed forces."

I wondered if my son was as impressed with my knowledge of recent history as I'd been with his university education, but I didn't ask.

"Over the next few years Hitler consolidated his power base and banned all political opposition. In 1936 his army reoccupied the Rhineland, in direct contravention of the treaty which had concluded the Great War; that act was conveniently overlooked by the politicians in England and France, frightened some might say to do something to provoke another conflict, but it was the events on the night of 9/10 November 1938 which shook not only Germany, but the whole world. *Kristallnacht*, the Night of Broken Glass, so called because of the number of Jewish owned shop windows which were smashed in towns and cities across Germany, and parts of Austria too, as the Nazi's began their persecution of the Jews. Hundreds of them were beaten to death that night, thousands sent to concentration camps, and synagogues everywhere were ransacked and set on fire. It was a terrible night, and it showed the rest of the world the kind of dictator they had to deal with."

It was getting late; we hadn't had any supper, and neither had we had much fresh air. With just a couple of pages to go, we settled down to what seemed to be the last part of a fascinating story.

Unbeknown to Anastasia, Dimitri had purchased a manor house in the Harz Mountains, near the village of Elbingerode, as a wedding present for her. They moved to live there almost immediately after the wedding, and while Anastasia recorded her sadness at leaving Cecilienhof, it was clear she was supremely happy; this was the first house she could call her own. High on a hill, and with a clear view to Brocken in the west, the highest point in the mountains, it was idyllic. No doubt she was pinning much faith on Hitler making good on restoring the Romanov's to the Russian throne, but meantime she could get on with organising her house, and settling down to married life.

Mikhail and Sophia had gone with them, and they occupied the dormer rooms set in the roof of the house; this was spacious accommodation, self-contained, with views from the front of the house across to the distant mountains, while from the back they overlooked the spacious and extremely well-stocked gardens. The ground-floor rooms in the front of the house were used for entertaining, not that they had many visitors; they had to be so careful. One room in particular Anastasia mentioned had two sets of windows looking west to the mountains, and a side window looking north, with a view of the delightful village of Elbingerode far below. Their private apartments were on the first floor, including a music room where

Anastasia could continue playing the harpsichord, as she'd been able to do at Tsarskoe Selo.

Together with Prince Dimitri, Mikhail would spend hours tending the various vegetable, fruit, and flower beds, and with the welcome addition of a chicken coop in the far corner, they soon became self-sufficient in most of their needs. Attached to the south side of the house was a very spacious conservatory, a real sun trap in the autumn and spring, and where Anastasia and Dimitri spent much of their time.

They had stabling for horses on the west side and a huge shed in which they stored vast quantities of wood, salvaged from the many trees which Dimitri and Mikhail had felled to make way for the vegetable and flower beds.

Anastasia told us that as you stepped out of the front door of the house, you were on a patio, set with paving slabs and with a colourful flower bed in front. From the middle of the patio a wide staircase swept down to the marvellous lawns below. The grass was a wonderful shade of green, which Mikhail kept so meticulously manicured you might be afraid to even step on it, while off to one side was a delightful lake, crossed by an ornamental bridge and stocked with brown mountain trout.

I asked Nicholas to read that paragraph again. I felt ill, perspiration rushed onto my brow, and my heart was beating wildly. This was the recurring dream I'd had for so many years. I knew that patio and those lawns. I'd been there!

Nicholas turned to look at me, a sad and wistful look, almost as though he knew what I was feeling, and then turned to the last page of the book. How would it end? I was visibly shaking, hanging on to every word he uttered. He was translating word for word:

"For my birthday that year Dimitri had bought me a wonderful horse; we called him Chestnut, it wasn't difficult to understand why. But I had an even more special present to give to him. A couple of days previously Mikhail had driven me to the village; I had an appointment to see the doctor. I was feeling just a little unwell. He promised to let me have the result later in the week, and in fact he telephoned just as we were sitting down to a birthday lunch.

"Princess Suvorin," which was how I was known locally, "I'm

happy to say I've completed my tests. There's nothing wrong with you." He'd paused at that moment; I remember it so clearly, like he was teasing me. "Oh, I almost forgot Your Highness, you're having a baby."

"They probably heard the screams of delight all the way back to Potsdam! To be married to a man I adore, to live in such a beautiful house, to have two such faithful friends as Mikhail and Sophia – and to add a baby to that list of privileges, because that's the way I thought of these things, made my life complete. All the suffering, the long days and weeks of imprisonment in Tsarskoe Selo, then at Tobolsk, and the house of death in Yekaterinburg, the deprivations of Moscow and St Petersburg, the years of patiently waiting in Potsdam – suddenly it was all worthwhile. If we could only return to Mother Russia and resume the Romanov dynasty, that would have made Papa so proud of me.

"Never did a husband care for his wife as Dimitri did for me those months of pregnancy. Night after night he would put his ear to my stomach and listen to our baby talking, or so he claimed. Eventually the time came, and you, my dear baby Alexei, who I named after the brother I'd left in that dark forest in Siberia, came into the world with a yell that brought Dimitri and Mikhail running into my bedroom. You were born at home, as was the custom in those days, on 27 January 1937. The village doctor was present, but it was dear Sophia who held my hand, and mopped my brow. Even in the agony of giving birth, and you weighed a solid 4 kgs, I was feeling sorry for Sophia. She and Mikhail were trying very hard to start a family, but to no avail, and maybe as things turned out that was as well.

"It was our custom every Sunday to attend morning service in a small church in Elbingerode. Mikhail would usually drive, with Sophie next to him in the front of the car, with your father and me in the back; you would sit on your father's lap in the car. He would never trust me to hold you safely. The journey to the village was only three kms, but it was down a steep hill, with lots of sharp bends, so Mikhail was always very careful.

"The tragedy came in October of 1940. It was a delightful autumn morning, and we decided to walk to church, while Mikhail and Sophia went in the car. That of course meant they would drive us back; we didn't want to walk up that hill. We started from the house a long time before them; it would take a good hour for us to walk, stopping from time to time to pick berries from the bushes growing at the side of the road.

"On that Sunday we heard the car coming; Mikhail was using the horn non-stop. Suddenly they came round the bend behind us, travelling very fast, far too fast for safety. We had to jump out of the way, and I remember I fell and cut my knee on a stone. Your father was very angry, and he was shouting after the car. Mikhail was going to be in trouble, but it wasn't like him at all, he was usually so careful.

"We heard the crash just a few minutes later. Your father ran down the hill, leaving me to follow with you in your pushchair. By the time I arrived, your father was trying to pull Sophia from the wreckage, but I could see it was too late to save her. Mikhail had gone through the windscreen; I could see his body lying in the ditch a little further on. He was dead too. It was terrible. The police arrived and took control.

The next week they came to see us at the manor house and told us the deaths were suspicious; the brake cables of the car had been cut. They never found out who'd done it, assuming of course it wasn't a genuine accident. They wanted to know if we would usually have been in the car with them, and of course we answered yes; had it been a cold or rainy day, we would have been with them in that car. Then they wanted to know if we had any enemies, but no, how could we have any enemies? We weren't hurting anyone; we were leading very quiet lives. Your father was convinced the police were wrong, and it was a genuine accident. We both hoped he was right!

"The deaths of Mikhail and Sophia hit us very hard. For some weeks we were both subdued, each wrapped up in our own thoughts. That was what made me write the letter at the front of this book, on the first of January 1941, to push myself to go on.

"We miss Mikhail and Sophia. They were our friends as well as our helpers in the house and garden, and they loved you very much, almost as if you were their own. Another couple has taken their place, but they live in the village, and anyway they could never mean to us what Mikhail and Sophia did – so much history we've shared together, so many trials and tribulations particularly for me and Mikhail. We've taken on a nanny too; she comes in three days a week, but she's not very reliable and your father wants me to get rid of her. I think I'll wait until after your birthday, then she can go.

"The dreadful war seems to go on and on, but the news for Germany is generally encouraging; their soldiers seem to be winning all the battles, Europe is falling at their feet. I speak with Cecilie on the telephone some days; she has no news about the German monarchy, and of course nothing about Russia. For your father and me, it is a constant dream that one day we can return to our own homeland, and make the Romanov dynasty great again. We talk of the things we'd change, getting rid of poverty, letting people feel proud, and free again. But for now it's only a dream.

"For your fourth birthday we gave you a wonderful cuddly teddy bear I'd seen in a shop in Wernigerode, which is where we go to buy most of our things these days. It was a very happy day; you are growing up to be such a lovely boy, so like your Uncle Alexei. You are so full of life, and you can run so fast I can't keep up with you. When I see you climbing trees I make you come down again, and your father doesn't think I notice when he winks at you, encouraging you to go back up!

"If it's nice in the morning we'll leave you with your nanny for a while, and your father and I will go riding our horses in the forest. After that, if it's not raining, we'll wrap up warm and have a picnic on the lawn; I know how much you love playing on the grass—"

Nicholas looked across at me. He'd finished the notebook. It was all over, but what did that mean? What happened to my parents? I was desolate.

Chapter Fourteen

I spent the entire night restlessly turning over and over in bed, trying to come to terms with what I'd learned. If the notebook was to be believed, my entire life had been a lie! Many years ago I'd learned that Geoffrey and Ann McCabe, the couple that I, as a young child, had assumed to be my parents, were nothing of the kind; in fact they'd taken me in and looked after me on the orders of the Duke and Duchess of Dumfries. Now I'm learning my name is not Alec Johnson either, and I'm not the orphaned child who was supposedly evacuated to the safety of rural Britain when his parents were killed in one of the bombing blitzes of London. Presumably the remains of the real Alec Johnson are buried somewhere in an unmarked grave, conveniently made to disappear so that I might live. How am I supposed to come to terms with that?

And who am I really?

I now knew, beyond the shadow of a doubt, who the notebook tells me I am. According to them, I am the son of Her Royal Highness the Grand Duchess Anastasia Nikolaevna Romanov, daughter of the murdered tsar of Russia, and His Royal Highness Prince Dimitri Suvorin. To give me my full title and name, I am His Royal Highness Alexei Dimitriovich Romanov Suvorin, the exiled tsar of Russia.

I was fairly certain that night, when I would have dinner at Rannoch Castle, the Grand Master would confirm this to me, and no doubt would fill in some of the many gaps, not least, what happened to Anastasia after she'd written that last entry in her book. But more than any of that, what the bloody hell had it got to do with him, the Grand Master of the Chivalric Order of St John of Jerusalem? How long had he known all this, and what did he hope to gain from it? Did I really have to go along with all of it? Did I have any choices? Who did I want to be? Given the choice, who would I choose to be? Still so many questions, but no answers!

I went into the bathroom to shower and shave. It was still early, but I couldn't sleep, and if I stayed in bed I'd go crazy. Randy cocked an eye at me from his blanket at the bottom of my bed, as if to ask what I think I'm doing, it's still sleeping time. Something he and I have in common – we both enjoy a full eight hours sleep every night. Well, most nights.

"How does it feel to know your master is the Tsar of Russia?" I asked him. With all the other turmoil going on around me, I wouldn't have been surprised if he'd answered.

I put on a clean shirt, a tie, and my only suit. I couldn't remember the last time I'd worn it; the trousers still had the old fashioned turn ups, and they needed pressing, especially if today was going to be showdown time, which in my present mood I was sure it was going to be, but there was no time for that. My shoes, however, were another matter. They were black and had traces of mud round the uppers, which I would have to clean before I could put them on; not all the habits I'd acquired in the army were bad ones. The shoe brushes and polish were kept in the cupboard under the sink, so I tiptoed gently, not wanting to wake my sleeping son, but I needn't have bothered; I'd forgotten the cupboard door creaks loud enough to awaken the dead. I saw him stir. Holding my shoes in one hand, I tried to creep through to the conservatory, but my efforts were in vain. He was curled up in his sleeping bag on the settee, one arm flopping lazily, the hand touching the floor. Randy had licked it; Nicholas was awake.

"Dad, what time is it?"

He sat up, the sleeping bag falling down to his waist, exposing his hairy chest. I don't know where he'd inherited that from, but most definitely not from me, my chest was as devoid of hair as a baby's bottom.

"And where on earth are you going dressed like that?"

I don't believe Nicholas had ever seen me dressed in a suit, at least not when he was of an age to remember. Probably the last time I'd worn this suit was at his christening. On my visits to him in America I always wore my blazer and flannels.

"Not too sure son," I answered, "but maybe to get some answers to some questions. How about meeting for lunch in the pub?"

He looked perturbed, almost as though he didn't trust me to go out on my own, or maybe he didn't want me doing anything too rash. Whatever it was, my mind was made up.

I went into the conservatory to polish my shoes, in the process managing to get some black polish on the cuffs of my shirt.

Damn, I don't have another clean one. This will have to do.

I returned the polish and brushes under the sink, took my heavy raincoat from the hook behind the front door, and my twelve-bore shotgun from its cupboard. Randy was still shaking his head, unsure whether he wanted to accompany me or not. It seemed both my nearest and dearest thought I was going mad. Perhaps I was, but at least I was doing something positive, which would be the first time since this all started a week ago.

"C'mon, Randy, let's go."

He looked at Nicholas, still sitting up on the settee, enquiring whether he was coming too. He wasn't invited.

Once outside, I felt the full force of the northerly wind. It was strong enough to take a man's breath away, but it's something you become accustomed to after spending a lifetime in these Highlands. Rain was threatening, and thunder could be heard in the mountains to the north.

"I hope that stays away," I muttered to myself.

I settled down into the long stride which the army had taught me was the most efficient way of quickly covering large amounts of ground. "Thirty inches wide, one hundred and twenty to the minute," was my old sergeant major's favourite expression. He'd yelled it at me and my fellow national servicemen so many times it had become part of the folklore by which I remembered those days.

I turned left out of the cottage to follow the track west to Loch Rannoch, a couple of miles further on. The loch is a great source of Loch Leven trout, which were introduced into Loch Rannoch many years ago and have thrived, mainly because so few fishermen come up here, preferring to fish one of the larger and more accessible lochs further to the west. As well as being a great game fish, it sits well on any dinner table, the black spots on its otherwise totally brown body giving it a nice rounded appearance, and since it can grow up to seven or eight pounds in weight, it easily feeds a complete family.

I have kept a small dinghy on the loch for many years, bought if I remember well with my very first wage packet when I returned from doing national service. I might not be best dressed to go rowing, and certainly not for fly fishing, which would be my usual pastime, but using the dinghy to cross the loch cut a couple of miles off the distance to Rannoch Castle, which was my destination. I'd never gone calling on the Grand Master without an invitation before, but there's a first time for everything, or so I was always told. Randy's not too keen on boats, perhaps because he's fallen into this loch on several occasions when he's become too excited at seeing me fight to land a good-sized trout, and the water is exceptionally cold at any time of the year, but today he jumped in the dinghy without hesitation and took his customary place in the bow. For me the physical effort of pulling on the oars was good therapy.

Thirty minutes later I beached the dinghy amongst some weeds, hidden from view of the young local lads who also like to fish this loch. The bank rose steeply, and then levelled off after a few minutes, which was where I joined the track to lead me to the Castle. This was the same track which Bonnie Prince Charlie had used as he was making his way to the Western Isles and where a local chief had used his men to cover for him, earning him the Prince's gratitude, and an eventual death sentence from the English. Many are the ghosts said to haunt the hills hereabouts, if you believe in that kind of thing of course.

A carrion crow, or corbie to use our word for it, was winging its way to a large tree near the top of the hill I was climbing, the remains of a young grouse clearly visible in its powerful beak. Carefully I watched where it landed and then stayed still as it surveyed the area, wanting to make sure no one was watching to see where its nest was hidden. I'd done this enough times to know what to do, and sure enough the bird soon betrayed its nest. A double blast from my Yeoman proved I'd lost none of my hunting skills, and the rest of the season's young grouse and lambs wouldn't be bothered by this particular predator anymore!

Maybe I'd lost none of my hunting skills, but the same could not be said for my stamina, particularly when climbing steep hills. By the time I reached the crest, and could look over to Rannoch Castle, my legs were thinking of giving way, and my lungs bursting to capture another gulp of oxygen. I stayed where I was for a good half an hour, less sure now about why I'd made the journey, and wondering whatever had possessed me to wear a suit. Randy too was feeling the pace, and he was content to sit and watch me, an enquiring look on his lovely old face, whereas years ago he'd have been off hunting for rabbits or ratting for which his breed is particularly useful.

Beyond the Castle I could clearly see the long driveway and the gatehouse lodge at the end, which had been my home for so many years. As I watched, a serving brother, as the security guards were all called, opened the gate. Seconds later I saw a Rolls Royce turning left off the Highland road, and into the castle driveway. Rolls Royce cars are quite rare up here, even the gentry preferring the flexible efficiency of four-wheel-drive Land Rovers and such like, so I assume this Rolls was the same that had collected me from the pub all those years ago. What a wealth of memories that brought back.

I watched as the Rolls started up the driveway, the brother closing the heavy gates once it was safely inside. I could clearly see the butler, Brother James, waiting at the entrance to the Castle, and he was suddenly startled to realise the Grand Master had come up behind him. James respectfully opened one of the rear doors of the Rolls, the chauffeur doing the same on the other side. From the passenger side came a young lady, her blond hair clearly visible from my vantage position, as too was the pink tracksuit she was wearing – not by any means the usual attire for guests of any gender visiting the Castle. From the other side stepped a man, seeming quite a lot older than his female companion, and much more appropriately dressed too. They were both greeted with an enthusiastic hug by the Grand Master, a sign of affection I personally had never witnessed from him before.

These must be special people, I thought, *but what do I do now? I can hardly go down there, demanding some kind of showdown, while they're with him.*

Reluctantly, I turned my gaze away from Rannoch Castle and contemplated the walk to the village. The shortest way would be to return to the loch and take the dinghy back to where I'd started earlier, but that would have meant rowing against the northerly wind, which I didn't fancy doing. The alternative meant finding a way to the Highland road without being seen from the Castle and perhaps hitching a ride to the village.

I'd better get going; it's going to take all of three hours if I can't find a ride with someone.

❊❊❊❊❊

Monika had exited the Hilton Hotel on Park Lane, the laundry bag clutched in her hand, wondering which way to go. Without warning, a hand had grabbed her shoulder. She turned in alarm.

"Majed Dajani. Quickly, my car is over there."

He was pointing to a black Rolls Royce, which was double parked next to one of the stretch limousines. A policeman was walking towards the car, notebook in hand, the car's distinctive registration number OSJ 1 already noted. Majed let go of Monika's arm, and together they walked to the car, just in time to make the policeman's journey unnecessary. A chauffeur had jumped out of the car and held a rear door open for them. He was wearing a strange-looking robe; anyway it looked strange to the policeman but not to Monika or Majed. They had similar robes, albeit of a different colour, as did all the members of the Chivalric Order of St John of Jerusalem.

Once safely inside the car, Dajani looked hard at Monika; he'd already decided he didn't like this girl, and now he was sure of it. She smelt awful! As they settled into the back seat of the Rolls, Dajani put his arm round her shoulder, and pulled her face towards his, as though to kiss her. This had taken Monika so much by surprise that she hadn't immediately resisted, and those precious few seconds were enough to ensure both their faces were shielded from the gaze of the policeman, a wise move on Dajani's part. As Monika pulled away from him she raised her hand, slapping the side of his face very hard, something she considered his action had richly deserved. Whatever kind of reputation she might have, it wasn't for him to take liberties with her, and she'd make damned sure he knew it.

Dajani ruefully rubbed the side of his face and gave a soft chuckle.

"Nice to meet you, young lady. I did that to protect your face from being seen by the policeman. In truth you smell so bloody awful I'd much rather have put you in the boot, but that would have attracted attention. Whatever have you been up to?"

Monika knew who Dajani was; the Grand Master had often spoken of him, always with deep respect. She felt she was safe here and could relax. She explained what had happened in the hotel, how she'd discovered the tiny tape recorder hidden inside the waist band of Abdullah Qahtani's trousers and how she'd had to fiddle to remove it, getting his vomit over her arm and dress in the process.

The Lebanese man had listened attentively to the Austrian girl's recount of her evening. He hadn't asked how she'd known the tape recorder was inside the trousers; he didn't want to know.

"We have to drive to Scotland tonight, but not with you smelling as you do. We're going to the flat where you can clean up while William and I find something to eat in the kitchen. Then we'll head north."

Brother William was very familiar with this part of London. Whenever he chauffeured the Grand Master to the capital he always used Park Lane, an easy point of reference, and convenient for any part of central or west London. As he pulled away from where he'd been double parked, he waved his hand in a half-meant apology to the policeman, an action the policeman would remember the following day when being quizzed by Detective Chief Inspector Bill Morgan, who was investigating the death of a Saudi Arabian government minister in the Hilton Hotel. William drove round the traffic circle at the side of the hotel and expertly joined the stream of traffic heading towards Hyde Park Corner, immediately cutting across the flow to the consternation of a tired, long-distance National Express coach driver who was looking forward to his arrival at the Victoria Coach Station.

There is a little-used road running around the south side of Hyde Park, appropriately enough called South Carriage Drive, which shortened the distance to the Grand Master's Kensington flat and avoided completely the usual traffic mess around Hyde Park Corner. "Twenty minutes from door to door, not bad for a busy Saturday night in London," thought William.

Seven hours after leaving the flat, Brother William carefully eased the large car off the Highland road and onto Rannoch Castle's driveway, his two passengers, who until that moment had been sprawled asleep in the back, both came awake. William had used the window controls in the console to lower both his own and the offside rear passenger windows to permit the brother on security duty at the gate to verify the occupants. By the time the car had passed between the two medieval knight statues and came to a stop by the entrance to the portico, they were both wide awake, a little surprised to see the Grand Master waiting to greet them, standing to the side of his butler, Brother James.

The smile of welcome on the face of the Grand Master was genuine. He was always pleased to greet these people. They always did precisely as he ordered; they never questioned why; and had never failed him – rare qualities indeed.

"Come on inside and have some breakfast with me, and then you can go to your rooms and rest."

Turning to his butler, he told him to take his guests' belongings to the rooms that had been already prepared for them.

As they were passing through the hallway, Monika turned and dashed back to the car. She'd forgotten the hotel laundry bag, which in her case had rather more inside than a set of used underwear! Dajani had looked a little surprised, and Brother James had told her not to worry, he'd put it in her room, but Monika insisted, she wanted to take it with her.

During breakfast, Monika briefed the two men about her date with Abdullah Qahtani. The anticipated order for 150 tanks had been much hyped by Mr Hamlyn in a press conference he'd given some days earlier, so it wasn't totally surprising that he would meet the Saudi that evening to sign the contract. What was surprising however, was when she mentioned the tape recording. They heard the British minister of defence telling his opposite Saudi number how the 150 tanks covered by the agreement they'd each just signed would open a new chapter in the relationship between their two countries. They also heard him say "All counted and correct, exactly as ordered dear Sir," which Monika told them was when he'd given the Saudi the two oblong packages, which were now resting on the table in front of them, and then even more damning, "the Prime Minister was very impressed that you will be using the money to set up a foundation for the underprivileged children in Africa."

"And do you happen to have any idea what is in those two packages," the Grand Master asked Monika, pointing at them on the table as he spoke.

Both the Grand Master and Majed Dajani looked on unbelievingly as Monika triumphantly removed the wrapping paper on one million pounds in cash, all except for six hundred and fifty, which had been the price of the Saudi's last dinner on this earth!

Dajani was perhaps even more impressed than the Grand Master. He himself was secretive by nature, but he doubted he could have kept quiet for so long about the unexpected wealth that she'd so casually carried in the laundry bag.

The Grand Master was quiet for several long minutes trying to decide how best to use not only the information that Monika had brought to him, but also such a huge sum of money, while his two guests looked on, expectantly. Suddenly turning to Monika, he asked if she'd had the foresight to get a contact telephone number for Mr George Hamlyn.

"We need to have a word with him rather urgently."

There was no disguising the malevolence in the way he'd uttered those few words.

Mr Hamlyn's mobile phone had rung just twice before he answered. Few people knew this number, it was after all his private mobile, nothing to do with his job as minister of defence, and it was unusual not to see a number displayed indicating who was calling him.

"Good morning, this is George Hamlyn."

"Oh, I'm sorry to disturb you, George. This is Monika Wolff. If you remember, we met at dinner last night. I hope you don't mind me calling you; is it convenient to talk?"

She almost cooed the words to him, sounding as sensual as she knew how.

George Hamlyn had never been quicker off the mark. He'd been having a row with his wife Madeleine; she was complaining he'd arrived home late again last night, smelling of wine, and a hint of perfume. She was well aware of his predilection for members of the opposite sex.

"Oh, good morning, Prime Minister. Of course it isn't inconvenient. Can you hold on a moment while I go through to the study and get the paper?"

He mouthed to his wife a quick apology and scuttled through to his private den, closing the door very firmly behind him.

Madeleine Hamlyn was a much smarter person than the man she was married to. Several things told her George wasn't talking to the prime minister. First, the PM never made calls himself; an aide always made the call and would put the PM on the line at the appropriate moment. Second, none of his work colleagues, including the PM, knew her husband's private mobile-phone number; and third, the PM was on a plane at that very moment flying to New York for a meeting of the UN Security Council, a fact her husband had told her at breakfast just one hour previously.

"Monika my dear, what a real pleasure, and so soon too; I mustn't stay too long on the phone, but when can we meet?"

A day that had started out pretty badly was suddenly starting to look decidedly better.

"Can you be free tomorrow afternoon – say at 2 p.m.?" she asked.

The minister consulted his diary. A cabinet meeting was scheduled for 9 a.m. every Monday, something Gerald Smith had instigated when he'd replaced Tom Lane at No 10 Downing Street.

"Get the week off to a good start," had been his justification, whereas what he'd actually been doing was setting his own mark on the office of prime minister.

Tomorrow's meeting would be chaired by the deputy leader, as the PM was at that moment flying to New York.

"Shit," George said to himself, realising he'd just told Madeleine that was the PM on the phone, when he'd already told her he was on his way to New York. Fortunately, she wouldn't connect the two; she really wasn't very smart.

At 11.30 a.m. he had a meeting scheduled with his deputy, a left wing moron who'd only been given the job to keep the trades' union people happy. He'd be free in plenty of time to meet with Monika..

"Two p.m. is no problem Monika; where shall we meet? I have a nice little pied-à-terre in Pimlico that would be most convenient for me. If you have a pen I'll give you the address."

He was excited at the prospect of seeing her again; the kiss she'd planted on his cheek as she'd handed him the Saudi's exquisite fountain pen was a nice memory, and the look down her cleavage as she'd dropped her napkin on the floor had haunted him all night! The little pied-à-terre he'd referred to was in fact a poky bedsit in the basement of what had once been a grand Victorian town house on Winchester Street, now largely occupied by students from Westminster College on Vincent Square, the other side of Vauxhall Bridge Road.

Oh, I bet your little pied-à-terre would do just great for you, Monika thought to herself. *Wham, bang, thank you ma'am, and now I have another meeting to go to. Can you see yourself out? No, that's not the way it's going to be.*

"No darling, I have a much better idea," she told him. There's a flight leaving Heathrow at 2 p.m. tomorrow for Edinburgh; I've already checked, there's plenty of room left so you won't have a problem getting a seat. I'll be waiting as you come out the gate."

The minister went cold. Suddenly there was no affection in her voice, despite the use of the darling endearment; that had sounded more like an order.

"I'm very sorry, my dear. Much as I'd love to do as you ask, it's impossible. Such a busy schedule you know. Come on down to London; I'll pay the fare."

Monika's voice had indeed hardened, and she wasn't through yet.

"George my pet, you don't understand. You remember the package you gave to my friend Abdullah – the one with a million pounds that has your fingerprints all over it? And you remember telling him how pleased the prime minister had been? I'm really sorry, sweetie,

I didn't know he was recording everything you said. Anyway, I can save your bacon because I took those things from him when he died, and I've got them here with me. See you tomorrow my darling; don't be late."

With that Monika hung up.

Both the Grand Master and Majed Dajani had been listening to Monika speaking with the minister of defence, and both were impressed by her coolness.

"There are a few things I need to brief you on, my dear, so you'll know how to deal with Mr Hamlyn when you meet him at the airport tomorrow, and I'll need you to take the Rolls. Majed, this would be as good a time as any for you to have a rest."

Majed took the hint. As he stood to leave the room he noticed a man skulking through the bushes on the far side of the courtyard. He was wearing a suit, and carrying a gun, and he had a dog with him too!

None of my business, he decided, *If he's up to something the security people will have him soon enough. I'm going to get some sleep.*

Down in London, meantime, George Hamlyn had gone into a blind panic.

Oh, my God, my fingerprints, a tape recording, I've implicated the Prime Minister – and what the hell did she mean about Qahtani having died?

Mr Hamlyn did the only sensible thing he could do. He booked himself on the 2 p.m. shuttle to Edinburgh for the next day.

✳✳✳✳✳

Fortunately, I'd been able to get past the Castle without being seen, or so I thought, and I knew of a gap in the wall behind the gatehouse lodge where I could cut through to the road without having to use the main gate. Even better, I'd barely been on the Highland road five minutes before Fred the postman came along in his delivery van, which was unusual, this being a Sunday, but was just as well for me, the rain was beginning to come down very heavily. Bang on the dot of 12.30 p.m. we arrived in the car park of the Speckled Grouse, and dashed inside. Nicholas was already there, chatting to, or being chatted up by Julie, I wasn't sure which, maybe both. I bought Fred a drink, he'd earned it, the lift had been more than welcome, but my suit was wet and my shoes muddy again.

Julie looked me up and down as though I was some kind of scarecrow, which someone had carelessly left behind, whereas I felt more like a drowned rat. "Here, you can't sit in those things, you'll catch your death of cold," she told me, "Matt, can I take a pair of trousers from your wardrobe for Alec to wear while I iron his own?"

She didn't bother waiting for the landlord to answer, but went behind the bar and through the door which led to his sitting room. She clearly knew her way around very well, because in a couple of minutes she was back, carrying a pair of trousers, a jumper, and some slippers.

I was very conscious that Nicholas and I were going to the Castle for dinner, and to have arrived looking like I was would not have been a good idea at all. Remember, I wasn't Alec the gamekeeper anymore; I was the tar of Russia in exile! Bloody ridiculous! I headed towards the toilet to change into Matt's trousers, only to find the door locked. Fred had beaten me to it and he was renowned for how long he would stay locked inside.

Julie was laughing at me.

"What's the matter, Alec? Are you a wee bit frightened the rest of us will see something we haven't seen a few times before?"

With that she walked over to where I stood and took my jacket, then my tie, and would have gone further had I not stopped her.

"I can manage quite well myself, thank you, Julie," I said, trying not to sound too huffy.

There and then in the pub, I stripped down to my underwear and pulled on Matt's trousers, jumper, and oversized slippers. Both Nicholas and I could have climbed into the trousers together and still left room for Randy, and the same went for the jumper too. But so long as no one else came in the pub it didn't matter too much. Julie had taken my things into the back from where she emerged half an hour later proudly carrying my suit and shirt on hangers and the shoes wrapped in a duster, nicely polished. What a gem this girl really is!

Nicholas and I had lunch together. I told him what I'd seen at the Castle and how I'd been unable to have the confrontation I'd been looking for. We had a problem though; by 3p.m. it was raining heavier than ever, and the wind was stronger than it had been when I'd crossed the loch. We didn't have a car to take us back to the cottage, and Fred was reluctant to take us in the Post Office van in case he got bogged down. John the taxi driver was out on another job and wouldn't be back until early evening. Matt was about to close the pub, which he always did on a Sunday afternoon, but invited us to stay as long as we needed, which was considerate of him, particularly as I was still wearing his clothes. We brought Randy in from outside and spent the afternoon sitting in front of the fire in the lounge bar, plotting our strategy for later than night, when we'd be with the Grand Master and Sir James Sinclair.

By 6 p.m. we'd exhausted everything we could think of to say and had resorted to just looking at the fire, which was when Nicholas's mobile phone rang. The caller was Sir James Sinclair. He'd tried calling us at the cottage to offer us a lift to the Castle, and when he got no response there, he tried on the mobile. He told us he would be passing the pub in a few minutes on his way to the Castle, and he'd be pleased to give us a lift. Rarely had an offer been more gratefully received.

Chapter Fifteen

The security guard stepped from his sentry box to open the massive gates as we turned in from the Highland road. I saw him press the bell to alert the butler at the Castle someone was on the way up the drive.

Brother James was standing just inside the portico, protected from the rain, which was now coming down very heavily. He came across and opened the rear door where I was sitting and held an umbrella open for me. Nicholas and Sir James Sinclair weren't afforded that luxury; they got wet! We were escorted up to the second floor.

The Grand Master was waiting for us in his private sitting room.

"We're having a buffet supper tonight, so please help yourselves to whatever you fancy. Brother James will be here in a moment to see what you'd like to drink."

As we'd entered the castle, I'd looked around for any sign of the two visitors I'd seen arriving in the Rolls Royce that morning, but if they were there, they kept well out of the way. That was a pity; I was intrigued by the pink tracksuit.

The buffet was only slightly more generous than the dinner I'd attended just after the Grand Master first arrived at the Castle, and the drink options that the butler had given us hadn't included alcohol at all. The settee that Nicholas and I were invited to sit on was poorly upholstered and lumpy, and the matching arm chairs, which Sir James Sinclair and the Grand Master occupied, looked to be similarly uncomfortable. The room was cold, too; as I learned when an opportunity presented itself for me to touch one of the radiators, the central heating was off. This evening was going to be a long one, long in more ways than one.

"Where to begin?" asked the Grand Master, probably more to himself than to Nicholas or me. "You've read Anastasia's notebook; if for the time being we can take it at face value, we can move on. Do you have any problems with that?"

It was time for me to speak up.

"I'd rather like to start from the end – the end of the notebook, that is; why did my moth—? Why did Anastasia finish her writing so abruptly?"

For the first time, I'd really wanted to refer to Anastasia as my mother, hoping that by doing so it would instil some sense of reality, of belonging, but it wouldn't come. It sounded unnatural.

"Ah, yes," was his measured reply, "but before coming to that there is something you both have to understand. Much of what you will hear this evening is conjecture on our part," indicating both himself and Sir James Sinclair, "and indeed on the part of many other people who, over the years, have been fascinated by this mystery. It all happened a long time ago of course, and sadly, once she'd gone, there wasn't another Anastasia keeping notes. Almost everyone concerned is long dead, except the two people who are now the principal players; Alec, that is you and your son Nicholas, of course.

"Another complicating factor is that under the British Official Secrets Act some of the documents that would help us unravel at least part of the mystery have been sequestered until the year 2017, and still others until twenty years after that. Only when, or should I say *if* and when, they are released into the public domain will anyone know for certain why some people acted as they did. I will have to come back to that very shortly, but I'll do my best to answer your question, Alec."

He was staring at me, his eyes wide like saucers.

"I regret to tell you, your parents were murdered."

I visibly shuddered; he'd said those words so dispassionately, so coldly, and yet that was my mother and father he was referring to.

"Murdered?" I asked, "Is that all you have to say?"

I hoped I'd sounded brusque, demanding that the Grand Master keep nothing back.

"No, Alec, there is much more. The date we can be sure of, that was the 4 February 1941, and the place too, that was on the lawn of their manor house in the Harz Mountains . Your parents had been out horse riding and were having a picnic, exactly as your mother had written they would. Your nanny, an elderly lady from the village of Elbingerode, had taken you inside to change your blouse; apparently you'd spilt some ice cream or something.

"That undoubtedly saved your life. While you were in the house she'd heard some shooting and rushed out to see what was happening. Two men were running across the lawn and disappeared into the trees on the other side of the lake. The horses, which until then had been munching grass near the picnic spot, had bolted into the trees on the other side of the garden. The police later said they'd found traces of a motorcycle and sidecar having been parked there. Your parents were lying on the grass, both dead, both shot in the head, clearly the work of professional assassins. If it's any consolation, death must have been instantaneous!"

I was finding it difficult to control my emotions. That dream I'd had so many times over the years, of that picnic, that lawn, the horses, and the panic!

I'd told Nicholas about it, but of course now I knew it wasn't a dream; it was real.

"And the murderers," I asked, "were they ever found?"

"No, Alec, they never were. Earlier, I said much of what we will say this evening will be conjecture, and sadly it starts now. You remember in her book Anastasia mentioned the brakes on the family car having failed on the hill when Mikhail and Sophia were killed? The police were certain that was no accident, and I suppose that would have been reinforced by the shooting. No one locally knew your mother's real identity; even the local police didn't know. The German royal family knew of course. Anastasia had stayed with them in Potsdam, and the ruling German politicians knew. We learned from the notebook how Anastasia had met with Hitler and several of his senior staff.

"One other person knew; his name was Richard Sorge. He was what today we'd call a double agent, a spy; he was working for the Germans but also for the Russians who'd given him the codename

Ramsay. He was based in Japan. He gave Stalin the actual start date of Operation Barbarossa, the German offensive against Russia; that was June 1941. He'd learned that from his relationship with the German Embassy in Tokyo, where he'd also learned that your mother was alive and living in Germany, and that Hitler had some ideas about restoring the Romanov dynasty, once the war against Russia was won. We have to assume Sorge passed that information on to his masters in the Kremlin as well, because they sent agents to finish the job that had been botched in Yekaterinburg twenty-three years earlier. We must also assume neither Sorge, nor the assassins who carried out the murders, were aware of your existence Alec; otherwise, they'd have killed you too."

That was a very sobering thought!

"So, if the German authorities found out about this double agent, what did they do about it?"

"Oh, he was hanged of course, by the Japanese on 7 November 1944 – they were allied with the Germans during the war. At the time of his arrest, the Russians had denied he was working for them, which they would of course. It wasn't until twenty years later, in November 1964, they awarded him the honorary title Hero of the Soviet Union. I'm sorry Alec, it was all rather tardy!"

I wanted to move on; the part I'd just learned was too distressing.

"And after that, Grand Master, I surely didn't walk to Scotland. How did I get here?"

"More conjecture I'm afraid. We know you were taken to Princess Cecilie in Potsdam, and then within hours of arriving there, you were moved on again, almost certainly to a convent in Augsburg. I believe the Nazi authorities would have done that for your safety. You stayed with the nuns there for three months, which is when we come to another bizarre twist in your life story. On 10 May 1941 you were taken to the Messerschmitt aircraft factory near Augsburg and flown from there to Scotland."

I didn't think that was any more bizarre than everything else I was learning and made the mistake of saying so!"

"The name of your pilot, Alec, was Rudolf Hess. He was Adolf Hitler's deputy. Isn't that bizarre enough for you, to know the deputy fuehrer of the Nazi Party flew a four-year-old boy to the safety of rural Scotland and was himself incarcerated as a prisoner of war for the next forty-six years for his troubles?"

Nicholas sat bolt upright and said, "I seem to remember there were, and probably still are, serious questions whether there was any collusion on the part either of Winston Churchill's government or the British royal family in persuading Hess to make that flight. What do you know about that Grand Master?"

At this point Sir James Sinclair intervened.

"Most serious analysts agree: it is absolutely inconceivable Hess would have taken that flight without the approval of the man he so admired – Adolf Hitler. Those two men went back a long way together; Hess had edited Hitler's book *Mein Kampf*. They'd been in jail together, and they'd plotted the rise of the Nazi Party together."

It was my turn to interject a question.

"In your opinion, Sir James, was Hess's only reason for making that flight to take me to safety or was there something else?"

Even while I was asking the question, another part of my brain had enormous difficulty accepting that this was anything more than a gigantic piece of fictional nonsense.

The Grand Master had that supercilious look on his face, which I was to come to hate in the next few days.

"Oh, I hope I don't disillusion you, Alec, when I say there was certainly more to the flight than merely transporting you to a place of safety. We've already mentioned that Hitler intended invading Russia, codenamed Operation Barbarossa, just four weeks after your flight to Scotland. Every military strategist I have read has been firmly of the opinion Hitler could not have successfully fought on two major fronts, that is against Britain and Russia simultaneously, and the severity of the Russian winters was a major issue in the planning of the Russian campaign. His generals had developed blitzkrieg to an art form; they'd rehearsed it in the Rhineland, Czechoslovakia, and Poland, and perfected it in Holland, Belgium, France, and elsewhere in Western Europe.

"Now Russia was the big one, but it had to be won before the winter set in, so he couldn't afford to divert any of his military resources to the Western front. He needed to have peace with Britain, and that I believe is why Rudolf Hess made that flight. He was aiming to land on a small airstrip next to Dungavel House, owned by the Duke of Hamilton who was lord steward of the Royal Household at the time. He'd allegedly had met Hess and other senior figures in the Nazi leadership at the 1936 Berlin Olympics.

"The suggestion was that Hamilton was in some way being used as bait to lure Hess to make the flight. What is clear is that someone from the aristocracy was waiting at the landing site and had to be rushed away due to Hess's alleged botched arrival! Hess hadn't made it quite as far as the Dungavel House airstrip; he'd crash-landed some miles away and was injured in the landing, yet you, in the rear seat, a frightened four-year-old child, appeared to have come out of it unscathed – surely a minor miracle!"

It was Sinclair's turn again; these two were so expert in the way they passed the conversation back and forth it was as though they'd rehearsed it all. Maybe they had?

"It is not disputed Hess was carrying some important papers with him, not least Alec the notebook and that exquisite locket, and while some of those papers have subsequently been released for public consumption, others remain closed. The intention, as the Grand Master has already said, is that they will remain closed until the year 2017. Ask yourself; what could have been so important almost seventy years ago, as to be denied into the public arena still today?"

Sir James continued: "What I believe they will reveal is the growing discord between the Churchill government and the British aristocracy, something Adolf Hitler believed he could exploit. Rudolf Hess was his messenger."

Almost as soon as Sir James had finished speaking, there was a discrete knock at the door and the butler looked in. The Grand Master glared at him disapprovingly. Clearly he didn't like unscheduled interruptions.

"What is it, butler? I hope it's important."

Brother James walked to stand behind his boss's chair and whispered in his ear.

"Are you absolutely certain about that?" he asked, looking quizzically at his butler, "Where did you hear that from?"

Again the butler whispered in his ear, at which, for the first time in my limited acquaintance with him, the Grand Master roared with laughter.

"Well, I'll be damned," he almost exploded, "even in my wildest fantasies I hadn't considered that. Thank you very much, James, you can go, but tell me if you hear more."

Sir James Sinclair's thoughts at that moment were divided between wondering what had caused the Grand Master to be so amused, and why he'd used language which, if his puritanical father had still been alive to hear, would have earned him the kind of thrashing James himself had incurred from time to time from his own sadistic uncle.

"Something funny, Grand Master?" he asked.

"More than funny, dear friends," he said, "The people who run the Suez Canal have decided it will be denied to tankers carrying oil to coalition countries. Such vessels will have to take the long way round, by the Cape. That's going to add extra days, and I would have thought, significant extra cost to the price of petrol in your country and mine."

Later that night, when I was back at the cottage and had more time to think, I'd tried to understand why something that was going to add even more problems to our countries' economies should be a source of such amusement. I failed, but that was because I didn't understand what was going on – anyway not then.

The Grand Master brought the discussion back to our topic.

"There's one aspect you've missed out, Sir James. One that has huge relevance to Alec here. Hitler never had any doubts he could win the war, but he'd understood very early on that in order to have a 'Thousand Year Reich', which was his goal, he must also win the peace, an altogether different problem. We know from history that Hitler's government had considered restoring the German monarchy, albeit as a constitutional monarch rather than the absolute monarchy enjoyed by Kaiser Wilhelm. The clue for that can be seen in his book, or should I call it his strategy document, *Mein Kampf.* Anastasia told us of her meeting with Hitler, and with other senior officials, when they discussed doing the same thing in Russia once that war was won. Wasn't it true that the Nazi government had ideas about doing something similar in Great Britain, restoring Edward VIII to the throne here? Tell us about that Sir James."

"Yes, you're quite right. There was much speculation about that at the time, and there is circumstantial evidence to back it up. It was clear that in the summer of 1940 Edward was trying to get back to England, though it is extremely doubtful that had the blessing of Mr Churchill, or even King George. We know he was heading for Lisbon from his temporary home on the French Riviera, and we also know that simultaneously his younger brother, the Duke of Kent, was flying to Lisbon, ostensibly to attend Portugal's 800-year anniversary. That was in a Royal Air Force plane, and I have to confess I have a problem believing such a senior member of the Royal Family would be allowed to fly to Portugal, at the height of the air war with Germany, indeed just a matter of three weeks before the Battle of Britain was to take place. However, he certainly did make that flight, but whether it was only to attend those celebrations or if there was a more brotherly motive as well, is open to intense debate. But Edward and Mrs Simpson were delayed in Madrid, apparently on the direct order of Winston Churchill to the then British Ambassador in Madrid, Sir Samuel Hoare, so it didn't happen, and sadly the Duke of Kent was mysteriously killed in a flying accident the following year, so we'll never know the truth about that!"

The Grand Master looked at his watch. "Alec, Nicholas, we've been very patient with you; we've done our best to tell you everything we know. It's getting very late so now we'll call it a day. I look forward to seeing you both at the service on Tuesday."

He was referring to the St John's Day service in the chapel.

I returned to the settee and sat down.

"No, Grand Master, we're not going to call it a day, not just yet."

The Grand Master's face lit up like a red traffic light; he wasn't accustomed to anyone questioning his decisions! Before he had a chance to stop spluttering and actually form coherent words, I carried on.

"I have listened very attentively to everything you've told me, and I have something to contribute to this conversation, too. I fully accept the contents of the notebook, which means, ridiculous as it sounds, that I accept I am the tsar of Russia in exile. I don't know how long you, and Sir James here, have known all this or what your motives were in keeping it from me until now, but I know beyond a doubt you haven't done it for altruistic reasons. Therefore I suspect the worst."

The Grand Master had stood up and glowered at me, speechless with rage. I put my hand up, indicating I hadn't finished speaking, he should stay quiet.

"As Sir James so eloquently reminded us, Hitler didn't win the war, so we are still a free country, and as citizens of a free country, we each have certain rights; I am exercising mine. For almost my entire life, and without me knowing anything about it at all, people in very high places have connived to keep my true existence from me, at least until such time as they can use it for their own ends. My actual existence has been as a humble gamekeeper, living in a cottage in the remote Highlands of Scotland. I have never known anything different, and I have always been content, which is perhaps more than I can say for either of you. I fully understand my birthright is to be the tsar of Russia, as it was also for my grandfather Nicholas II. It is my intention to follow his example, though for entirely different reasons.

"When Tsar Nicholas abdicated in 1917, it was initially in favour of his son Alexei, after whom I was named. I've never been crowned, so therefore I can't abdicate, but here and now I relinquish my right to the throne of Imperial Russia. I don't want to be the tsar, whether that is in exile or in reinstatement. I intend to stay as I am today. So far as you are concerned," and here I was looking at Nicholas, "I relinquish the right to the throne in your favour. It is for you to decide your place in whatever scheme these people have in mind, and whatever you decide, I will continue to love you as I do today."

The room was totally silent. The Grand Master had sat down again and was silently drumming his long, bony fingers on the arms of his chair. Sir James Sinclair was looking down at his feet, too embarrassed to look at any of us. It was Nicholas who finally broke the silence.

"I presume, Grand Master, that somewhere in this castle you keep a bottle of whisky. It may not be your habit, but from time to time it is mine, as I know it is my father's too, and I suspect Sir James, you wouldn't want to be left out. May I suggest, respectfully of course, that you ask your butler to bring a bottle and four tumblers. I too have something to say in this matter, and I need time to think."

The Grand Master pressed the bell by his side, and when Brother James appeared, asked him to bring a bottle of whisky. The butler's eyes opened wide, he stood in the doorway, transfixed, staring at his boss as though he'd taken leave of his senses.

"Brother James, let me say it again. I would like you to bring a bottle of whisky from the cellar, and bring six tumblers, and you can ask Chevalier Dajani and Dame Wolff to join us. Do it quickly, man; we are all in need."

Still the butler stood in the doorway.

"The key, Sir. Can I have to key to the cellar please?"

The Grand Master took a bunch of keys from his trouser pocket, selected one and held it for James to take.

"Just one bottle mind. We don't want people to get the wrong idea as to how we behave when they've all gone home!"

As the butler turned to do his bidding, the Grand Master came over to where I was sitting. He had a wide smile on his face, his thin, cruel lips drawn tightly against his teeth. What on earth was going through his mind? He reached for my hand, and pulled me to my feet, then held his arms out, and hugged me in the same way I'd seen him hug the girl in the pink tracksuit, and her companion this morning. He didn't say a word, and certainly I didn't. This was so unexpected. Silence continued for several minutes until two faces peered round the doorway, looking inside, trying to guess if it was OK to enter. The Grand Master turned to face them.

"Dajed, Monika, come on in, it's time for a small celebration. Let me introduce you to three very important friends."

Saying that, the newcomers came to each one of us, introduced themselves and we shook hands. Monika was still wearing the pink tracksuit and Majed a pair of slacks and a jumper. To be honest, they looked as though they'd jumped straight out of bed, and as I found out later, that's exactly what they had done, though not the same bed of course! Brother James returned with the whisky, Johnny Walker Black Label.

My oh my, the Grand Master was really letting his hair down, what little he had left!

The butler poured reasonably generous measures for all the guests, then a very large double for his boss, something noted by every other person in the room.

"Friends," the Grand Master was still standing, holding his tumbler at arm's length in front of himself, "let's drink a toast to a really momentous day, and for the benefit of our newcomers, let me explain. You are my inner circle; I have no secrets from any of you."

OK, so he was telling lies.

"Chevalier Alec, who you all know to be the son of Anastasia, herself the daughter of the last tsar of Russia, has renounced his right of succession to the Imperial throne of Russia in favour of his son, the Tsarevich Nicholas. He has done that of his own free will. Let's drink a toast to Alec."

I swallowed mine in one go and looked expectantly at the half empty bottle which the butler had left on the coffee table.

"Help yourself, Alec, and the others too if they wish."

Having said that, he was the first to push his tumbler forward for a refill,

"Alec, you wondered for how long Sir James and I had known of your real identity. The answer is for twenty-five years, before I bought this castle. Indeed, the reason I bought the castle was because of you. Sir James has been my dearest friend since our days at Harvard University. By chance, I was staying at his house just after his father died, which was when he found the locket and notebook. What started out then as nothing more than an intrigue, quickly became more of a quest, a quest to see justice done and a mission to right the wrong which had been done to your mother Anastasia, and to you.

"A few minutes ago, Alec, you voluntarily relinquished your right of succession to the throne, and without being disrespectful to the lifestyle you've been living, Alec, it would have been totally unfair and unrealistic to expect you to suddenly become the ruler, albeit in exile, of a country as vast as Russia, so you've done the right thing. When you and Maria fell in love, and Nicholas here came along, we realised that through him we could discharge the obligation we felt to you. In other words, Nicholas could become the tsar, and we would do all in our power to have him restored to his rightful position on the imperial throne.

"Alec, this Tuesday is St John's Day; it is also Nicholas's twenty-first birthday. Under the terms of the constitution of our Order, that is the age when an esquire, which is what Nicholas has been since the day of his Christening, can be invested as a fully-fledged knight. This is the day that Sir James and I, together with other friends, have been working towards all these years. This Tuesday, you Nicholas will be invested as a full knight of our Order and will then be inaugurated as the protector, filling the vacuum created by the murder of your great grandfather Tsar Nicholas II."

The Grand Master turned to look at me, a benign expression on his usually severe countenance.

"Alec, you've saved me the distressing duty of having to ask you to renounce your succession in favour of your son Nicholas, who has been trained all his life to expect greatness. Knights," and turning to Monika, "Dame, of the Chivalric Order of St John of Jerusalem, a massive toast to our new protector, and also to our dear friend Alec, without whom none of this would have been possible."

Once the toast had been drunk, the Grand Master suggested it was time for everyone to go home and get some sleep.

"Everyone that is, except for you Nicholas," he said, "I need you to remain here tonight. We still have much to talk about in preparation for the investiture on Tuesday. James, would you be kind enough to ask your chauffeur to drive Alec back to the cottage?"

It says something about the air of authority, which the Grand Master naturally wielded, that no-one raised any objection; I hadn't, and it was only later I would realise how cunningly he'd manoeuvred me into the position of resignation he'd wanted, and Nicholas hadn't either. He hadn't even said whether he wanted to inherit the mantle of tsar.

Sir James's chauffeur drove me back to the cottage without a word being spoken between us. As he then roughly accelerated away, the heavy-duty tyres threw up a shower of dust and stones, one of which I saw the next day had cracked a pane of glass in the conservatory!

✽✽✽✽✽

Tom Lane's plane from Dulles Airport near Washington, DC, landed at JFK airport in New York just a few minutes late, at 6.30 p.m. As he descended through the centre door he was met by a uniformed chauffeur and escorted to a waiting people carrier, which whisked him back to his hotel.

No police escort this time, he thought to himself, *probably in New York it's better to keep a lower profile than in the capital.*

His wife Carol had left a note for him at reception, to say she'd taken the opportunity to have a private dinner with a lady friend.

Once in his room he made a telephone call to the White House and left a message for the president to express his thanks for helping secure him the new job at the United Nations. Next, he called the UK ambassador to the UN, who congratulated him on the post and offered every cooperation in resolving the present crisis. The ambassador had gone on to explain it had suddenly become more complicated; CNN had just reported the Suez Canal Authority had declared the Canal closed to tankers carrying oil to coalition countries, which was something Mr Lane hadn't been aware of. He went on to tell him his colleagues at the UN realised the new deputy's first priority had to be an urgent meeting with the Russian president, and they understood he expected to be flying to Moscow the following morning. They agreed to meet when he came back to New York, at which time he would hopefully report mission success to the General Assembly.

✽✽✽✽✽

Fifty nautical miles south of the El Ballah bypass in the Suez Canal, Captain Julian Springer of the Bahamian registered oil tanker *El Paso* had heard the news broadcasts on his short wave radio that tankers carrying oil to what were termed invader-countries would not be allowed to transit the Canal. He was carrying one hundred and fifty thousand tons of crude oil from Qatar to Houston in Texas, where it would be refined to suit the gas guzzling cars and trucks pounding the interstate highways of his native America. He'd e-mailed his parent company asking for advice, but all he had in reply was an instruction to wait and see. It was early Sunday morning over there; maybe everyone was in church. How was he supposed to wait? He was approaching the assembly area in Suez Bay, or Bahr el Qulzum as his Egyptian chief officer called it, where he should join tomorrow morning's north bound convoy to transit the Canal. "Hello Port Control, this is the Bahamian oil tanker *El Paso*, en route to Houston in Texas," he'd said. "I've heard on the radio that certain tankers will not be allowed to transit the Canal. I don't want to be caught like that. Can I have your assurance that my ship will be allowed to transit the Canal without interference please?"

"Captain Springer," Port Control had replied, "I know your voice and you are a good friend to everyone in Egypt. You are welcome Sir. Please do not worry, of course you will be allowed to transit. We have no problem with you, or your cargo. Your pilot will be waiting for you, and you will be first in the morning convoy."

Captain Springer was still undecided. "Chief, you're an Egyptian; you understand how their minds work. What do you think we should do? Tell me the alternatives."

Chief Officer Ismail Wahba had absolutely no doubt what was the right thing to do. He'd had enough of this arrogant American captain already, and he'd only joined the ship in Doha. His home was in Ismailia, and the sooner he left this ship and went back there the better for him. *What the hell!*

"Captain, from Qatar to Houston through the Canal will take us thirty-nine days, allowing we keep an average of 10.5 knots. We have an assurance from Port Control we'll be allowed to proceed; they've even told us we'll be first in the convoy, and the pilot is waiting. Plus of course, if we have a problem with them, I can soon sort that out; it might cost us a few more Marlboro cigarettes than usual, but that's not a big deal.

"On the other hand, from where we are now, if we have to go round by the Cape, the journey time will be fifty-two days. With due respect, Sir, the answer is too obvious."

That was really what Captain Springer had wanted to hear. This was his last ship; his wife Emily back home in Phoenix, Arizona had given him an ultimatum last time he was home.

"The kids have all married and left home!" she'd yelled at him. "They're all over America now, everywhere except here in Phoenix. I never get to see my grandchildren unless they come here on holiday, which they don't like to do, and my husband spends his life at sea. For God's sake, even my dog died, and that was probably from boredom, and so will I unless I do something. Either you quit, or I do."

There was nothing unequivocal about that, and Captain Springer did not want to spend the rest of his days living alone; he'd told the company he was calling it a day. Now he'd had enough, and if going through the Canal was going to give him an extra two weeks at home in retirement, that's what he would do.

"Maintain course, Chief. Call me when we arrive at the waiting area."

Every day of the year the northbound convoy departs from Suez at 06.00 hours, and steams non-stop in daylight the entire length of the canal to Port Said. Captain Springer didn't want to be late at the assembly area, particularly because it was to be his ship which would have the honour of leading the convoy safely through the waterway.

Chapter Sixteen

For all my adult life, no sooner had my head hit the pillow than I would be asleep; I'd never had things on my conscience which kept me awake worrying, and except for the time when my marriage was falling to pieces. I'd always slept really soundly. Until now! Last night again my mind went round and round in circles, not wanting to let go of the discussions in the Castle. If I'd thought that by simply relinquishing my right of inheritance to be the tsar, I could put the disturbance of the past week or so behind me, I was mistaken.

It was coming light outside when I gave up the unequal struggle and got out of bed. Randy was snoring. Whatever was bothering me wouldn't be allowed to disturb him, anyway not two mornings in a row. He'd made his own way home from the pub last night and was standing outside the conservatory door waiting to be let in when I came back from my dinner date at the castle.

I tidied away the debris left behind when I'd gone to bed and made breakfast, a couple of boiled eggs I'd brought in from the chicken coup and would have made toast, only to discover I had no bread left.

"Thanks Nicholas," I said, speaking aloud, which is what I tend to do when I'm alone, "next time you go to the village, you buy some more."

I'd turned the television on in time to catch the 8 a.m. news. The very first item, unsurprisingly, was the problems caused by the increased oil prices. The London Stock Market was about to open, but if it followed the lead given earlier in the morning by the Asian markets, and then by the European markets, it was going to be a bad day. The cameras were waiting outside the headquarters of the world's oldest stock market, in the very heart of the City of London; they'd already filmed anyone they could find, from the chief executive to the porter who stood by the door, eager to ask their opinion on what the day was likely to bring; all had been tight lipped, no comment to make, except wait and see. At the beginning of trading, both the Frankfurt Dax and the Paris Cac 40 had actually climbed a little from their lows on Friday; the financial wizards who manipulated the stocks had suddenly realised their countries didn't have any fighting troops in Iraq, so it looked like they would escape the punitive sanctions. But that little piece of euphoria was short lived; the world of stocks and shares, of company ownerships, mergers and the like, transcend national boundaries. Everyone was going to feel the pain. I watched as the reporter described the way the Footsie in London was dropping, already down 8 per cent from the Friday close and with no apparent end in sight, mirroring the Dax and Cac.

After giving sombre warnings of worse to come, the cameras moved on. Eight a.m. was bang in the middle of rush hour across the country. The reporters in London, Manchester, Leeds, Edinburgh, everywhere, all described the same phenomenon: the roads were virtually empty! The M1 south from Watford to where it joined the North Circular Road, the M25 with its four lane ribbon of concrete snaking its way round the capital, the M6 north past Birmingham and Manchester, everywhere roads which at this time of day would normally be chock-a-block, were almost deserted. There was the occasional truck, often with foreign registration plates, hoping to get to Dover without having to replenish their diesel tanks at inflated prices, and a few coaches whose owners had shrewdly realised people would be looking to find a cheaper way to get to work, but otherwise the roads were empty. The cameras switched to the train stations. London's Kings Cross, Waterloo and Paddington stations, Birmingham New Street, Edinburgh Waverley were all packed with frantic commuters desperately trying to force their way into already crowded carriages, while long queues of impatient businessmen and women, from the most senior managing directors down to the lowliest of clerks, formed at ticket offices, hurling abuse at anyone desperate enough to try to jump a place or two.

I continued watching, fascinated to realise that the actions of just a few governments or individuals in the oil producing countries so many miles away could produce such panic and chaos in this country and in other countries, too, of course.

I was watching the BBC news channel in time to hear the newsreader tell of a flash news item coming in from Egypt. Colin Jackson, who I remembered reporting on the suicide of the secretary general of the Arab League, was on camera. He was holding up a copy of an Arabic newspaper, which he called *Al-Ahram*, and which he told us meant "Pyramids" when translated into English. He was speaking about a suicide letter. I automatically assumed this was the one he'd already reported on, but no, this was another. What on earth was going on?

This suicide letter, which had been re-printed in *Al-Ahram* in full, was from the president of OPEC, who'd committed suicide in Vienna on Friday. It was addressed to a Saudi Arabian government minister.

"This can't surely be the same Saudi who was mentioned in the Arab League suicide's letter, can it?" Jackson asked rhetorically.

The answer was a clear "Yes, it could, and it was".

The letter talked about the formation of a unified Islamic Self Defence Force, and that the Arab world would in future be responsible for its own security; Arabs wouldn't have to rely on the Americans and their allies any longer.

I'm no politician, I thought to myself, *but it seems a very reasonable thing for them to do, and I'm sure both the Americans and the British will be more than pleased to bring their own troops home.*

How little did I know!

The reporter went on to say OPEC would use the extra income generated from the increased oil price to fund the purchase of equipment for the new Islamic Defence Force. I did wonder why the OPEC man had committed suicide; that didn't seem to fit in at all, until he mentioned the million dollars in a Swiss bank account. I also wondered why it had taken almost three days before the letter had been made public.

Someone must have been sitting on it all this time, I thought, *presumably the police in Vienna.*

I wasn't nearly right; it was the president of America.

Colin was interrupted by the newsreader back home in London, "Colin, what's the name of the Saudi — does the report tell you that?"

The look of annoyance on the young reporter's face was easy to see; he'd been stopped mid-flow. Never in his wildest dreams had he imagined his very first foreign assignment could have given him such immediate prominence, and he didn't want to waste a single second of it.

"Abdullah Qahtani — he's the Saudi deputy minister of defence."

"You mean he *was* the deputy minister, Colin. He was found dead in his hotel room here in London yesterday morning. The police appear not to be treating it as suspicious, at least not yet. It will be very hard for them not to change their minds in view of this latest development."

I turned away from the television to make a cup of coffee. The newscaster had moved on from Egypt and was telling his audience that Gerald Smith was in New York, attending an emergency session at the United Nations, while his predecessor in office, Tom Lane had now been confirmed as deputy secretary general of the UN, with specific responsibility for the oil crisis. He would shortly be on his way to meet with President Schumakof in Russia.

Jobs for the boys, was my thought about that, not that anyone cared.

The one thing I'd learned about the news was that it was hardly ever about something good that had happened, and today's was no exception; I'd heard enough.

"C'mon, Randy, let's go walking."

The poor old dog reluctantly struggled off his blanket, peering up at me through eyes still half closed in sleep. Good thing dogs can't talk; he looked as though he wanted to give me a real mouthful. I needed to stock up on essentials from the village, and collect my pension from the post office. It was a cold morning, but there was little wind and the smell of the morning dew on the heather was enough to raise even the lowest of spirits. Randy too seemed to cheer up once he realised where we were heading, and I confess, much as I love my son, it felt good to be just Randy and me again, at least for a few hours until the Grand Master had finished with Nicholas, and we could have him back.

It should go without saying I'd timed our little shopping expedition to coincide with lunchtime at the Speckled Grouse; the Monday menu always started with a very traditional cockaleekie soup, followed by steak and kidney pie with a wonderful apple pie and custard to follow, all washed down with a pint of best bitter. It takes more than the long walk home afterwards to digest that lot.

Matt let me have a bottle of Johnny Walker Red Label, at a price considerably lower than I'd have to pay in the nearest supermarket in Pitlochry, a service he's given me for more years than I care to remember, as he had my father before me. My visit to the pub also cost me the price of a pint of bitter for Fred the postman, after he reminded me how grateful I'd promised to be when he'd rescued Randy and me from the rain yesterday.

٭٭٭٭٭

Monika stood in the arrivals hall at Edinburgh Airport and watched as George Hamlyn waddled through from his flight. He had the look of a worried man, as indeed he might. He had no idea how this afternoon was going to progress, but of one thing he was certain, she hadn't brought him up here to have sex. On the plane he'd drunk a couple of large whiskies, whether to calm himself down or give him Dutch courage, was irrelevant. He saw Monika waiting for him, wearing a black trouser suit, a white blouse underneath, with a frilly neckline. It looked extremely smart, but was hardly the slinky black skirt and the low neckline blouse she'd worn for the Saudi. If he needed proof this was not an afternoon for casual playing, he had it now.

"George, it's so nice to see you again, and how kind of you to make the journey."

She looked and even sounded sincere as she offered him her outstretched hand in greeting.

"The car's outside."

They walked to where a black Rolls Royce was parked in a no-waiting zone, a uniformed policeman standing guard.

How on earth had she managed that? he wondered.

The chauffeur stood in the front, busy spit polishing the heavily chromed radiator. His appearance was attracting attention from passers-by. He was tall and very slim; his head was completely shaved. The brown cloak he wore, floor length, a coarse material, with a white, eight-pointed cross on the left side, massively different from the traditional uniform of a chauffeur, and his skin, black as ebony, shocking to a community still trying to come to terms with European integration. No way for this man to pass unnoticed. He moved to open the nearside rear passenger door for Monika and her reluctant guest and then held it closed once they were safely seated, his cloak flapping round his ankles in the wind.

The minister was full of questions; he was a frightened man, totally out of his depth.

"Monika, what is this all about? Why have you brought me all this way?"

Dame Monika Wolff didn't answer.

"Let him stew for a while," she'd been told.

The car turned from the airport and followed the signs to the Forth Road Bridge, that marvel of mechanical engineering with a 1,000-metre main span, which crossed the Firth of Forth and which permanently occupies a team of painters to keep it looking pristine and to stop the salt water corroding the steel girders. Once across, they joined the M90 motorway north, and thirty-five miles later, bypassing Perth on the west side, joined the A9 trunk road, still heading north towards the Scottish Highlands.

The minister took a packet of cigarettes from his jacket pocket. He hadn't smoked a cigarette for more than five years, but by God he needed one now. He'd bought the packet on the plane, which was a bit of jingo commercialism, since you weren't allowed to smoke on board.

"Tch tch, no smoking in this car, George!"

Monika took the packet from him and tossed it into the front seat.

Again he demanded to know.

"Monika, what is going on? You must tell me."

Giving a not too heavily disguised sigh, the lovely Monika turned to the man sitting beside her, a man who'd had ambitions to be in a very different position in relation to her heavenly body but who was realistic enough now to know that wasn't going to happen.

"George, even I don't know all the answers, but I'll tell you what I can.

"I'm taking you to Rannoch Castle, to meet a man I only know as the Grand Master. He wants to talk to you. Then we leave the chauffeur behind and I will drive you to another castle, to Blair Castle, where you will meet with two gentlemen, both Knights of the British Realm. One of these gentlemen will be on your side, one will be against you. Your job is to persuade the one against of the wisdom of the other's arguments. I will then drive you back to Edinburgh, where you are booked on the 9.05 p.m. flight tonight back to Heathrow. The tape recording and the packaging from the money you gave to Qahtani which bears your fingerprints will be destroyed. Your job will be done, and you will never hear from us again."

"And if I fail? Suppose I'm unable to convince the other gentleman of the merits of the first's arguments?"

Monika placed her left hand on the Minister's crotch, clenching her hand, and in the process his crotch, into a tight ball.

"All I know my dear, it would be a lot better for you if you didn't fail!"

Just two nights ago, George Hamlyn, Minister of Defence and lover of young ladies, had lain awake for hours, dreaming of how this beautiful girl would caress his private parts. In his dreams he'd moaned with anticipated pleasure as her hand had circled his growing member; in this car he yelled in excruciating agony as he felt his testicles being squeezed until he felt they would pop out!

*****

The captain of the 30,000-ton, Marshall Islands registered, heavy-lift freighter *Rickmers Tokyo* wasn't best pleased. They'd been delayed leaving the port of Genoa by four hours, caused by the late loading of a luxury yacht. His ship's immediate destination was Port Said, where they would transit the Suez Canal southbound en-route to Dubai. He'd ordered best speed across the Mediterranean, covering the 1,419 nautical miles to Port Said in 77 hours, but even so the adverse sea currents south of the Greek island of Crete had delayed their arrival to the North Anchorage Area by more than an hour, making it touch and go whether they'd be able to join the first southbound convoy of the day.

At 6.45 a.m. his Filipino third mate, Lourmel de Castro, was waiting at the pilot boarding area on the main deck to welcome the sea pilot on board, and able seaman Rolando Relojas was on the bridge, ready to hoist the pilot-on-board pennant. Overweight Egyptian Pilot Ibrahim Abdel Malek hated these Rickmer freighters, one of which came through southbound every two or three weeks. They didn't have a lift, which meant not only did he have to scale the fragile pilot ladder to the main deck from the tug boat which had brought him out from Port Said, he then had to climb ten sets of stairs to reach the bridge.

Croatian Captain Kresimir Biljan was on the bridge, waiting to greet his first pilot of the day; there would be four more before his transit of the Canal was done. Dawn had already broken with a bright sun in the cloudless sky promising another typically warm day.

"Good morning, Pilot. Welcome on board," he said, "the *Tokyo's* draft forward is 9.30metres, and aft 10.42metres. Can I get you a cup of coffee?" The captain was dressed in his tropical uniform, the four gold bars on each epaulette of his whiter than white shirt seeming to glow in the early morning light, further enhancing the duskiness of his sunburnt complexion.

Ibrahim was always mollified when a ship's captain accepted him as an equal.

"A cup of coffee would be most welcome, Captain, and perhaps a little breakfast, cold meat or something like that, to start my day," was his response. Turning to Able Seaman Rolando Relojas, he instructed "Course 160."

"160, Sir," repeated Rolando, and almost immediately, "160, Sir," indicating they had reached that heading.

"Proceed at 6.5 knots please," advised the pilot.

"6.5 knots, Sir," replied the officer of the watch, confirming the instruction.

Pilot Abdel Malek had turned to the Captain.

"You're number three in line, Captain, behind the British tanker *City of Lincoln*, which is travelling in ballast, and in front of the Italian freighter *Messina*. There are nine ships in the convoy total."

Two things the pilot had just told him pleased the good captain: they would be part of the first southbound convoy of the day, and they would be in front of the Italian ship Messina – they'd been berthed next to the Messina in Genoa and had left that port an hour after the older ship. It was always a matter of pride to get to be number one in the convoy if possible, but anyway to beat a rival.

An hour later and the sea pilot's job was done; his responsibility had been to take the freighter safely from the Mediterranean Sea to the town of Port Said, where the Suez Canal, or Qanat el Suweis as it is known in Egyptian, began. A Canal pilot would take over from here. Captain Biljan was standing on the starboard wing of the bridge, paying close attention to the Port Said breakwater, which was only five metres away from the side of his ship. Ibrahim Abdel Malek came over to say goodbye, saluting the captain, and receiving from him a larger than usual reward of cigarettes for keeping his ship safe and particularly for getting them on the first convoy. Not for nothing is this sometimes disrespectfully referred to as the Marlboro Canal!

Suez Canal, a lock-free, sea-level waterway runs north-south across the Isthmus of Suez, connecting the Mediterranean and Red Seas, and separating the continents of Africa and Asia as it does so. In its 100-mile length the Canal utilises four lakes, Manzala, Timsah, and the Great and Little Bitter Lakes, easing the enormous problems of construction in the first instance and creating huge areas of manoeuvring room for shipping should it be needed.

The new pilot, Captain Abdul Ashraf, was a much younger man than his predecessor on board; he hadn't come up through the ranks of the Egyptian Navy, as most of his older colleagues had, and he'd never even been to sea, much less had command of a ship. He was very conscious he'd only been given this job because his father-in-law was a senior official at the Suez Canal Company, which caused him to feel inferior to his more experienced colleagues. He usually took this out on the junior seamen manning the bridge, and today was to be no exception.

Abdul Ashraf took his seat in the high chair on the port side of the bridge, giving him a commanding view of the *Tokyo*, and forward to the *City of Lincoln*, ignoring completely the presence of the ship's captain. It was his practice not to move from his chosen seat until arrival at Ismailia, where he would hand over to a replacement pilot, his job done.

"Six point five knots, midships," he instructed the officer of the watch, the arrogance in his voice clearly indicating his lack of respect for anyone of lower rank than himself.

"Six point five knots, midships," was the automatic reply.

Captain Biljan smothered a grin; normally this OOW never failed to use the courtesy "Sir" whenever acknowledging an instruction. Until today that was.

"Standby on VHF Channel Twelve," the pilot ordered.

This was the channel designated by the Suez Canal Authority for all vessels to maintain a listening watch.

Over to starboard, Port Said was coming awake. People living in the tall blocks of flats were throwing open the shutters, welcoming another gloriously warm day. The minarets dotting the city skyline were impressive, and the noise and pollution from the traffic crowding the narrow streets of this free port were only too obvious to those crew members on the ships who were passing this way for the first time.

The nine ships proceeded in convoy, all keeping in the maintained centre line of the west channel, where the maximum guaranteed draft was sixteen point five metres. On the bridge of the *Tokyo*, Abdul Ashraf stared eastwards, malevolently eyeing the rugged and arid Sinai Peninsula, scene of heavy fighting in the Arab-Israeli War in June 1967, such a bleak moment in Egypt's otherwise glorious history. His thoughts were rudely interrupted by the voice coming from the VHF radio.

"Captain of the tanker *City of Lincoln*, this is Port Control, you are not authorised to proceed. Please return to the north holding area."

From his high chair on the *Tokyo* bridge, Abdul Ashraf was galvanised into action.

"Stop engines," he ordered.

Captain Biljan raced from the starboard wing on the bridge deck to where his chief officer was standing.

"Ignore that instruction, Chief. Maintain dead slow ahead. Pilot, if you will Sir, please step to the starboard wing."

The chief officer was pleased his captain was on the bridge, relieving him of the responsibility to countermand the pilot's instruction, which if he'd followed would have placed the ship in a position of danger.

"Dead slow ahead it is, Sir."

Captain Biljan was profuse in his apologies to the pilot.

"I'm sorry to have countermanded your instruction Sir, but the freighter behind is travelling at 6.5knots and until he too orders his ship to either slow down or stop, I cannot stop mine. What is the problem with the *Lincoln*?"

Captain Biljan knew something irregular was going on; he'd been listening to Radio Zagreb on his short wave radio the previous evening, and had heard the Suez Canal Company order denial of transit to tankers delivering oil to countries having troops stationed on Islamic soil. It didn't affect his ship of course; his was a freighter, not an oil tanker, and he was surprised that it should affect the *City of Lincoln*, which after all was travelling in ballast, so it wasn't carrying oil either. He'd brought ships through the Canal on many occasions, and was fully aware that things were not always as they might seem in this part of the world. He wondered if this was an attempt to squeeze baksheesh out of the British tanker.

Abdul Ashraf felt humiliated. Never before had anyone countermanded his orders.

"Captain, I would remind you I am the pilot of this vessel. Day after day, month after month, I safely bring people like you through my Canal. How dare you change my orders?"

The Captain returned to the bridge and took a manual from the ship's extensive nautical reference library.

"I'm perfectly sure I do not need to remind you of the regulations concerning usage of the Canal – that under Article 2.64 of the Admiralty Sailing Directions," and here the Captain had thrust the *Pilot's Handbook for the Red Sea and Gulf of Aden* into Ashraf's hand, "it says, and I quote, 'pilots only give advice on manoeuvring vessels. They place at the Master's disposal their experience and practical knowledge of the Canal, but the Master is responsible for his vessel and any damage that may accrue in an accident.' I will continue to listen to your advice, Sir, and then I will order my officers to do as I think best."

The pilot huffed his way back to the high chair, red in the face. Meantime, the English captain of the tanker *City of Lincoln* was using Channel Twelve, informing all the ships in the convoy he was ordering his ship to stay at dead slow ahead while he tried to sort things out, and suggesting they do the same. He then asked Port Control to switch to Channel Sixteen, so as not to overuse the emergency channel. Of course it went without saying, every other ship in the convoy also switched to Channel Sixteen; they were just as curious as the Englishman to find out what was going on.

"Captain of the *City of Lincoln*, this is the Port Control Superintendent. Under instructions from the Suez Canal Authority, access to the Canal is denied to all shipping carrying oil to those countries with soldiers stationed on Islamic soil. You are an English registered oil tanker, and your country has many soldiers in Iraq and Afghanistan, therefore I order you again to return to the holding area north of Port Said."

Mark Taylor was the English master of the *City of Lincoln*. In his thirty years at sea he'd passed through the Canal more times than he could remember, and while he'd experienced petty bureaucrat problems before, never anything like this.

"Port Control Superintendent, this is Captain Taylor. I have to inform you, not only would it be unsafe for me to turn this ship and return to anchorage, it is impossible. Perhaps you should consult the navigation chart to learn the width of the canal, and the depth of water away from the maintained line. If I did as you instruct, I would go aground. Can I also inform you I am currently travelling in ballast; I don't have any oil on board, unless you count that in my engines! I cannot and will not comply with your instruction."

For several minutes there was absolute radio silence, everyone both on land and on water waiting to see what would happen next, how they would unlock this impasse. On the *Lincoln* the mobile telephone carried by the pilot had rung. Port Control, aware they were being made to look foolish on the radio, had resorted to calling the pilot on his mobile phone. The pilot had an angry exchange in Arabic, and then went to talk to Captain Taylor.

"Captain, your concerns are understood. They're now asking you to stay with the convoy to the El Ballah By-pass, where all nine ships will make fast on the port side of the west channel, and wait while the northbound convoy clears on the east side; our anchorage is by the signal tower. After the northbound convoy has cleared, we will all proceed to Ismailia and from there to the Great Bitter Lake. Only there will you separate from the rest of the convoy. You will drop anchor just before the Suez Canal Authority Signal and Radio Tower at El Kabrit, that is at the 119 kilometre point, where we will await further instructions."

Captain Taylor picked up the VHF handset.

"Port Control Superintendent, I have received your message from the pilot. May I remind you, under the Convention of Constantinople, which has been in effect since 29 October 1888, and which your Company has ratified, the Canal is open to vessels of all nations, and is guaranteed free from blockade except in times of war. I demand to be allowed to proceed."

The response from the control tower was as immediate as it was precise.

"Captain Taylor, you clearly spend too much time at sea and are not aware of what is going on in the outside world. We are at war Captain; soldiers from your country have invaded Iraq and Afghanistan. I confirm that as an act of war, and as allowed under the Convention you quoted to me, your ship and crew will be arrested at El Kabrit."

*****

The Grand Master was watching television in his private study on the second floor of the south east turret, his attention riveted to the BBC news channel. Colin Jackson was back on screen, reporting from Cairo.

"Reports are coming in," he was saying to the camera, "that a British registered oil tanker has been seized in the Suez Canal. Details are sketchy for the moment. All we know is the name of the ship, the *City of Lincoln*, and that she is being escorted to a point in the canal near Ismailia, where she and her crew will be formally arrested. The offence I understand, is illegally transiting the Canal in contravention of the ban which came into effect yesterday, on tankers carrying oil to what they term are invader-countries."

The Grand Master could not believe his luck! It is a fact of life, what is bad news for one person is generally good news for someone else, and so it was in this case. What was a crisis for the poor ship's captain and his crew was a sheer bonus for the Grand Master; he hadn't even thought of using the Canal as a weapon.

The telephone on the side of his desk rang, interrupting his musings. It was his chauffeur to say that Monika and the British minister of defence were in the Rolls and would be at the castle in just over an hour. The Grand Master was looking forward to the meeting with the minister. Blackmail was an ugly word, but as far as he was concerned, it was a weapon to be used to achieve your objective. If your opponent didn't like it, he shouldn't misbehave. Simple really!

*****

Colin Jackson, meantime, was doing his best to marinate the few facts he had into a longer story, a reporter's trick to gain more air time. His cameraman needed his hands free to use his mobile telephone, so he'd rested the heavy camera on its tripod, where it gave a distant shot of the ancient Pyramids and Sphinx.

Colin glared at the cameraman.

"What are you doing? Put me back on you fool," words clearly heard by the Grand Master, and everyone else tuned in to that news channel.

Cameraman Mohammed Wahba spoke a few words into the phone in Egyptian, and then passed the instrument to Colin.

"Listen to what my friend is saying, Colin. He's a pilot on one of the ships in the Canal. He speaks good English."

The audience at home heard those words too.

Colin held the instrument to his ear.

"The tanker *City of Lincoln*," he heard a voice say, "is in convoy immediately in front of my ship. We are travelling southbound in the Canal; the tanker is on its way to the Gulf to take a cargo of crude oil. It is travelling in sea water ballast just now. It is empty of oil; therefore, it is not in contravention of the new law and – wait. Something else is happening."

Mohammed turned the camera back on the young Englishman, giving the thumbs up to go ahead. Colin wasn't slow to catch on. He repeated the words he'd just heard over the telephone, and while his mouth was working, his ears were tuned to listen to more words from the voice of the unnamed person on the phone.

"More news is reaching us by the minute," Colin went on, "I'm hearing a second ship is about to be arrested in the Canal."

There was a pause while Colin digested the words coming through the telephone speaker.

"It seems the second vessel is the Panamanian registered tanker *El Paso*. She is travelling northbound through the Canal, en route from Dubai to America, carrying a full load of oil."

Colin had put the bit in about Dubai himself; in fact the tanker had come from Qatar, but that didn't alter the fact that Colin Jackson had just successfully scooped his media rivals for the second time in as four days. He passed the phone back to his cameraman, flushed with the success of the broadcast.

Mohammed spoke into the telephone, using his own language to thank his cousin, Canal Pilot Abdul Ashraf on board *Rickmers Tokyo* for the information and wished him a safe journey to Ismailia. Mohammed actually disliked his arrogant cousin Ashraf intensely; even as a young child, when they were growing up together in the Canal port town of Ismailia, he'd been a bully, and now that his father-in-law had got him the pilot's job, he was worse than ever.

However, he was a useful source of information, so it was as well to stay on good terms.

On board *Rickmers Tokyo*, the bridge was very quiet. The pilot was sitting in his high chair. He was sulking, and he was angry with himself for not demanding interview money from his cousin Mohammed for the news about the arrests he'd given him over the telephone. *Rickmer's* Chief Officer Ernesto De Garcia Escobar was listening intently to what was going on. For him it was a particular worry; the nine months he'd contracted to serve on board this ship were almost over; he was due to fly home to his family in the Philippines from Dubai. He didn't want a delay.

In an ancient castle in a remote part of the Scottish Highlands, the Grand Master rubbed his hands in glee! Things were getting better and better, but now he had to prepare himself for the meeting with the minister of defence.

Meantime, the Panamanian registered tanker *El Paso* had dropped anchor on the Great Bitter Lake, joining the British registered tanker *City of Lincoln*. They were both under arrest. Chief Officer Ismail Wahba had told his captain on the *El Paso* he would go ashore to negotiate their way out and had been given $2,000 to help pave the way. In fact, he was already on his way home where he'd be greeted joyfully by his wife and two kids, happy not only to see the head of the house come home unexpectedly early, but with $2,000 to spend on them as well!

Chapter Seventeen

The walk back home was very pleasant. I even found myself whistling and feeling quite carefree, but that hadn't lasted long! The peace and quiet of the moorland was rudely disturbed when a helicopter, painted white with a red stripe running the length of the fuselage – the mark of an aircraft on long-term charter to the British government for use by senior members of royalty and such like – flew low overhead. *These people really should be more considerate*, I thought to myself, *they'd behave differently if they had to earn their living up here, looking after the wildlife, instead of scaring it to death fancying around in expensive toys, all at the taxpayers' expense of course!*

The meeting between the Grand Master and Minister of Defence George Hamlyn hadn't lasted long at all, just enough time for the minister to receive his orders for the meeting that was to follow, and to listen to the sound of his own voice on a tape recording in which he'd bribed a Saudi government minister in return for an order for a number of British made tanks. There was no room for doubt in the minister's mind what would happen if he failed to do as the Grand Master had instructed him.

The highly polished Rolls Royce turned left, off the B8079 and onto the long tree-lined driveway leading to Blair Castle. The car had been waved through the entrance to the driveway by the police officer on duty, for which he'd received a warm smile of appreciation from the female chauffeur. It was rare to even see a Rolls Royce up here in the Scottish Highlands; he'd never seen one driven by such a lovely young girl.

Even with so many other things on his mind, Sir James Sinclair took the time to admire the impressive 800-year-old building, begun in medieval times and transformed through the ages into its present magnificent state. Usually the castle and grounds would have been thronged with visitors, but today there were closed signs everywhere, and the police presence as the car turned into the driveway emphasised that point better than any other. On the lawns to the right of the castle sat a helicopter of the Queens Flight. It would have made the short journey from Balmoral Castle, where the gentleman he was about to meet had started his journey, in even less time than it had taken the Rolls to drive from Rannoch Castle, further west over the high moors.

Sinclair's companion in the car was the Right Honourable George Hamlyn MP, minister of defence in the Gerald Smith government, who had only one thing on his mind: to faithfully carry out the instructions he'd just received from the man calling himself the Grand Master, and tonight to fly back to his comfortable existence in London, putting this nightmare behind him.

Sir James had a tiny microphone concealed behind the Windsor knot in his tie; this he knew was tuned to a micro-transmitter hidden in the back of the Rolls Royce, which in turn transmitted the sounds for a distance of five miles with absolute clarity. Somewhere beyond the now silent helicopter, and camouflaged to avoid being seen, would be the Grand Master, radio receiver clenched tightly in his hand, eager to hear how the forthcoming meeting would progress.

As the Rolls Royce approached the steps leading down from the patio, the butler, not wearing traditional Highland dress as he might have if there'd been tourists thronging around, but instead a pair of black trousers and a very ordinary white, open-necked shirt, walked across to open one of the rear doors, fortunately the one where Sir James was sitting. That gave Monika, now playing an unaccustomed role as a chauffeur, the opportunity to open the other door where George Hamlyn was sitting and whisper words of encouragement to try and calm his nerves. She doubted it would work.

The actual entrance to the castle was a disappointment. For one such as this, you would expect a really wide, open staircase, climbing from the lawns to reach an impressive patio area, with lots of shrubs carelessly dotted around to create an atmosphere of grandiose elegance. Not here though; there was a patio, true, but it had seen better days and needed grouting between the paving stones. The doorway was very ordinary too, but perhaps this was intentional because once inside, the view was far from ordinary. Sir James Sinclair and the Right Honourable George Hamlyn MP were escorted into the entrance hall which resembled an ornamental armoury, similar to that at Rannoch Castle, though perhaps less made to measure, more natural looking, with targes and muskets dating back many years, a veritable museum chronicling the castles' more violent past.

"I assume you would be Sir James Sinclair," the butler asked, correctly identifying Sir James, "but I was led to believe you would be alone. Will your friend be attending the meeting upstairs, or do you wish him to wait down here?"

George Hamlyn would have liked nothing better than to have been excluded from the meeting – perhaps to sit down here, as the butler had asked, with a cup of hot tea to keep out the slight chill one gets when waiting in such draughty places. Sir James on the other hand was only too pleased to have the Minister with him. He'd be the one to carry the can if the meeting went badly.

Sir James answered, "This is the minister of defence, the Right Honourable George Hamlyn. He will be with me in the meeting with Her Majesty's representative."

The butler wasn't fazed even for a minute. It was only a politician, and he'd seen many of them come and go, like the leaves on the gigantic oak trees in the castle grounds every autumn.

Together they were escorted up the medieval staircase. The plasterwork was simply magnificent, and the paintings of family members through the ages were too numerous to count.

"Please follow me, the other gentleman has already arrived and is awaiting you in the Tea Room."

Fortunately, the Tea Room in question was not the coffee shop, used on normal days by members of the visiting public, but instead was a wonderfully elegant room on the first floor, its high ceilings and walls displaying fine ornamental plasterwork and an unusual frieze in the section above the mantelpiece containing musical instruments. The Chippendale display cabinets showed a fabulous display of Sevres china, whereas the cups and saucers already laid out on the circular shaped table were plain white – perhaps these had come from the public restaurant.

"The other gentleman" the butler had referred to, stood as the two men entered the room.

"James, how wonderful to see you again. It's been far too long, but I understood there would be just the two of us. Who is your friend?"

Sir James Sinclair and Sir Norman Fitzgerald had known each other since their days in the Guards Division in the 1960s. They'd been adversaries then, competing with each other for top honours in the various ceremonial duties the division routinely undertook, most notably at Buckingham Palace. They were to be adversaries again today.

"Norman, what a pleasant surprise," James said. "I knew of course you'd entered service in the Queen's Household, and indeed that you were very close to Her Majesty, but I certainly hadn't expected it to be you I was meeting today. May I introduce –"

Sinclair's attempt at introduction was cut short by an exclamation of surprise from Sir Norman Fitzgerald. He knew George Hamlyn very well; they attended many meetings together in London, though, as today, on opposite sides of the conference table.

He addressed himself to Sir James Sinclair.

"James, you know how the Palace works, old chap. You yourself were quite close to Her Majesty at one time. You requested a meeting with a senior officer of the Venerable Order of St John of Jerusalem, *et voila, c'est moi!*"

The attempt at jollity was as forced as it was inappropriate.

"I am the bailiff of the Order," he went on to say, "the sovereign's representative, and you and I are friends of old. Who better old chap? But Minister, what on earth are you doing here?"

While he was talking, Fitzgerald had dismissed the butler with a wave of his hand, indicating they could serve the tea themselves. He was very conscious the meeting had suddenly taken on a very ominous tone, much different from what he'd anticipated.

George Hamlyn was as much taken by surprise at seeing Fitzgerald, as the other had been. So far as he was concerned, Fitzgerald represented the old order, the landed gentry who'd been gifted life on a silver platter, while people like himself had had to fight to get even one step on the bottom rung of the ladder.

"Sir James and I are old friends," he lied, "I chanced to be visiting with him and he told me of today's meeting. I am interested in the works of charities such as yours, and asked if I could attend. Nothing more than that, actually."

The Grand Master meantime was listening in, hidden behind a magnificent stand of noble fir trees in an area of the castle grounds known as Diana's Grove. His shoes and the bottom of his trousers were still wet, from having had to wade across the Banvie Burn, but the alternative route, across one of the very attractive bridges, could have meant being spotted by one of the gardeners. His face displayed a characteristic frown. As a Bostonian man born and bred, he'd always found trust to be something alien; it inevitably led to a weakening in your own personal armour, and would leave you vulnerable to attack. Such was his attitude to most things human, and knowing that 'his own man' was at this very moment exchanging pleasantries with an old friend, when instead they should be discussing something for which he personally had sacrificed too many of his years and where it was so important his own man should win the day, was as unwelcome as it was unexpected.

Once they'd taken their seats, Sir Norman Fitzgerald again spoke, only this time any traces of familiarity were gone.

"If I've been briefed properly, I understand the reason you requested this meeting was to explore the possibility of establishing a relationship between the Most Venerable Order of Saint John of Jerusalem in the British Realm, of which the Queen is the head, and the so-called Chivalric Order, which I understand you claim to represent. I will come straight to the point. Her Majesty had consented to this meeting taking place because, and only because, of the very high personal regard she has for you, and had for your father.

"I am instructed to tell you there are only two organisations today that can legitimately title themselves Orders of St John of Jerusalem. The Sovereign Military Order of Malta, which as you know is a strictly Catholic organisation based in Rome, and the Most Venerable Order, which is best known for its work around the world as the St

John's Ambulance. All the other so-called Orders are false, including the one which you claim to represent. I trust you find no ambiguity in the words I've been instructed to use?"

Sir James Sinclair had sat in silence, listening to words that could be so damning to his cause. When he did speak it was with measured authority, from a man who knew exactly where he stood and was not afraid to put forth his point of view.

"The organisation, which, as you so rightly say, I represent, can prove direct legitimate descent from the Russian Grand Priory, which was created by Tsar Paul I in 1798. Perhaps Her Majesty is not aware of this?

"Furthermore, I respectfully suggest you tread with care when using the word 'false' in connection with claiming the right to a name," he said. "People who live in glass houses shouldn't throw stones. I needn't remind you the family name of Windsor was adopted as an act of convenience by King George V in 1915, because his true family name, Saxe-Coburg-Gotha, reminded his faithful British subjects that it was his cousin, Kaiser Wilhelm II of Germany, who was reputed to have started the Great War and which was killing thousands of allied soldiers every day. Just because you change the cover of a book, it doesn't mean the inside has changed."

Sir Norman had become almost apoplectic. What right had anyone to threaten the Royal Family, whereas the Grand Master, sitting in the back seat of his Range Rover, was rubbing his hands in glee – this was going precisely as he'd hoped.

Fitzgerald continued: "I can promise you, dear sir, that Her Majesty is well acquainted with all the historical and modern-day ramifications. The very best that your so-called revived modern order could have done was to fall back on historical evolution with the Russian Hereditary Knights of which Grand Duke Alexander Mikhailovich became the Grand Prior in 1928 in Paris."

Sir James was not to be put off.

"I beg your pardon Norman, I haven't explained myself fully enough. The Supreme Council of the Chivalric Order is well aware of the so-called Paris Order, which, in their opinion, was a group of exiled aristocratic Russians who saw a chance to gain access to the untold wealth which their royal family left behind when they were so cruelly murdered. To be able to claim true descent from the Russian Grand Priory, you must be able to claim direct descent from the original Russian Grand Prior himself, Tsar Paul I, which they certainly could not do, and which we do."

Fitzgerald stood to leave the room, waving his finger in anger as he turned to face his adversaries.

"This tomfoolery has gone on long enough. Her Majesty was concerned enough for you that she wanted this meeting to take place in the hope that you could be persuaded to see sense. That clearly is not going to happen. I can see no point in continuing our discussion further. This meeting is closed."

Underneath his posturing, however, Sir Norman Fitzgerald was a rattled man. Sir James Sinclair had remained calm throughout the meeting; he was an educated man; he came from a family which had given valuable service to the Crown over many generations. While the claims he was making were preposterous, he'd maintained that look of absolute certainty about him. He actually believed what he was saying.

"Sir Norman, what if the Grand Duchess Anastasia had survived that massacre, and what if she'd given birth to a son, Alexei Romanov, the grandson of Tsar Nicholas II, and what if that grandson were alive and well today. What message would you then take back to the monarch?

Sir Norman Fitzgerald stopped in his tracks and turned to face his adversary.

"What you say Sir is astounding and beyond belief, and yet I cannot suppose that you would make such a statement, in the full knowledge that the whole of society will demand irrefutable proof, failing which, you and your entire family will be consigned to ridicule."

James Sinclair rose from his seat. He was cool; he knew he had Fitzgerald on the ropes.

"The proof will be made public in good time. The DNA has already been tested against the Romanov remains that were exhumed in Russia in 1991 and also against the DNA of our own dear Queen's husband. It is beyond doubt. In the meantime we have this message for you to take back. As you are aware, OPEC has confirmed its decision to savagely increase the price of oil to those countries that participated in the invasions of Iraq, Afghanistan, Lebanon, and other Islamic countries. That is a financial catastrophe, not only for our country, but for the United States, Australia, and many of our other closest allies. Siberia has enough undeveloped reserves of oil and gas to keep all of us supplied with all our needs for more than a hundred years. By historic proclamation of Tsar Paul I, certain of those reserves belong to the legitimate Order of St John that can prove actual descent from him. Only the Chivalric Order can do that. The Supreme Council has instructed me to tell you, they wish to share the wealth with those noble allies who are participating in the fight for democracy in the Middle East. In return they have certain minor demands, which you are easily able to satisfy.

1. That Her Majesty and the government declare Rannoch Castle and all its moorland an independent bailiwick, to be called the Bailiwick of the Knights of St John. It will have its own laws and the right to issue its own passports.

2. The tsar will be the absolute ruler, taking advice from its legislature, which will be the Supreme Council of the Chivalric Order, under the chairmanship of the Grand Master.

3. I will be appointed bailiff of the Order, as coincidentally Norman, you are of the Venerable Order, and so you and I will need to meet very often.

Sir Norman Fitzgerald had visibly paled. What was being demanded was preposterous and totally without precedent, and yet the offer of a solution to the country's energy needs could not be ignored. He turned to look at George Hamlyn.

"You've stayed silent so far, Minister. What is the reaction of the government to these demands? Will the prime minister accede without a fight, or will he negotiate for more reasonable terms?"

"The prime minister is at this very moment meeting with his opposite numbers in the United Nations in New York in emergency session," Hamlyn informed him. "They have only one topic on the agenda: the energy crisis that is threatening the stability of the entire world, and if unchecked, will result in conflagration unseen since World War II. This time it will be between Moslems and Christians, as it was all those years ago at the time of the Crusades. The demands of our mutual friend here, and of his Supreme Council, seem to me to be minor if, as they claim, they can prove the descent from Tsar Paul, and can prevent that conflagration from taking place."

"I can inform you privately," he continued, "that Mr Tom Lane had been confirmed by the UN as its representative, with the authority to find a way out of the crisis. I can also tell you that in just a few short hours he will be in a United Nations plane, on his way from New York to Moscow to meet with the Russian president. Siberian oil is the only item on his agenda. My recommendation to the prime minister will be for the government to give immediate recognition to the legitimacy of the Chivalric Order of St John of Jerusalem, and to recommend very strongly to Her Majesty that she does the same on behalf of the Venerable Order."

Minister of Defence George Hamlyn was actually beginning to enjoy himself, which he most certainly had not expected. It was rare indeed that he could talk to one of the landed gentry in this way.

"I consider that any attempt at negotiating down the demands being made by the Order will only result in a hardening of their position, which will, I am absolutely certain, lead to them making other demands that may not be so easy to satisfy. As a minister of the Crown, I will not be party to petty squabbles of the type you appear to be suggesting. There will be no negotiating, you can be sure of that. The prime minister will adopt my recommendations, and I strongly suggest you advise Her Majesty to do the same."

The drive back to Rannoch Castle was less strained than the journey to Blair Castle had been. George Hamlyn was pressing Sir James to confirm the meeting had been a success, and that the blackmailing which the Grand Master was doing would now stop. Sir James would love to have been able to put the minister's mind at rest, but he knew once the Grand Master had his talons into you, he never let go. The Polaroid photograph which the Grand Master had taken of him and his American friend Charles Weinberger at Harvard half a century earlier was evidence of that.

Once back at Rannoch Castle, Monika moved to sit in the back of the car with George Hamlyn, and the regular chauffeur replaced her behind the wheel. Sir James had gone inside; he'd wait for the Grand Master to return with the Range Rover and for the inevitable post mortem on the afternoon's activities.

"So, Monika," Mr Hamlyn started, "I've done as your boss demanded. Now if you'll just give me the tape recording and the wrapping paper from the banknotes, I can put this terrible experience behind me."

Monika had been prepared for that.

"George, take my word for it, the Grand Master will probably be burning those things right now. Please don't let it worry you ever again."

Even she didn't believe what she'd just said, never mind the minister of defence.

"There is one more thing the Grand Master has asked you to do though."

Monika removed an envelope from her handbag.

"This is a draft of a letter from you to the solicitor representing the Chivalric Order of St John. You are to have it typed on ministry of defence letterhead paper and sign it."

She smiled across at him.

"And please don't look so worried, my dear. It's only the confirmation of the things you told Sir Norman Fitzgerald you would do: that you will recommend to the prime minister that his government give immediate recognition to the independent bailiwick of the Knights of St John and to the legitimacy of the Chivalric Order of St John of Jerusalem and to recommend very strongly to Her Majesty that she does the same on behalf of the Venerable Order. Oh, and that letter has to be couriered to the solicitor by tomorrow lunchtime. And that's it, George. Not a big deal?"

George Hamlyn was street-wise enough to realise that for him this nightmare was far from over. Back at the airport, Monika walked with him as far as the departure gate, where she turned to give him a kiss on the cheek in farewell, but he pulled away. He'd learned this young lady was not his type; she was bloody dangerous, and anyway he had no intentions of flying anywhere that night. As soon as he'd judged she'd have left, he went back outside and took the first taxi in the rank.

"Edinburgh, Caledonian Hotel, please." It was a hotel he knew well, and was reasonably sure that, as a minister of the Crown, they'd find a room for him somewhere. George Hamlyn didn't take too kindly to being blackmailed, and was going to fight back. From things James Sinclair had told him, he understood that tomorrow was going to be an interesting day, and he intended to play a big part in it. He wanted his revenge on the Grand Master."

*****

Saeed Al Turki, Saudi Arabian ambassador to the United States and brother-in-law of Abdullah Qahtani, the now deceased deputy minister of defence, had just finished his audience with His Majesty the King. He returned to his own home in Riyadh, a palace, smaller than His Majesty's of course, but impressive nonetheless. He disappeared into the study without even pausing to greet his two young daughters, a sure sign something was seriously wrong. He dialled a number in Washington, DC, and was rewarded to hear Dr Deborah Adams's voice.

Deborah recognised the telephone number displayed on her mobile phone and in fact had been on the point of calling him, anxious to hear if he had any more information about the crisis.

"Ambassador, I'd almost given up on you. Do you have any news?"

The ambassador had been brought up as a Bedouin tribesman, where everyone's place in society was well ordered; the man was master outside the home, the woman was very definitely in charge indoors. But the world had moved on, and, with some regret perhaps, so had he. When angry, he was more than capable of equalling the legendary brutality practiced by his Bedouin forefathers, but given the choice he much preferred the more gentle, but equally damning, English way of using carefully chosen cold words to defeat his opponents.

Dr Adams did not fit into either the old or the new ways; she was a quite exceptional woman who was never afraid to show her femininity, but who left even a man such as him in no doubt who was in charge. When she'd said "Ambassador, I'd almost given up on you," it was a reprimand, which he had no choice but to accept.

"Dr Adams, I left His Majesty the King just minutes ago. We were together for more than two hours. I can tell you, he is as confused about what is going on as you are. Together we spoke to the rulers in Kuwait and each of the Emirates, the presidents of Egypt and Iran, and others. All of them deny having anything to do with this crisis. We telephoned everyone who'd attended the OPEC and Arab League meetings; each one of them confessed they'd supported the resolution put forward by the respective head of the organisation, demanding the withdrawal of foreign troops from Islamic soil, and as you know very well, that is nothing more than an often uttered rhetoric. They know nothing about an Islamic Self Defence Force.

"It is His Majesty's opinion that someone is deliberately fermenting tension between the Christian and Islamic worlds, though who that person might be and what he hopes to achieve, we can't even guess at. The incident going on at this very moment in the Suez Canal – the detention of two oil tankers – does not have the support of the Egyptian president or his government, but curiously, neither is it coming from whoever is propagating this crisis. It is individuals inside the Company itself, Egyptian Islamists, who have seized on this crisis to further their own religious ends, and therein lies our real problem Dr Adams. At this very moment, here in my home city, a demonstration is taking place, demanding the withdrawal of foreign troops, and the same is happening in other cities in the Middle East."

The American secretary of state was well aware of the demonstrations taking place, not only in the Middle East as the ambassador had declared, but all around the world. In the United States, Great Britain, Australia, Denmark, Poland, and many more countries that were supplying troops to the allied coalition, demonstrators were demanding their troops be brought back home and thereby end the massive price hike imposed on them by OPEC. In those same Western countries, the Islamic activists were joining the marches, because their demands were the same, the withdrawal of foreign troops, though for different reasons. The world was upside down!

"Ambassador, there is a real easy solution here."

This was Deborah Adams at her no-nonsense best.

"Why don't all those OPEC and Arab League committee members you spoke to simply put out a statement denying their role in this, and OPEC rescind the decision to impose price sanctions on each barrel of oil? Why doesn't your king and the emir in Kuwait and the other leaders in the Arab world remind their peace-loving subjects that it was their own representatives at the United Nations who voted their agreement for the troops to be sent in? Why doesn't your own king remind his subjects it is the very presence of those foreign troops that is keeping him and his family in power?"

The Ambassador knew the conversation would turn this way; in Western eyes what she asked was such a simple solution, but not so from the Arabic perspective, and Dr Adams knew that very well too.

"Deborah, there are those in my country and throughout this region who oppose any form of cooperation with Christians. They are the ones who deliberately inflame Islamic passions by misquoting from our Holy book, the Koran. They are the ones who demand Jihad from their followers; they are the people your own president is fighting in his war on terror, and their numbers are growing.

"Every one of those activists is as confused as you and I about what is behind this crisis; they are wondering if their own governments are secretly endorsing the action, as perhaps even you and your president are too. If we now do as you want, if we put an end to the crisis in the way you suggest, as I agree we so easily could do, those activists would feel cheated, and they would want revenge. There would be a Jihad, Dr Adams, unlike anything we've ever known before. I'm very sorry to say it to you this way, but you have to find the solution to the crisis in Western ways, while we in the Arab world must endorse the actions of OPEC and the Arab League."

The American secretary of state hit the disconnect button on her mobile phone. She had an appointment with the president in an hour, and before that she needed to brief her special adviser, Dr Charles Weinberger. She wanted him to travel with Tom Lane for the meeting with President Schumakof. She was determined to have her own man at the meeting; not that she didn't trust Lane, but better safe than sorry.

*****

Minister of Defence George Hamlyn had checked into an ordinary room at the Caledonian Hotel; he'd asked reception to send up a razor and toothbrush and then gone to the bar downstairs. More than anything, he needed a drink. He'd had a couple on the flight up from London earlier in the day, but the effect of those had worn off; he needed topping up, and he also needed time to think. He sat at the bar, and was barely into the first double before a heavily painted woman took the next bar stool. She was wearing a tight jumper, which showed her rather plump breasts off to perfection, a tartan mini-skirt, which did much the same to her legs, and a pair of bright-red shoes with ridiculously high heels, signposting her profession as clearly as though she had a sticker on her forehead saying "for hire", like the taxi he'd left not long before. The makeup on her eyes was smudged, her lipstick looked as though it had been painted on with a paintbrush – all told she looked as though she'd just left one customer and was looking for the next, which was in fact what had happened.

"Hello dear, would you care to buy me a drink? My name's Leila."

George didn't know what her accent was, but with a name like that she certainly wasn't Scottish; in fact the lady had come from Albania to work in a bar – her pimp hadn't specified precisely what the work was, if he had, maybe she wouldn't have come.

George Hamlyn had had enough of women, especially women who used their sex to lure tired politicians looking for nothing more than a few minutes relief away from the pressures of government business, into their web of blackmail and extortion. He'd learned his lesson. Without saying a word to the prostitute, he signalled for the bar bill, signed that to his account, and went back to the safety of his bedroom. He could think more clearly up there, and perhaps he'd spend a minute or two watching the free previews to X-rated porn films on the television, but first he had several telephone calls to make.

❊❊❊❊❊

Captain John Maguire of the Argyll and Sutherland Highlanders had called into the guardroom at Redford Cavalry Barracks on the outskirts of Edinburgh on his way home from a social evening in the officer's mess. He was orderly officer that night, and as was his usual custom, he liked to make sure that all was peaceful before returning to his married quarters a mile away. The guard commander was about to hand him a cup of coffee and brief him on the evening's activities when the telephone rang.

"Captain Maguire," he said, motioning to the guard commander to set the coffee cup down, "orderly officer."

As he listened to the unexpected caller giving his instructions, the officer could have been forgiven for thinking someone was winding him up.

"By 1600 hours tomorrow I want you to position thirty of your men on the hillside facing the south door of Rannoch Castle. They must be well concealed and act only under the instructions of a police officer, which I will arrange tonight. There will be a strong police presence as well as your soldiers. I don't expect resistance, but it would be better if at least some of your men could be armed. I also want a military helicopter to be positioned at Blair Castle at the same time."

Never before had Captain Maguire been telephoned by the minister of defence, if indeed he was who he claimed to be. He had to play this cool.

"I can of course make the arrangements you are asking for, Sir, but without being disrespectful, how can I be sure you really are Mr Hamlyn?"

The minister grudgingly admitted the young officer had a good point.

"Five minutes from now, I want you to call the ministry in

London, ask for the operations duty officer, and he will confirm the orders I am about to give you."

George Hamlyn disconnected from that call, and then telephoned Sir Norman Fitzgerald, the local dignitary and magistrate he'd met at Blair Castle earlier in the day. After explaining to him his concerns about the following day's activities at Rannoch Castle, the minister asked that the two men meet the following afternoon at Blair Castle and requested him to organise road blocks on the A9 trunk road, half a mile north and south of the turning to Rannock Castle, at 4 p.m. the following day. After that, Mr Hamlyn had just one more call to make, to his wife back home, to tell her how much he loved her, and how he was looking forward to celebrating their golden wedding anniversary that weekend.

Mrs Madeleine Hamlyn couldn't believe what she was hearing; her husband actually saying those things to her, things he hadn't said in more than ten years.

"Tony," she said, looking adoringly into the eyes of her husband's parliamentary private secretary," I think your boss has finally met his match. Turn the light off again darling. I hate it when you watch me doing that to you!"

Chapter Eighteen

The sun's rays were beginning to emerge over the top of the distant hills, evaporating the early morning dew that coats the thin, woollen fleece of the baby lambs. It wakes the young grouse, so they can resume their incessant scratching for the fine quartz grit which they use to grind into pulp the tender young shoots of heather sitting heavily in their stomachs. The cock grouse is already awake; he's watching the young chicks, ready to give the alarm call at the first sign of any playful but deadly fox cubs or the fluttering of newly grown wings on baby carrion crows. The gamekeeper won't be far away either, gun at the ready, listening for that alarm call, ready to kill anything that threatens the lives of the young grouse; less than two months from now people will pay good money to kill for pleasure what the fox cub and carrion crow kill so they can live.

Those same sun's rays illuminate the flag proudly flying from the roof of Rannoch Castle, a soft breeze doing just enough to cause it to ripple very gently, the flag's red background contrasting sharply with the azure blue of the morning sky. A man is standing in the paved courtyard, his back to the castle door, his long cloak fluttering silently round his ankles, the white, eight pointed cross on its left side accentuated by the blackness of the cloak itself. The man has a decoration hanging from his neck by a red ribbon, the enamelled motif of the Malta Cross topped by a double-headed eagle, indicating he is a person of high rank in the Russian Grand Priory of the Chivalric Order of St John of Jerusalem.

He is quietly surveying the area around the castle, making sure everything is as it should be before his guests start arriving. This is 24

June and St John's Day, the day the Order of St John commemorate their patron saint; it is to be a very special day for the Grand Master, a day he has worked for tirelessly since learning of the existence of the grandson of Tsar Nicholas II a quarter of a century ago.

Looking outward from the courtyard, past the statues of medieval knights, the long driveway runs in a perfectly straight line until it comes to an end by the enormous gates, gates that today are standing open, miniature flags of the Order strategically placed atop each of the pillars. Turning left out of those gates onto the main road would take you deep into the sparsely populated Scottish Highlands, whereas turning right is to return to civilisation, to cities like Perth, Edinburgh, and Glasgow, and onward to London. His guests will be coming from the south in time for a buffet lunch in the large marquee, which had been erected just inside the gates.

The Grand Master returned to his private study on the second floor of the castle, satisfied that everything was arranged as he'd ordered. He was waiting for some very important telephone calls, the first of which came as he walked back into the room. It was his solicitor in London, confirming he'd received a letter from the minister of defence, the Right Honourable George Hamlyn MP, copies of which had gone to Her Majesty the Queen, to the prime minister, and to the former prime minister, Tom Lane. The Grand Master smiled confidently. Step one accomplished, exactly as he'd ordered.

✳✳✳✳✳

Tom Lane was on his way back to New York's John F Kennedy Airport, the second time in as many days. He was travelling in a rather unusual people carrier, unusual in that it weighed a little over three tons, and was heavily armoured, while the four police motorcycle escorts, two in front and two behind, were under very strict instructions concerning that gentleman's safety. Dr Deborah Adams wasn't taking any chances of something going wrong on her patch on today of all days! Carol Lane was sitting next to her husband in the car, delighted that her time in the limelight, which she'd so enjoyed as the wife of the prime minister, had been renewed now he was the deputy secretary general of the United Nations. Pity he didn't have the top job, but there was time enough for that to happen.

The convoy swept through the VIP entrance to the terminal building where an airport security vehicle was waiting to escort them to the chartered Boeing 757, which was to take Mr Lane to Moscow for his meeting with President Vladimir Schumakof. This was the part the Lanes liked best: an airplane at their disposal. They'd travelled extensively round the globe during their last few years in Downing Street, usually in a chartered airplane, something the press hadn't always approved of. No one would like going back to sharing public transport once they'd had that kind of privilege.

The captain of the plane and the senior steward were waiting to greet their VIP guests as they climbed the steps. Mr Lane would have preferred a British crew, but the UN was making efforts to contain expenses, and Russian owned aircraft and crews came a lot cheaper than British ones. Six other people were already on the Boeing, sitting in what would, on a scheduled flight, be equivalent to business class. They were all UN people with expertise in the appropriate areas of Russian politics and energy supplies. The secretary general had also sent his own personal assistant along, to lend whatever services he could to his newly appointed deputy, and of course to report back to him on what he was up to. He wasn't about to let Mr Lane steal a march on him.

The Lanes went back to introduce themselves to their fellow passengers before settling down into their first-class armchairs, and were fastening their seat belts ready for take- off just as Mr Lane's mobile phone rang.

"Hi Tom, it's Charlie Weinberger. Deborah thought it would be a good idea for me to accompany you. I've just arrived on the shuttle from DC, it'll probably take me twenty minutes to change terminals, can you wait for me?"

"Sure Charles, no problem, we'll wait for you. Must go; I've got another call waiting."

He pushed the recall button: "Tom Lane."

The new caller was from his private office in London. He wanted the boss to know the contents of a letter they'd just received from George Hamlyn, recommending to Gerald Smith that his government give immediate recognition to the independent bailiwick of the Knights of St John and to the legitimacy of the Chivalric Order of St John of Jerusalem and to recommend very strongly to Her Majesty that she does the same on behalf of the Venerable Order.

To say that Tom Lane was mystified by the message he'd just received was an understatement, and why Hamlyn should feel it necessary to copy it to him was equally strange but he had far weightier things on his mind just now. He dismissed it. The engines on the 757 had been turned off while they waited for Dr Weinberger, who at that moment was taking his shoes and trouser belt off, ready to go through the security scanner before being allowed to proceed to the private boarding gate. He also had another telephone call to make, only this time rather further afield than before.

"Oliver, it's Charles Weinberger."

No one, but no one, used Oliver Charles Edward Emerson's name except Weinberger; to everyone else he was the Grand Master, and it always infuriated him when Weinberger did it, a fact the American scholar knew very well. It was his own little act of rebellion against a man who'd been blackmailing him ever since they were at Harvard together, when Emerson had returned to his room in time to catch Charles in a very compromising position with young James Sinclair.

"Just to let you know, Tom Lane has delayed the departure of his plane to Moscow, he's waiting for me. I'm through security, just waiting for a car to take me out to the plane."

The great American public would be surprised, and in some cases gratified, to know that even in this enlightened age, if someone has a photograph of you doing what Weinberger and Sinclair were doing to each other, even though it was half a century earlier, your security clearance would be trashed. If that happened to Charles Weinberger his whole career as a political academic would be worthless. The Grand Master had been playing on that more and more as Weinberger's career had progressed..

"Charles, I don't need to remind you, Mr Lane must not go to Moscow. His business is here in Scotland. It's up to you to persuade him of that. I also don't need to remind you what will happen if you fail – this is too crucial to our plans!"

*****

At the same time in Moscow the Duma was sitting in emergency session, deliberating the crisis caused by OPEC increasing the price of oil to certain invader-countries. To Vladimir Schumakof it was a God send. Ever since the breakup of the Soviet Union he'd been working flat out to secure international respect for Russia consistent with her size on the global map. Oil and gas, and to a lesser extent, gold and diamonds were the keys, and OPEC's surprising move had given Schumakof the opportunity he'd been looking for. He was about to play the same card he'd played in 2006, immediately prior to the G-8 Summit in St Petersburg: getting the Duma to deny foreign companies the right to participate in Russia's mineral wealth.

Tom Lane had called him yesterday, explaining the new role he'd been given by the UN and asking for a meeting to discuss the oil crisis. He knew Mr Lane wanted Esso, Shell, Exxon, and BP – all these European and American owned companies – to have oil exploration rights in Russia, so the politicians could use their power of patronage to persuade them to be lenient in times of crisis, like now. The president of Russia wasn't about to let that happen; he was going to close the door in Mr Lane's face before his plane even touched down at the airport, just as he'd done in St Petersburg those years earlier.

It was rare for Russian presidents to attend Duma sessions, but today was an exception. He wanted to be there in person. No sooner had he taken his seat than the speaker of the parliament addressed him, holding a paper aloft as he introduced a speaker's motion.

"Mr President, I have here a report, which has been filed by the Moscow Judiciary today, confirming the legality of a document signed by Tsar Paul I in 1798. This document purports to give mineral exploration rights across a wide belt of Siberia to an organisation known as the Chivalric Order of St John of Jerusalem. Do you know of that ruling, and is it something that you and this Duma must abide by?"

Vladimir Schumakof was a master of facial expressions. Had he chosen to be an entertainer rather than a politician, he would have been an exceptional performer. He took his place in the box to give his reply, a cheeky grin serving to broaden his handsome face.

"Mr Speaker, I can confirm I am aware of the ruling, as I also confirm, on behalf of all the Russian people, and of this Duma, that all this Order has to do, assuming it is still in existence after two hundred years, is to produce a legitimate successor to Tsar Nicholas II, which means someone in the direct line of succession to him. If they can do that, they are welcome to the full exploration rights as decreed by Tsar Paul, without incurring even tax liabilities in Mother Russia. Now can we debate the oil crisis, and find a solution that helps our American friends, and at the same time increases the Russian voice in world politics?"

But the speaker wasn't finished.

"Mr President, if as you say the judiciary ruling is confirmed by you in the form of a Presidential Decree, it is necessary it bears your signature before it can be considered lawful."

The president was becoming increasingly impatient.

"I will sign the paper right now, Mr Speaker, if you will then allow the more serious business of this parliament to proceed."

As he spoke he walked over to where the speaker presided over the Duma and took the paper from him, signing it with an extravagant flourish that characterised the flamboyance of his mood.

"There you have it, Mr Speaker, but perhaps it would be even more legal if you signed it too."

The sarcasm in the president's voice was wasted. The speaker of the Russian Duma, Yakov Mikhailovich Yurovsky, had every intention of signing the paper, and in so doing, fulfilling a pledge he'd made to his namesake grandfather many years earlier, atoning for the terrible deed which that man had perpetrated in the name of Bolshevism!

The speaker handed the paper to an orderly, whispering instructions as to what he should do with it. President Schumakof meanwhile had returned to his place, and was addressing his parliamentary colleagues. He was at his eloquent best as he skilfully cajoled his less-enthusiastic supporters to agree it was in Russia's national interest not to allow foreigners to exploit the Siberian mineral resources. He reminded them how the British, closely followed by America and France, had for years raped the oil fields in Saudi Arabia, Iraq, and Kuwait, changing national borders and imposing ruling families absolutely at will when it suited their greedy purposes. It was only now that OPEC had found the courage to say enough is enough.

"Is that what you want to happen here too?" he asked. "For the sake of the few miserly dollars we'd get by granting mining rights, we would be losing our independence to those same countries which have finally been kicked in the teeth by the Arabs."

*****

As Mr Schumakof was ranting at his colleagues in the Duma, two-thousand miles west, in a very much calmer atmosphere, the warning lights on a fax machine started to glow, and the soft whirring of the mechanical insides heralded the arrival of a single piece of paper. It was written in the Cyrillic alphabet used in Russia and bore two very important signatures. The Grand Master knew exactly what it was; he'd been expecting it.

*****

Charles Weinberger was breathless as he entered the aircraft by the forward cabin door. Even as the senior steward was pulling the security arm into place, the free-standing steps were taken away, and the twin engines started. Dr Weinberger hadn't waited to be invited, he'd chosen to sit immediately opposite Mr Lane in the forward cabin. As the Boeing began its long taxi to the departure runway he began his pitch, knowing that if he failed to convince Lane, his own reputation would be at stake.

"Tom, we need to revise our plans."

He was interrupted by two very different sounds. One was Mr

Lane indicating his annoyance that this American academic was muscling in on his carefully thought out plans; he wasn't about to let that happen, anyway so he thought. The other sound was the tone of Weinberger's mobile telephone, indicating there was a text message waiting to be read. He examined the message from the Grand Master; everything was on course!

"Tom," he began again, overriding Mr Lane's attempts to speak, "there has been a significant development I have to make you aware of."

The voice over the aircraft's public address system managed to do what Mr Lane had failed to do; it stopped Weinberger talking. It was the Russian captain, speaking in excellent English to his passengers.

"Ladies and gentlemen, we are number three for take-off, which should be in two minutes from now. Immediately after take-off we will be making a fairly sharp right turn northeast, passing overhead Boston and continuing our climb to a cruising altitude of 38,000 feet as we begin our journey to Moscow."

The steward came to see his guests immediately the seat belt sign was extinguished, offering a cooling face towel and refreshments.

"A cup of tea for me please, English breakfast tea if you have it, and coffee for my wife. Will you be serving breakfast? We were late to bed last night and up early to get the flight this morning; we're both very hungry. What about you, Charles?"

No way could Tom Lane use the familiar styling of Charlie, as Dr Adams had done the day previously.

"No breakfast for me thanks, Tom; I grabbed a bite on the commuter flight from DC this morning, but black coffee would be great. While we're waiting for that, I need to talk with you."

Some people are better in the mornings, and others at night. The former prime minister of Great Britain was of the latter type, and not having slept too well either of the last two nights he wasn't feeling at his brightest, and he was hungry too.

"If you don't mind, Charles, we'll have breakfast and perhaps a bit of shut eye, then we can talk. It's a long flight to Moscow, we have plenty of time."

That should have settled matters, but it didn't.

"But that's the point, Tom. We're not going to Moscow."

The United Nations deputy secretary general looked hard at Dr Adams's special adviser.

"Mr Weinberger, we are going to Moscow, where I – and I will repeat that in case you didn't understand – I will meet with Vladimir Schumakof. If you want to play a role, it is to be my adviser on technical matters within your competence. If you don't want to play that role, then I suggest you stay in your hotel room in Moscow, and I'll let you know when it's time to leave. Now I'm going to have my breakfast, then a nap. We'll talk later."

This wasn't going the way Dr Weinberger had planned it at all; this Brit wasn't the pushover he thought he'd be.

"Mr Lane, I'm sorry, Sir. I haven't done this very well at all, but it is crucial I bring you up to date on a development which happened in the Russian Parliament within the past couple of hours. Mr Schumakof has done exactly the opposite of what he said he'd do; he has signed away mineral exploration rights in part of Siberia, coincidentally the very same part of Siberia I briefed you on yesterday lunchtime."

Mr Lane was understandably flabbergasted, as anyone would be who understood the absolute pig-headed way the Russian president had consistently refused to give way to opening up Siberian mineral rights. Breakfast was forgotten. He moved across the aisle, to sit next to the American.

"OK, Charles, you'd better take this from the top. Tell me what you know."

Twenty minutes later Mr Lane was standing on the flight deck arguing with the Russian captain, while far below the island of Newfoundland could clearly be seen, its capital city of St John's being the closest city to Europe from North America. The captain didn't want to divert his aircraft to Edinburgh; he was looking forward to being back home in Moscow, where he could see his wife and kids, but as is the way of such things, he didn't really have a choice. If the client wanted Edinburgh, then that's what it had to be, but he'd give him the most uncomfortable damn airplane ride he'd ever had in his miserable life in revenge!

Back in the cabin Mr Lane got to thinking about the letter

his private office had received that morning from George Hamlyn. He was particularly cynical by nature, and naturally suspicious of coincidences, and in this case he had far too many. Dr Weinberger being on this plane with him, which Dr Adams certainly hadn't mentioned; the briefing yesterday which had narrowed his choice of oil location to just one chunk of land in the middle of Siberia; the Russian president apparently signing away mineral rights of that same chunk of land to an organisation he personally had never heard of until today, and lastly, a copy of a letter from his political ally in his days at Number. 10 recommending that same organisation be granted independence of a piece of Scottish territory. There was something very wrong going on.

"Carol, what do you make of all this?"

It had always been their way, ever since student days at university, to mull over problems together. Whatever other faults the popular press liked to find in this lady, they had to agree she had a very analytical brain.

"I think you need to broaden your vision, my dear," she told him. "So many things have happened in the past ten days or so – things that have combined to put us on this plane today. First there was the announcement from the Arab League, followed by the suicide of their secretary general. Next day was the OPEC press conference, followed by the suicide of the president of that organisation. Hours later came the apparent death from natural causes of that nice Saudi minister, Abdullah Qahtani – you remember he invited us to his beautiful palace in Riyadh on our last visit there; he was linked in both suicide letters. Then the Suez Canal was closed to certain oil tankers, and two of them were arrested, and now we have all that Charles here has told us! For sure you will find that organisation, what was it called – the Chivalric Order of St John of Jerusalem, is behind this, making it all happen in ways, and for reasons I can't fathom just yet."

Dr Charles Weinberger sat back in his seat, he was relaxed. Mrs Lane had laid it out precisely the way it was.

One very shrewd lady! Let's see what happens when we get to Edinburgh.

On the flight deck, Captain Vassilyevski was speaking with his co-pilot.

"Valerij, I'll monitor air traffic control while you call Gander Oceanic on HF, to see if the company has filed our new flight plan to Edinburgh."

Gander Oceanic has a certain reputation amongst the more experienced trans-Atlantic pilots for always seeming to be one step ahead of the game; it was almost as if they were in the jump seat behind the captain, advising him of routing and conditions.

"Yes UN 554, we have your new clearance; are you ready to copy?"

The co-pilot looked across at the aircraft captain.

"The clearance is coming through now; will you listen in while I copy it?"

It's generally accepted policy that both pilots listen in to clearances such as this, to preclude the possibility of mistakes.

"Mr Lane, this is Captain Vassilyevski; just to let you know we have the clearance for Edinburgh. Flying time will be four hours and twenty-six minutes."

*****

In Moscow, the Duma had given President Schumakof his way; foreigners would not be allowed a stake in the Siberian oil fields, except for anything covered by ancient treaty. Those last few words had been added at the suggestion of the speaker, mindful of the Proclamation signed by Tsar Paul in 1798. Mr Schumakof had looked across at the speaker, a puzzled expression on his face, but it seemed that he alone of all the members had realised the significance of what the speaker had done. As the president turned to leave the chamber he looked across at the speaker and inclined his head to one side, indicating they should meet outside.

"OK, Yakov Mikhailovich, what the hell was that all about?"

Vladimir Schumakof was angry that one of his own closest supporters should have been instrumental in forcing him into a compromise.

"You're up to something. What is it?"

They were in the president's room; no one could overhear what they were talking about.

"Mr President – Vladimir – I will explain. I am named after my grandfather; I was his favourite grandson. Right from my earliest memory of him he liked to talk to me about what life was like when he was a boy growing up in Tomsk and later years when he moved to Perm, where he was employed as a watchmaker. My grandfather was a very gentle man, which made what he told me in 1938 as he was dying all the more shocking.

"I was just turned fourteen. I sat with him at his deathbed, in his little room above the workshop. For a while he was rambling, talking nonsense things; he had difficulty breathing, and his voice was hoarse. Suddenly, he grabbed hold of my hand, and held it very tightly.

"'There is something I will tell you Yakov Mikhailovich,' he said to me, 'it has been my secret from the family all these years, but someone has to know.'

"He told me he had supervised the massacre of the imperial family at Yekaterinburg in 1918; he'd actually been the one who fired the first bullet, killing Tsar Nicholas II outright. He described to me the events of that night and the hours that followed; how he and his comrades tried to dispose of the bodies. He told me two of his prisoners, Alexei and Anastasia, had escaped, helped by the guard on door duty, while he and his team were meeting in the basement deciding how to carry out the killing. They had panicked, knowing their own lives would be forfeit if their superior comrades found out what had happened. The original plan to dispose of the bodies had to be scrapped, because that required the Chairman of the town executive committee to supervise the burial; he would realise at once two bodies were missing. One of the team, a Cheka man called Medvedev, suggested they make a fire and pretend to burn two bodies, which was what they'd done. My grandfather thought the two escapees had probably died of hunger or maybe been killed by a bear in the Siberian forest, as no-one ever heard of them again!"

"Vladimir, my grandfather was carrying out his orders, as a soldier should. It was only as he grew older he appreciated the terrible deed he'd committed. All the promises that Lenin and later, Stalin made, how the working people would rule the country, the wealth would be shared equally by everyone. Bolshevism was the way, not the pampered lifestyle of just a few nobles, but those promises came to nothing. Things got worse, but you know this very well; they had mass starvation, thousands, hundreds of thousands of people were sent to camps in Siberia for no reason. Families turned against each other. He'd lived with the cruel realisation that, while he'd followed his orders, it was the people who'd given him those orders who were the real murderers; these people now had the fancy houses and food for their children, while everyone else starved. Russia had exchanged one failing system for another."

"Mr President, my grandfather made me promise to make up for the terrible deed which he had perpetrated in the name of Bolshevism! That was why I came into politics, and why I've always worked so hard to fight for the common man in the street; why I was amongst the first to rejoice when you became the president, knowing you had those same values. Last year, when I was with you on the visit to the American president in Washington, I received an unusual message in my hotel room. It was from Dr Weinberger; you'll remember, he was an adviser to Deborah Adams. You had an argument with him; he told you he knew more about the Russian oil reserves than you did!

"His message asked to meet me privately; he'd enclosed a very beautiful gold locket with his note, a locket which I understood was a gift from Tsar Nicholas to his wife when she gave birth to Alexei. I was curious, so I met with him in his room. He knew about my grandfather, and when he saw my name on the attendance list to meet President Riles, he made enquiries about me. He found out I came from Perm, as did the man who'd murdered the Tsar. He put two and two together: an unusual family name, Perm, and what else I don't know, and he made four."

The Speaker was interrupted by the ringing of the green telephone on President Schumakof's desk, but other than hearing him utter monosyllabic responses, he was unaware of the subject.

"Mr President, Dr Weinberger confirmed to me exactly what my grandfather had told me on his deathbed: that Alexei and Anastasia had escaped. He also told me that Alexei had died in the forest, as my grandfather had always assumed, but that Anastasia had survived; she'd lived long enough to have a child herself, a child she called Alexei, in memory of her brother of course. That child, now a grown man of course, is alive and well, living in Scotland. Vladimir, we have a tsar!"

"Well, well, so that's what it's all about" Mr Schumakof said, almost to himself. "Carry on with your story, my friend."

"The American offered me money if I would help him to prove the tsar was genuine. There was a document, the one I mentioned in the Duma today, that Paul I signed more than two-hundred years ago. He told me he had the original. He gave me a copy, and asked if I could get it authenticated in our Supreme Court, and then try to trick you into confirming you would honour the agreement, assuming there was a tsar of course. That was what I did to you this afternoon, Mr President, and I would do it again if I had to, for the sake of my grandfather, and for my country."

The president had that look on his face similar to how a bird of prey would look when it knows it has got its prey at its mercy.

"So, how much money did Dr Weinberger give you Yakov, and where is the locket?"

The speaker denied accepting the offer of money. The American had given him the opportunity to avenge his grandfather, and he believed it was for Russia's good, too. As for the locket, he had given that back, as he'd been asked to do.

"Yakov, the telephone call a few moments ago was from our ambassador in London. It seems my friend Mr Lane has cancelled the appointment to see me here in Moscow tomorrow. He tried to phone me while I was in the Duma, He wanted to explain, but as you know I don't accept calls in public meetings, so he called the ambassador. He's asked me to fly to Scotland instead, to meet the tsar of Russia.

Chapter Nineteen

This is the day my son Nicholas will celebrate his twenty-first birthday, and when, under the terms of the Constitution of our Order, he becomes eligible to be a fully-fledged knight, but is that what he wants? I confess I was worrying about my son; did he understand what he was getting involved in, what it would mean for the rest of his life, to be known as the tsar of Russia, albeit in exile! I'd told him whatever he decided to do, I would respect his decision, and it would make no difference to our relationship, but how sure was I about that? Frankly, I didn't know.

Today was going to be a big day, but for who? Nicholas of course, the Grand Master certainly, what about Sir James Sinclair, and last, but not least as far as I was concerned, me? The Grand Master had tactfully suggested it would be better if I didn't attend the Grand Priory meeting; it would only confuse the rank and file members of the Order to know I was the true tsar, but Nicholas was taking my place. Maybe there was something in that, and I tried to tell myself I didn't care anyway, but whether I was being honest with myself was another matter.

I decided to go into the garden and do some manual work to take my mind off these other matters. It wasn't too late to dig the last of the new potatoes crop, so perhaps egg and chips for dinner tonight. Not quite what the people attending the meeting in Rannoch Castle would be getting. They were in for a banquet, but I wasn't complaining.

I'd gone into the chicken coop to top up their drinking bowl when I felt someone watching me. It was Sir James Sinclair, standing erect as always, his hands clasped behind his back; he looked very tired, and it seemed to me he had aged even in the short time I'd known him. I was surprised at my own feelings – suddenly I felt sorry for him, whereas earlier my feelings had almost been of contempt.

How had he got here? I asked myself, and in the same instant I received the answer: an old model London black cab was parked on the side of the track, a logo on the driver's door advertising a London gaming casino. The cab belonged to John, our local taxi driver; he'd had it for ten years to my knowledge, and it was well used even before that. It was his pride and joy, and he was forever doing precisely what he was doing just now, polishing the paintwork.

I left the chicken coop, being careful to latch the door closed behind me – foxes like chickens as much as they do rabbits – and walked over to where Sir James was standing. I had to place the basket of eggs I'd collected on the ground before we could shake hands.

"I never thought I'd live to see the tsar of Russia walking out of a chicken coop in Scotland with half a dozen eggs in his basket," he said, laughing at me. "How does it feel?"

Despite his apparent relaxed good humour, he hadn't forgotten to bow his head; some habits die hard.

"It feels just the same as it did two weeks ago, before you came into my life," I answered. I immediately regretted the implied criticism. "Why don't you come in and have a cup of coffee, Sir James?"

"Alec, if I may still call you that, and you should drop the formality as well, please just call me James. As for something to drink, it's still a bit early for me to be drinking coffee, but if you have some tea it would be most welcome."

We went into the conservatory where he sat in one of the armchairs while I made the drinks. By the time I reappeared, the smile on his face had been replaced by the more familiar aloof look which I'd noticed the very first time we'd met. I preferred him smiling!

"Alec, perhaps I've already left it too late, but there are still things left unsaid between us, things you should know. I confess I also have a great desire to unburden myself, and that is something I've put off for more than fifty years. Do you mind?"

How could I mind? On the mantelpiece in the next room was a

beautiful locket, one which the tsar of Russia had given to the tsarina the day she presented him with a baby boy, an heir to the Romanov throne. That boy had died in a dark forest in Siberia, and his sister had then looked after the locket until she too had died, murdered by a Russian assassin in Germany. The deputy Fuehrer of Nazi Germany had then chosen that locket to accompany me on the flight to Scotland, where a knight of the British realm, Sir James Sinclair's father, had safeguarded it until such time as it could be given to me. How could I possibly mind after all that?

"Alec, everything I'm about to tell you concerns myself and the Grand Master. I'd first met him at Harvard University; we'd come from a similar background, perhaps neither of us actually unloved by our parents, but of a certainty they were of the same mould, very strict disciplinarians. At that time I was sexually confused, not sure where I belonged, and it was while I was indulging in a moment of sheer stupidity with an American student Charles Weinberger that Oliver Emerson, to give the Grand Master his real name, came into the room and saw what we were doing. He had a Polaroid camera with him and used it to good purpose – he's been blackmailing me to do his bidding ever since."

Wow! Whatever I thought James had wanted to tell me, it most definitely wasn't that!

"Even today," I asked, "when there's no shame being homosexual, and it isn't against the law, how can he still have a hold over you?"

He went on to tell me how, after university, he'd come back to Britain and found employment with the Security Service.

Some years later, he'd been in the attic going through some of his father's old papers which had been stored there after he died. There was a small chest, the kind travellers used in the early part of that century, and in there he found Anastasia's notebook and the locket, and a letter explaining why he kept them. James foolishly mentioned it to the Grand Master during a telephone conversation, and the following day the Grand Master arrived at his door, completely unannounced.

By this time Sir James had progressed in his career, eventually coming to head the secret service, a remarkable achievement. It was his habit to take work home, which he'd done that day. The

Grand Master saw Sir James's briefcase on the table in the hall. He opened it and amongst the papers inside was one stamped Top Secret. Unbeknown to Sir James, the Grand Master photocopied it; this was during the 1960's when spies Burgess and Maclean were still fresh in people's minds. The Grand Master threatened that if James didn't give him the locket and notebook, that classified document and the Polaroid photograph from his Harvard days would be sent anonymously to the authorities. His career would be over and he would probably be sent to prison.

"I felt I had no choice, Alec; had I not given them to him he would have denounced me. What you see at Rannoch Castle today is the result of my weakness all those years ago. I'm ashamed of what I've done, but perhaps I can yet find a way to make amends."

It was taking me time to get used to calling him by his first name; each time I'd done it so far it had sounded so false, but I felt I had to persevere. He was sitting in an armchair, looking completely dejected, a tired, worn out old man. No wonder I felt sorry for him!

"Why are you telling me this, James? Nothing you've told me changes anything."

"It will, Alec, oh it will! The Grand Master has been obsessive about the Order of St John ever since his father introduced him to it, which coincidentally happened when we were at Harvard. His father sent for him to come home, to be invested into the Order. He would usually stay the night, and return to the university the following day, but not this time. He returned unexpectedly and found Charles and myself lying on the bed together, which is where that Polaroid photograph comes in.

"Alec, the Grand Master has spent years researching the Crusades, 'the most glorious moment in our history,' he's fond of reminding anyone who'll listen, remembering of course that his ancestors did originate in England. He's visited all the cities which the Crusaders held, and the islands of Cyprus, Rhodes and Malta as well, always trying to discover untold history.

"His hero is King Richard I; he's convinced if Richard's brother John had not been trying to usurp the English throne, Richard wouldn't have returned home and would have successfully accomplished his mission to recapture Jerusalem from Saladin's hordes during the third Crusade. As he sees it, Jerusalem wouldn't be the divided city it is today. He hates Moslems for the defeats they inflicted on the Order, and he's determined to have his revenge. Alec, the Grand Master is totally crazy, and he's dangerous."

"He once told me about a secret room in the castle, a room he discovered by chance, and where he claims Bonnie Prince Charlie hid from the Royalists. I told you, he's mad! He says in that room is his entire strategy, his operation plan he calls it, which will lead the Christian Knights to a final victory over the Moslems. He told me there are three pictures on the wall of that room; one is a painting of King Richard in his uniform as a Crusader, a second is a copy of the portrait of Tsar Paul which hangs in the Great Room on the third floor, and the other that he swears is an almost identical look-alike of Tsar Paul, is of his own son ..."

Sir James Sinclair stopped talking mid-sentence. He gave a huge sigh as though to expel every last bit of air from his lungs, his head dropped so he was staring at the floor, his arms seemed lifeless, something was terribly, terribly wrong.

"James," I shouted, "James, the Grand Master doesn't have a son." I stood up, towering over his almost lifeless body, then my voice dropped to a whisper; I was suddenly afraid; "James, tell me the Grand Master doesn't have a son. Please, James, tell me what you just said was a mistake? James ..."

After what seemed like an eternity he looked up at me, shaking his head from side to side as though desperately wanting to deny something, but no words came. His eyes were looking at me, the saddest eyes I've ever seen, almost imploring me to forget the words he'd foolishly uttered; he was sobbing.

"Alec, I'm a sick and foolish old man. When I tell you what I know, my life will be forfeit, the Grand Master will demand that, but it's better you hear it from my lips than never hear it at all. Twenty-one years ago today, when your wife Maria gave birth to Nicholas, the Grand Master celebrated with a bottle of champagne. He wasn't accustomed to alcohol, it loosened his tongue and made him boastful. I said how happy you would be, Alec, now you had a son. That was when he told me that shortly after you and Maria were married, you'd had an argument about something and she'd run to the castle to beg the Grand Master to buy her a plane ticket so she could go home to Boston. Instead of doing as she asked, Alec, he raped her. You will remember, after Nicholas was born she disappeared some afternoons, and when she arrived back home at the gatehouse she was often drunk. She was ashamed of what she'd done to you, Alec; the reason she went back to America was not to escape from you, it was to escape from him! The Grand Master is Nicholas's biological father, not you."

The bottom dropped out of my world.

After what seemed like an eternity Sir James Sinclair stood from his chair.

"Alec, I think it's best for me to leave you now. I came here to unburden myself, not thinking what that would do to you. I'm truly sorry. Try, I beg of you, to find it in your heart to forgive a sick old man."

He moved to open the conservatory door, and then stood transfixed. The taxi which brought him here had gone; in its place stood the Range Rover; the chauffeur leaning against the bonnet smoking a cigarette, a huge smile on his flat, ugly face.

"Well, well, the old queer came here to unburden himself, did he? I do hope you feel better now, you faggot!"

Hawk stood upright, reaching into his pocket as he did so. In his hand he now held a gun, its short barrel menacingly pointing at James's head.

"Did the Grand Master forget to tell you I installed a microphone in the Tsar's cottage, and it is linked to the radio in this car? That was so forgetful of him, but then he's never trusted you, you know. 'Watch the queer,' he always told me.

"Did you know that's what he calls you? Not to your face of course, dear me no; you are Sir James Sinclair, a Queen's knight, but does she know you're also a knights queen?" The Hawk gave a dirty snigger as he continued taunting James Sinclair; "I'm talking about your American sweetheart, Chevalier Charles Weinberger. You know he's on his way here, don't you? In fact the Grand Master wanted you to meet him at the airport, maybe he thought it would be a nice reunion after all these years; kiss and make up, maybe even more than that, but that can't be allowed to happen now, can it?"

James turned white as a sheet, but he wasn't going to allow this obscenity of a man the pleasure of seeing he was frightened, and most certainly had no intention of begging for his life.

"Hawk, you are as twisted and evil as your master. My life is nearly done, what matter if it is the cancer eating my inside, or a bullet from your little gun tearing my outside, the end for me is the same, so get on with it man. Soon your little games will catch up with you, and you'll have to start running again, as you did once before. I don't think Alec here knows your heroic background, does he, Hawk? Because you are a half-breed with an American father and a Mohawk mother, nobody wanted you, did they? The Mohawk tribe expelled you and your mother for bringing shame on the tribe, so you went to the white man, and what happened then? He put you in a uniform and wanted to send you to Vietnam, but you were frightened, little man; you ran away from the Army, suddenly being a white man wasn't such a good idea after all!

"That was when your Master found you, wasn't it, stealing money from the offerings box in his father's church. You killed his father and were standing over his body, and what did the son do? Did he send for the police, as he should have done? Oh no, that's not the way he operates, as I know to my cost. He made you into his slave, like he does to everybody who falls into his evil web. And what do you think he calls you, when you're not listening? Does he call you Hawk, the brave Mohawk warrior? Nooo - you're the half-breed thief, a bastard Indian no-one wanted; so, do your worst, little man, but be sure your time is not far away."

I was watching the awful scene being played outside my conservatory. It was one of life and death. Hawk walked up to Sir James and prodded him with the pistol, forcing him to walk away from the cottage onto the track and turning towards Loch Rannoch. I watched, traumatised. Sir James turned his back on his adversary and walked, in fact almost marched away, as though he was again in the Guards Division, his shoulders square, head held high, his arms swinging, the defiant last act of a very proud man. I had no doubt in my mind how this would end.

"That's far enough, Sinclair," I clearly heard Hawk command, "now get down on your knees, poofter, pray to your Maker."

The gunman was continuing to mock his victim, enjoying the power which the little pistol gave him, but Sir James Sinclair refused to be intimidated. "I will never descend to your level, little man. Kill me, as I believe you killed Sandy Hutchinson when he wouldn't sell the castle to your Master all those years ago; shoot me in the back as you did him."

The noise of the shot was surprisingly loud from such a little pistol, and it was probably that, more than the fact Hawk's shot apparently missed him, which prompted James to turn round. His adversary was in the process of falling to the ground, the pistol already slipped from lifeless fingers. Now he was on his knees, the look on his face one of total bewilderment. Blood began to trickle from a corner of his mouth. Then he fell forward, lying full length on the rocky track; he was absolutely still.

I strode across to check the body; he was dead. I'd shot many different animals in my life as a gamekeeper, but never a human being before; I was surprised how easy it was, but then a Yeoman twelve bore is a very versatile weapon in the right hands.

James came back to where I was standing next to the body of Hawk. He had tears in his eyes. I'd never been embraced by a man so fervently. His whole body was shaking as though he was in spasm, much as a deer will do when it becomes transfixed, too frightened to run from danger. He clung to me for several minutes, not saying a word, and then pulled away, seeming to be embarrassed at the shared intimacy.

"Alec, you saved my life." It had come out almost as a whisper. Those words seemed so insignificant considering the ordeal he'd endured so bravely. He was alive, and his antagonist was dead, a danger no more.

I wanted to move the corpse from the track as quickly as we could; it was highly unlikely anyone would come by, but better safe than sorry. We each took hold of an ankle and dragged the Hawk's lifeless body into the lee of the cottage, its head bouncing drunkenly on the rocks as we did so. I covered it with a tarpaulin which I keep as a cover for the logs in the wintertime, and secured the edges with stones; I didn't want the wind blowing it away, but now what to do with the body?

"James, I think a drink of something a little stronger than tea is called for now, and then I suppose we'll have to call the police?" That had come out as a question—I wasn't too sure how you go about telling a policeman you've just shot someone!

Once inside the cottage I made coffee, and laced it strongly with whisky, and then James started to take charge; "maybe he's done this before," I thought to myself, "when he was in the Secret Service." He seemed to have composed himself very quickly. I wasn't to know his entire career in the Service had been office bound, he was as much unsure what to do as I was.

"I don't think we should call the police just yet," he told me. "More things are going to happen today which will be of even more interest to them . It's better if we let them learn everything at the same time."

He outlined his ideas.

"Those members of the Order attending the St John's Day celebrations are due to arrive at twelve noon. A buffet lunch has been organised for them in a marquee that is situated next to the gatehouse. Sharp at 1pm they will assemble in the driveway, from where they will march to the chapel.

"After the service, the Supreme Council and the priors from each country will meet in the Great Room on the third floor of the castle. While they are doing that, the rank and file members will be taken by the security team to the ranges, where they will be given the opportunity to fire the latest weapons from the castle armoury. At 6pm everyone will assemble in the courtyard, which is when the Grand Master will give his address. He will have informed all the priors of Tsar Nicholas's existence during the Supreme Council meeting, but then comes the moment he's been working towards for so many years; Nicholas will appear from the castle door, and the Grand Master will introduce him to the knights."

"Alec, I propose that you and I make our way to a point overlooking the castle from where we can observe the preliminary activities. Immediately after the service in the chapel, when the Supreme Council members adjourn to the room on the third floor and the others go to the ranges, we can sneak into the castle and try to find that so-called secret room which the Grand Master has boasted about. There we will learn his true intentions, and we can decide what we are going to do, including now of course informing the police about the dead body outside!"

It was time for me to admit something I'd never mentioned to a soul in the past sixty years.

"James, when the Grand Master spoke of a secret room, it wasn't an idle boast, there really is such a room. A young friend and I discovered it by accident when we were barely in our teens. It was so well hidden I don't believe the then owner, Mr Hutchinson, even knew of it, because it contained some, shall we say, rather exotic wartime memories of the Duke of Dumfries, a previous owner of the castle. Even though it has been so many years, I have no doubt I can find it again."

That's what we did. James very confidently drove the four-wheel-drive Range Rover over the moorland, crossing the rock-strewn gully and then up the sharp hill immediately opposite to reach a vantage point I often used in the past when I wanted to see what was happening at the castle. He parked the car behind a clump of bushes. The time was 11.55am.

Men were on guard duty at the gates to Rannoch Castle, men whose colour and dress were out of keeping with the traditions of Scotland. Today such people are commonly referred to as African Americans, but these four would prefer to be referred to somewhat differently; they are serving brothers of the Chivalric Order of St John of Jerusalem, and their uniform of floor-length brown cloaks, with the eight pointed Maltese Cross boldly emblazoned on the left side, sets them apart from the local population. The duty of these men is to serve the Grand Master to the point of death, and to make sure they never forgot their duty, another man should be present, a monster of a man known as Hawk; if he had another name, none knew it. Never before had he failed to appear when needed, and that it should happen today of all days would be a real problem for the rest of the team.

One of the guards spotted the first of the coaches as it breasted the slight rise, about half a mile down the road. The coach driver knew the road well - but couldn't recall ever before seeing the sign to the Independent Bailiwick of the Order of St. John of Jerusalem, but it looked freshly painted so it was obviously something new! He moved the turn lever by his right hand upwards, causing the left indicators to flash, warning the drivers of the three coaches behind they were approaching their destination. One after the other the coaches turned into the driveway, the cream-coloured paintwork on each gleaming in the noontime sun, the motif of the Order of St John of Jerusalem prominently displayed in the windscreen of each.

A serving brother went to each of the coaches as they came to a stop in the parking area, his duty to check the identity of the occupants against a list of names, but therein lay a problem; the Hawk had the lists! They weren't to know the Hawk was dead and those lists were less than half a mile away, in a Range Rover parked behind some trees on the near horizon! As the passengers disembarked, unchecked by the brothers but all wearing a cloak signifying their membership of the Order, they were directed to the large marquee which had been erected nearby, and where Brother James and Sister Martha were waiting with the buffet lunch.

One of the brothers closed the gates behind the fourth coach, keeping curious passers-by from getting too close, unwilling to respond to the many questions thrown at him as to what was happening. He stood to attention, not as colourful as those British soldiers who undertake a similar duty at Edinburgh Castle, or indeed at Buckingham Palace, nor perhaps so well trained in regimental drills as they are, but what he lacked in glamour he more than made up for in mystery. What was he doing here in the heart of the Scottish Highlands, what was the robe he was wearing, and for those few that recognised it, what was the significance of the Maltese Cross so tantalisingly displayed on his robe? Their curiosity would have to wait for the next morning's newspapers!

A short while later there was a rare moment of activity as one of the security guards reopened the gates to admit yet another coach, this one carrying a group of musicians brought in from their base near the wonderful castle at Stirling.

Those spectators still there at 1pm were treated to a sight beloved in Scotland; the lead drummer, dressed in full Highland regalia, began to play the drummers call, a signal to his colleagues in the pipe and drum band to assemble in the driveway. The drum major looked magnificent as he took his place in front of the band; well over six feet tall, a real barrel of a man, his steely eyes glued to an imaginary centre line in the driveway down which he would lead his band of Highland musicians. The mace he carried, equally as tall as himself, would shortly be the centrepiece of his theatrical demonstration of timing as he sent it spiralling into the air, spinning not once, not twice, but three times on its own axis before falling back effortlessly into his heavily gloved hand. The men of the band of pipes and drums assembled behind their drum major, standing proudly at ease, resplendent in their tartan uniforms, instruments held loosely at their side, silently waiting for the signal to begin the procession to the chapel.

Once the band was in position, the spectators behind the gates, and two other, not so easily visible watchers, were treated to a sight unseen anywhere since the Emperor Napoleon defeated the Knights of the Order of St John, and took possession of their island base of Malta in 1798. Almost two hundred modern-day knights of the Order, successors in title if not in deed to their forbears, formed up in separate groups, or priories as they are more properly known, behind the band. There were six priories, each comprising thirty men and women, the Prior of each group standing in front of his own national contingent. Immediately behind each prior stood his national flag-bearer, the flags of Austria, Germany, Lebanon, Canada, the United States and the host nation, the United Kingdom gloriously rippling in the early afternoon breeze. To say everyone in the group was dressed the same would not be entirely accurate. All wore the cloak of the Order, and every one of the cloaks bore the Cross of Malta on its left side. However some, like those of the UK and Canada, were of a simple black material, while others differed in colour and texture. The knights and dames of the Austrian Priory looked most striking, their scarlet lined black cloaks held together at the neck with a solid gold clasp. The Germans looked impressive too, their traditional black cloaks having white collars, and the American contingent, alone in the Order having hoods attached to their cloaks, added further to the mystery of the spectacle. Another group fell in behind the main procession, this one numbering just ten men and women, the serving brothers and sisters of the Grand Priory Headquarters, the parade was assembled, awaiting their leader.

The only noise to be heard was the clicking of cameras wielded by the group of tourists gathered behind the gates as the parade waited patiently for their leaders. A black Rolls Royce appeared from the direction of Rannoch Castle, the motif of the Order prominently displayed on the top of the radiator grill, and pennants fluttering either side of the bonnet.

The drum major came to attention as the two passengers disembarked from the Rolls Royce, his left foot slamming into the tarmac driveway clearly heard by the increasing number of spectators. He raised the mace above his head, holding it at an angle of forty-five degrees to his own body. That was the signal for the lead drummer to come to attention and tap once on his drum which brought the whole parade to the same state. They stood absolutely silent as the two men from the Rolls Royce took their places immediately behind the band. The flag-bearer first, the Grand Master next, rigid, his regalia as austere as the Austrians were ornate. The parade was assembled; it was precisely 1pm on St John's Day.

The drum major correctly judged the moment to whip his mace to the fully vertical position, the unspoken command to the band to begin playing. The drums beat out their tattoo, and were then joined by the shrill skirl of the bagpipes, the whole parade standing rigidly to attention, waiting for the moment when the drum major would let the mace fall to the hold position, which was when the knights and dames would begin the half mile march to the chapel, stepping off with the left foot as they had all been taught over the years by Hawk.

This was the proudest moment of the Grand Master's life; in his dreams he lived this many times, always wondering if he could bring it off, and now today it was happening. How he wished his father could be there, to see his son leading this awesome procession, but his father had died at the hands of the Mohawk Indian many years ago when he caught him stealing the contents of the offertory box in his church.

Anyway, where is the Hawk," he asked himself, as the entire

parade took their first step forward into what the Grand Master was certain would be a glorious future. The Hawk should be there to open the door of the royal car, but he had to do that task himself. "No matter, I'll sort that out later." Punishing the Hawk was one of the Grand Master's greatest pleasures.

We watched, enthralled as the procession began its half mile journey to the chapel. The sights and sounds of a pipe and drum band are enough to stir the heart of the most hardened cynic, and the colourful spectre of the various contingents of knights, all marching perfectly in step, added an almost medieval quality to the proceedings. The Grand Master would have likened the spectacle to that of their Crusader forbears nobly beginning an arduous journey to the Holy Land, their sworn duty to free Jerusalem from the Moslem hordes. The air had suddenly become very still, as though mighty Thor was holding his breath, waiting to see what would happen next, and while immediately above where Sir James and I were sitting the sky was a lovely clear blue, dark clouds were gathering to the west.

The band worked its very own particular brand of theatrical magic; the drum major threw his mace fully forty feet into the air as he passed between the statues of the two knights guarding the entrance to the courtyard, and as he did that the giant bearded bass drummer gave an extra loud clout to his instrument, as did the more diminutive cymbal player, while the pipers gave their shrill support to Scotland the Brave.

The spectators cordoned off behind the gates craned their heads to catch a final glimpse as the last contingent disappeared from view behind the west side of the castle. Unseen by those spectators, the parade came to a halt in front of the entrance to the chapel. From our vantage position we watched as each contingent in turn marched in single file through the porch door, kept in step by the tapping of a drum stick from a solitary drum. By ancient tradition serving brothers and sisters do not participate in the religious ceremonies of the Order, leaving them free to resume their normal duties. Brother James closed the door as the last of the contingents, that from America, passed from our sight, their final act being to remove the intimidating hoods of their cloaks, paying respect to a place of worship.

The musicians, still in band formation, obeyed the unspoken

command of the drum major's mace and performed a countermarch, enabling them to return to the starting point next to the marquee, and board the coach for their journey back to base, their duty done.

We returned to the Range Rover concealed behind the clump of bushes from where we still had a partial view of the castle, and gladly took a drink of coffee from the vacuum flask I'd thoughtfully prepared before leaving the cottage. Now we had to wait for the church service to finish, and for the knights and dames to move on to the next part of their programme.

"They're coming out of the chapel, we should get ready." That was Sir James, his nervousness showing. A gamekeeper's most important attribute is patience, the ability to stay perfectly still, unseen by his quarry until it is time to strike, a quality not shared by my companion—perhaps he had more reason to be nervous than I!

The Grand Master was walking back to the castle, escorted by the chaplain, with the priors tagging on behind. My father-in-law, who'd been carrying the flag of the Order in the procession, was some way back, speaking with a wizened looking old man I'd never seen before. As the leaders passed through the portico, the rank and file stayed in the courtyard where the brothers from the security team were trying to organise them into groups but once again without the Hawk's lists to guide them it was chaotic. Eventually however they were all led off, west from the castle to the rifle ranges, a walk of almost a mile. One of the brothers parked my old Land Rover next to the portico, and loaded rifles and ammunition into the trailer attached to the back. The Grand Master must have gone on a spending spree for weapons judging by the number of journeys he was making to and fro, though how he would have got permission to buy so many was beyond me. There is only one private army anywhere in Europe allowed to bear arms, and that coincidentally is at nearby Blair Castle, where the Atholl Highlanders gained Queen Victoria's Colours in 1844.

It was only later, when I met up with Nicholas again, that I learned the Grand Master had taken for granted the Government's approval for the independence of the Bailiwick of St John, and therefore as the head of a sovereign nation he could do as he liked!

We decided to risk taking the Range Rover as close to the castle as possible rather than arriving with muddied clothes. The danger of being seen was very slight; all the security guards bar the one left on the gate would be on the rifle ranges with the guests, and the windows in the third floor Great Room, where the Supreme Council meeting would be taking place, were set high up. I wondered how Nicholas was getting on, and why he wasn't on the parade; by now he would surely be sitting in the chair reserved for the Protector of the Order in the Great Room, dressed in whatever design of robe the Grand Master organised for the occasion; I was fairly certain he would have had a tailor create something similar to those worn by the original Protector, Tsar Paul the First, back in 1798, illustrated by the portrait on the wall behind that seat. Amongst the officers in the meeting he would of course know his grandfather on his mother's side, but was he by now aware that his biological father was also in the room, and equally did his grandfather know the Grand Master raped his daughter, and fathered Nicholas? More than all that though, the real question that, so far at any rate defied an answer, how did the Grand Master think he would get away with passing Nicholas off as the great grandson of Tsar Nicholas the Second? The authorities in Russia would demand the right to test Nicholas's DNA themselves. Still so many questions waiting to be answered!

James parked the vehicle out of sight behind the chapel and walked to the portico entrance. We discussed whether we should ring the doorbell to gain admittance, but that raised the possibility of the Grand Master hearing us so we decided to bluff our way in should it become necessary. Sir James was a frequent visitor to the castle so Martha wouldn't be too surprised he should be there, especially on a day as busy and confusing as this one. In fact we needn't have worried; Martha was nowhere to be seen, and we knew her husband would be on duty in the Great Room, attending to refreshments for the meeting. Both James and I had been to the Grand Master's study on the second floor on many occasions, so finding our way there wasn't a problem, and the door wasn't locked, so far so good! I felt as though we were burglars, which in a way I suppose we were, though we had no intention of taking anything, we just wanted to learn what the Grand Master's plan was all about.

James closed the study door behind us and looked at me,

questioning if I remembered where to look for the secret room, but I did, even after sixty years I went straight to the corner where an ornate coffee table was placed on a heavy Persian rug. It was a simple matter to move them aside and lift the ring set in the stone floor, and reveal the opening. I vividly remember the last time I looked into that room and saw the girlie pictures on the walls and the magazines strewn over the floor, but it isn't like that today. Now it is fully carpeted, though the furniture consists only of two fairly uncomfortable looking armchairs and an occasional table. On one wall is a copy of the magnificent portrait of Tsar Paul the First which hangs in the Ball Room, and next to that is the painting of Richard the First, which James had already told me about, alongside a blown-up photograph of Nicholas. On another wall were several documents covered by a large sheet of what looked like perspex, but it was none of those things which held our attention.

Nicholas was sitting bolt upright in one of the chairs, dressed pretty much as I'd envisaged he would be, a full length robe, bright red in colour, made of silk, heavily embroidered and with numerous medals on the left breast. He had a blue sash going from one shoulder down to his waist, on which the eight pointed Cross of Malta had pride of place, but that was where any resemblance to a Tsar ended. Each wrist was handcuffed to one of the chair arms, he was wearing only one shoe, the other I could see on the far side of the room; he had deep scratch marks on one cheek, and his bottom lip was swollen. His hair was awry, confirming the impression of a young man having been involved in a fight, and coming out of it badly! He looked up at me, giving the forlorn look of a lost child; he hadn't recognised me! He was drugged, that much was obvious, but with what, and why, more unanswered questions!

Chapter Twenty

"James, quickly man, help me down." Maybe I wasn't as sprightly as the last time I climbed down into this room, but never before had I needed to act with such urgency. Sir James followed me into a room that was secret no more. I knelt in front of Nicholas, trying to get him to talk to me, but the only responses were babylike gurgles, accompanied by drops of saliva falling from the corner of his mouth onto the beautiful robe he was wearing, while the frightened look in his eyes would haunt me for the rest of my life..

Sir James walked across to where I was kneeling. "My God, what has he done to him?" James was holding a set of keys he'd found lying on the coffee table and which he correctly assumed would unlock the handcuffs; "these should at least help us to get him out of here."

We freed Nicholas's arms and left him sitting in the chair while we examined the documents on the wall, well aware we must act urgently lest we be discovered. Two of the documents were written in Cyrillic, and one of them was very old and had what appeared to be an English translation next to it. It was headed with the word 'Proclamation' and had been signed by Tsar Paul the First in 1798 when he agreed to become the Protector of the Chivalric Order of St John of Jerusalem. The proclamation granted to the Order the rights of exploration and mining rights to a part of Siberia east of the Ural Mountains. The second paper was a faxed document, and the imprint from the Grand Master's fax machine indicated it only arrived earlier this morning.

James Sinclair put on his reading glasses and was studying the faxed document. I interrupted his reading.

"James, this ancient document which my ancestor signed, is it really worth killing for? Does this single piece of paper justify the murder of Mr Hutchinson with which you taunted the Hawk; or the chicanery with my mother's notebook, my marriage to Maria, not to mention doing this to Nicholas? Surely there must be something a lot more valuable, something we're missing!"

Sir James Sinclair looked very thoughtful as he put his glasses back in his jacket pocket. "Alec, you've been a gamekeeper all your working life. Your relationship with people like him has been, if I may say so, one of master and servant; up here in the Highlands you've been insulated against the kind of trickeries and deceptions I've had to deal with all my life. This document is worth billions of dollars to the Order, but only if two things can be proven."

"One, that there is continuation of the Imperial family. Tsar Paul wrote that document and he very clearly had an eye to the future. See here," James pointed at the translated copy, "on the last line of the main paragraph, where it says 'and shall remain forever the same'; he very cleverly committed not only himself, but all his successors to the conditions of this document."

He turned from pointing at the document to looking at me. "You, Alec, or Alexei to give you your christened name, are his successor in title. This document binds you just as much as it did your grandfather, Tsar Nicholas. The first of the conditions I mentioned is proven."

I protested. "No, no James, I might not have the devious nature which you city types seem to thrive on, but what we Highland folk lack in sophistication, we more than make up for in good old-fashioned common sense. While I agree the document does indeed commit me to being the Protector of the Order, that land to the east of the Ural Mountains to which it refers now belongs to the Russian Government, and to its people. It isn't mine to give away."

By the size of the smirk on his face I understood he was about to trump my argument, and do it convincingly.

"And there my dear Alexei, you are very wrong. At the time he signed this Order the land did belong to him. See here," he pointed in the middle of the translation, "he refers to 'My City of Serov and My City of Surgut', both founded by his forbear, Peter the Great, as the gateway to the exploration of Siberia. As things stood in those days Siberia belonged to him, and this faxed paper," and he pointed to the second paper on the wall, "if my very rudimentary knowledge of Russian is correct, is the Russian Parliament's acknowledgement of that fact. Therefore the second condition I mentioned, ie, the present day legality of Tsar Paul's document, has also been met, signed this very morning by Vladimir Schumakof, and someone called Yakov Yurovsky, the Speaker of the Russian Parliament. You know who Mr Schumakof is, don't you?"

"James, I may be an old Highland man but even people up here read newspapers and watch television. Of course I know who he is, but do you know who Yurovsky is?" I could see a light beginning to dawn in Sinclair's eyes so I hastened to finish.

"Anastasia had told us in the notebook the name of the man who'd led the execution squad; that was also Yakov Yurovsky. I am willing to bet that the Speaker of the Russian Parliament is the grandson of my grandfather's killer."

I can't even begin to describe the eerie feeling I had as I studied the signature of Mr Yurovsky, and began to wonder if, after all these years our two families were about to cross swords again.

James continued to examine the contents of a folder lying on the coffee table, but I was nervous, I wanted to get out before we could be discovered. Goodness only knows what the Grand Master would do if he found us in this of all places.

"James, you've got to help me get Nicholas up the ladder, I can't manage on my own and he's in no condition to help."

He stuffed the folder inside the waistband of his trousers, and between us we managed to get Nicholas up the ladder and out of the castle without being seen. By the time we reached the portico entrance we were both too tired to carry him any further; Nicholas is a muscular young man, certainly weighing more than thirteen stones , and my friend and I are a bit too long in the tooth to be carrying such a load, particularly in those circumstances. James ran behind the chapel, and returned with the Range Rover, keeping the engine running as we struggled to get Nicholas on board, discretion thrown to the wind; urgency was the master just now.

James gunned the powerful engine and pointed the car through the gap between the two statues, and raced the length of the driveway.

As we approached the gates we could clearly see the puzzlement on the guard's face, he presumably couldn't remember seeing the Range Rover coming in to the castle this morning! He obligingly opened one side of the gates, and then perhaps thought better of it, so instead of opening the second, he signalled to us to stop. Nicholas was lying on the back seat, the guard couldn't help but see him; this could be trouble! James's reactions were very quick, especially, it crossed my mind, for someone so old, but then I checked myself, he was no more than a couple of years older than me! He flashed the lights and hit the horn, his intentions very clear—he had no intention of stopping, and I joined in by waving my hand at the guard, indicating he should get out of the way. In a matter of just a few seconds it was all over; for the guard, discretion overcame valour—he jumped clear and we were through, scraping the side of the car on the one open gate as we did so; James had misjudged the width of the Range Rover! We turned left, and a mile further up the Highland road turned left again onto the track which leads to my cottage. I breathed a huge sigh of relief; we were safe, at least for the time being, but would the guard inform the Grand Master what had happened? As it turned out he didn't, no doubt afraid of being accused either of letting us escape, or of being the cause of damaging the car and the gates! A classic case of condemned if he did, condemned if he didn't, so he chose the lesser of the evils!

Now we had to turn our attention to Nicholas. Once we were back in the cottage I made a telephone call to Dr Edwin, the village doctor. I'd known him for some years, in fact ever since he retired from what I understood had been a very lucrative Harley Street practice, and then just wanted to escape the pressures of big city life. He certainly succeeded in that; he spent more time looking after his chickens, and growing all his own vegetables than he did worrying about sick people! "Practicing self-sufficiency is more rewarding that practicing medicine," he was fond of telling anyone who'd listen, "did you ever hear a carrot complain?" He was a man with a very peculiar sense of humour! Anyway, he promised to come straight away, and was true to his word. The time was 4pm.

James was studying the contents of the folder he'd removed from the secret room. "This," he exclaimed, holding up a Polaroid photograph, "is the root cause of half a century of my misery and blackmail, something I'm almost too ashamed to let even you see." I took the photograph from him; it was of him and another man lying together on a bed, both their faces clearly recognisable as they'd turned to see the cause of the interruption. "And this," he was pointing to a document in the folder, "is the copy of the top secret paper he took from my briefcase. What do you think I should do with them, Alec?"

The answer was so perfectly obvious that words weren't necessary. I took them from him and consigned them both to the fire, poking the paper as it charred to make sure it could never be reconstituted. "The other young man in the photograph, James, is this the American that Hawk mentioned, the man who is flying into Edinburgh this afternoon, and who the Grand Master wanted you to meet at the airport?"

The answer of course was yes, it was the same man, Dr Charles Weinberger. No doubt he too would be very relieved when he found out the incriminating photograph had been destroyed!

❊❊❊❊❊❊

The Russian captain's heavily accented voice came over the PA system.

"Ladies and gentlemen, we'll be landing at Edinburgh International Airport in a few minutes. Please return to your seats and fasten your seat belts. Cabin crew: five minutes to landing, five minutes."

With so few passengers on board the normal bustle associated with an aircraft landing was at a minimum, but the cabin crew went through the motions nonetheless, checking that all the seats were in the fully upright position, the tables stowed, and seat belts properly fastened.

The trans-Atlantic flight had been quite rough, almost as though the Captain had deliberately sought out the most turbulent flight level, which indeed he had. He'd taken his revenge on Mr Lane and now reconciled himself to spending the night in Edinburgh instead of being back home in his native Moscow with his lovely wife Anna and their young baby. It also meant he had one more chance to try his luck with Olga, the Ukrainian junior flight attendant; she'd resisted his rather heavy-handed flirting in last night's hotel near JFK airport in New York, so he'd gone off to the bar in a huff and drank too much cheap vodka. Tonight he'd invite the whole crew to dinner, and brief his co-pilot to suddenly fake an immigration problem, which meant the entire crew, except himself and Olga of course, would have to return to the airport to have their passports rechecked. Then, using the father-figure approach, he'd tell her he was concerned about her welfare, ask about her family back home in Odessa, if her salary high enough—not that he could do anything about it, but he could drop hints so she'd believe he could, meantime feeding her full strength Russian vodka from a flask he'd conceal in his jacket pocket. Then he would pounce, like a cat pounces on a mouse when he's finished toying with it, and he would have his way! The only problem with his plan was that the co-pilot had tasted Olga's charms in their hotel last night after the captain had gone to the bar, and tonight she'd promised him more of the same!

Carol Lane gazed out of the plane window, savouring the last few peaceful moments before she and her husband would be thrown into the hurly burly VIP reception, which she secretly enjoyed, but wouldn't admit to of course! Less enjoyable would be the nail biting negotiations Tom would be having with this strange organisation which had come from nowhere to further aggravate the oil crisis. She'd asked the Russian captain to radio ahead to book a hotel for them in the village of Pitlochry, and was surprised when he came back to say all the hotels were full. She hadn't expected that, not so early in the tourist season, but then he told her there was a convention near the town, something about the Knights of Malta, and they'd booked all the good hotel rooms.

Her husband for his part was admiring the view of the Firth of Forth still some ten thousand feet below, the famous road and rail bridges, gateways to the Scottish Highlands, clearly visible in the middle distance

They'd overflown the city of Dundee a few minutes earlier as the plane had gone a short way out to sea before making a westerly approach to Edinburgh Airport. He could make out Castle Rock and, of course, Edinburgh Castle, dominating the city skyline, and then the Royal Mile, descending Castle Hill and leading to the heart of the new town with its multiplicity of modern shops, hotels and coffee houses. Waverley train station was down there somewhere, slightly to the south of the Royal Mile, he remembered, which was where he and Carol would usually arrive when coming to Scotland's capital city.

An immigration officer came on the plane to check the passports, and the passengers and crew then disembarked into a fleet of cars waiting on the tarmac. Charles Weinberger asked to be excused as he wanted to visit an old friend before getting down to the business at hand, to which Tom Lanc had been only too pleased to agree—he'd had enough of this American academic for one day, and was hopeful he and Carol could have dinner somewhere nice and quiet, followed by an early night in bed. He'd had a busy few days in the States, and having to cope with jet lag as well didn't auger well for tomorrow's meetings.

✻✻✻✻✻

The hired Jaguar car carrying Dr Weinberger, the American secretary of state's special adviser on Russian Affairs, left the airport and turned west, and then north to Queensferry where it crossed the Firth of Forth. It continued north, travelling fast, the chauffeur doing his best to comply with his American passenger's request to be in Pitlochry within the hour. They would have made it, albeit with just a few seconds to spare, but his passenger suddenly had a change of heart, and asked instead to be taken to nearby Rannoch Castle. Both the chauffeur and passenger had visited the area before, and both knew there was a sign off the A9 trunk road to Rannoch Castle, so they'd been somewhat surprised to see the sign now directed them to the Independent Bailiwick of St John in its place. The chauffeur's surprise was then compounded when his passenger asked to be let out near the gate, saying he wanted to surprise his friend who lived in the gatehouse. That of course was a lie; Dr Weinberger did indeed want to surprise someone, but that would be in the castle, not in the gatehouse, and it most definitely was not a friend!

The time was 5.30pm, and the sky was becoming overcast as he furtively made his way up the long driveway. He went to the west side of the castle where he found concealment behind a clump of bushes next to the chapel. He waited there patiently, the suit he was wearing totally inappropriate for this kind of exercise, but that was of secondary importance. He would wait until the Grand Master left the castle to address the knights, as the programme he'd been sent told him would happen, and then he'd break a window and make his way to the man's study. He hoped to find a certain photograph there, a photograph which had been his nemesis for the past fifty years, but he'd be disappointed. It had already been taken.

All six of the national contingents, as well as the headquarters staff of the Chivalric Order of St John of Jerusalem were formed up in front of Rannoch Castle, the prior of each contingent standing in front and centre of his own group, the flag-bearers taking their positions as right markers on the front ranks. Brother William stood in front of the headquarters contingent, taking the place usually occupied by Hawk. "The Master would feel humiliated that one of his disciples was missing," William told himself, "Hawk would be in for another beating." He knew the Master took sadistic delight in beating Hawk, though he didn't know the reason why. He'd often heard Hawk begging the Master to stop the beating, always to no avail. Once William had seen Hawk with his shirt off, straight after he'd received a particularly vicious thrashing. The welts on his back had cut deep into the man's brown skin, looking even worse where the blood had started to congeal, forming a series of nasty scars. He'd run from the castle and was hiding in the bushes behind the chapel, whimpering as a child might whimper. "He'd get more than that today," William told himself, "the Master will have his revenge."

The entire contingent stood at ease, their cloaks hanging lifeless in the still June air. Shortly before 6pm the senior prior, by tradition always the prior of the host nation, came to attention. He shouted the command to the rest of the parade to do the same, the refined tones of his very high-class English accent contrasting sharply with the aged roughness of his surroundings. After a pause of a few moments a figure marched out from the castle portico. He was the wizened-looking old man Alec and James had seen accompany Maria's father back to the castle after the church service. Charles Ray was partially crippled with rheumatoid arthritis, a disease which Green Peace luminaries declared was God-sent in revenge for the pollution his single-hulled oil tankers had caused all over the planet. As a major figure in the Earth Oil Corporation in the 1990's he'd opposed the purchase of double- hulled oil tankers, saying it was a Chinese Communist plot to expand their own ailing shipbuilding industry. His opposition had delayed the eventual purchase of the double-hulled vessels, a delay which had cost the company dear, and had cost him his place on the Board. By way of revenge he'd created a shell of an oil company which he called Ural Oil, in which he and Oliver Emerson, the Grand Master, were the only shareholders. It hadn't traded in its eight-year history, but he was confident that would soon change.

He came to a halt in front of the parade, and executed as smart an about-turn as the painful inflammation in his knees and shoulders allowed. He looked an incongruous sight, the lines of his misshapen body exaggerated by the way the cloak hung from his hunched back, and the hood, worn by knights of the American Priory, completing a very sinister-looking appearance, not unlike the menacing hunchback rumoured once to have alarmed visitors to the Church of Notre Dame in Paris. While he might have looked totally out of keeping in those militaristic surroundings, his voice when it came belayed any other criticisms. "Flag- bearers to me," he bellowed, at which all six bearers left their positions and marched smartly to form a line immediately behind him.

Precisely at 6pm the Grand Master himself stepped out from the Portico and took up his designated position on a small rostrum which had been erected in the courtyard. Where Bailiff Grand Cross Charles Ray looked incongruous in his robe, the Grand Master looked utopian; his particular advantage over his deputy was in being tall and thin, rather than misshapen. For this special occasion he sacrificed his strict interpretation of the knightly codes of dress and the mantle he wore today was made of black merino, laced with scarlet silk, the cross on the left side had a double eagle superimposed on the top, the sign of the Russian Grand Priory, as too did the emblem suspended on a scarlet ribbon from his neck; the mantle was held together at chest height with a gold chain. He looked a very worthy successor to those grand masters who'd preceded him in centuries past. He was perfectly confident the speech he was about to deliver would be as inspiring to the knights assembled in front of him as anything those other great leaders had been able to achieve!

"Bailiff, priors, fellow knights, dames, brothers and sisters in Saint John, followers of Christ," he began, "today, the Chivalric Order of St John of Jerusalem will regain its rightful status as a sovereign nation. Remember if you will that very first Crusade, proudly undertaken by our forebears to protect those good, honest European Christians wanting to make pilgrimage to the Holy Land. They were being attacked and robbed by the Seljuk Turks. Our forefathers bravely took the battle to these Moslems and defeated them, then went on to lay massive siege to Jerusalem itself which they captured in 1099 and banned Moslems and Jews from living there, reserving to us the most important shrine in Christianity. For almost two hundred years our Order was all-powerful, keeping the City of Christ unpolluted by heathenistic purveyors of lies and trash, but the sacrifices so willingly paid by those magnificent Crusaders were in vain." The Grand Master paused to create effect. "Remember the valiant triumphs of our greatest warrior king, Richard the First; he thrashed the pagan Saladin and his hordes at the Battle of Arsuf in the Third Crusade, but was then forced into making a truce, and why?" Again he paused, the silence broken only by a distant roll of thunder. "Because while he was leading an austere existence on distant battlefields his brother John, arrogantly putting his own selfish desires above duty, usurped Richard's role as King. Even modern-day monarchs would do well to remember the fate that has befallen so many royal houses when they've put their own selfish desires and unwarranted family advancement before their duty to the country they've been privileged to rule, blatantly ignoring the edicts of church and state in their pursuit of ever more lustful pleasures!"

James looked across at me from the driving position in the Rover. "The Grand Master is clearly on a crusade all of his own coming out with statements like that. He's going to be hoisted with his own petard before the day is out." We listened to the speech through the radio which the Grand Master had obligingly installed in this car for his own purposes. Back in the cottage we'd discussed our next move and agreed I should try to take Nicholas's place in whatever nefarious schemes the Grand Master was planning. James therefore busied himself writing what we hoped would be an appropriate speech while I put on the beautiful robe. We then left Dr Edwin while we got back into the Range Rover with the intention of returning to the castle. Our progress however was short-lived as we were brought to a halt at a road block manned by the local police just north of the gateway to Rannoch Castle. The officer in charge had stared aghast at me, dressed as I was in the magnificent robe which, together with the blue sash and the various medals, was clearly an unexpected sight in these remote Highlands. This was one step too much for a man who was already confused about what was happening on his patch. The Chief Constable had telephoned him at home the previous evening, telling him to organise road blocks north and south of the castle driveway on the authority of Sir Norman Fitzgerald. Anyone attempting to enter the castle grounds was to be held in temporary custody until further orders were given, and here he was faced with a man dressed fit for a king—should he arrest him, or should he bow, a predicament he resolved by using his radio to call for advice. His call was patched through to Sir Norman Fitzgerald who at that moment was sitting in a military helicopter parked on the side of a disused quarry a short distance further west, with Minister of Defence George Hamlyn sitting beside him. Once Fitzgerald was made aware who the occupants of the car were he instructed the police officer to give us every cooperation and he needed no extra bidding; he signalled to one of his constables to join him, and together they climbed into the back seat of the Rover. He didn't know what was happening on his patch, but he sure as hell wasn't going to be left out of any action!

"Excuse me gentlemen," the inspector was speaking to us; "whoever it is making statements like that can be arrested and charged with treason. Please can you tell me what is going on, and who are you sir?"

He was talking to James Sinclair, but looking quizzically at me. His colleague meanwhile was sitting silently on the back seat; I could see the reflection of his head in the driving mirror moving from side to side as he looked from me to Sir James, and back to me again, his mouth wide open in amazement. Poor man, this was something to tell his wife about when he got home that night! It is doubtful that a Highland policeman such as he would have arrested sinners for anything much worse than drunken behaviour after watching Scotland thrash arch-enemy England at football, or perhaps poaching a deer, the property of nearby Atholl Estates.

Sir James did his best to inform the inspector what was happening while at the same time continuing to listen to the speech the Grand Master was making to the assembled knights. A wind sprang up, bringing a distinct chill to the evening air.

"After King Richard" the Grand Master continued, "our leaders replaced knightly bravery with cowardice, corruption and decadence, and their sinful lust for personal pleasure led to the downfall of our once mighty Order of Chivalry. At the battle for the city of Acre in 1291, our last mainland stronghold, we were defeated by the Mamluks and forced to flee the Holy Land; many of the survivors from that shameful battle were deservedly taken into slavery by the victorious Moslems, and our downfall didn't end there. Our illustrious forebears then sought exile in Cyprus, Rhodes and finally Malta where they continued to live the decadent lives they so enjoyed until the Emperor Napoleon put an end to our shame in 1798 when he ingloriously threw them off our island home of Malta."

"We can thank God there are still men of honour in our Order, men who recognise the valiant deeds of our forebears and who understand the work of the Crusader Knights is far from done. Tsar Paul the First recognised the good that still existed in our Order; he took us under his protection, and his imperial successors continued his good work until that fateful day in July 1918 when the Bolshevik hordes murdered Tsar Nicholas the Second. They said we were finally vanquished, they said we were leaderless, but they were wrong, as Saladin was wrong, as Suleiman the Magnificent was wrong, and as Napoleon was wrong. Our Order was not dead, it was asleep."

We continued listening to the Grand Master, his voice becoming higher pitched as he prattled out his message of duty and sacrifice, wondering what the assembled knights would be thinking. Was this what they had joined the Order for, to sacrifice themselves for the glory of God, or for the more earthly pleasure of wearing regalia which for just a few hours from time to time raised them above the level of the common man?

"I've dedicated my entire life to restoring our Order to its former glory, humbly accepting sacrifice of earthly pleasures in pursuit of a far greater goal, but today I willingly relinquish that leadership in favour of a young man who will be all powerful, merciless in his determination to succeed; he will demand your absolute obedience as he takes the Order on its path to greater glory. Not since the murder of Tsar Nicholas II has anyone sat on the royal throne of St John, that is not until today, for, dear friends, today the Order is reborn. Fellow knights, once again we have a Protector, His Royal Highness Tsarevich Nicholas Romanov has graciously consented to continue the patronage initiated by his Imperial predecessor, Tsar Paul the First. His Royal Highness is at this very moment here in Rannoch Castle deciding on the strategy for what will become The Last Crusade which in his name I promise will be the greatest crusade of all time. Jerusalem is once again a divided city, and once again all Christianity will look to our Order to restore the true faith to the City of Christ. Our Crusade will use the very same weapons which the non-believers, the heretics use against our civilised world today. Terrorism, but of a kind even they couldn't dream of, martyrdom with the conviction that God is on our side, assassination with the moral certainty that we are on the right path to glory. Go to your homes, dear brothers, keeping our secret safe until you hear my call when it will be the time for you to make the sacrifices your brave forbears did so many years ago, when like them your sacrifices will be for the good of all Christendom."

The Grand Master was coming to the end of his tirade; it was time for us to make our move. James started the engine and we drove forward. The police officer used his radio to warn his colleagues: "we're going in now."

As we turned into the castle driveway the sentry signalled to us to stop. It was the same man on duty as had been thwarted by us earlier in the afternoon; he wasn't going to let it happen again, and short of battering down the heavy gates we had little choice but to obey his signal. James wound down his window, attracting the sentry's attention, and as he did that so the constable jumped out of the car and folded his massive arms around him, preventing him from doing anything to summon assistance. I took the opportunity to change places with the officer on the back seat, and we then continued our journey to the castle, leaving the constable to take care of his charge. The sky which had been so blue during the day suddenly darkened as thick black clouds rolled in from the west, completely obscuring the sun, and we heard a distinct roll of thunder coming from the same direction.

"There's going to be more than one storm tonight," James said; the look on his face of steely determination, his jaw thrust forward in a characteristically aggressive attitude told its own tale. His own personal nightmare was a mere two hundred yards away, and the gap closed as we drove forward. The Grand Master was about to leave the parade when he heard the motor. He turned to face us in alarm, worried something was going wrong. James drove the car right up to the dais and then rushed round to where I sat in the back, opening the door for me as a true chauffeur would, the cloak he wore a signal to the assembled knights that he was of their ranks. The inspector played his part, standing next to the car as though he was my security officer. The involuntary gasps which came from all sides of the gathering as I stepped out of the Rover fully justified our decision for me to wear the robe. The drops of saliva which Nicholas had spilled on the robe had been cleaned off with washing-up liquid, and although the lad is much heavier than me we are of about the same height, so the robe fitted well enough for the occasion. When I'd put it on in the cottage and looked in the mirror I'd confessed to feeling like royalty—in seconds I'd been transformed from a Highland gamekeeper into an aristocrat! The blue sash added a final touch of imperial arrogance to the outfit, which otherwise was spoiled only by the un-Tsar like shoes on my feet; unfortunately Nicholas's feet are like huge slabs of meat, whereas mine are much smaller, so wearing his highly polished shoes was out of the question. Still, I doubted that in the gathering dusk, and with everything else going on, anyone would notice.

The look on the Grand Master's face as I approached him will be something I will treasure to the end of my days. He'd turned deathly white, his mouth was agape, whatever words he was trying to use were incomprehensible gibberish. Both Bailiff Ray standing to attention immediately in front of the Grand Master, and my father-in-law who was in his place as the head flag-bearer, had similar looks on their faces too. Everyone on that parade was trying to understand what was happening.

"Thank you, Grand Master," I said, "they are truly a magnificent sight and you've done a wonderful job bringing them together in this way. Would you mind if I addressed a few words to my knights and dames?"

The Grand Master had recovered his composure sufficiently to try to take advantage of the situation. I could only imagine how hard his feverish brain was whirring round and round as he worked out all the permutations of what I was about to do and say.

"Your Majesty, I am sorry if the young Tsarevich is not feeling well enough to address the Order personally. I know, of course, he's been feeling unwell most of the afternoon, but your presence here today adds even more grace to our proceedings. I am sure everyone present will treasure your words of encouragement."

I turned to face the parade, doing my best to remember the military bearing my old sergeant major had tried so hard to instil into me all those years ago.

"Knights and Dames of the Chivalric Order of St John, it was my ancestor Tsar Paul the First who took upon himself the duty to protect this ancient and distinguished Order of chivalry. The glorious past to which the Grand Master so eloquently referred a few moments ago is something each and every one of us must treasure. The noble deeds done in the name of Christ by our illustrious forbears are a talisman to which we must all aspire if we are to carry out His work as successfully as our noble predecessors.

"I want us to carry on the deeds initiated by our forebears all those years ago. The war to which the Grand Master referred, however, is not one between Christians and Moslems, or between black and white peoples, it is between the haves and the have-nots of this world. It is our duty to reach out, to pluck from the graveyard of despair those people less fortunate than you or me, because those are the people the deranged fundamentalists that exist in all religions exhort to do their foul deeds, promising a better life in the next world, a life where all men are equal. My own family know better than most the cancerous wounds that such megalomaniacs can help fester; my own family was sacrificed on the altar of Bolshevism, but the land promised by the leaders of that Revolution, men with names we all recall, Lenin, Stalin, Beria, did not materialise except in their own fevered imaginations."

I turned to face the Grand Master. "The Last Crusade to which you referred will indeed happen and it is we, those of us gathered here today, who will be the vanguard of that Crusade, but you will not be there to bask in its reflective glory. It was your own personal forbears who through their wickedness and depravity caused knights of great integrity to be consigned to oblivion, and an Order so illustrious to be defeated time and time again, not by those of other religious persuasions as you insisted in your speech, Grand Master, but by the bigotry and hatred practiced by you and your kind. You have no place in this Order; in front of these witnesses I now strip you of your robe of office." Saying that I advanced on him and pulled at the gold clip holding the two sides of his robe together; it fell to the ground and as it did so the air throbbed with the roaring sound of the helicopter swooping in low over the castle, its powerful searchlight suddenly coming to rest on the pathetic figure in front of me.

At the same time from the driveway police cars appeared, driving at speed and coming to a halt in a squeal of brakes; policemen dashed out to surround the parade, while from the bushes at the back of the courtyard a squad of soldiers dressed in full camouflage uniforms mysteriously appeared, all carrying rifles which were pointing unerringly at the knights on parade. Two of the police officers advanced on the former Grand Master intending to take him into custody, but he wasn't for taking! He pulled away from his captors, pausing for just one second to pick up his beautiful cloak from where I'd dropped it at his feet, and raced to the portico, slamming the heavy wooden door shut in the face of his pursuers as he went. The crashing sound of the wind and the noise of the hovering helicopter drowned out the sound of his footsteps, echoing on steps made of stone, to all but the policemen standing by the door. They heard the sound coming from higher and higher as he ascended the ancient staircase, seeking refuge from the calamity which had befallen him, until eventually he came to the turret room on the south-east facing corner of the castle. He flung the window wide open and climbed out onto the narrow ledge which in years gone by would have been the support for a bucket of hot tar waiting to be dumped on any potential aggressor.

The thunder which had been threatening for some time finally gave vent to its anger, rattling its way across the darkening sky, and the rain took that as a signal to unleash its deluge onto the crowd watching below, but no-one moved. Everyone was entranced by the figure standing on that narrow ledge, once again wearing the cloak which I'd ripped from his shoulders just moments earlier and now flapping wildly in the strong wind, his face, white as a sheet, illuminated by the spotlight from the helicopter which was hovering above the courtyard. That spotlight also illuminated a box about the size of a book which the Grand Master was holding in his outstretched arm.

"You fools," he screamed down at us, "you think you can defeat me." His voice was an ear-splitting shriek. "This castle is impregnable. There is food and drink enough to feed an army against a siege, as it has done before, and will do again, long after your puny efforts have failed. There are booby traps in every room, the doors and windows are all mined, I have only to press the button on this control box in my hand and this entire castle, and all of you fools waiting below will be blown to smithereens. You will never get me."

The thunderstorm was now directly overhead, the rain, from the pitch black sky, was beating a tattoo of its own as it hammered into the stone forecourt; the wind, roaring in from the mountains behind Loch Rannoch, tore at the branches of the trees surrounding the chapel. The knights were still in parade formation, desperately holding onto their own cloaks, everyone looking upwards at the figure of the Grand Master crazily gesticulating on the ledge forty feet above us, continuing to scream his threats down to where we were standing, his voice clearly audible even above the noise of the thunder, the wind, and the roaring of the helicopter. The lightning when it came dazzled us all, a vivid slash of pure electricity forking down to the castle, outshining even the spotlight from the helicopter. Dazzled as they were by the lightning, few of the spectators would have seen the arm which suddenly appeared from the open window behind the Grand Master, but I did, and so too, I think, did Sir James Sinclair, though he was later to deny it. Whether the owner of that arm had said something to attract the Grand Master's attention, or something else had happened, I don't know, but the raging lunatic suddenly turned round to look behind him, and for the briefest moment I clearly saw the head of a man emerge from the window as he leaned out to lightly push the Grand Master in the back. The Grand Master struggled to regain his footing, which was when I saw the man for the second time now seeming to push with much more energy than before. The Grand Master didn't stand a chance. He teetered on the side of the stone ledge for a moment, and then with arms and legs flailing like the sails on a demented windmill he fell to as gruesome a death as anything which his knightly forbears had had to endure. Maybe it was my fevered imagination but for just a brief moment I seemed to hear the sound of gushing air, much as an inflatable ball will make when it is punctured, as the Grand Master's body was pierced by the lance held by one of the statues guarding the entrance to the courtyard, and hung there, blood gushing from the wound and smearing the cloaks of those knights nearby.

To Majed Dajani, standing in the ranks with his knightly colleagues from the Lebanese Priory, the scene he'd just witnessed was reminiscent of a similar scene at the Marriott Hotel in Cairo just over a week ago, one which the man whose broken body was now horribly suspended not ten paces in front of him had demanded, and he himself had orchestrated. In the gathering darkness he couldn't make out Dame Monika Wolff standing in the ranks of the Austrian Priory, but he knew she was there, and she'd be as worried as he that somehow their best-laid plans had gone horribly wrong. This was confirmed when one of the police officers spoke briefly into his radio telling anyone listening that the subject was well and truly beyond medical help, and then picked up the microphone which had fallen to the floor. He flicked the switch on the side to reactivate it, and then looked at the people standing on parade. "If Miss Monika Wolff is present, please come forward."

Monika was stunned, this wasn't how it was supposed to be; all the promises she'd been given by the Grand Master, how her role was going to be to nurture the young Tsarevich, to keep him occupied while they searched for a suitable bride for him, and then she'd become a royal lady in waiting, living a life of glamour in the Royal Court. Her mother would have been so proud of her, she could have come and stayed at the castle if she'd wanted, but now it was doubtful she'd even get to wear the Rolex watch her daughter had so thoughtfully taken from the bedside table in Sheik Abdullah Qahtani's hotel bedroom! All her dreams had come to nothing. Monika stepped forward from her place on the Austrian priory's front rank, walking as if in a stupor to where the police officer stood waiting for her. The two officers who'd tried and failed to catch the Grand Master as he'd fled back into the castle walked across to join their senior officer, and stood either side of Monika.

"Miss Monika Heidi Wolff, I hereby arrest you on the charge of the murder of Sheikh Abdullah Qahtani at the Hilton Hotel in London on the nineteenth of June this year. You are also under arrest on a warrant issued this morning by Interpol at the request of the Austrian police, suspected of the murder of Mr Ahmed Khalifa, a Kuwaiti national, at the Sacher Hotel in Vienna on the eighteenth of June this year."

Monika heard the rest of the officer's statement advising her of her rights in a daze and started to giggle. "I suppose you want the million pounds back but you can't have it, he's got it;" she was pointing at the body of the Grand Master now grotesquely spinning round and round on the blade of the lance, "and he can't tell you where he's hidden it, not now he's dead, can he?" She was still giggling hysterically as the two officers led her away to one of the waiting police cars.

Majed Dajani was frantic. Did the police know about him too, and was he also about to be arrested? He was a Lebanese businessman, and a damned good one at that. When the Grand Master had approached him at a Crusaders meeting in Jerusalem five years earlier, and asked if he would be prepared to lead the negotiations for the sale of oil exploration rights in Siberia on behalf of a company called Ural Oil, he'd jumped at it, particularly when he understood he'd be entitled to one percent of the selling price! Later, when he'd learned he would first have to attend to certain other duties on behalf of the Grand Master he'd still gone along with it. After all, scum of the earth like Mamdoubh Rifaat deserved to die. He, Majed Dajani, wanted to avenge all the young boys Rifaat had abused over the years.

He was standing in the rear rank of the Lebanese Priory. The rain was still pouring down, getting heavier if anything, and the sky even darker. With a bit of luck he'd be able to slip away without being noticed, but he'd have to watch carefully for a suitable opportunity, he'd only get one chance at this! His chance actually came almost as soon as he'd thought of it; the military helicopter had circled away from its place above the courtyard, and was hovering above the grassy lawns, which was where the four coaches were still parked. The helicopter was being buffeted quite badly in the strong wind and rain, and the two civilian passengers were beginning to complain; he needed to land! There is a tradition in the army that if a passenger pukes up in a helicopter they either clean the mess themselves, or give the pilot twenty pounds and a crew member does it for you. The pilot doubted that either of these two would go along with that tradition; the gentleman with the la-di-da voice, Sir Norman Fitzgerald according to the name on the passenger manifest, didn't look as though he'd ever got his hands dirty in his entire life, and judging by the suit he was wearing, the other passenger, Mr George Hamlyn, technically his boss as Minister of Defence, didn't look as though he had any money for himself, never mind to give away.

Eventually two of the police officers realised what the pilot was trying to do and turned their cars so that the headlights illuminated the lawn, giving the pilot just the help he needed to make a safe landing. The distraction caused by the landing gave Majed the opportunity he was looking for. As he started to slip away from the parade the knight standing closest to him realised his intention and cleverly moved very slightly sideways so as to close the gap between himself and the man on the other side, doing his best to cover for Majed. The ruse worked and within a matter of seconds Majed was scrambling over the immaculate hedge surrounding the square, being careful not to be seen by the soldiers guarding the perimeter area, and disappeared into the nearby trees.

The cloak would have to go; it was a hindrance in the strong wind, and would attract unwanted attention if and when he found somewhere inhabited. He made a cavity under one of the gorse bushes and pushed the cloak inside, wondering if he'd ever be able to find it again, and then realising that was the very least of his problems - he had to get away. He had little idea of the geography of the surrounding area and it was too dark to get any bearings, so he'd have to follow his nose! It took him almost an hour before he came upon a petrol station on the main road which fortunately stayed open late to catch any motorists unwise enough to want to be driving around in such filthy weather. The forecourt attendant was a bit surprised to see such an unruly figure coming to him, but decided it was none of his business especially when Majed spoke to him with a foreign accent and had his wallet open.

"Excuse me," Majed said, "do you happen to know if I can get a taxi anywhere around here?"

The attendant scratched his head. "I suppose John'll be in the pub about now. If you don't mind the smell of whisky on his breath, he can be here in less than five minutes. It'll cost you a pound for the phone though, the boss don't like anyone using the phone. He's a bit tight like that."

Majed was so desperate to get out of the area he would willingly have paid the telephone bill for the entire month, and if the driver had the smell of alcohol on his breath, so much the better—he'd less likely want to be caught speeding or do anything that would attract attention to him, which suited Majed admirably. Within five minutes John's old London taxi had pulled into the forecourt, loaded Majed into the back seat, and he was on his way again. A job to Edinburgh Airport was always welcome; when going out of the area he was allowed to turn the meter off and charge whatever he felt the passenger would stand, especially because Bill on the forecourt had told him this gent was a foreigner.

They arrived at the airport in time for Majed to catch the last shuttle to Heathrow; in London he'd stay in one of the airport hotels for the night and take an early flight out the following morning, perhaps to Africa or the Middle East, though definitely not to Cairo, anywhere except to his home in Beirut—if anyone was trying to find out where he went, that would be the first place they'd look. In fact what he actually did, was fly with Emirates to Dubai, took a taxi across the desert to Abu Dhabi, where he holed up in a hotel for several days until he'd judged it was safe to return to his home.

The helicopter touched down very lightly on the castle lawn, a textbook landing particularly in such awful weather. The pilot waited for the rotors to stop turning before opening the rear door for his passengers to disembark; he'd done that from his own seat, he wasn't about to go out in this weather, even if one of the passengers was his boss! One of the police cars bumped across the grass to where the two gentlemen had alighted, checking to see what their business was in being there. The driver recognised Sir Norman at once; he was a local bigwig, and a magistrate. "Jump in sir," he'd suggested, "come in out of the wet."

The two did just that and it was quite fortunate for George Hamlyn that the police car with Monika in the back seat had returned to the parking area. She would certainly have recognised him and that would have been really messy, but for all she knew he was back in London. Just twenty four hours earlier she'd accompanied him to Edinburgh Airport for his flight back to London.

--*-*-*

The initial joyful reaction of the crew of the UN plane in finding they were staying in the same hotel as their passengers didn't last long, anyway not for all of them. Usually they would be accommodated in a cheap motel close to whichever airport they happened to have parked their plane in, so the Caledonian Hotel, just off Princes Street in Edinburgh's Golden Mile was a pleasant surprise. It is an old fashioned hotel, providing exceptionally good old fashioned service at fairly modern prices - not that that would bother the crew, their bills were all paid by the office in New York. It was the Captain's responsibility to do the check-in formalities, which was when he'd learned they'd been allocated two double and one twin bedded room for the six person crew, and there was no possibility of changing as the hotel was absolutely full. That, so the Captain thought, had played right into his hands, but he was wrong. He'd collected the three room keys, then gone back to brief his crew on the sleeping arrangement.

"I'm sorry guys," he explained, "but we've got to bunk up together tonight. Volodya, you and Semyon," indicating the two male flight attendants, "you share the room with two single beds, Valerij and Vasya," indicating the co-pilot and the third male flight attendant, "you get to cuddle up together in a double, and I'm sorry Olga, but you have to put up with me." He'd dropped the other room keys on a convenient table and then turned quickly away, ostensibly to collect his overnight bag but in reality so his crew wouldn't see the salacious grin on his face. "Olga, we're on the third floor, you'd better follow me now."

The Captain was in a hurry, but in fact it wasn't Olga who'd followed him, it was his Ukrainian co-pilot Valeriy Rokotyanskyy. "Sorry to disappoint Chief, but Olga's with me. It's you who gets to cuddle Vasya."

The Captain turned round to insist, but thought better of it when he saw the determined look on Olga's young face. "Shit, this was turning out to be a real lousy trip," he muttered half aloud, "come on Vasya, let's drop our bags in the room, and then we'll find a bar with some good vodka." For the second night in a row he'd gone off in a huff, but all was not lost. As he and Vasya plonked themselves on their bar stools, Leila came and sat next to them.

"Would either of you gentlemen care to buy me a drink? My name is Leila." In fact they both bought her a drink, and another, and another, and then took her and a bottle of cheap vodka to their now rather cramped hotel room.

)( )( )( )( )(

Back at Rannoch Castle the rain was still coming down as fiercely as ever, and the wind definitely hadn't abated. The knights had broken ranks and sought shelter in the lee of the castle. Detective Chief Inspector Bill Morgan of the London Metropolitan Police had taken charge of the proceedings. "Gentlemen," he shouted into the battery powered megaphone, "it's enough for tonight. Please go back to your coaches. One of my police officers will be on board for the journey to your hotels. He will be taking your names and addresses, and we will contact you at some future date, should it be necessary. Thank you for your cooperation."

The knights didn't need any further prodding, they'd really had enough. Whatever their reasons for making the journey, or pilgrimage as some preferred to refer to it, it most definitely was not this. They'd seen their leader standing tall, showing them a way forward that had been missing for centuries. He'd promised them the greatest Crusade of all time. They'd actually seen with their own eyes a figure they'd only whispered about in secret conclave, the exiled Tsar of Russia, the Protector of their noble Order. Then they'd witnessed the collapse; the Grand Master screaming obscene abuse at them from high on the castle walls, the awful moment when his body was impaled on the statue's lance, the arrest of one of their number by the police on a charge of murder; every one of them wanted nothing more than to go home.

As the last of the coaches turned back onto the main road, and all the police cars did likewise, including the one taking Dame Monika Wolff to the security of the police station in Perth, the small crowd left behind gathered together, aware that their every move was being watched very carefully by the soldiers still guarding the perimeter of the courtyard. The soldiers were awaiting the arrival of someone their young officer had referred to as 'Ato', which I later learned referred to the bomb disposal officer who'd been summoned to disarm the devices with which the Grand Master had mined the castle. Sir Norman Fitzgerald, the Queen's personal representative in matters concerning the Venerable Order of St John, Mr George Hamlyn, Minister of Defence, Sir James Sinclair of the Chivalric Order of St John, and myself, Alec Johnson, gamekeeper and child evacuee from wartime London, or Alexei Romanov, the exiled Tsar of Russia, whichever you choose, took shelter in the lee of the castle, each of us drenched to the skin, shaking with cold, and uncertain what to do next. It was the shout of alarm from the soldier who'd taken up guard position by the door of the castle that alerted us to something unexpected happening and we watched with baited breath as the heavy door slowly opened. The Grand Master had assured us all the doors had been mined, the whole castle booby trapped, how was this possible? An uncertain head peered round the doorpost, looking enquiringly to discover who was on the outside. Dr Charles Weinberger, special adviser on Russian affairs to the American secretary of state, blackmail victim of Grand Master Oliver Emerson, former very close friend to a much younger James Sinclair, was standing there. In his hand he had a box about the size of a book, a box he'd snatched from the hand of the Grand Master just before he'd pushed him to his death from the small ledge on the third floor. Although we couldn't see it in the dark, the single switch was pushed to the off position; the castle was safe!

Chapter Twenty-One

And the rest, or so the saying goes, is history. Two days after the dramatic events of St John's Day, a meeting had convened at the Castle under the chairmanship of Mr Tom Lane, the United Nations deputy secretary general. The president of Russia had reacted to the telephone call from Mr Lane and had arrived in Scotland, as too had Saeed Al Turki, the Saudi Arabian ambassador to the United States. All the other people in the room that morning, the bailiffs of the Chivalric and Venerable Orders of St John, Sir James Sinclair and Sir Normal Fitzgerald, the British minister of defence George Hamlyn, and the special advisor to the American secretary of state Dr Charles Weinberger all had something to contribute, and Mr Lane had insisted that both I, and Nicholas, who by now had recovered from his shocking treatment by the Grand Master, should also be there, much against my better judgement I might add!

President Schumakof asked to be allowed to speak first as he had an important announcement to make. He informed us the Russian Government would honour the Proclamation signed by Tsar Paul on 21st December 1798 subject to being given scientific proof that I really was the grandson of Tsar Nicholas the Second, and with one further stipulation, - and it's worth recording that in detail here.

Mr Schumakof wanted to ask me what he termed an impertinent question. "Alexei," he'd asked, "have you fathered any children who could claim inheritance to the title of Tsar when you die?"

Just twenty-four hours earlier I would have told him that Nicholas was my son, he was the Tsarevich, but that was before the devastating news which Sir James had given me, that the Grand Master raped my wife Maria, and fathered Nicholas. "Mr President Sir, sadly I can indeed confirm to the very best of my knowledge I have never fathered a child. I am the last living descendent of Tsar Nicholas II." Nicholas was staring at me as I gave the answer to the Russian President, his eyes wide open, a look of horror on his young face as he listened to me denying our relationship. When they were together in the castle, the Grand Master had already told him he was his biological father, which was why Nicholas had refused to go along with the crazy man's plans, and why he'd been drugged and beaten. Now it was as though Nicholas desperately wanted to keep alive the hope the Grand Master had been lying, but instead he'd heard me destroy it; all the love and affection which had passed between us as father and son over many, often difficult, years had been false. As I watched him walk from the room, desperately trying to retain some dignity, I knew how he felt; after all, hadn't I too been deceived as to who my parents were, but then as now the truth had to be told. I also have to confess that even while these thoughts were going through my mind, and while giving Mr Schumakof the answer to his question, another part of my mind had gone back to my only other sexual encounter, the driving lesson given by the corporal in the Women's Royal Army Corps, but my contribution to that had been washed away in the army laundry. Anyway to claim legitimate succession both parents had to be of royal blood, and for sure the good corporal didn't list that quality amongst her other rather more dubious assets!

The President had then embraced me in what I can only refer to as a bear hug, and I swear there were tears in his eyes when he informed the gathering he was privileged to be able to make amends for the terrible deeds perpetrated in Yekaterinburg ninety years earlier. However, he went on, "you can be certain that immediately the right of Royal succession dies, so too will the Russian Government's agreement to the Chivalric Order being able to benefit from the mining in the Urals. That revenue," he told us, "would then be for the benefit of the Russian people."

Tom Lane spoke next, reminding us he'd been given the responsibility of finding a solution to the present oil crisis. "Am I right in assuming that the granting of oil exploration rights in the Ural Mountains can help resolve that problem," he'd asked. He'd expected Charles Weinberger to answer his question, repeating for the benefit of the audience the briefing he'd given President Riles at the weekend, but in fact it was the Saudi diplomat who'd spoken next.

Until that moment Saeed Al Turki hadn't said a single word! I'd been watching him, wondering what his role would be. His eyes had fascinated me - they were darting around the table, minutely examining the face of each speaker as though trying to read their minds while listening to the words they were uttering, which was precisely what he was doing. This is a Bedouin skill, honed in the blazing heat of the vast Saudi Arabian Empty Quarter, where knowing if your adversary was telling you the truth or a pack of lies could mean the difference between life and death.

"Mr Lane, in my opinion it is perfectly obvious that the mineral deposits in that area of the Ural Mountains represent a hugely significant contribution to the world's energy reserves. In my country we are aware of those deposits, and far from viewing them as a threat to our own trading position, we welcome them, as we do all major oil finds, including I might add" and he'd transferred his gaze from Mr Lane to Dr Weinberger, "the Arctic National Wildlife Refuge, which is causing Mr Riles so many headaches just now."

"We are also well aware," he went on, "that the oil consumers, particularly those in the west, are quite content to continue draining as much of the oil reserves in the Gulf States as we will allow, caring not a jot what will happen to my country, to Kuwait and all the others once the oil has run out, as one day it must. Perhaps they're hoping that we Arabs will then resume our nomadic lifestyle, following our sheep and goats across the desert sands? Rest assured, gentlemen, we will not allow that to happen and therefore if America and Europe can take some of their energy needs from elsewhere, we will be delighted."

The attention of every person in the room, me included, was riveted on the Saudi diplomat. Where was he going with his argument, was he being constructive, or was he on some kind of mission to further complicate the energy crisis? None of us knew, but we were about to find out!

"As you may know, I was on my way back to Washington when I

received the instruction to attend this meeting on the way. I was not however returning to continue my post as ambassador to the United States; in fact I was going to inform Mr Riles that my appointment in Washington is over, and a new ambassador will be appointed in due course. Yesterday, His Majesty the King of Saudi Arabia informed me I am to be the new president of OPEC, replacing Ahmed Khalifa whose death last week was such a tragedy for that organisation. On behalf of the OPEC member states, he has urged me to search for a solution to the present crisis, which is why I'm happy to be sharing this room with you, Mr Lane, since the secretary general of the United Nations has asked you to do the same thing."

There was something incongruous about Saeed Al Turki. If I closed my eyes and simply listened to him speaking, which I confess I'd spent some minutes doing, I could believe he was a typical Old Etonian, plumb in mouth, an articulate and confident member of the British upper class I'd spent so many years following over the high moors. Then when I opened my eyes it was to see an Arab, swarthy-skinned, slightly hooked nose, tight thin lips, jet black hair, all set against an amazingly white thawb.

"Gentlemen," he continued, "let me speak frankly. It seems to me perfectly obvious that the events in Cairo and Vienna, carried out in the name of the Arab League and OPEC, were orchestrated from this very castle, presumably by the man you all refer to as the Grand Master, now deceased I'm given to understand. The same man, no doubt, was behind the terrible murder of my own brother-in-law at the Hilton Hotel in London last weekend."

That last piece of information had shocked everyone in the room; none of us had cause to connect the dead Saudi Government minister and this ambassador. The Grand Master had known, he was meticulous in his research, and he'd told Monika, but no-one else had known. Sir Norman Fitzgerald had led the chorus of sympathy to the diplomat, who, it seemed to me, had taken it all totally in his stride; there'd been no emotion whatsoever in his voice when he'd told us of the connection!

"I don't believe," he'd continued, "any of us can doubt that this Grand Master had a hand in the writing of both the so-called suicide notes, the one in Cairo and that in Vienna. I am also certain that he faked the document which purported to have discussed the formation of the Islamic Defence Force. However, perhaps I should confess here and now, I had removed that document from Abdullah's briefcase before the police had chance to find it! The Grand Master, as you call him, sought to create uncertainty about the future of oil supplies from the OPEC states so that he could manipulate the selling price of the oil exploration licences in the Ural Mountains, to which, through the Knights of St John and an ancient proclamation, he was laying claim. "

So, if this diplomat's assumptions were correct, I finally knew what this was all about. The way the Grand Master had nurtured me, my marriage to Maria, the birth of Nicholas, everything had but one purpose, the vast sums of money to be made by selling those licences to the highest bidder. As Mr Al Turki had intimated, the Grand Master had indeed possessed a twisted and devious mind!

"Unfortunately," the diplomat went on, "there are very serious repercussions to his actions in the Arab world. Militant Islamists have seen this as an opportunity to exploit their own agenda of hate and division, and it's not going to be easy to stop that. It's not enough for us to go on television, and in the newspapers, and tell everyone that it was all a gigantic hoax, its gone way beyond that. The seizure of those two ships in the Suez Canal is an example of militant Islamists taking advantage of a situation caused by someone else, and using it to their own ends. We must tread very carefully if we are to resolve this crisis successfully and peacefully, and a good start to that, Mr Lane, would be for you to meet with me in Vienna next week and address the members of the OPEC Committee. If you, at your eloquent best, could persuade those members to reverse their decision concerning the price of oil to what they termed 'invader-countries', the whole dilemma can slowly recede.

The Russian President stood from his seat round the table and came to stand by me. I was half expecting another of his bear hugs, but not this time. "Friends and colleagues, I would like to make a further announcement, something which I hope will bring closure to the murderous event which took place in Yekaterinburg all those years ago. In the city of St Petersburg, just to the east of the Peter Paul Fortress, the Russian cruiser Aurora is in a permanent mooring.

It was from that very ship in 1917 that the canon was fired to signal to the waiting revolutionaries to storm the Winter Palace. That was the start of the Bolshevik Revolution."

"Your Royal Highness, half an hour ago I sent a text message to the Speaker of the Russian Parliament, the man whose grandfather led the execution squad that murdered your family. He was waiting at the cruiser for my signal, and has just responded. The cruiser has just fired that canon again, the first time in ninety-one years. The Bolshevik Revolution is finally over!"

Epilogue

Six months have flown by since those extraordinary June days when Grand Master Emerson turned my whole world upside down. The OPEC meeting to which Saeed al Turki had referred did indeed take place; Mr Lane had been at his eloquent best and had persuaded the OPEC members to reverse their decision regarding oil exports to the invader-countries, the two ships which had been arrested in the Suez Canal were freed immediately the OPEC agreement had been reached, and all mention of the Islamic Self Defence Force slowly disappeared.

Now it's Christmas Eve; I'm sitting in the conservatory, putting the final touches to the story, a story that began when a seventeen-year-old Russian girl and her fourteen-year-old brother, escaped from that terrible house of death in distant Yekaterinburg. Outside the snow is beginning to settle, we're in for a white Christmas. Unfortunately Nicholas is not here to enjoy it; he's on holiday for a week in America, staying with a well-to-do family in New York. Their ancestors were distantly related to the Romanov family; they'd fled from Russia at the time of the Bolshevik Revolution, as you'll remember Maria's ancestors did too; the two families have been friends ever since. They have a daughter, same age as Nicholas, 'a true-blue royal princess', as Maria described her to me, ignoring the fact that she also seems to be exceptionally pretty, and clever with it. The two mothers are busy trying to matchmake their offspring; quite why they have to interfere, why they can't leave the pair of them to get on with it is beyond me, but Nicholas doesn't seem to mind, so why should I?

Rannoch Castle is now officially described as the Headquarters of the Chivalric Order of St John of Jerusalem, and Martha and her husband James still work there, though they only dress in their brown robes on visitor days, and the security guards and the chauffeur have all returned to America, as they are no longer needed. Nicholas has moved into what had been the Grand Master's rooms in the castle from where he looks after the day-to-day business of the Order. He's restored the secret room to how he thinks it would have looked in the days when Bonnie Prince Charlie slept there—visitors love the story! For me, I prefer to remember it as it was when my friend Jimmy and I saw it all those years ago—those were innocent days, before the Grand Master came and corrupted all our lives.

"You're probably curious to know what happened to Monika? She was never tried for those two murders, you know; she was judged to be insane and spent a couple of months in a mental hospital before being sent back to her native Austria. I'm given to understand she's in a convent now, preparing to take her vows. I only hope she doesn't have too much trouble with the one about chastity!"

"Majed made it safely home to his family in Beirut. The British police weren't interested in him once they'd decided not to charge Monika with the Hilton murder, but the Egyptian police are after him for the murder of that paedophile, and the Saudi's are vaguely interested in him too, something to do with a hotel bill at the Cairo Marriott they've had to pay!

Majed knows I'm writing this story so he's a bit afraid, but he needn't be—his name isn't really Majed Dajani, I made that up, I'm protecting him. You see, I happen to agree it was the right thing to do, killing that obscene paedophile, and anyway, as we all know, he's an excellent businessman and he's coaching Nicholas on business techniques. The oil exploration licence negotiations start in January and Nicholas is leading for our side, so you could say we're helping each other!"

"You're asking about Sir James Sinclair? Oh, the cancer finally got him, towards the end of the summer. I was sitting with him when he passed away in a hospice in Perth; it was a peaceful death, the way we'd all like to go when it's our turn. He's buried in the chapel graveyard behind the castle and I go there from time to time, usually when I'm feeling low, just to talk to my friend. I hope he hears me. He did become my friend, you know; towards the end we became very close."

"And that's about it I guess. You'll remember at the very beginning I asked that you keep an open mind, taking my words on trust where proof was hard to find, and leaving any judgement as to fact or fiction right until the end. That's about now, but please bear in mind the following things:"

"Despite a massive search of the area, the human remains of Anastasia and Alexei were never found. Yakov Yurovsky, the killer watchmaker from Perm, lied in his report; he didn't burn them there, and he didn't have time to hide their bodies anywhere else, therefore it is not unreasonable to believe they got safely away.

Move on: it is a fact that Adolf Hitler did consider reinstating the German monarchy, and there is strong circumstantial evidence to suggest the Nazi leadership wanted to reinstate the Duke of Windsor to the throne of Britain when the war was won.

It is also a fact that in May 1941, Hitler's Deputy Rudolf Hess flew himself to Scotland in a Luftwaffe airplane. Why, you are quite entitled to ask, after the landing was he taken to Buchanan Castle instead of to a military hospital to nurse his ankle which was broken in the landing, and why, after more than half a century, are some of those documents which Mr Hess had with him on that plane, still embargoed to the British public? What did Rudolf Hess know that was so secret he had to be kept in virtual isolation in Berlin's Spandau Goal for forty-one years, and can you really believe this frail 93 year old man then committed suicide, hanging himself from an electric light cable? Was there a conspiracy amongst the aristocracy all those years ago against the wartime Prime Minister, Winston Churchill, to make a peace agreement with Nazi Germany, is that what all the secrecy is about? Did that conspiracy perhaps also involve a four year old Russian boy, evacuated not from war-torn London, as he'd always been led to believe, but from Nazi Germany? A little boy who'd been in the second seat on that Luftwaffe plane, who was spirited quickly away from the landing site by whoever was waiting there to receive him? If Mr Hitler planned to restore the German and British monarchies under his own rule, wouldn't he even more have valued controlling the Russian throne—with Anastasia's child he could have done that?

Most of the things I've told you about are on the Internet. Check them for yourself, and then ask yourself did they really happen, or are they merely the foolish dreams of an old gamekeeper, who'd spent too much of his life alone on the high moors?

Have I told you everything? No, I've kept the best bit till last. I was sitting in the garden of my cottage having tea with James and the American, Charles Weinberger, a few days after that final meeting at Rannoch Castle. That was the first time they'd met socially since that fateful afternoon at Harvard University all those years ago. I'm happy to tell you, they didn't dwell on that sad part of their lives, and while Charles didn't actually admit he'd given the Grand Master the fateful push that sent him to his death, I think both of us knew it was him!

Anyway, the good news: Nicholas, who was still recovering from his encounter with the Grand Master, had taken a room at the Speckled Grouse where he said he wanted to rest and come to terms with the devastating news about his parentage. He'd left his mobile phone with me. It had rung; it was a friend of his, a Dr John Allen, who asked me to pass a message to my son Nicholas. I'd interrupted him, telling him that sadly Nicholas was not my son.

"Mr Romanov," he said to me, and I can't tell you how weird that sounded, "Nicholas most definitely IS your son. He had sent me a cutting of your hair, and his own, and a third cutting he told me you'd found in a locket. He'd asked me to test them for DNA. I should explain," he went on, "I am the director of the leading DNA laboratory in the United States. I can tell you, sir, unequivocally, that Nicholas is your son, and both you and he are related to whoever that third strand of hair belonged to."

The third strand of hair he was referring to was presumably that of my uncle, the young Tsarevich, Alexei. I'd noted it was missing from the locket, and had intended asking Nicholas if he knew anything about it, but with so many other things going on hadn't got round to doing it.

"Sir," he went on, "I can tell you even more. I remember the excitement back in 1991 when the Romanov remains were discovered in Russia. Their DNA was tested here in the States, so I was able to compare your figures with those of Tsar Nicholas, his wife, and the three daughters. It's all on the Internet you see; you can't escape the science sir. You are all family."

I was flabbergasted, practically speechless, but from the massive grin on my face, both my companions understood I was hearing good news. Good news? That is an understatement; it was the best news I'd ever had in all my life, though unfortunately the same couldn't be said for Mr Schumakof; he was going to learn we Romanov's were going to be around for a lot longer than he thought! I do hope he won't think I lied to him!

✼✼✼✼✼

"So, finally that's my story, and now you can do with it as you will. It's getting quite late and Maria will be back soon, she's taken old Randy for his evening walk, and I want to wrap her Christmas present while she's out. Oh, didn't I tell you? Yes, Maria came back four months ago, and we are very happy living in the cottage, not that you'd recognise it anymore! It's been extended yet again; we now have a purpose built and very modern kitchen, a wonderful bathroom, and two bedrooms instead of just the one. Even more, she's had central heating installed, which I'd told her she could do, but only over my dead body; she'd told me that could be arranged as well! My wife wants grandchildren, lots of them, and she wants them now, so she is pushing our son hard to get married, and she makes no secret of that. Poor lad, he doesn't stand a chance!"

"Did you ask what I was giving her for Christmas? Well, if I give you some clues, you can hazard a guess. It's jewellery, and quite old; it's about the size of my thumbnail, heart shaped, made of gold with an enamel inlay. It opens, and inside is a picture of a very young baby, looking like Nicholas when he was that age."

"You still can't guess? More clues then: on the opposite face of the locket, the initials 'N' and 'A' are engraved, intertwined in gold letters and surrounded by diamond chips in the form of a crown.

They are the initials of the baby's parents. Now do you know what it is?

I'm sure the answer is yes, it's a beautiful locket. I hope she likes it—it's been in my family for a hundred years!

Alexei Nikolayevich Suvorin-Romanov

About the Author

The author was himself a Knight Commander in the European Grand Priory of the Sovereign Order of St John of Jerusalem. His particular interests lie in travelling, which he does extensively, and researching items of historical interest from his home in Suffolk, England, where he lives with his Swiss wife Liliane.

Lightning Source UK Ltd.
Milton Keynes UK
UKOW041401270313

208288UK00001B/36/P